The Sp.......
the Man in the Street

Eimar O'Duffy

THE SPACIOUS ADVENTURES OF THE MAN IN THE STREET

DALKEY ARCHIVE PRESS

Originally published by the Macmillan company in 1929.
First Dalkey Archive edition, 2018.

Library of Congress Cataloging-in-Publication Data
Names: O'Duffy, Eimar, 1893-1935, author.
Title: The spacious adventures of the man in the street / Eimar O'Duffy.
Description: First Dalkey Archive edition. | Victoria, TX : Dalkey
Archive Press, 2018.
Identifiers: LCCN 2018000191 | ISBN 9781628972801 (pbk. : alk.
paper)
Classification: LCC PR6029.D76 S63 2018 | DDC 823/.914--dc23
LC record available at https://lccn.loc.gov/2018000191

www.dalkeyarchive.com
Victoria, TX / McLean, IL / Dublin

Dalkey Archive Press publications are, in part, made possible through
the support of the University of Houston-Victoria and its programs in
creative writing, publishing, and translation.

Printed on permanent/durable acid-free paper

QUOTATIONS A PROPOS

DARIUS ON THE RELEATIVITY OF MORALS

Darius, after he had got the kingdom, called into his presence certain Greeks who were at hand, and asked: "What he should pay them to eat the bodies of their fathers when they died?" To which they answered that there was no sum that would tempt them to do such a thing. He then sent for certain Indians, of the race called Callatians, men who eat their fathers, and asked them, while the Greeks stood by, and knew by the help of an interpreter all that was said: "What he should give them to burn the bodies of their fathers at their decease?" The Indians exclaimed aloud, and bade him forbear such language. Such is men's wont herein; and Pindar was right, in my judgment, when he said: "Law is the king o'er all."

(HERODOTUS. Rawlinson's Translation.)

LUCRETIUS ON CURRENCY

Bronze once was precious, and edgeless gold despised;
Now bronze is scorned, and gold supremely prized.

GREAT THOUGHTS FROM THE CONCRETE AGE

There is not a single commodity this world uses that someone or other at some time or other hasn't made a fortune out of it.

(MR. GORDON
SELFRIDGE, Junior.)

PROCRUSTES ON UNEMPLOYMENT

That difficult problem of the boys will help to solve itself in the next few years, because of the fall in the birthrate.

(The Right Honourable STANLEY BALDWIN)

CONTENTS

"Light and the night, and the awful symbols of night."

CHAPTER 1

Mr. Aloysius O'Kennedy, sprawling across a table in an attic in Stoneybatter, his tongue straining out almost to his nosetip, his pen spluttering like a tarbrush, addresses the Manager of Mac Whatsisname's grocery

GOD HELP ME, MR. GALLAGHER, it wasn't me that gave you that outrageous blow and wrecked the shop on you. Honest to God it wasn't. I couldn't nor wouldn't do such a thing. I was always a quiet respectable lad that never wanted anything but to be let alone and to better himself by hard work, civility, and strict attention to business, and wasn't it just my bad luck to be sent stravaguing round the universe, while other people were standing in my shoes—yes, in my very skin, Mr. Gallagher—and taking advantage of this incognito to blacken my name in the eyes of my employers. Honest to God, Mr. Gallagher, I didn't know what I was up to when I let that cracked old humbug downstairs start monkeying about with my ego. A learned gentleman like you, Mr. Gallagher, will know what an ego is; for I don't rightly understand it myself; but from what they've told me it seems that your ego is a part of you that isn't yourself: something like your soul, you know, only your soul is in the Catechism and this isn't. Anyway, what happened was this. This fellow Murphy, as stupid an old ass as ever stepped, and it's the greatest gas in the world to pull his leg for him, walks in to me in the morning when I was washing my face, and says he: "Will you lend me your body for two pounds ten?" Of course I was used to him saying queer things, so I said: "Done, Philosopher" (which is a nickname they've given him on account of being

3

cracked), and with that he put me sitting in a chair and began waving his hands at me in the silliest sort of way till I was ready to burst with laughing. But presently his hands seemed to go slower, like, and his left eye seemed to grow larger. Then I began to feel a bit queer, and tried to stand up, but he just pushed me back into the chair, and I hadn't the strength to resist him. I just sat there helpless, gazing into his eye, which grew larger and larger, while everything around went black, till at last there seemed to be nothing in the world but the eye and the darkness, and an infernal thumping in my ears. Then, all of a sudden, I seemed to fly right out of myself, and I thought my last hour was come and that I was going to slip off this mortal plane altogether, as the poets say: not that I've much use for poetry as a rule, but sometimes these birds put a thing in a snappy way that just gets it. Anyway, that's how I felt. And I said to myself: "No. I'm not going to die. I'm not going to die. I won't die. I won't. I won't," and set my teeth, in a manner of speaking, hard. And at that I stopped dying; which shows there's something in will-power after all.

Next minute I was flying through the darkness faster than an airplane. I went so fast that I wanted to shut my eyes: only I hadn't any eyes to shut, and no head, and no limbs, and no body, nor anything. It was the funniest feeling in the world. There was I, a little wisp of nothingness, blowing through space, without wish to move or power to stop, and nothing but the stars about me, shining big and clear like electric lamps. The Philosopher johnny tells me I wasn't moving at all. He says that the world had simply gone on its way and left me behind, having no pull on a spirit. He may be right for all I know or care. I can only tell the thing the way it seemed to happen at the time.

CHAPTER II

He warms with the Zest of Authorship

ANYWAY, WHEN I LOOKED at the earth it was far beneath me, shining like a silver plate, with the continents marked on it like on a globe at school. In a few minutes it had shrunk to the size of a shilling, and in a few more it was just a star like all the rest. Then it got mixed up with a bunch of others, and I couldn't tell which of them it was. I can tell you I felt lonely then, and an awful cold fear got a grip on me like once when my mother lost me when I was a kid, only this was a million times worse, for I was lost, I thought, for ever in the middle of God knows where.

But I wasn't left alone for long. For presently one of the stars began to get bigger and brighter, and I knew it was coming nearer. It grew and grew till it was as big as the moon, and bigger and bigger, till it filled half the heavens, and I could see that it was all a swirling mass of molten stuff, white hot, and spitting vapours. I could have screamed with horror if I'd had a throat, but instead of running me down it sort of curved off and swept away again, with nine other little bodies trailing after it like chickens round a hen. I suppose it was Mars or Jupiter or one of these planets they tell you about. Anyhow, it passed away and left me alone again.

Now that I was beginning to find my feet, so to speak, I began to wonder what had become of the sun. You'd think that when you got away from the earth you'd find yourself in a blaze of perpetual sunlight. But you'd be wrong. The Philosopher—who, though he's an ass in most things, knows a lot about astronomy and things of that sort—has since told me why. But I couldn't understand him. Anyway, after thinking a bit, I worked it out that the biggest star in sight must be the sun, and it wasn't hard to pick him out, though he was getting smaller every instant. I kept watching him sinking into the well of the night until he too vanished like the earth before him, and you can guess what a poor lost lamb I felt like then, out in the universe all on my lonesome.

What happened after that I'm not quite certain. I seem to remember great stars and comets and things that went rushing and sweeping past me, and always leaving me behind. On they went, hundreds of them, and thousands, till I was tired counting. Great God, I thought to myself, what will I do when they've all gone by and left me alone in the darkness? For it's strange what a comfort there was in the light of them. Still they went racing by, but getting fewer and fewer and farther between, till I was half mad with fear. You know the sort of fear you feel when you're alone on a dark road and you think there's something creeping behind you, and you daren't look round to see. That's how I felt, only a thousand times worse. Out in the black cold emptiness of space there was an awful something waiting for me: and here was I flying faster and faster, as I judged, into its jaws.

A few stars were still passing by; and now I noticed one, smaller than the rest; and duller. It was sort of homely, like our own earth, and it came nearer to me than any of the others—so near indeed that I could almost see the waters of its oceans moving. Then it too went past and sailed away from me.

I became desperate. I must catch that world, I told myself, like as if it was a train I was missing.

"I will catch it," I said.

By jove, there's a lot in will-power. The instant I put my foot down like that everything became all right in a flash. I stopped drifting out into space. The planet stopped rushing away. It stood still, as if it was waiting for me. It grew larger. It came nearer.

In a few minutes more I was under a blue sky, with a golden sun shining in it just like our own. And far beneath me was a great world just like our own, with hills and rivers, and green fields, and roaring oceans breaking on its beaches. It was just lovely to see after all those nightmares I'd come through.

I came nearer and nearer, till I could see the roads and houses, and little towns. Rather foreign, they looked, but quite human, and all glistening very bright in the sunshine. I thought of coming to rest in a nice-looking field near a lake, but I miscalculated a bit, on account of the rapid motion of the planet. A broad belt of trees passed under me, and next instant I found myself in a huge plain covered, as far as I could see, with skulls and bones.

CHAPTER III

He comes to Rathé

SKULLS AND BONES, SIR. Not even skeletons, but bones picked clean, lying in heaps all over the place, with rank weeds growing around and between them. Acres and acres of them; just think of it: white dry bones, and dismal-looking weeds like great nettles, and huge purple and yellow funguses. And there were horrible-looking animals too, prowling about, something like hyenas to look at, only much smaller, and their heads and shoulders and front legs were bald—like vultures, you know. They had long thin tongues which they darted in and out like snakes, and I saw one of the creatures crack a bone and lick up the marrow out of it in a way that would have made me sick if I'd had a stomach. As it was, it made me feel so shuddery that I moved off again into the upper air to refresh myself.

I can't tell you what a delicious sensation it was to be floating about so free in the air and going up or down, backwards or forwards as you liked, by merely wishing. Who hasn't dreamt the dream of floating down the stairs with just a hand on the banisters? I know I have, scores of times. This was a million times nicer, and there was no waking up in the middle to spoil it all. Up, up, up I went until the plain of bones lay far beneath me, white and shining in the sun. I saw now that it was surrounded by a high stone wall, inside and outside which were two belts of trees, very tall and rather clumsy-looking, with large heavy leaves nearly black in colour. At four points in the wall there were gates, made, as far as I could judge, of solid brass, and from each of them a broad straight road of dazzling whiteness

8

stretched out into the warm green countryside. I was just about to fly off to one of those pleasanter fields when one of the gates swung open, and a group of people came through into the plain of bones.

They were savages, I could see at once. They had nothing on their bodies except a pair of running shorts, with a belt of some shiny stuff at the waist; but on their heads they wore a sort of helmet, which flashed and sparkled like huge diamonds. One of the men was walking a little bit in front of the rest. I thought he must be some kind of a chief, for he was less naked than his fellows, having a short white cloak hanging from his shoulders. The other two were carrying something heavy between them: and what do you think it was but a corpse, though it might have been a sack of potatoes for all the respect they showed it. When they had lugged it about a hundred yards from the gate they let it drop, and one of them picked up a bone from the ground and flung it at a hyena-beast which had come sneaking up. You never saw such a shot, though it seemed quite carelessly done. The bone caught the hyena on the head and knocked it clean over. Whether it was killed or stunned I couldn't tell, but anyway the man must have had the strength of ten, for the throw was a hundred yards if it was an inch. The man in front now gave each of the others a cloak—I hadn't noticed that he had been carrying them over his arm all the time—and, slipping them on, the three of them walked off the way they had come, as cool as a picnic party. The moment their backs were turned a dozen or so of the hyena-beasts made a rush for the corpse and began to tear it in pieces.

That philosopher fellow used to be always telling me that there were people in the stars—"beings, probably, far more advanced than we," he'd say in that booky way of talking he had. I thought to myself I'd have a rare laugh on him if ever I got back to earth and told him what barbarious people lived on this star. After all, a funeral shows people at their best. You've got to be decent and solemn then, no matter what sort of an oojah you may be the rest of the time; and said I to myself: "If this is the way these heathens bury their dead, what must their ordinary life be like?"

While I was thinking like this, lo and behold, out of the blue came sailing a huge airplane. I call it an airplane, but it was very different from any we have in our world. It was shaped almost exactly like a bird, with great spreading wings which folded up when it grounded, and wheels that yielded like as if they were made of rubber, and then stiffened up as it ran a few yards before stopping. Next minute four men jumped out smartly, and dash my eyes if they weren't savages also. You wouldn't expect to see savages in an airplane, but there they were, half naked like the first lot, with the same sparkling helmets on their heads. I can tell you I was clean bewildered.

But listen to what happened next. Two of the men walked off together, deep in some confabulation, while another went round the airplane examining it and tinkering at it with an oilcan or some such gadget. The fourth man reached into the body of the machine and fetched out something like a camera on a tripod. This he fixed up very carefully, squinting into the view-finder, and generally adjusting things like a photographer. Presently the two in front halted and shook hands. Then one of them stood off a few paces, while the other turned to face the camera. I couldn't help thinking it was a queer place to choose to be photographed in, but I was past astonishment by this time. There the man stood, bolt upright, with his heels together and his hands by his sides, like a soldier on parade. A fine-looking fellow he was too, whatever his notions of good taste. His naked brown limbs and chest were sleek and muscular, and his short white breeches and cloak edged with purple, with his silver-studded belt and shining helmet, made a very handsome costume. There he posed as I say, but only for an instant. The photographer bent over his camera and pressed a button. But instead of an innocent click the thing gave a sharp hiss, like steam rushing out of a valve, and spat out a streak of blue fire. At the same moment the man in front staggered, fell forward, and lay still among the bones. It was the meanest and most treacherous murder ever committed; and when it was done the scoundrels never gave as much as a glance at their victim, but just packed up their infernal machine and jumped aboard the plane. The third man—who, I noticed, had never once looked at what was happening, but simply went on tinkering as coolly as if he was in hangar—clambered in after them, and with a whirr of wings they were off, leaving me alone with the dead.

It was pitiful to see the poor limp body lying there so still. Only a minute ago it had been brimming full of life, the very picture of health and strength. There the poor devil had stood, all dressed up and smiling, so to speak, for his photograph. Then whiss-ss! and a corpse ready for the hyenas. This was no world, thought I, for a civilized man; and anyway it was high time for me to be making tracks for my own, considering that I was already a bit on the late side when that philosopher chap came bungling in on me, and I didn't want to lose my record for punctuality and strict attention to business, to say nothing of displeasing you, Mr. Gallagher. Now that I was accustomed to being a spirit I could face the homeward journey as naturally as a penny tram-ride. The nightmarishness of space worried me no more than the bogey tales I'd heard as a child; and as for the distance—well, when I could travel faster than a flash of lightning merely by wishing, it seemed like a stroll down Stoneybatter. The only difficulty was that I hadn't the faintest notion what direction to take, and while I was puzzling out this problem a ghostly voice butted in on my reveries.

CHAPTER IV

Conversation with a Ghost

"So DEATH IS NOT the end," said the voice.

"Not on your life," said I, guessing that it was the ghost of the murdered man that was speaking. But you must understand it wasn't English we spoke, or any other language, or any words at all. I have to set it down as language for want of a better way; but in reality we sort of wirelessed our thoughts to each other, and what passed between us was more like pictures than sentences.

"Stretch out thy power to me, kindly spirit," wailed the Ghost, "I am borne away on a potent wind and know not how to stop."

"Use your will," said I, remembering my own predicament.

"Spirit of Wisdom," said the Ghost, "I have used it, and here I am."

"Death is not the end," said I.

"So I perceive," said the Ghost, "But what is the end? Is there rewarded and vengeance? Is there eternal rest? Is there life everlasting? Does the Devil rule, or God? Or does Chance solve all the riddles?"

Before I could answer there came out of the emptiness around us an awful Voice. It came out of everywhere and from nowhere in particular. How my stomach would have sunk and my hair bristled if I had heard that voice in the flesh. Even as a spirit I was horribly disturbed.

"I have the answer to all questions," said the Voice. "Will you be satisfied?"

"I will," said the Ghost, rather meekly, I thought.

"Spirit of ignorance, think again," said the Voice. "What you ask shall be answered, but dare you face the answer?"

"I don't know," said the Ghost uneasily. "It depends on what the answer may be."

"If you fear what May be," said the Voice, 'you may fear what Is. So think well, fearful spirit."

"What if I ask nothing?" said the Ghost.

"You shall have Nothing," said the Voice.

A long silence followed while the Ghost deliberated. If the Voice was dreadful, that silence was more dreadful still. It was like the silence in a court of law when the judge puts on the black cap—only a million times more so. It was the deepest, darkest, ghastliest silence that ever was. The whole universe seemed to be holding its breath in expectation of the Ghost's decision.

Then, all of a sudden, out of some unimaginable distance, came a tiny pinpoint of sound, which swelled slowly to a high, hard, piercing note. I felt at once that there was some frightful deviltry in that sound. It was more dreadful than the silence; more dreadful still than the Voice. Harder and louder it grew, and the louder the flatter, till suddenly it split in two and became a bang—bang—banging, as if some gigantic hammer were battering on a slab of unbreakable stone. Harder and louder and quicker grew that infernal clangour, so that all the frights I had ever felt were like cool gallantry to the terror that gripped me now. All the wickedness and hate that I had only known as words in a catechism seemed to flash into life and meaning in that devil's tattoo. The Powers of Evil were abroad, raging and masterful. Satan was coming to judgement, and his majesty was impatient.

All this was in the beating of that awful hammer, which still grew louder and louder and louder until, just as it came to be utterly unendurable and seemed to have been going on, and likely to continue, for all eternity; and just as I was beginning to feel that death and annihilation would be preferable to another instant of it, it stopped dead, with never an echo, leaving only the silence and the memory of the words of the Voice: 'You shall have Nothing.'

Then came the voice of the Ghost, very thin and weary in the stillness:

"Nothing is easy to think upon" said the Ghost. "Nothing is soft and soothing. O gentle Nothing, warm and drowsy Nothing, draw me into thy dark and silent womb. Shade me from the horror of life, from the terror of God. Lull me to rest."

"Rest" said the Voice; and then there fell another silence, but now the presence of the Voice was gone, and I began to feel at ease again. I was glad that the Ghost had been a sensible ghost and not pressed his inquiries home. I perceived him, indeed, to be a very decent fellow, after my own kidney, and so proceeded at once to strike up an acquaintance with him.

"Who are you?" I asked him.

"The spirit of one, Ydenneko," said the Ghost. "A dweller in Rathé, in the city of Bulnid."

"Was it you that they murdered just now in the plain of the bones?" said I.

"Not murdered, spirit of good or evil, whichever you be. Executed," said the Ghost.

"Spirit of evil, as you plainly are," said I, "what was your crime?"

"I pointed a gun at a friend of mine, not knowing if it was loaded."

"Spirit of carelessness!" said I, "So you killed him?"

"O no," said the Ghost. "The gun wasn't loaded."

"Why, then, were you executed?" I asked.

"Pure spirit that knows not the ways of men, for my carelessness. If I had slain my friend, as happened in a similar case many years ago, remorse for my folly would have been deemed

sufficient deterrent against a repetition of the offence. But having been convicted twice before of minor acts of carelessness, I
was declared to be incorrigible and a danger to the community.
What else could they do but shoot me? That is the law."

"It seems to me rather severe in proportion to the offence,"
I said. "If they executed you for not shooting your friend by
mistake, what would they have done if you had shot him on
purpose?"

"In that case the remainder of my life would not have been
worth living."

"But what would the law have done with you?"

"I don't know."

"You don't know?"

"No. One can hardly be expected to know all the intricacies
of the law in so exceptional a case as that."

"Well," I said, "it seems to me frightfully savage to execute a
man for a mere piece of carelessness."

"Foolish and sentimental spirit," said the Ghost, "there must
surely be some deterrent against careless practices?"

"Yes, but it needn't be quite so severe."

"Ah," said the Ghost wisely, "that is an impracticable dream,
which does credit to the angelic heart of a pure spirit like you,
but must be rejected by the sane heads of practical-minded
men. Mitigate in the smallest degree this salutary severity, and
carelessness would increase to a most alarming extent. There
would be buckets left in every doorway for people to fall over,
fruit-skins dropped on every pathway, cyclists riding everywhere
without a light, slaughter in every thoroughfare by reckless motorists. Indeed nobody would be safe from peril to life and limb
except when in bed."

"You people certainly have vivid imaginations," said I. "Are
there any other offences to which the death penalty is affixed in
this fortunate sphere?"

"Some few," said the Ghost. "I am told it has been inflicted

for persistent uncleanliness, ill-manners, and even for the possession of an unpleasant voice."

"Good lord," I said, "that's the limit. A man isn't responsible
for a defect like that."

"The law is not concerned with a man's responsibility," said
the Ghost. "Its concern is the protection of life and property,
and the amenities of life."

"I'm not surprised," I said, "to observe that the slaugh-
ter-ground below is so well stocked with skeletons. The marvel
is that there's anyone left alive in the country at all."

"You mistake," said the Ghost, "Those bones did not all support the flesh of the careless and unclean. Most of them died a
natural death. Indeed we have but few executions—not above
ten or a dozen in a year throughout the whole world. That plain
below is the cemetery of the city of Bulnid."

"Cemetery!" said I, horrified. "What sacrilege was this? To
execute you in a cemetery?"

"Why, what better place could they have chosen?" asked the
Ghost. "They were thus saved all the trouble of a funeral."

"Not that there's much fuss over funerals in this part of the
universe," said I, remembering the sample I had seen.

"Questioning Spirit," said the Ghost, "what part of the
Universe do you come from that matters of course seems so
strange to you?"

I told him all about myself, and he was sorely disappointed
to find that I was only the ghost of a man, like himself, and not
a pure elemental spirit as he had thought. As he showed but
little curiosity about me, I set to work questioning him again
about himself and the world he belonged to, but he would tell
me no more.

"Restless spirit," said he, "question me no further: for already I sink into the everlasting slumber promised me by the
Voice. But first let us descend, that I may view my body once
more before I sleep."

We sank to the ground beside the chilling corpse, and a

couple of hyena-beasts which had come sneaking towards it backed away from our invisible presence, snarling and bristling. We silently gazed on the face of the dead, as the poem goes in the school books; and then I noticed a queer thing. The helmet was still on the corpse's head, but it seemed to have got knocked forward over the eyes, and it had gone quite dull and filmy like a dead fish. That, I thought, was curious, for you couldn't imagine a silk hat changing colour for anything that might happen to its owner; but looking closer I saw that the thing wasn't a helmet at all, but actually a part of the head. "These were my eyes," said the Ghost, answering my unspoken question. "A queer sort of eyes," said I. "Why? What sort of eyes have you in your world?" asked the Ghost. I explained to him as well as I could. "Then how can you see around you and above you and behind you?" asked the Ghost. "Why, by turning our heads, of course." "A clumsy and insufficient method," said the Ghost. "And how strange it must be to see things only in bits, instead of as a whole, like us." I said No: it seemed quite ordinary to us, and that to see everything all in a lump must be rather bewildering. The Ghost left it at that, not being fond of arguing, apparently; and then after another gaze at the corpse, registered a sudden flash of joy.

"Look, look," says he. "This body of mine shows no mark or sign of injury. I must have died of fear before ever the shaft was loosed." I could not see why this should cause him any joy, and said so. "Why, thou dull spirit," says he, as proud as a film star, "it means that, however infamous my life, I ended cowardly." I flashed surprise at him. "What?" says he. "Do you not admire cowardice in your world?" "Quite the contrary," I told him. "What cynical perversity," says he. "And by the same token am I to take it that you honour bravery?" I admitted it. "You have misnamed your planet," says the Ghost. "Call it no longer Earth, but Topsyturvydom." "No," said I, "it's your planet that's topsyturvy. Cowardice a virtue! my hat!" "Bravery a virtue! my breeches!" "A bags of a virtue!" said I. "It is useless to bandy exclamations," said the Ghost. "Can you defend your position?" "Of course I can." "Why then do you consider bravery a virtue?" I found that I had never really considered the question before. "Why—" said I, "Why—why—because it *is* of course." "I can defend my position better than that," said the Ghost. "because the coward is more agreeable, more useful, and lives longer than the brave man. He is more agreeable because he takes care to offend nobody; he is more useful because he takes proper care of his health and safety; and he lives longer for the same reason. Contrast him with the brave man, who from his boyhood is always climbing trees that are too tall for him, running races that are too hard for him, swimming in water that is too deep for him, and in a thousand ways wasting his strength and risking his limbs and life. Brave men spend weeks of their lives recovering from wounds and hurts, and are generally cut off in their youth or their prime, leaving their work undone and their children unbegotten. If final proof of their inferiority be needed it is to be found in the words of our immortal poet:

The brave die many times before their death:
The coward never tastes of death but once.

I let the fellow have it at that, knowing that it's waste of time arguing with a lunatic. Besides, an idea had occurred to me. I thought it would be fun to go and explore this mad world, and that the best way to do it would be to slip inside the Ghost's body. You must excuse me, Mr. Gallagher, if I confess that I had quite forgotten that I was due at the shop. After all, the chance of seeing another world doesn't come to a lad in my position every day of the week. So I said to the Ghost: "Spirit of Ydenneko, will you lend me the loan of your body for a while, so that I may walk up and down in this world of yours and see for myself its manners and customs." "I have no body now," answered the Ghost. "What I have left I have left." "But tell me," I said, "Supposing I was to get inside this body and travel around in it, would I be safe? I mean, would they execute me again if they thought I was you?" "I do not think so," said the Ghost, "so long as you do not repeat my offence. But, in any case, none will make such a mistake, for it is by the soul, and not by the body, that men recognize one another in Rathé." "Then I'll risk it," I said. "But advise me first. When I am asked who I am and where I have come from, what sort of lie shall I tell?" "Tell the truth, of course," said the Ghost. "But nobody will believe it," I said. "Why?" asked the Ghost. "Is not the truth its own guarantor? Base spirit from a baser world: see that you tell no lies in Rathé." "Why?" I asked. "If you neglect the advice you shall soon learn," said the Ghost. "But take my body now, and do as you will with it. I am for my eternal sleep."

The Ghost was gone and I was alone. I wasted no more time, but glided into the body. Thump! went the heart. Thump—thump—thump—slowly and heavily. Then, with a frightful pang the clogged blood stream began to move, and, as I gasped in agony, the air, rushing into my lungs, nearly overwhelmed me. After that, however, the beating of the heart came easier, and the distressful symptoms passed slowly away, leaving me prostrate but pleasantly tingling. With a great effort of the will I managed at last to sit up; and instantly, with yelps of dismay, a dozen of the hyena-beasts who had gathered around, went scuttling away over the plain, their tails between their legs. Shuddering with horror I rose quickly to my feet; but there was no need to be alarmed, for the filthy brutes made no attempt to come near me. I regained my confidence at once, and did a few dumbbell exercises to make sure of my limbs. Needless to say I felt a little strange at first in the new body—rather like as if I was wearing clothes a couple of sizes too large for me—but I soon got accustomed to it, and stepped out in the direction of the nearest gate, wondering a little fearfully whether I should find it locked.

CHAPTER V

The Road to Bulnid

PICKING MY WAY THROUGH the litter of bones, I reached the gate, which was closed with an ordinary spring lock, and passed through to the road beyond. I call it a road; but the finest road I ever saw in Ireland was like a boreen beside it. It was about a hundred feet wide, and all paved with great blocks of marble as white as snow. Instead of walls or hedgerows to divide it from the fields, there were fine long borders, like in a park, planted with the most wonderful flowers you can imagine; and at the back of each was a row of tall trees with light lacy foliage that just shaded the road from the sun without altogether cutting it off. The fields were different from ours too. They were very big, and divided from one another by ornamental fences made of some white metal that shone like silver. In some there were sheep grazing; others were under crops, which I thought to be grain of some kind, but afterward discovered to be flax; and far in the distance was a huge rolling meadow of yellow flowers. It was just the loveliest sight I had ever seen.

Before me the road ran, not quite straight, nor yet all twisty like an Irish road, but with a graceful sort of sweep that followed the lie of the land, towards a range of low hills about two miles away, where it passed through a gap and disappeared. These hills were the one blot on the landscape. They were of an ugly lumpy sort of shape, and coloured in streaks and splashed with flat reds and blues and yellows like the refuse of mine workings. They looked like nothing in nature, and it struck me as queer that the people who could make such beautiful roads and fields should have hashed up a mountain so abominably.

There was no sign of traffic on the highway; yet when I started to walk, my feet seemed to carry me by a sort of instinct to the pathway. To my surprise I found that this, though paved to all appearance like the road, was really surfaced with a soft springy substance like rubber, very pleasant to walk on. It was the queerest feeling in the world to be walking like that, half naked, through the strange countryside, and to be seeing everything in front and behind and on both sides of me all at once in that tremendous pair of eyes. They were a terrible nuisance at first, those eyes, bewildering me so that I hardly knew whether I was on my head or my heels. However, I got used to them in time—far sooner indeed than I got used to being without them later on when I came back to earth. If you'll believe me, Mr. Gallagher, it's half blind I feel now, with my two miserable little bits of eyes that can see nothing unless it's put straight in front of them.

Well, anyway, I set off down the road, stumbling and swerving a bit, and sitting down now and then so as to steady my giddiness, until, after I had gone a quarter of a mile or so, I came to an awfully nice little fountain by the wayside. It was like this. There was a basin of green marble, shaped irregularly like a lake. In the middle of it was an island, with tiny hills and valleys in it, and a waterfall that ran from the hills to form a river, which flowed into the basin. The basin stood on a pedestal, and its overflow dripped all round into a pond full of water-plants, which here took the place of the flower border. It was a lovely sight, and you may be sure that on such a hot day it made me feel thirsty. There was a cup standing on a marble table close by. Not an ugly iron cup like you see chained to public fountains down here, but a handsome electroplate goblet: at least so I thought at first, but, when I picked it up for a closer look, I found that it was no electroplate, but real silver. On my honour, Mr. Gallagher, for I know the difference, having worked for a pawnbroker for a while before I came to you. "More lunacy,"

said I to myself, and wondered why it hadn't been stolen long
ago. I dipped it in the fountain, however, and took a long drink,
after which I went on my way.

There were more fountains at various intervals along the
road; but a stranger thing still was the bicycle sheds. I came
upon the first when I had walked about a mile. It was like a
little model of a Chinese pagoda, so that I hadn't a notion what
it was for until I looked inside and saw two bicycles propped up
there, and vacant stands for more. I thought this rather a queer
idea, as you may guess; but when I came later on to another,
like a little Roman temple, I was fairly jiggered, and couldn't
help wondering which was the biggest fool—the man who built
bicycle sheds like temples and pagodas, the man who left his
bicycle lying there for anyone to walk off with, or the man who
let slip such an opportunity of helping himself.

The road was now climbing towards the gap between the
hills, so I had a chance to look at these more closely. I saw
that their ugliness was not due to mining operations, as I had
imagined, but was natural. It was the rocks themselves that
were coloured in those dead yellows and blues. They stuck out
everywhere through the thin soil, which grew nothing but moss
and some miserable weeds, except in a few small valleys where
there were clumps of wretched trees, stunted and twisted, with
dull slaty leaves. When it comes to mountains, said I to myself,
this blinking star doesn't hold a candle to the old country: for
I've been on a couple of picnics in my time on the sides of
Kilmashogue, and you'd be hard to please in mountains after
that, though they do say the Alps are bigger. But give me the
heather and the frochan, and I won't ask for avalanches.

Anyway, I topped the rise, and down before me lay another
stretch of beautiful country, with broad meadows of flowers,
and plantations of young trees, and here and there a house set
among shrubs and lawns, with the great white road winding
along to a town about two miles away, and only one ugly little

hill in the whole prospect to spoil it. I didn't waste any time in gazing, however, because I was beginning to feel hungry, and the sight of the town and the houses made me think of a meal. So I pushed on down the other side of the saddle. The road here cut right through a plantation, and, as I have said, took a winding course. Consequently I could not see as far ahead as before, and so came quite unexpectedly upon a man who was standing in the pathway. He was staring up at one of the trees, so intently that he didn't notice my approach until I was close upon him. When at last he saw me he went very red in the face and looked in another direction, like someone caught in a guilty act. Turning with some curiosity towards the tree at which he had been gazing, I saw that it was loaded with fruit of the size and colour of melons. I jumped at once to an obvious conclusion.

"Hello!" I said: but not in English, mind you. Ydenneko's brain still carried Ydenneko's faculties, so that his own language flowed from his tongue as readily as if he was wagging it himself.

The youth blushed deeper. I could see that he was very young: much younger than I or Ydenneko.

"Is that tree private property?" said I.

"What tree?" says the lad.

"O come," said I. "I won't give you away. I'll give you a back if you'd like to shin up and gather us a couple of those melons."

You should have seen the change that came over the fellow when I said that. He clenched his fists, and his enormous eyes flashed with rage as he said: "You filthy hound, how dare you speak to me like that."

"No offence, old chap," I replied. "I didn't mean any harm. I've had a long walk, and I'm tired and hungry, and I just thought a bit of fruit would be refreshing—" There I stopped dead, for the lad was positively foaming with rage.

"Begone, you foul-mouthed rascal," says he, "or, coward as I am, I'll stuff your vile insinuations down your throat." Here he doubled his fists and stepped towards me with a menacing look in his eye. Plainly he was mad, and not half such a coward as he boasted; so, not to be outdone in nobility by a native, I turned round and galloped away at a pace that must have raised me a hundred per cent in the idiot's esteem. For half a mile I sprinted. Then, as he didn't pursue me, I dropped again to a walking pace—not a bit breathless, though, for Ydenneko's body was in the best of training, but hungrier and thirstier than ever, and just raging with disappointment. To think of those beautiful luscious melons kept from me by a brat of a half-witted boy! I felt I could have killed him.

Worse still, I had been turned back in my course, and, as I didn't want to encounter the lad again, I had to beat it across country and try to strike the road further on. So with weary steps and a steadily growing appetite I plodded through fields and plantations with occasional distant glimpses of the town to guide me until at last I reached the level ground and began to think I might safely take to the road again. I was casting around to put this decision into effect, when suddenly—O joy!—what should I see ahead of me but a little grove of melon trees, with the golden fruit hanging from their boughs in gorgeous profusion. What a sight for hungry eyes. With a shout of delight I dashed forward and forced my way through a thicket of flowering shrubs, until I was brought to by a high wooden fence which surrounded the grove. I hesitated a moment; then went circling round to look for a gate. But there was none, nor any opening of any kind, though I ran round twice to make sure. For an instant I stood baffled, looking helplessly up at the smooth brown face of the barrier, and the treetops and the inviting fruit that peeped above it. Then suddenly I remembered that the legs I was wearing were fit for feats that my own on earth would have quailed at. So, gathering myself together, I gave a spring upwards, hoping to catch hold of the top of the fence and haul myself over. It was a good jump—never had I

done its like before—but it wasn't high enough for the purpose.
I tried again, and again fell short. Then I went back a dozen
paces or so and took a running leap, but though I just managed
to get the fingers of one hand over the edge of the boarding, I
fell to earth once more, with a bruised knee and a splinter in
one finger to add to my troubles. But I wasn't beaten yet. In the
hope of finding a low spot in the fence I went prowling round
it again, to be rewarded at last by discovering, not what I was
looking for, but something better—a fallen tree trunk lying half
hidden in the shrubbery. In three seconds I had it propped up
against the fence. In three more I was on top of it and looking
over into the grove. Then a hoist and a spring, and I was down
under the shade of the melon trees, with the tasty fruit hanging
in thousands over my head, waiting to be devoured.

"Up boys and at 'em!" says I, and started to shin up the
nearest tree; but the moment I laid hands on it I knew it was
no go. The bark of that melon tree was like no bark on earth. If
you'll believe me, Mr. Gallagher, it was as smooth and slippery
as a pillar of greased ice, and not a branch or a snag to give you
foothold or handhold up to a dozen feet. I went from tree to
tree looking for a more likely one, but they were all the exact
same. At last, however, I found a fairly young one, which I was
able to get some sort of grip on. With tremendous labour, and
many a backward slip, I managed to work my way up this until
I was almost within reach of the lowest branches. Then my
strength gave out, and, even as I stretched up my hand, the grip
of my legs relaxed, and I went slithering to the ground again
with a frightful crash. Battered and stunned I lay there for a
while wondering was my back broken, and not daring to move
lest my fear might be confirmed. I was soon reassured, however,
and sat up to find that my worst injuries were a bruised behind
and a rawness of the insides of the thighs where the friction
had rasped the skin off. But it was quite enough to put me
off melons for the day. Painfully I hobbled back to the fence,

wondering how I was to get over it again. But there was no difficulty in doing that from the inside, as the beams which braced it up gave ample assistance. With a flop that jarred all my aching bones I landed on the far side, and set off once more in the direction of the road.

Disappointment combined with my recent exertions had given me a worse thirst than ever. My tongue felt like a clothes-brush against my parched lips and palate, and I was tormented with visions of the glorious drink that I was going to have at the first hotel I might come to. Then all of a sudden a doubt struck me, and I clapped my hands to my breeches pockets—I mean of course to the place where they should have been; for there wasn't a sign of one in the thin sateeny stuff of Ydenneko's shorts. Quickly my hands went to the belt—a very handsome one of soft leather, with a silver clasp and ornaments. One little pouch hung from it, but it was as light as a feather. Tearing it open I found a handkerchief and a box of matches. Nothing else. Not a sou; not a stiver; not a brass farthing nor a red cent.

I felt nicely sold I can tell you, and just thanked my stars I had made the discovery in time, instead of waiting till the bill for a good dinner was put before me. I now saw clearly that I had bitten off more than I could chew in this business. I was devilishly hungry, absolutely penniless, hadn't yet thought out a way of explaining myself, and more than certain that I was in a land of lunatics. If I pushed the adventure any further I might find myself completely in the soup, whereas, if I returned to earth, I had already gathered enough queer experiences to make my fortune as a lecturer—of course only as a sideline, Mr. Gallagher, for you mustn't think I'm the smallest bit dissatisfied with the place, or likely to get above myself on account of my travels. So I made up my mind to quit then and there; and standing still in the middle of the road, tried to shake myself free of Ydenneko's body. I thought it would have been as easy as putting it on, but it wasn't. I wiggled and waggled this way and that. I jumped into the air. I did the motions of flying with my arms. But it was no good. Then I lay down on my back and willed as hard as I knew how. Still no good. I shut my eyes and opened my mouth and willed again like the very devil. But it was all useless. After half an hour of the most ridiculous efforts I lay exhausted in that damned body, literally and metaphorically at the back of god-speed.

I don't suppose anyone was ever in such a desperate position before. Think of it. There I was, in another man's body, stranded in a strange world, penniless and starving, not quite sure whether the first person I met mightn't hale me off to execution, and in danger of losing my job in the heel of the hunt. When the full horror of the situation came home to me I sat up and cursed. I cursed my own folly and curiosity. I cursed Ydenneko and his carelessness. I cursed the whole world of Rathé. Above all I cursed that meddlesome old ass of a Philosopher. That made me feel a lot better, and cleared my mind for action, so to speak. I saw that there was only one thing to do at the moment: to walk straight on into the town and beg or steal something to eat. If I could dodge the police I mightn't be recognised by anyone else. I should have to chance that anyway. When I was fed I could enquire for Ydenneko's house, or look it up in a directory. Then I could slip in by a back way after dark, and surely my own family would shelter me from the law. After that maybe I could find a hypnotist or some such fakir who could rid me of Ydenneko's body as the Philosopher had rid me of my own. By jove, the position's not so hopeless after all, said I to myself as I rose to my feet; and with a lighter heart in spite of my empty stomach, I made my way towards the curving line of trees that marked the position of the road. To reach this I had to pass through a dense shrubbery, after which there was the flower border to cross. I had barely set foot on the latter when I heard a warning cry, and I looked up to find myself face to face with a Rathean girl.

CHAPTER VI

The Gardener's Daughter

SWEET YOUNG SLIP OF a girl she was, though her dress, according to our standards, was far from proper: but then it was the fashion of the place, and no fault of hers. She had nothing on but a kind of chemise of some white silky stuff, cut low in the neck, and reaching barely half way to her knee; which showed off her figure to perfection, as you may guess. A pretty figure it was too, though I haven't the skill—nor the conscience—to describe it. There, however, her beauty ended, for no face could be pretty with those dreadful Rathean eyes in it. Can you imagine them? Great bulging jellies, curving up from the cheek bones to the crown of the head, they fixed you with an awful unblinking stare that seemed to see right through you and read your very thoughts. There was also another feature which I now noticed for the first time. The mouths of these people were very small; so were their jaws; while their chins were almost non-existent. So you see that even with her peach bloom complexion and the daintiest of noses this Rathean girl didn't greatly appeal to me.

She stood in the pathway on the other side of the flower bed, leaning on a hoe, having evidently stopped working at the sound of my approach. "Have you lost your way, stranger?" she asked. I nodded, my mouth being too parched to utter a word. "O," she said, "you seem exhausted. Come over here and rest. You may cross the flower-bed. I can set it right again at once."

I picked my way over, the girl smoothing out my footprints with the hoe. Then I dropped upon a bench close by, while she took up a cloak which had been lying there—a gorgeous affair of blue silk lined with yellow—and threw it around her shoulders. Then, stooping to a basket under the seat, she took out a little silver flask and offered it to me. I took a long pull at it, and what do you think was in it, Mr. Gallagher, but wine! How did I know, you'll ask. Well, there was a fellow once kept an illicit cellar under the house I live in, and when he was raided there was a couple of bottles overlooked, and I and another lad found them. But this wine was in another class altogether: heavenly stuff that set my blood racing, my spirits soaring, and my tongue as free as the clapper of a bell.

"My fair preserver," I said—for in Rathé I used words quite naturally that you'd only read in books down here—" My fair preserver, if blessings were flowers, there'd be a garland of my weaving round your neck at this moment."

"I'm glad you are recovered," said the girl simply. "Have you travelled a long way?"

"A mile and the rest of it." I said.

"Why did you not cycle?" she asked.

"Because I haven't a bicycle," I said.

"You might have used the public ones," said the girl.

"Those ones in the sheds?" I asked.

"Of course," said the girl, looking rather astonished at my ignorance.

"I never thought of it," I said. "But no matter, I'd walk the whole distance twice over to be where I am now."

"Where's that?" says the girl with a blush.

"Why, outside this wine, of course," says I, taking another swig.

"I'm afraid," says the girl, "it's the neck of the flask and not mine, wears that garland of yours."

"Maybe I've a better tribute for your own neck," says I sootheringly.

"How dare you!" says she, not much displeased, but moving

away a bit, though not very far. I said no more, having my lips to the flask again, till presently she asked me where I had come from. This was a poser, but that wine had so sharpened my wits that, without more delay than you'd give to a two-figure tot, I said: "I'll give you three guesses."

"From the Twilight Lands perhaps," suggested the girl.

"How did you know?" I asked.

"Easily enough," said she. "A person who has never heard of public bicycles can only have come from some backward region. Have you come to stay here, or are you taking a holiday?"

"I've come to look for work," I said.

"Wouldn't that be easier to find in your own country?" asked the girl.

"O no," I said. "It's too poor and backward. There's nothing to do there."

"What did you say?" asked the girl in a puzzled tone.

"I said there was nothing to do there," I repeated, "because the country is so poor and backward."

The girl looked at me with the blankest astonishment in her enormous eyes. "Do you mean that?" she said. "I thought I hadn't heard you aright at first."

"Of course I mean it," I said.

"But it's nonsense," said the girl. "How can there be nothing to do when the country is poor and backward? There must be everything to do."

"Well, I suppose that's true enough in a sense," I admitted. "But of course the more advanced and prosperous a country is the more employment there must be for its people."

"Quite the contrary," said the girl. "There must be less."

"More, surely," I protested.

"Not at all," she declared.

"O come," I said. "Can't you see that it must be more?"

"I know perfectly well that it actually is less."

"Well, prove it then," I said triumphantly.

"Why, you stupid boy, can't you see—" She paused and broke off. "O, it's too childish to argue about. One might as well start proving that night is darker than day."

"All right," I said. "We must agree to differ, that's all."

"But it's too absurd!" she cried. "There must obviously be more work to do in a backward country whose resources aren't fully developed than in one like ours where we have the latest machinery to help us and can reap the benefit of the works of previous generations. Mustn't there?"

"Well," I said, rather dashed, "if you put it that way I suppose there must be. But if machinery and progress generally are going to cause unemployment, well, all I can say is that I'm against them."

She gave me another of those astonished glances, but at this moment our conversation was interrupted. Over the fields behind us—I could see it, of course, without turning round—came flying what I took at first to be a small airplane. As it drew nearer, however, I saw that it was really a bicycle with wings. Closer and closer it came, flying less than a dozen feet above the ground, banked skillfully, and after hovering for a moment like a bird, settled lightly on the road. I saw the rider press a lever on his handle-bar, the wings immediately closed down, and he went pedaling swiftly along the road for a couple of hundred yards. Then at a bend he took to the air again and was soon out of sight. The whole performance was a treat to watch.

"Would that be a public bicycle?" I asked the girl.

"I don't know," she replied. "It might be his own."

"Then the public bicycles are fliers too?"

"Yes."

"I must try one," I said, jumping to my feet.

"You'll find one in that shed down there," said the girl, pointing down the road. "But why hurry?"

"O, I'm in no hurry," I said; for I found that, ugly as she was, she was beginning to sort of grow on me, and when one is

stranded in a strange world one is naturally inclined to hang on
to anybody who acts friendly.

"Well, then, sit down," said the girl, "and tell me something
about yourself."

Here was a poser; but again my wits, thanks to that wine,
were equal to it. "There's nothing about me worth telling," I
said. "I'd rather hear about you."

"Well, you see what I am," said the girl, indicating the hoe.

"Are all these flower beds your work?" I asked.

"O no. I only weed them. I'm not out of my apprenticeship
yet. My mother is head gardener over this road, and it's all her
design. That's her house over there."

I had barely noticed the house before this, being too much
occupied with the girl. It stood back some distance from the
road, and was approached by a narrow graveled path which
wound through the road border, passed under a flowery arch,
and meandered on through a glorious rock garden to reach
it. The house was built long and low, bungalow-fashion, with
broad spreading eaves, a verandah running along the whole
frontage, and a three-storeyed tower with a high conical roof at
one end. With its white walls and green pilasters and its large
open windows it looked deliciously cool and airy, and so altogether delightful that I was scarcely surprised to hear it tinkle
musically at a sudden freshening of the breeze. I saw an instant
later that the sound came from some little bells hung at intervals
from the eaves: but the first impression was that the house was
a sort of musical instrument played by the wind. Well, thought
I, if this is a mad world, at least it's a beautiful one. And then
a fresh notion struck me. Maybe these people weren't really
mad, but only artistic. I'd often heard that musicians and artists
and people of that sort were generally a bit queer in their ways.
Maybe this was a world of artists. Quite likely, indeed. That was
why all this flowery talk came to me so easily. It would be quite
natural to Ydenneko. And this girl talked in a bookish style that

no gardener's daughter on earth ever used. Unpractical notions she had too—

She was still talking. "My mother is one of the greatest gardeners that Bulnid has ever produced, and they say I have inherited her skill. But I shall not work with her when I am out of my apprenticeship. Our ideas clash so. She breeds for bold and startling colour effects, whereas my taste is for subtle shadings. See those mauve delphiniums there? They are my work, and it was all I could do to induce mother to give them a place in the border. Do you like them, stranger?"

"They're awfully nice," I said. "But a clever girl like you oughtn't to be content to be a gardener all your life. You should try and raise yourself."

"I am not ambitious," replied the girl. "Besides I cannot paint or compose music or write poetry."

"Well, they aren't the only professions in the world, are they?"

"They are the only ones that rank above gardening," said the girl.

"You astonish me," said I. The girl laughed. "What queer ideas you Twilighters hold. Apart from these, could there be any work more dignified than the care of the beauty of the world?"

"Lucky beauty that has so beautiful a guardian!" I said, letting Ydenneko's tongue run away with itself.

"Am I beautiful?" says she, dimpling.

"Like one of your own flowers," says I. (Jove I was going it, but I wasn't responsible. It was my brain and body acting in accordance with habits implanted in them by their previous owner.)

"That is only your fancy," replied the girl. "No artist is as beautiful as his own works. I know, because once I loved a poet through reading his songs, but afterwards I met him, and now I am heart whole."

"Then there's a chance for somebody else?" I hazarded.

I don't know how it was, but not long after that I had her
hand in mine—or rather in Ydenneko's. I think I can leave it
all on Ydenneko, for I'm a shy lad myself. There it lay, anyhow,
quite contentedly, fair spoil of the first advance in the love game.
Rather embarrassing position, wasn't it? because I didn't want to
hurt the girl's feelings by withdrawing, and at the same time I
didn't want to commit myself to anything serious. Not that I'm
anyway conceited— for I know I'm not the kind of chap that
girls run after—but, you see, this girl obviously wasn't the kind
that goes in for flirting: you'd only have to look at her to know
that. So it was embarrassing as I say. At the same time I won't
deny that it wasn't altogether unpleasant. After all, a girl's hand
is a girl's hand, and this one was very nice and friendly: soft,
you know, though a bit roughened in spots by garden work,
and very expressive, if you understand what I mean. In fact I'll
confess that I began to feel very sweet on her.

"Do you like our country, stranger?" I heard her say, slipping
a little nearer to me.

"Very much," I replied. "Indeed I've never seen anything to
match it. But what a pity your hills are so ugly. They quite spoil
the picture."

"You are right," said the girl. "I'm afraid they'll never do
us credit, though we have done our best with them. Have you
done better in your country, stranger?"

A comical picture came into my mind of the Dublin mountains covered over with scaffolding, and gangs of workmen
improving the shapes of them with trowels and mortar. It
wasn't a bad guess at her meaning, as I found out later on; but
for the moment I was so bewildered that I could only mum-
ble something about their being indifferent also, and covered
up my confusion by squeezing her hand. At that she smiled so
encouragingly that I made so bold as to slip my arm around her
waist, which she yielded gracefully. What a waist it was! And
how delicious was the feel of her supple body through her thin

tunic. We sat like that in blissful silence for some time. Then "What may your name be, stranger?" says she. "Ydenneko. And yours?" "Nadimé." "Nadimé. Why, it's the sweetest name that ever I heard, and well suited to the sweetest girl I ever saw." "Am I that?" says she, smiling her delight. "Indeed," said I, "if I were a poet itself my tongue would be unworthy to sing your praises. Being none, I am struck dumb, and can tell my love only in the old way of lovers, with my lips on yours." She tilted hers up to me, murmuring something like "Well, why not?"

I turned to kiss her: but the sight of those great shining eyes, with their hard shell-cases languidly closing over them, and the remembrance of who I was and where I was, and a sudden cold douche of common sense made me pause.

"Alas!" I said. "I cannot do it. I am married."

Was she shocked? annoyed? disappointed? Not a bit of it. "I am afraid you are not very loyal to your wife," she remonstrated mildly, as if she were reproving a child for stealing sugar. "Aren't you ashamed of yourself?" I said I was, but that the temptation of her beauty had been too strong for me. The girl sighed regretfully. No heartbreak in the sigh though: just a sort of wistfulness, as if she had seen a pretty frock in a window and couldn't afford to buy it.

"Marriage is a bit of a nuisance at times isn't it?" she said. "But on the whole I should think the balance of advantage is in its favour. My mother, for instance, has lived with five different men, and she says now that she'd have been happier married." Cool as a cucumber she said it, Mr. Gallagher, as if she thought her mother's shame of no more account than her taste in chocolates. "And this," said I to myself "is the girl I nearly got myself engaged to." "But then," she babbled away, "she also says she could never have married any of the men she lived with. One was a handsome humbug; another was a bore; another was cold and couldn't satisfy her; another was too sensual; another mean and unkind; and another quite decent, but they simply couldn't get on together. I think her case only proves the necessity of choosing one's mate with the greatest possible care. At any rate mother's example has made me and my sisters convinced monogamists."

"Indeed?" I said, sarcastic like.

"Yes," she said. "The four eldest are already married, and I shall do the same when I meet the right man. Najé—she's the youngest—talks of becoming a courtesan, but she's only fifteen and doesn't really know her own mind. Besides, mother and her father have always spoilt her . . . What's the matter, Mr. Ydenneko? Are you ill?"

I was, but whether it was due to horror or hunger I couldn't be sure. However, as I was undeniably hungry I welcomed the opportunity to escape from this improper young woman's society.

"Madam," I said, as politely as my disapproval for her would allow, "I am a little faint from long fasting. Would you be so kind—?" But here I stopped. Nadimé had shrunk from me suddenly, and now rose to her feet with an expression of cold disgust on her face. She said not a word, but, pulling her cloak about her, turned me her back and walked sedately away. The suddenness of the change in her left me dumbfounded. One would have imagined that it was I who had said something improper and not she. But perhaps those great eyes of hers had really seen into my mind and found out what I thought of her. That must be it, I told myself, as I sat there looking after her. As for Nadimé, she never turned her head, but walked straight up the path to her house, went in, and shut the door.

There was nothing for me to do but to go on. I made for the shed she had shown me, and took out one of those flying bicycles.

Chapter VII

Singular Reticence of the Bulnidians

IT WAS QUITE LIKE an earthly bicycle, but longer and lower, and
extremely light: made of aluminum, I guessed. The wings, which
were neatly rolled up, sprang from the front fork just above the
wheel, and were worked, I saw, by a very complicated system of
gears operated by the pedals. I mounted, and after a short quick
run, pressed the lever on the handle-bar which controlled them.
The wings opened out, and I felt the machine slowly rising.
Then, as I pressed the lever down further, the gears changed,
and the wings began to flap like a bird's. I was flying about a
dozen feet above the road, rather clumsily and zig-zaggily, but
still genuinely flying. Steering and balancing were very difficult
at first—rather like one's early efforts to ride an ordinary bicycle,
only more so. However, I stuck at it, and soon began to feel quite
at home. I turned off the road for a bit and did a few stunts over
the fields, soaring up twenty feet or so, then diving down and
skimming close to the ground like a swallow. I felt as if I had
become a bird myself, and darted this way and that way as if
I was chasing insects. They call our airplanes flying machines:
but lord! they don't fly. No more than a steam boat swims. This
was real flying, like what you dream about when you're a child.

As I flew I could see the city of Bulnid spread out before
me; and a pleasant place it looked, though not exactly what
we'd call a city in our world. It was more like a suburb; still
more like an enormous garden with houses scattered through it.
Anyway, the sight of it reminded me once more of my need of
rest and refreshment; so I glided down to the road again, and,

after pedalling close up to the place, wheeled the bicycle into a convenient shed, and walked on into the main street.

Such a street! It was twice as broad as any street in Dublin; and down the middle of it was a row of trees and flower beds, separating the two streams of traffic. The pathways were broad in proportion, and screened from the carriage ways by lines of flowering shrubs. Between them and the shops—which were all detached buildings either one or two storeys high—were wide strips of lawn with more flower beds. Neither street nor pathway was crowded, and there were no signs of bustle or hurry anywhere. The people sauntered about, chatting in pleasant gentle voices, as if they hadn't a care in the world; and the traffic—which was all motor—rolled along in the most leisurely fashion. By no means a go-ahead place, I judged. Perhaps the most curious feature of the street was the lamp-posts. They were made like small trees with red and white fruits on them. The red fruits were large jewels of some sort, and the white were electric light bulbs. The bark of the tree was most cunningly wrought in bronze, and the leaves were of metal foil stained green. As I strolled along I noticed that each lamp post was modelled after a different kind of tree, with different coloured fruits, and so on. There was one, I remember, had huge drops of amber hanging from its branches; and there was another whose bark seemed to be of silver. By this tree there sat a young man playing a harp amid a small group of listeners. But he was as well dressed, and looked as well fed, as anybody else. He seemed to be just playing for his pleasure; for people would stop to listen for a while, and pass on again with a word or two of praise or thanks, but never an alms. I supposed he must be a municipal entertainer (like the bicycle), and thought he must be scandalously overpaid to be so well dressed and fed. However, music is thin diet for a hungry man, so, after hearing a tune out, I pushed on rapidly, keeping a sharp look out for an eating house. The street was certainly a fashionable shopping centre, though from a first glance one would never have guessed it, the Rathean shopkeepers apparently knowing nothing of the art of Salesmanship. Not a single house had a window display or a skysign—nothing but the name of what it dealt in written up over the door: tastily done, of course, but not what you'd call appealing. "Furniture, Paper, Ironware, Shoes," I read as I passed along. "Books, Pictures, Bicycles, Clothes, Music, Optical Instruments, Tapestry, Jewellery, Paint," and so on through the gamut of human wants and luxuries, but never a sign of anything to eat. At last I took courage to speak to a nice-looking young fellow in a green bordered cloak, who stopped and bowed politely, and listened to me with the friendliest possible smile on his face. No lunacy about this lad, I told myself.

"Excuse me for troubling you, sir," I said, "but I am a stranger here and don't know my way about."

"I am entirely at your disposal, sir," said the youth very politely. "If there is anything in which I can assist you, you have but to name it."

"Thanking you kindly, sir," said I, "I'm starving with the hunger, and if you would be so good as to direct me—"

But there I stopped, for my simple words had had the most extraordinary effect on the young man. The smile froze up on his face, he gave me a look of surprise and horror, blushed red through the tan of his skin, and "I'm afraid you've come to the wrong person for that information," says he stiffly, and walks off with his head in the air.

As I stood looking after him, and wondering what I had done to offend him, I felt a tap on the shoulder, and turned round to face another man, somewhat older I guessed, who said with a bow:

"My friend, I think you must be a stranger in this town?"

"Very much so," said I.

"Then," said he, "it is yours to command me. What can I do for you?"

"Well," said I diffidently, "I was thinking of getting something to eat—"

"O indeed," said the man, a bit taken aback. "Then in that case—er—I beg your pardon, I'm sure," and he hurried away in the most acute embarrassment.

As for me, I was beyond being astonished at anything by this time, and too stupid with hunger to try and think how I had given offence, so I just blundered along in hope of finding what I wanted on my own account. In my distracted state I managed somehow to collide with a man walking in the opposite direction. He was a pleasant-looking fellow, and accepted my apologies in good part. Then, as I was about to proceed, he said:

"You seem to be a stranger here, sir?"

"I am," said I.

"Then I am entirely at your service, sir. My name is Dobyna. Have you any commands?"

This time I didn't dare mention what was nearest to my heart, but stood dumbly looking at him.

"What about a drink?" says he.

This looked like business at last. I thanked him heartily, and we strolled along together, turned down a side street, and went in at the first gate we came to.

The house which we approached, like all the others I had seen, was of white marble, long and low. In design, I had noticed, that while every house was in harmony with its neighbours, no two were quite alike. This one had a verandah along its whole front, in the shade of which about a dozen people were sitting. Over the doorway was the word DRINK in graceful letters of blue enamel; and, as we walked up the garden path, I could see through the open door a comfortable hall, and beyond it a sunlit courtyard, with a fountain playing. Into this courtyard I was led by my guide. It was a pleasant spot, paved with tiles of a most restful green, with shady trees here and there, and under them little marble-topped tables and comfortable wicker chairs.

I sank into one of these with a sigh of relief, as my friend rang the silver bell which stood on the table beside it.

Almost immediately a waiter appeared. But I say waiter only because he waited upon us. He might just as well have been a gentleman for any difference I could see. He was dressed exactly like ourselves, and he had the same equipment of good looks, good health, good spirits, and good manners which characterised everybody in this unnatural world. He showed no signs of deference either, but shook hands warmly with Mr. Dobyna, who promptly introduced us as "Mr. Elyod: my friend Mr. Ydenneko, a stranger to this town." "Welcome, stranger," said the waiter, giving me a mighty handshake, "and may your sojourn here be long and happy. How are your geraniums doing, Mr. Dobyna?" "Poorly, I'm afraid," my friend replied. "I knew you'd taken the cuttings too late," said the waiter. "What's your drink, friends?"

Having no notion what the habits of the place might be I waited for a hint from Mr. Dobyna. "Shall it be wine or beer?" says he as I hesitated. "Beer," says I, and presently it was brought to us foaming high in a pair of tall tankards of cut glass. "Here's to you," said we both and put our lips to it. Oh, but that was the great drink of my life. Never, before or since, have I tasted one like it. For not only was the beer in Rathé like no beer on earth, but never was any beer poured down a throat that needed it sorer. Up, up, up went the tankard, and down, down, down went the rich brown fluid like water through a sluice. In half a second I was looking at the sky through the bottom of a dry tankard, and licking the last lingering drop from its edge. "Another?" says Dobyna, who had barely begun on his own. "Yes, by God." It was brought instantly, and I tossed it after its forerunner. "Another?" says Dobyna, looking at me with a sort of admiration in his eye, his own tankard being still more than half full. Decent fellow Dobyna, thinks I, pitying him for a softy. But I'd had enough to be going on with. "No thank you, old chap," I said. "No more drink, thanks. But as you are so kind, I've a great wish for something solid. What I mean to say, old oyster—" But here Dobyna cut me short with a "Thank you, I am not interested," and a look like an iceberg. But I wasn't going to be denied any longer, and the beer had given me courage; so I said: "I dare say not: but I am. Will you kindly tell me where in this inhospitable town I can get a bit to eat?" "No, sir," says Dobyna firmly, "I cannot." "Now look here, old chap," I pleaded with him, "I've come a long journey—longer than you can imagine—and I'm half mad with hunger. You'll excuse me if I'm not up to your rules of etiquette: but in such a necessity what on earth is a poor devil to do?"

"Well, sir," said Dobyna with a look of cool disgust, "If you insist on taking me into your confidence on such a delicate and personal matter, I suggest that in future you should limit your journeys to a distance from home proportionate to your self-control. Good morning."

He stood up to go; and I saw that it was a case of tell the truth or starve. So I laid a hand on his arm and said: "One minute. You don't understand the position at all. I haven't come from just over the hills: I'm from another world." "I thought it would come to that," said Dobyna scornfully. "It is the usual clap-trap with which so-called philosophers and self-styled thinkers bolster up their attacks on morality and social order."

"Easy! Easy!" I said. "Who's attacking morality? I'm no philosopher nor thinker, thank God, but just an ordinary respectable man as good as yourself. Yes: and better. When I said I came from another world I meant another world like this: another planet as you might say."

If a casual stranger told a story like that down in our planet, I've a pretty good idea how we'd take him. Eh? But this fellow believed me, right on the nail. "Indeed!" he said, brightening up in an interested sort of way. "Which planet?" and sat down again quite friendly.

"I don't know what name you'd call it here," I said. "We just call it the Earth."

"Have another drink?" said Dobyna. "I'm delighted to have met you. You know I've always felt that the stars must have some other purpose beyond looking pretty in the evening. But I imagined they must be populated by wonderful beings quite different from ourselves."

"Well, we're different over beyond, of course," I said. "But not very wonderful. In fact we're more ordinary than you." Then I had to explain that I hadn't brought my body along from earth, and to tell him how I had come by the one I was wearing, and so on— in fact the whole story of my journey, to which Mr. Dobyna listened with the greatest interest and attention.

"But tell me about your own wonderful world," he said when I had finished. "That's what most interests me. Tell me all about it."

"That's a rather large order," I said. "I wouldn't know exactly where to begin. Consider after all, if you were in the same position—"

"Quite right," he interrupted. "It was an unreasonable request. Perhaps when you've looked around a bit here and seen how we differ from you. But there was one thing I seem to have gathered from your first remarks." He hesitated a moment, and I saw a slight flush rise in his cheeks. "Aren't your people—er—a little—well, free and easy in—er—gastronomic matters?" He spoke with extreme hesitation and embarrassment, but was, I could see, most frightfully curious and excited.

"Well," I said, "we certainly can get a meal much easier than seems possible here."

"Indeed?"

"Yes. In fact, we can eat whenever we want to."

At this Mr. Dobyna's face took on such an expression of mingled delight and horror as you'll see in an audience at an improper filmplay. "Whenever you want to!" he said.

"Certainly."

"And—and—*what*ever you want to?"

"Of course."

"Er—eggs, for instance?"

"Rather."

"And—and—flesh?"

"Certainly."

"Do you mean that one man can have both?"

"Obviously."

"Eggs one day, I suppose, and flesh the next?"

"Or both together on the same plate," I added.

"What an orgy!" cried Mr. Dobyna. "How filthily revolting!" and his cheeks went blazing red and his eyes bright with excitement.

"Why? What do you eat here?" I asked.

Mr. Dobyna's face reddened deeper than ever, and he said: "Please, please, Mr. Ydenneko moderate your language. Someone might hear you."

"What's wrong with my language?" I asked.

Mr. Dobyna coughed apologetically behind his hand. "Well—er, it's a little outspoken, isn't it? Narrower minds than mine would be inclined to call it coarse."

"Coarse?" said I.

"We do not talk of such things as—er—eating in Rathé," explained Mr. Dobyna.

"Well, by Hell," said I. "I'll talk about it pretty strongly before I'll starve. I'll obey any etiquette in reason, but eat I must."

"Quite so, quite so," said Mr. Dobyna, nervously soothering me. "Say nothing more, and all will be well," and he looked this way and that, with an expression of absolute panic on his dial, as if he thought there were spies behind every pillar.

"Good lord," I said as I watched this pitiable exhibition, "you must be devilish cranky about your eats in this planet.

What's your worry, old chap?" But the fellow held up his hand with an imposing gesture, saying: "No more, I beg you. We have discussed this question quite long enough. It was my fault, I admit, to raise it, and for that I beg your pardon. Now let us change the subject."

"No, by your leave, Mr. Dobyna," said I, "we'll do nothing of the sort. A dish of bacon and eggs—"

"Please! Please! Mr. O'Kennedy."

"A dish of bacon and eggs," I repeated firmly, "may not sound very appetizing to you—" here Mr. Dobyna made a face of disgust—"but it's just the very thing I'd like to get outside of at this minute. However, if your local etiquette is against it, I won't press that. I'll take whatever I'm given and be thankful for it, but for pity's sake get me something quick or I'll go mad."

"This is really a most awful problem," said Mr. Dobyna, who indeed looked much distressed. "There's nothing for it but to take you to the Chief."

"The Chief?" I exclaimed.

"Yes. The chief of our Tribe."

Chiefs and tribes! said I to myself. Dash me if I haven't landed among cannibals after all. Mr. Dobyna went on to explain that it was the common rule for strangers who were in any difficulty to put themselves under the protection of the Chief; and as this seemed to offer some remote chance of a meal I consented to be led to him at once. My friend accordingly drained his tankard, slipped his arm through mine and led me to the door. He asked for no bill, I noticed, and left no money on the table; but as the waiter, who came into the courtyard at the same moment, waved us a cheery good-bye, I concluded that he must have an account there.

A little further along the street I nearly cried out with joy to see the word "Grocer" over the door of a shop. Now at last, I thought, I could get something to eat. "Excuse me a minute," I said to Mr. Dobyna, "I want to get something here," and I walked inside. It wasn't as much unlike a grocer's on earth as the outside view would have led you to believe. There was a counter in its proper place and a cash desk, and goods displayed quite tastefully. But one thing I took in at a glance. There were no eatables on view. I saw soap, and matches, and candles, and paraffin oil, and furniture polish, and suchlike household requirements, but not a thing else. For a moment I thought that perhaps the eatables might be on sale, though not on show: but listening to what the customers ordered soon put the idea out of my head. Feeling kind of sickish, I was turning to go away when one of the shopmen came up to me.

"Good morning, sir," he said very politely. "What can I get for you?"

I asked for the first thing that came into my head, which was matches.

"I am sorry I was unable to attend to you before, sir," he said, handing me a box off the counter, "but we are shorthanded today. One of our partners—a Mr. Ydenneko—was executed this morning."

"Not at all," I said.

"The curious thing is that when I first saw you come in I thought it was he. You are extremely like him, sir."

"Indeed?" I said.

"In fact," said the man, "in face and figure you are exactly the same. But of course that's not what one goes by."

Without thinking I went to my purse only to realise afresh that it was empty.

"I'm sorry I have no money—" I said.

"Money, sir?" said the man with a look of surprise. "O, I know what you mean! Well, I should hope not, sir. Good morning," and he held open the door.

More puzzled than ever I rejoined Mr. Dobyna outside.

CHAPTER VIII

A Number of Queer Happenings

WE TURNED SOON ONTO another broad street much the same as the first one I described, but with different trees and a different colour scheme in the flower beds: red and white predominating instead of blue and yellow. The lamp-posts were different too, being statues of men and women, some of them holding the lamps in their hands, others wearing them as ornaments; and there was one man posed like a juggler, the lamps being hung by thin wires from a canopy over his head, so that at night it must have looked as if he was playing with balls of fire. The statue of a boy a little further on held a scroll with the words: "Wait here for Omnibus"; which we did; presently boarding one marked "Palace." The buses, I may explain, were just like private cars, only bigger, and painted a uniform grey. Not being plastered with advertisements, they looked quite nice; but what a difference it must have made in their profits. We rolled along in no great hurry—nothing ever did hurry in Rathé—so that I had plenty of time to look at the streets. Everywhere were the same long low houses in their pretty gardens, the same broad sweeping thoroughfares and shady trees, the same cheerful gaily dressed people. But in each street there was some new beauty of flower setting, some fresh ingenuity of building or lighting. There was one street lined with images of strange beasts with lamps in their great eye sockets or on the tips of their horns, or in the depths of their roaring throats. Here the flower beds gave place to rockeries covered with extraordinary plants such as I had never seen before. In the next street the beds held ferns and mosses, the trees were tall straight larches, the pavements were of a cool green shade instead of the prevailing white, and the lamps were mounted on columns of old grey moss-covered stone. In yet another there were no trees at all, but creepers climbing on poles, some with flowers, and some with leaves coloured no less brilliantly. In this street the lamps were affixed to graceful columns of brass, which, though not highly polished, were nevertheless so bright that I asked Mr. Dobyna how they were kept so.

"Why," said he, "they are not brass, but gold."

"Gold!" I said.

"Yes. Brass, as you have observed, would require constant cleaning. Besides, gold looks nicer."

"But isn't it rather—?" I was going to say "expensive," but found no word of that meaning on my tongue. "Isn't it rather wasteful?" I amended after a moment's thought. "We wouldn't dream of making gold into street lamps in my world."

"Why? What do you use it for?"

"We don't use it. It's too precious. We keep it locked up in cellars underground."

Mr. Dobyna looked astonished. "And you talk of waste!" he said. "Yours must be a mad world. What do you make your street lamps of? and your outdoor seats? and your palings? Iron, I suppose. Absurd! It looks abominable and requires constant painting. Now gold is pre-eminently suitable for these purposes. It is durable, resistent to the atmosphere, looks handsome, and requires no attention. —But here we get off."

The bus had stopped where the street ended in a huge open space, from which other streets radiated in all directions. There were more flower beds here, and statues, and fountains; and right in the middle was a house, the largest and handsomest I had yet seen in the city. Mr. Dobyna told me it was the palace of the Chief, and that our journey was at an end. If you'll believe me Mr. Gallagher, the pavement we now walked on was all over pictures done in little coloured squares—mosaic I'm told they call it—representing what must have been stories from history. But I didn't get the chance to observe them closely for Mr. Dobyna hurried me on towards the Palace. We walked in at the open door and right through the hall to the courtyard without meeting a soul: rather strange, I thought, in a palace, where I had been led to believe you wouldn't be able to go two steps without knocking into a servant or a soldier or a courtier or some such fowl. In the courtyard, sitting in a plain wicker chair, was a man reading a book: a very fine figure of a man, taller by a head than either of us, with a square-cut grey beard, and eyes deeper and larger than any I had seen yet in Rathé. He was dressed in the usual fashion except that his cloak was crimson, with gold fringes. Rising at our entrance he waited for us to approach. Mr. Dobyna, drawing near to him, with me in his wake, raised his hand in salute, saying: "Greeting, my Chieftain," and presented me as a stranger who claimed his protection.

"You are welcome, Stranger," said the Chief. "Be as my son in Bulnid," and he laid his hand for an instant on my shoulder. He then asked me what land I came from.

"From no land of this world," I replied. "I come from a distant star which we call the Earth."

I hardly expected the Chief to be as gullible as his subject: but he was, every bit. Without a start of surprise or a sign of doubt he bowed as low as if I had been a king, and says he: "Sir, you do our planet much honour. Dare I to hope that your first impressions of it have not been unfavourable?"

"Not altogether," I said, very grandly, feeling that with a little show of neck I should soon get the whip hand of these people. "Of course you aren't up to our standards, and never could be, but I don't see why you shouldn't improve yourselves a lot if you were shown the way."

"Sir," said the Chief with another bow, "if your wisdom will but condescend to instruct us, you will find us very willing to learn."

"Good," I said. "Just give me a day or two to look round, and I'll soon show you where you're wrong."

At a reminder from Mr. Dobyna I now told my full story to the Chief; who, I found, knew all about poor Ydenneko, having confirmed his sentence of execution that morning. I remarked that I was surprised that he had not taken me for the man himself; to which he replied that he certainly had done so at first sight, but that he had very soon observed that the resemblance was only physical. There was no danger whatever, he assured me, of anybody taking me for the deceased criminal: least of all (as I had suggested) his own relatives, who would be the last to be deceived by mere outward show.

Mr. Dobyna now interposed to say that he had some business to attend to, and, begging to be excused for taking his leave, he promised to call on me again in a few days. When he had gone the Chieftain begged me to consider myself his guest for so long as I might choose to remain in Bulnid, and, if I had any immediate need, to name it, and it would be an honour and a pleasure to him to gratify it. I had the sense now not to blurt out an immediate demand for supper; but after a few tactful preliminaries about the difference in habits between the people of my world and his, more particularly in the matter of etiquette and social custom, I asked him not to be shocked if I told him, in the plain blunt language of the Earth, that I was hungry. The Chief didn't make quite such an ass of himself over the phrase as Dobyna had done, but I could see quite plainly that he was embarrassed. For a moment he was at a loss for words; then he began:

"Hm. Yes. Put bluntly, as you say, that is a rather common condition with young fellows of your age. We all have to go through with it. Doubtless, in a week or two, you'll fall in with something that you fancy, and then—well—" here he laughed nervously and broke off, leaving the sentence unfinished.

"You don't seem to understand," I said. "I'm not worrying

about next week. I want a good square meal now—this very minute."

At that the Chieftain frowned angrily, and his voice went hard with contempt as he said very decisively: "Nonsense, sir. Nonsense. Try and exercise a little self-control. Pull yourself together now and forget this. I want to introduce you to my family."

Utterly blanked and dumbfounded I could only follow him into the house. We walked along a corridor past two doors and through a third into a large room flooded with the late afternoon sunlight, and in a minute I was being introduced to a whole bunch of ladies. There was the Chieftain's wife, handsome and stately; his eldest daughter, Camino, the very image of what her mother must have been thirty years ago; his second daughter, Ianda, long-limbed and athletic; and Ytteb, his youngest, a sweet girl just out of her teens. Glorious creatures they were, every one of them, though rather embarrassing to look at, standing about like that in their chemises (they left off their cloaks indoors) like advertisements in a newspaper.

Lastly I was introduced to the Chieftain's son, Ensulas, a sly-looking youth whom I didn't like at all. He was fattish, with an unhealthy complexion—the first person I had met in Rathé who was noticeably out of training. He looked me over in an irritatingly superior way, as if I was a dog he was thinking of buying; and afterwards stood apart, while I talked with his mother and sisters, as if he took no interest in what I was saying, but listening with unconcealed contempt, which upset me most horribly. The three girls, when they had heard from their father that I was from another world, closed round me at once, demanding to be told all about it. I did my best, for all my aching stomach, to comply, but must have made a poor hand of it; for presently their mother, guessing part of what was wrong, cut in saying that it was a shame to bother me when I was so tired, and asking me if I would care to go to bed. In spite of a little insistence from Ytteb I grasped at this opportunity to escape, and went off with the contemptuous Ensulas, whom his parents told to show me to my room.

The young man led me further along the corridor and round the corner into another wing of the house. The first door we came to after that he threw open to show me a bathroom—an affair of white and green tiles and shiny nickel and glass like you see in millionaires' houses on the films—and then, passing a couple more doors, he took me into my own room further on. I was expecting this to be on the millionaire scale too; so you can imagine my disappointment on finding it quite small and simply furnished. It was bright and cheerful, however; the walls being done in snow-white shiny enamel, while the large window looked out on a garden and the great circular space beyond. The floor was of the same sort of rubbery material as the public paths, patterned like a carpet: and all the furniture in the place was a small bed, a chair, a table, and a wardrobe. There was no wash-stand: apparently one had to use the bathroom. Exhausted, I sank down on the bed and lay sprawling, while Ensulas stood looking down at me with a look of cynical compassion.

"I know what's wrong with you," he said presently. Then, as I looked up: "Hungry, eh?"

"Rather!" I cried, my heart giving a sudden bound of hope.

Ensulas came closer to me, and with his mouth almost at my ear, said in a hoarse whisper: "Like something to eat?"

His breath was far from pleasant and my instinctive dislike of the fellow was not diminished, but here, I felt, was an ally, and I grasped his hand. "I'm dying for it," I said; whereupon Ensulas put a cautionary finger to his lips, and tipped me a knowing wink. Such a wink! The eyelids of the Ratheans, which are made of a hard brown glossy stuff like the wingcases of a beetle, fit close to the back of the head when out of use, and can be slid forward over the eyes as quick as the shutter of a camera if necessary. But there was no such snap in Ensulas's wink. Quite slowly the lid rolled itself over one eye till only a slit was visible between it and the twitched up cheek. Then, just as slowly it slid back again. You've no idea what a world of archness that wink suggested, though where the joke lay I hadn't a notion. "Not a word," he cautioned me. "I'll get you fixed up all right. There's a jolly little place quite near here, and as soon as it's dark we'll make a bolt for it. In the meantime you'd better lie low and pretend to be asleep. Would you like a book or a newspaper to pass the time?" I asked for a newspaper, which he fetched promptly, and then left me to myself.

The newspaper, I found, was called *The Bulnid Record*, and was the queerest sheet I had ever set eyes on. How it ever paid its way is a mystery beyond my solving. Under the title the following sentence was printed in capital letters:

> We cannot guarantee the Truth of anything in these pages. We do our best to be fair and accurate, but allowance must be made in all cases for our human liability to error and prejudice.

A joke? No, sir. And, if it was, it was the only one, for the rest of the paper was as dull as a book of history. There were no flare headlines; no gossipy pars; no murder or divorce news; no sporting news; no advertisements; no pictures except for a couple of silly landscapes—jolly well done, of course, but who cares about such dud stuff? The most featured item in the whole concern was some stuff about a new chemical discovery. Next to that in importance came a notice of a new book, an account of an exhibition of pictures, and an essay on some jaw-breaking subject that I can't remember. How anybody could think it worth his while to print such dry rubbish; still more how anybody could ever be induced to buy it, are questions that are quite beyond me.

I threw the rotten rag on the floor and went to look out of
the window. The sun was setting. It rested on the horizon like
a huge dome of hot copper under a dully glowing sky. There
were no rosy clouds nor strokes of apple green like we have in
Ireland: just the same uniform red growing deeper and deeper
towards the sharp rim of the sun. There was a heavier sadness
about it than I had ever felt on earth: a keener reminder that
days and worlds must die. And there was a dreadful look about
the sun itself that I had never seen in our own old orb: it was
like a hungry eye glaring on its prey.

Two hours later, it being now dark, Ensulas tapped softly on
my door. When I opened it he crept stealthily into the room,
and, after whispering me to put on my cloak, softly opened
the window and stepped out on to the balcony. I followed. We
let ourselves down on to the lawn, passed swiftly and silently
through the garden to the great square beyond, and made
for the nearest street. Looking up at the sky I saw the stars
twinkling in unfamiliar groupings, and over the distant hills
the rising of two moons. The fantastic lamps were everywhere
alight, but few people were abroad, and they but flitting figures
discreetly wrapped like ourselves. We had not gone very far
when my companion caught my arm and stopped in front of a
house which was darkened and shut up like its neighbours. A
side door, however, proved to be unlatched, and I followed my
guide through it—not without a good deal of misgiving—into
a dark passage, on through another door, down a dimly lit stone
winding stair, and along another passage to a third door, on
which Ensulas rapped with his knuckles. After a short pause
the door was opened by a horrible-looking man: the first really
unhandsome being I had met in Rathé. He was fat and under-
sized. His eyes were bleared and fishy. His teeth were black and
rotten, and his breath stank.

"I've brought you a new customer, Mr. Radnap," said
Ensulas.

The fellow gave an odious laugh. "Walk right in," he said. "Any friend of yours, Mr. Ensulas, is doubly welcome. Stomach in good condition, eh?" he said, poking me in that neighbourhood with his claw of a hand, and laughing again.

As he closed the door behind us I looked around the room which we had entered. It was large and low, and lit only by a tallow candle. There were no windows, and the air was damp and oppressive, with a strong smell of bad food. All round the walls were tiers of shelves, laden with various kinds of fruit, with here and there a pile of eggs, and a few chunks of doubtful-looking meat.

"What'll you have, sir?" asked the odious old man. (Mr. Ensulas, I noticed, had slipped away.) "I've the loveliest and juiciest fruit in every variety. Prime tender lamb in the best condition. New-laid eggs fresh from the hen."

If I hadn't been desperately hungry I couldn't have touched any of his wares, or eaten anything at all in such a place. But I was in no condition to be squeamish. I was frightened of the eggs, and beastliness was written all over those greasy lumps of mutton; so I decided to try my luck with a collection of assorted fruit. From those musty and decaying piles I picked the best specimens I could find; after which the old man led me to a smaller room, furnished with a solitary chair and table, and left me to myself to make what cheer I could with my choice.

Over that feast I'll draw a veil. In half an hour Ensulas returned and said it was time to go home. So once more we passed through the deserted streets and regained my room without mishap. We had been so muffled in the streets that talk had been impossible, but now I turned to Ensulas for an explanation of our adventure.

"O, don't worry me with moral problems," he replied wearily. "I dare say you're less hypocritical than we are in the world you come from. But this is no time for religious conversation. Good night, old chap." He yawned, and was gone.

Tired and replete, I now undressed and fell into bed. But I couldn't sleep. The unsavoury mess of fruit which I had eaten sat on my stomach like a load of lead, and nauseating memories kept forcing themselves on my attention. I twisted and turned; I sighed and groaned; I rolled myself in the sheets; I cast them off on to the ground. Thus hour after hour went by, the little clock in the room serenely chiming the quarters.

At last I could stand it no more, and in a fever of restlessness left my rumpled bed to look out of the windows. The few stars were paling, and a grey light like that of dawn was in the sky. But it could hardly be dawn, I realized, because it was in the wrong quarter of the sky. What else could it be? Wrapping myself in a blanket I sat down by the window to watch. The light steadily grew brighter. The features of the silent houses beyond the square became gradually distinguishable. Presently a breeze rustled through the shrubbery beneath me, and a bird gave a wakening chirp. Then, as I yawned, a bright ray shot up from the horizon which so lately had hidden the copper disc. There was no longer a doubt of it. The morning sun was rising in the west.

CHAPTER IX

Further Peculiarities of the Ratheans

WHEN I FIRST EMERGED from my room in the morning my first object was to get hold again of Ensulas, whom I now regarded as my one safeguard against starvation in an inhospitable world. But as I entered the hall I was hailed by the voices of the three girls, who were sitting round a table on the verandah sipping white wine. Of course I joined them at once, taking a chair between Ytteb and Ianda, while the tall and stately Camino poured me a brimmer of the wine—lovely stuff, the colour of sunshine, and tasting like nothing that ever was brewed on our old sod. It was better than a dozen breakfasts, and drove all thought of Ensulas clean out of my head.

"This is the finest world in the universe," said I with enthusiasm as the girl refilled my glass.

"What? Have you visited many?" asked little Ytteb eagerly.

"O, no," I said carelessly. "I just glanced at a few in passing."

"So the stars are really and truly worlds?" she said.

"No. The stars are suns, and the worlds revolve around them."

"Of course," the second girl, Ianda, interposed impatiently. "The child meant the planets. They really are worlds like this, then?"

"More or less."

"And yours?"

"Quite like this."

"With land and sea?"

"Yes."

"And flowers and animals?" said Camino.

"Yes," I repeated. "And men and women."

"And cities and governments I suppose," said Ianda.

"O yes. And motors and airplanes and all the rest of it."

Ianda turned a satisfied look on her elder sister and said: "Well, that pretty well settles the Scientific Revival, doesn't it?"

Camino laughed and said, "Poor old Science!" half affectionately and more than half contemptuously.

I asked what they meant.

"What?" said Ianda. "Have you no conflict between Science and Religion in your world?"

I had heard some such phrase somewhere or other—in a sermon most likely—and I know that Scientists are bad men who go about digging up facts to overthrow the truths of religion. But I thought the best way to get an explanation out of Ianda was to say No.

"Well," said she, "it won't last much longer even here. At one time our scientists used to teach that the sky was a metal sphere revolving around Rathé at a distance of 4004 miles, and that the sun, moons, and stars were fixed to it. Of course all this was exploded long ago by the imagination of poets and religious thinkers, and only the most lowly-evolved people continued to believe in it. But lately the scientists have been trying to regain their influence by pretending that they never taught that the old theory was *literally* true, and claiming that it is true in a figurative sense and therefore doesn't really clash with modern religious discoveries. They've regained some ground in consequence—that's what they call the scientific revival—but their real grip is gone for good, and your coming will finish it. . . . But tell me about your own world," she said. "What are your men and women like? Are they very different from us?"

I told her no. We were much the same except for our eyes, of which I was beginning an elaborate description when she cut me short, saying: "I know. Like a dog's. Then what have you on top of your heads?" "Hair," I said. "O," says she rather contemptuously, "like monkeys. You must be very low-ly-evolved. Are your eyes much use to you?" I said they were, but she couldn't believe it. Weren't we always getting bumped into from behind? she asked. And wasn't our field of vision even in front very narrow? And how could we see any very big thing as a whole? I argued and argued, but couldn't convince her. She'd a devilish tough mind, had Ianda, and a tongue of steel. Then off she went again on a different tack. How ugly and bestial we must look; how difficult it must be for us to distinguish one another from monkeys.

But here Camino broke in with a kindly laugh. "I daresay you seem all right to yourselves," she said sensibly.

"And of course monkeys have tails," Ianda reflected.

"But what *frights* your women must be," cried little Ytteb.

"Not at all," I said stoutly.

"O come," she persisted. "Aren't their eyes very *inexpressive*," and ogled me gigantically. Boys-o-boys, what a come-hither. I foresaw that little Ytteb and I were going to get on famously.

Just at this point a little boy came running in from the garden and jumped into Ianda's lap, crying, "Hello, mummy." Ianda kissed him and said, "Go and shake hands now with the gentleman from the stars." So down the child scrambles at once, and "Are you from Alpha or Beta or Gamma?" says he, as cool as a cucumber, putting his little hand into mine.

"He is not from the Solar System at all, dear," said Ianda. "He comes right from the other end of the universe."

"You'd never think it," said the kid. "He looks quite ordinary. Is yours a nice planet, Mr. Stranger?"

"He's a clever youngster," said I to his mother. "How old is he?"

"O you rude man!" cries young hopeful at this. "I asked you a question, and instead of answering it you make personal remarks over my head. I shan't speak to you any more."

He turned away from me, and I looked up at the girls

expecting to find them amused at the child's cuteness. But not a bit of it. They all looked annoyed, and Ianda said quite snappishly that I'd no business to give the child a bad example. Then Camino intervened with some patronizing tosh about my knowing no better, perhaps, for which I could have hit her, and which had no effect on Ianda, who got up and walked off into the garden with the kid in tow. Even Ytteb seemed to be a little displeased with me, though she at once began to make allowances. "I dare say etiquette is different in your world," she said, "but here it's considered very rude to ignore a question like that and to ask about a person's age—especially to ask it of someone else before his very face."

"But surely with a child—" I protested. "And to its own mother—"

"That's what makes it so much worse," said Camino. "To be rude to an adult is merely rudeness. To be rude to a child gives it a bad example."

"I'm sure I meant no harm," I said.

"I can quite believe it," replied Camino with exasperating indulgence, as if she thought me half-witted.

"You see," I explained, "I thought the boy so advanced for his age. I don't supposed he's more than four years old, but—"

"Four years old!" cried Camino and Ytteb in a breath. "Why, he's only eighteen months."

"Eighteen months!" I said.

"Nearly nineteen, as a matter of fact," Camino admitted.

"Well," I said. "I thought we knew something about hustling in our world, but this has us beaten to a frazzle. Eighteen months! Why, in our world a child of eighteen months would only be beginning to crawl on hands and knees, to say nothing of talking."

It was now the turn of the girls to be astonished. They told me that in Rathé children could walk and talk when they were first born, and that some could even sing or play the piano. At a year old they could read and write; at two they went to school; and at seven they were grown men and women. When I proceeded to describe the helpless condition of infants on earth Ytteb could not help laughing, and Camino, with gentle pity, said that we were evidently in a very lowly-evolved state.

"O no," I replied. "The lower the animal the quicker it develops"—which was a jolly smart extempore and sent her away very thoughtful.

I was now left alone with little Ytteb, who, to my great delight, suggested presently that she should take me on a tour of inspection round the city. I was half afraid her parents might object; but not they. The Chief asked had he not taken me as his son; and his wife—My Lady, as everyone called her—thought it "too much honour" for her daughter to enjoy the company of a gentleman from my starry sphere. So off we went together. I have already given you a fair idea of the general layout of the city of Bulnid: its long streets with their flower borders and shade-trees and their quaintly varied lamp-posts; its low white buildings and handsome gardens; its air of ease and cheerfulness. We now wandered off the main streets into delightful by-ways where there were all sorts of nice little shops. Here there would be a silversmith selling his own handmade wares; there a toymaker polishing up the last of a family of wooden animals, or showing a child how to work an engine; further on a painter's apprentices would be exhibiting his pictures while the great man himself could be seen at work through the window above. Some of the nicest private houses were in quiet blind alleys at the end of these by-ways. There was less formality of arrangement here than in the big thoroughfares. The streets curved and climbed hills, and you came on little parks in unexpected places. But everywhere there was the same bright neatness and prosperity. I looked out for a working quarter in vain. There were no factories, no tenements, no workers. Nothing but beautiful buildings and well-dressed people. At last I put a question to Ytteb.

"Factories?" she said. "Why of course we have factories. Come and see," and she led me into the very next house. From the outside it looked like any other house in the street, and there was the usual hall and courtyard; but in every room there were hand looms, with men and women hard at work on them weaving the beautifully coloured stuffs out of which they make their clothes. You mayn't believe me, Mr. Gallagher, but these workers were as well dressed, as well fed, and as happy looking as the people I had seen on the streets and lounging on the terraces of the wine shops. It was a model factory if ever there was one, and I guessed that the mug who ran it must have very little profit to show after he had paid these hands their wages.

"I'd like to meet the owner of this place," I remarked to Ytteb.

"Nothing simpler," she replied. "There are two of them," pointing to a young man and a girl working in the room we had just entered.

"Are they shareholders?" I asked.

"Naturally," replied Ytteb. "Why else would they work here?"

This answer didn't seem to apply exactly to my notion of a shareholder; and my notion of a shareholder puzzled Ytteb altogether, so that we got into a pretty muddle in trying to explain things to each other. I couldn't get any idea of industrial conditions on earth into Ytteb's head, but from her I gathered that in Rathé the factories all belonged to the people worked in them, and that the managers and other officials were elected from among themselves. Such things as employers and employees were unknown in the planet: in fact there were no such words in the Rathean language. Very primitive state of society, don't you think? Altogether, as I found out later on, industry and commerce in Rathé were in a very unprogressive state. The people seemed to have no idea of the value of mass production. Factories were few and small, most trades being carried on by individual craftsmen, or at best by half a dozen working in partnership. Newspapers, theatres, retail shops were all on the same scale. They made little use of machinery, and what they had was nothing like as good as ours. They had us beaten, I admit, in airplanes, at any rate as far as quality goes: but in quantity they were years behind us. As for their motors and railways, they were a joke. When I first saw the leisurely way the traffic rolled along the Bulnid streets I thought it was from choice, or because the legal speed limit was low. But the real reason was that they had no engines capable of going any faster—and didn't want them. It was the same with the railways. There were few lines, the trains were small, and services execrable. They were all electrified, but the fastest trains crawled along at a maximum speed of twenty miles an hour. And the Ratheans didn't desire any better; nor were they a bit impressed when I told them of our achievements on earth. Regular stick-in-the-muds they were, without a spark of enterprise in their composition, and absolutely void of the spirit of competition. However I'll leave the subject here, as I am going to deal with their whole economic system later on.

Shortly after leaving the factory we came to a most extraordinary-looking erection. It was an enormous heavily constructed pile of black marble towering high above every other building in the city, and lavishly decorated with carvings and sculptures, but simply hideously ugly. I don't mean to say it was badly designed, or clumsily carried out, or anything like that. Quite the contrary. I'd say it was a jolly clever bit of work if my opinion was worth giving. But the feeling it gave me was that it had been planned wrong on purpose by someone who liked ugliness for its own sake, who had had to labour against difficulties—against lapses into beauty perhaps—so as to make it as completely ugly as possible, and had triumphantly succeeded. The whole shape of the thing was an offence. The sculptured figures that crawled over it were ghastly mockeries of living things. The patterns of the carved traceries that covered the surface seemed to convey some diabolical meaning. I was half afraid to enter the place, but Ytteb led me towards it quite unconcernedly, and turned the handle of the iron door.

"What is it?" I asked.

"A Church," said she.

Next instant we were inside, the door closed heavily behind us, and we stood in the pitchiest, blackest, coldest darkness that ever appalled a human soul. A chill shudder, as if I had plunged into an ice bath, shook me all over. For a moment I stood frozen to the ground. Then with a gasp I darted to the door, pulled it open, and flung myself into the sunshine outside. I had a few minutes in which to recover my composure before Ytteb reappeared, looking somewhat edified and apparently unaware that I had left her side. As we walked off together I looked up at the massive frontage, and saw, what I had not noticed before, that it was unbroken by a single window. It was more like a tomb than a church, and, as I was to learn later on, only too well suited to the abominable religion to which it was consecrated. But that subject I must also postpone for the present.

Soon after this I saw a young man and a girl smiling and bowing to Ytteb as they came towards us. "Here are two of my greatest friends," said she, delighted. "I must introduce you." An instant later we were shaking hands, Ytteb presenting me quite coolly as "Mr. O'Kennedy, from the stars." Would you believe it, Mr. Gallagher, they showed as much surprise as you would if you were introduced to a man from Drumcondra. "Welcome to Rathé," says the man; and, "I hope your stay here will be a pleasant one," says the girl.

When they had passed on I asked Ytteb why it was that people accepted my story so readily.

"Would such a story not be believed in your world?" she asked in return.

"Not likely," I said. "Not without some sort of proof."

"You must be a very deceiving race to be so un-believing," said she. "Here we believe because we don't deceive."

"What?" said I. "Are there no liars in Rathé?"

"I didn't say so," replied Ytteb. "I suppose there are some, but what of that? We have short-tempered people too, but we don't wear armour for fear of being stabbed, so why should we wear distrustful minds for fear of being deceived?"

"But surely," I said, "no matter how truthful your people are as a whole, the chance of being deceived is greater than the chance of being murdered."

"Perhaps," said Ytteb carelessly. "But then if one is deceived one has a remedy: one goes to law and gets damages: whereas there is no compensation for being murdered. Besides, a distrustful mind is a heavy weapon to carry about. I'd sooner wear armour."

"Do you take an action against a person who tells you a lie?" I asked, rather amused by her simplicity.

"Naturally," said Ytteb. "It is a graver abuse of the ear than a stone could inflict."

I was prevented from carrying the argument further by the sight of a strange procession which at this moment came round a corner ahead of us. First of all came two rather pompous middle-aged men dressed in brilliant yellow and covered all over with jewels. They had ear-rings in their ears, necklaces round their necks, bracelets and bangles on wrists and ankles, blazing buckles in their shoes, and more pendants and brooches than a prince in a pantomime. They danced and skipped along to a tune played by four lads with flutes who followed behind. After these came a dozen or more men and women marching two by two; and after these a crowd of children of all ages, skipping and laughing. Last of all came a chariot drawn by two white horses, in which sat a man and a young woman with a baby in her lap. As they passed by, all the people in the street bowed or waved their hands, so that, between this and the general gorgeousness of the turn out, I thought it must be the King and Queen of Rathé out for an airing. But what do you think it was? Only a young couple taking their newborn child to be received by the Chief. Such a fuss over nothing! I remember the time my

youngest brother was born. He was our ninth. There was my
father sitting in the corner grumbling at having another mouth
to feed, and my mother not knowing whether to be glad or
sorry, and dying undecided, and the baby itself dying next day.
I suppose it was just as well so, and we gave them the grandest
funeral that ever was seen in Stoneybatter. —But to return to
this christening procession.

"I suppose the other children are the brothers and cousins,"
said I. "And are those the relatives beyond?" Ytteb nodded.
"And who," I asked, "are the two playboys in front?"

"Priests," said Ytteb.

I should have been prepared for any kind of lunacy by now,
but this was so totally unexpected that I really thought, in spite
of our recent argument, that Ytteb was pulling my leg.

"O come," I said. "This is too much."

"Well," said Ytteb, quite seriously and in a judicious sort of
tone, "perhaps their piety is a little ostentatious; but I believe
they're quite sincere."

I had no answer to that, so we pursued our way in silence
for some minutes. Presently ahead of us I noticed a man whose
walk and appearance singled him out at once from the cheerful
well-dressed crowds. His face was pale and sad, his tunic soiled
and faded, and instead of the usual silver-buckled belt he wore a
plain one of red leather. As he slunk along the pathway towards
us he seemed suddenly to recognise my companion, and turned
a timid, half expectant face towards her. Ytteb at once, with the
most insulting deliberation, looked the other way, which plainly
wounded the poor devil to the quick.

"What has that fellow done to you?" I asked when he had
passed by.

"Nothing," said Ytteb. "He's a murderer."

"So one cuts murderers in Rathé," I observed, rather amused.

"Well," said Ytteb, "one must draw the line somewhere. I
dare say Camino would find it in her heart, and Ianda in her

philosophy, to be more charitable, but as for me"—primly—"I draw the line."

"But has the law nothing to say in the matter?" I asked.

"Of course it has," said Ytteb. "He was put on trial in the ordinary way, but his crime was such an unusual one that the judges didn't know what to do about it. At first they thought of making him do the murdered man's work as well as his own, by way of compensation to the tribe; but this was found to be impossible, as his victim was an architect and he was a tailor, and anyway, if a man has double work to do, he'll do none of it right. I don't know how many other plans they considered, but they couldn't decide on anything, and in the end they just deprived him of his citizenship and let him go."

"They might at least have locked him up," I said.

"Where?" asked Ytteb.

I found that there was no word in their language for prison, so I couldn't answer. "Do you never lock up your criminals?" I asked.

Ytteb laughed. "What would be the use of that? Instead of making reparation, they'd be wasting other people's time in looking after them."

"Well," I said, "why not execute the fellow and have done with him? You're none too squeamish about executing in this planet, are you? Poor Ydenneko, for instance—"

"Ah, that's quite another matter," said Ytteb. "By executing careless people one saves valuable lives. But this man had done all the harm he could do already."

"He might commit another murder," I objected.

"No," said Ytteb. "The psychological examination showed that he had gone through such agonies of horror and remorse that he was unlikely to repeat the offence. Besides, that red belt is enough to put people on their guard against him."

"What if he didn't wear the belt?" I asked.

"I suppose his breeches would come down."

"O, look here," I laughed. "Do be serious."

"I'm perfectly serious."

"Do you mean to tell me that in the whole of Rathé that man couldn't get another belt?"

"I do. You see, the belt is the symbol of citizenship. Everybody gets one from the Chief as soon as he comes of age. There are no others made. If a man is convicted of something that renders him unfit for citizenship, it is forfeited, and he has to wear whatever is decreed by the judges."

Somehow I didn't feel quite satisfied with this position.

"But surely something ought to be done to the fellow," I said. "Some sort of—" I was going to say "punishment" but could find no Rathean word handy. "Some sort of vengeance," I amended.

"Vengeance?" said the girl, as if she didn't understand. "That sounds like some antiquated word out of the classics. What does it mean?"

"I'm afraid I can't explain it," I said, at a loss. "Hello! Here's another criminal. What has he been up to?" and I pointed to a man a few yards ahead, in a white belt this time.

"He's an idler," said Ytteb.

"The white belt stands for uselessness, I suppose."

"Exactly," said Ytteb. "And while he wears it nobody will speak to him or have him in their houses; he can't enter a wine-shop or a theatre; he loses his vote and his seat in the Assembly; and no shop will serve him with anything but the necessaries of life."

"So you have a different coloured belt for every sort of crime?" I said.

"O no," replied the girl. "Most offences can be atoned for by compensating the person wronged. These things are only given to people whose crimes entail loss of citizenship, and are really a kind of mitigation of the hardship of forfeiting the belt. In sterner days, I'm told, the penalty used to be exacted in full.

It was found, however, that this left people no way of distinguishing between such comparatively harmless delinquents as murderers and the really dangerous type of idler. It came to be recognised also that even the worst malefactor should be allowed—in the public interest as well as his own—some practical means of keeping his breeches up. So these coloured substitutes were invented."

"You Ratheans are beyond me," I said. "Do you really think an idler worse than a murderer?"

"Of course," said Ytteb. "A murderer only takes a life or two, but idlers are a danger to the whole tribe."

"Why?"

"Obviously," replied Ytteb, really sharply this time. "There's so much work to be done, isn't there? to keep the tribe going. Therefore everyone who idles puts more work on the rest. Do you allow idling in your planet?"

I was going to answer that that depended on the income of the idler—smart, eh?—but the idea wouldn't translate into Rathean, so I got stuck in the middle of it. Ytteb, however, didn't press for an answer to her question because at this moment she spied a wine shop, which inspired her to invite me to a drink. A few minutes later, as we sat on the terrace with a carafe of rose pink wine between us, a gay-looking youth, whose yellow cloak jingled with bells, came up the steps with a smile and a wave to Ytteb.

"Good afternoon, Mr. Selesu," said she. "Have you been taking the air?"

The young man looked up anxiously at the sky. "Have you missed any?" he asked with grave concern.

"Don't be silly," laughed Ytteb. "Sit down and have some wine."

"I will sit with you, dear lady," said the fellow familiarly, perching himself on the railing of the terrace, "but I will not drink."

"Why not?" asked Ytteb.

"Because my heart is broken."

"What? Again?" cried Ytteb with a smile.

"I cannot see why a second, or even a tenth heartbreak should be deemed less tragic than the first," said the young man. "It's more so, really. Would you rather have your toe trampled on ten times or once? And is not the heart the tenderer organ?"

"You are very gaily dressed for a lovesick man," observed Ytteb.

"Ah! That is because I learn from experience. I don't want to lose the next love for the same reason as the last."

"Indeed. What was that?"

"I neglected to press my suit."

"Take a drink," said Ytteb. "Fancy spinning out all that yard to lead up to a joke like that. If you can't do better than that, young man, you'll be asked to take up an honest profession."

"I shouldn't mind," said Selesu, pouring out some wine. "In fact I've been thinking of taking up a job for some time."

"O, what sort?"

"Window-cleaning. You see, I'm anxious to get a rise in life."

"You're too bad altogether," said Ytteb.

"Seriously speaking though," said Selasu, "have you heard about Thims?"

"Who's Thims?" asked Ytteb.

"I haven't the slightest idea."

"Then what have you heard about him?"

"Nothing."

"Mr. Selesu," said Ytteb in mock indignation, "I don't mind your jokes, bad as they are; but I object to having my leg pulled. Give us a verse or a story for a change."

"Certainly," said Mr. Selesu. "Anything to oblige." He slipped down from the railing and went on solemnly: "I will now recite you a philosophical poem in one hundred and fifty cantos entitle Transcendental Affirmations."

"Help!" cried Ytteb.

Mr. Selesu cleared his throat and declaimed:

> There was a young man who said: "Oh!
> I don't know, I don't know, I don't know."
> They replied: "Think like us.
> Things are thus, thus, and thus,
> And in consequence so, so, and so."

"Go on," said Ytteb.

"That's all," said Mr. Selesu.

"But you said there were a hundred and fifty cantos."

"So there are. But they're all the same as the first. It's what's called a repeating poem."

Here the young man resumed his seat on the railing, and took notice of me for the first time. He had a little stick in his hand with an ivory top carved like an ass's head, with the long ears of which he tickled himself under the chin as he favoured me with a protracted stare. "You haven't introduced me to your friend yet," he said at length.

"O, I quite forgot," said Ytebb. "It was your fault for talking so much. Mr. O'Kennedy—Mr. Selesu."

I bowed, but the gentleman didn't return the courtesy. He merely went on speaking, as if to himself, in a musing sort of way. "Here's a curious phenomenon. Some folk, which is to say most folk, don't know. I and fools like me know we're wrong. But here's one who knows he's right. Beware of him, gentle lady. Here's one with shrunken sight, who values scarcity above abundance, is careful about trifles, and has no concern bigger than his own; who sows carefully, and reaps with a scythe bigger than the crescent moon; who is perfectly satisfied that the first thought that comes into his head is a valid judgment upon everything, and thinks you and I and all the world a pack of fools for not thinking with him; who is now half amazed, half infuriated because—"

"Mr. Selesu!" interrupted Ytteb. "You are rude to our guest."

"Not I," said the fellow. "I'll bet you an even kiss that he'll find no more of offence in my words than you of profit."

"Then that will be nothing," said Ytteb. "But I won't take your bet, for you would be the gainer either way."

Mr. Selesu sighed in comic resignation. "How true it is," he said, "that the poor are more generous than the rich. Here have I been lavishing upon you all the fruits of the little wit I was born with; and you, of all your beauty will not grant me a sip."

"No," said Ytteb, "nor half a sip, since you are so rude to my guest."

At this Mr. Selesu jumped off the railing again and made me an exaggerated bow for which I should have loved to kick him. "A thousand pardons, Mr. Stranger," said he. "You will pardon a fool, will you not?"

What the dickens could I say to that?—without being downright rude I mean, and making a bad impression on Ytteb. I sat dumb, but the little girl came to my rescue in fine style. "Be off with you," she said to the zany. "Your little bit of wit is so rusty and your charm going so threadbare that you will find yourself beltless one of these days."

"You think so?" says the jackanapes imperturbably. "Then mark how sweet I can be if I try. Most noble signor,"—here he turns on me with a smile like a chorus girl's—" I will not ask pardon of a mind that is above resentment, nor oblivion for an offender too insignificant to be remembered. Deign but to laugh at me, and you will confer happiness on a fool."

"If you only knew who you're trying to flatter," said Ytteb. "Mr. O'Kennedy comes from the stars."

"What? From all of them?"

"No, silly. From one of the planets."

"Indeed? I paid a visit to the sun once myself. Shall I tell you how I did it?"

Ytteb tipped me a wink and if to hint to me to humour him, so I said "yes".

"Well," said he, "it was this way. I often used to wonder where the sun's rays go to in the night time. Now they must either go on into space, or else go get lost for ever, which is impossible, for that would argue an ultimate dispersal of matter, which is undesirable and therefore unthinkable. Therefore the sun's rays go back to him. So one evening I sat on the edge of the world waiting to see them do it. I chose a good stout one with a kink in it that made a comfortable seat, and as soon as it started to go back I threw my leg over it, and off we went, whizz bang into the sun."

"How did you find it?" asked Ytteb.

"Damned hot," said the joker, and with that he vaulted the railing and was gone.

"What sort of fellow is that?" I demanded.

"Could you not see for yourself?" said Ytteb. "He is a charming idler."

"Then why isn't he disenfranchised?"

"Why, because he is amusing, of course. He is almost worth his keep, isn't he? What do you do with charming idlers in your world?"

Why the devil was she always asking me questions I couldn't answer? What the dickens *do* we do with them?

CHAPTER X

A Lesson in Archaeology: and the Shameless Behavior of Ytteb

WHEN WE HAD FINISHED our wine Ytteb said, "What about a trip into the country?" So we took out a couple of bicycles and in a few minutes were flying towards a low range of hills about eight or ten miles from the city. Once more I was struck by the two characteristics of the Rathean landscape which I had noticed on my first arrival: the ugliness of the mountains and the artificial neatness of everything else. There was a river running straight as a canal between a pond in a city park; a forest planted in lines like a cabbage garden. Every field was a square; and every road a dazzling white ribbon bordered with flowerbeds. There wasn't a patch of wild or waste land anywhere, except for the forbidding desolation of the hills to which we were speeding.

"This is the most unnatural landscape I've ever seen," I remarked to Ytteb at last, as we sat on the grass by the side of the lake, our bicycles propped against a tree.

"Yes," she said. "It's a wonderful sample of the handiwork of man."

"So it actually *is* artificial," I said, being now ready to believe anything.

"Well of course," said the girl. "You couldn't imagine nature producing anything as beautiful as this, could you?

"Perhaps not in this world," I said. "But in my world it is different."

"What?" she cried in surprise. "Is nature beautiful there?"

"I wish you could see it," I said. "Why, all this landscape beside a bit of County Dublin scenery is like a gate post beside the figure of a beautiful woman."

"What a wonderful world it must be," said Ytteb. "Here nature is stern and ugly, and it has cost us thousands of years of toil to make our world even as handsome as it is. If you would have some idea of what it was once like, look at those mountains. They have defied all our efforts to improve them, and stand there still almost as the hand of nature left them. Did you ever see anything so hideous? I can't bear to look at them. I wish we could blast them out of existence. But never mind it. Tell me about your own beautiful world."

Well, Mr. Gallagher, I'm not a bit artistic, as you know, but I do like nice scenery as much as anybody, so I did my best. I told her about the cliffs and hills of Howth, with their furze and heather and tall bracken, and the gulls wheeling and screaming over the sea, and the white foam round the rocks below. Maybe you know that view, from the Summit, of the harbour and the islands beyond. I described it to her as you see it on a summer's day: Ireland's Eye with its great slope of bracken (looking like grass or moss on account of the distance), and its curved beach gleaming white in the sunshine, and the little ruined chapel close by, and the tiny yachts racing towards the Martello tower at the point, and Lambay sprawling in the distance. The other view too, from the Sutton side: Dalkey Island and the Muglins, and all the stretch of mountainy coast down to Wicklow Head: I told her about that. And I told her about the Velvet Strand and the links of Portmarnock, with its wild roses and pansies and the queer sound of the wind in the bent grass on the sand-hills. And I told her about the sleepy old river Dodder, with its weirs and mill streams, and the leaning willows and aspens on its banks, and the leafy roads around Rathfarnham. And I told her of the twisty road that climbs from Windy Arbour between

Three Rock and Tibradden to drop into Glencullen with its tumbling streams, and home again by Enniskerry and Bray. It was only now, when I called them up to memory, that I realised how nice those places were, and wished I had seen more of them when I had the opportunity instead of wasting nine weekends out of ten playing cards in some fellow's digs.

"Go on. Go on," said Ytteb, who had listened enchanted to it all, as I piled up grand poetic phrases out of Ydenneko's vocabulary, which I can't for the life of me remember now. "Go on. Tell me more. What about your mountains? Are they beautiful too?"

I thought of the rolling lines of the Dublin and Wicklow Mountains, as pictured in some old prints I had seen in a shop window, and of the mess that had since been made of them: how they had been blasted by the MacWhelahan for stone for his Castle; and by the Irish-American Mineral Trust for copper and iron; how the Undergrowth Utilisation Syndicate had carted away all the timber which had been left by the Mammoth Pulpwood Trust; how the valleys had been dammed and flooded by the Water Trust; and Lough Tay and Lough Bray drained dry by the Alluvial Slime Development Syndicate. I made no mention of that, however, but kept the old prints in my mind while I reeled off a description that would have made your heart ache.

"It's all too wonderful," said Ytteb when I had finished. "It reminds me of some of those obscure poems that clever people like—or pretend to like—but which I have never been able to understand. They put no picture before my mind. They seemed to be only strings of fantastic words woven into mazes in which all sense got lost: but I think I could understand their meaning now." She sat silent a few moments, gazing before her with pensive eyes. "No!" she said suddenly. "I'll tell you what your world is really like. It's the thwarted dream of our landscape-gardeers: the ideal conception they never can carry out."

I wondered what this world could have been like before the Ratheans started their improvement schemes. Nobody could be certain, Ytteb said, because it had all been done thousands of years ago. But according to tradition it had originally been a world of naked rock, hideously wild and ugly, with a few small scattered valleys in which the primitive human tribes had their dwellings. As mankind increased in numbers they had been forced to cultivate the wilderness around them, and to begin, not like the pioneers in our world by sowing seed in virgin soil, but by manufacturing the soil in which to sow it by pulverising the rocks. Forests had to be planted to hold it in place and give shelter from the winds. Courses had to be dug for the waters that wandered over rocky flats too hard for them to channel. Thus, by the constant labours of hundreds of generations, the wilderness had been rendered habitable, and finally transformed into the wonderful garden in which I now found myself. The mountains, however, had defied all efforts to improve them, and still stood up amid the surrounding civilisation as monuments to the desolation it had superseded.

"But this is no afternoon for archaeology," the girl broke off impatiently. "What about a swim?"

Without waiting for me to answer she jumped to her feet, threw off her clothes, and began to undo sandals, all with no more concern than if I had been a fish. Lord, Mr. Gallagher, I didn't know what way to look. And as for stripping myself— well, I couldn't. In an instant she had plunged into the water, and, coming up from the dive, was calling to me to follow. There was nothing to do but obey; and fortunately, as soon as she saw me unlace my sandals, she turned over and swam out towards the centre of the lake. In another second I was in the water myself; but I kept at a respectful distance from her, and came out again very soon, slipping into my tunic as quickly as possible after a hurried wipe down with my handkerchief that didn't half dry me. As for Ytteb, when she came to land a few minutes later, she dusted herself down with a bunch of fern leaves, and sat about in her bare skin till the sun dried her. She was such a pretty sight that way that I quite forgot it was sinful to look at her. However, I thought it wise to preoccupy myself with the gear of my bicycle until she saw fit to dress herself.

CHAPTER XI

The Barbarous Sports of the Ratheans

REFRESHED BY OUR BATH we took to our bicycles again and
flew on towards the mountains. These grew more and more
forbidding the nearer we approached. Vast clumsy masses of
rock, they rose almost perpendicularly out of the plain, offering
us no landing place, and the icy currents of wind that blew
down their desolate gorges made flying so difficult that we were
obliged to keep quite close to the ground. In this way we flew for
about an hour, keeping always within a few hundred yards of the
sheer grey cliff, and skimming over the brightly coloured flowers
planted in regular rows up to its very foot. Presently I noticed
that the barrier had become rather less sheer, and that ahead of
us it fell away considerably, both in height and steepness, until
at length it was no more than a very steep, but still stony, slope.
Still further on I espied, far up the heights, a patch of greenery,
which gradually resolved itself into a covert of stunted trees with
some undergrowth. It was bounded on one side by a stone wall
which, instead of continuing around it, ran perfectly straight
down the three or four miles of the declivity to meet at right
angles with another at its foot. This one stretched for a mile or
more ahead to meet a third, parallel with the first, which was
partly hidden by the lie of the land. We were in fact approaching an immense enclosure, at the upper end of which was the
plantation I had first observed, the slope beneath being covered
with thin grass and occasional patches of scrub.

"That's a game covert," Ytteb called to me. "Let's come down.
We may see some sport."

We descended; and, wheeling our machines along the narrow strip between the fields and the slope, soon came to the bounding wall. It was about ten feet high, and constructed of huge, regularly-shaped stones with no cement between them, which made climbing easy. Ytteb was up first, and standing aloft, after a swift glance at the plantation, called down to me: "Quick! Quick! They're off."

In an instant I was at her side, and, guided by her pointing hand, saw a flash of red in the scrub not far below the trees. What it was I couldn't tell for a moment. Then came a distant growling noise, and out of the covert burst a pack of white animals. Hounds, I thought: but what huge ones they must be: almost as large as horses. This must be a tiger hunt, I concluded. The quarry was hidden from view for the moment, but presently came another red flash out of a clump of scrub, and . . . good God! I nearly dropped from the wall in horror. It was neither fox nor tiger. It was a man: and the great white beasts were chasing him.

"Ytteb!" I cried. "Ytteb!" and could say nothing more, but only point frantically at the desperately running figure.

"Steady!" said the girl, gripping me by the arm. "They'll be here soon. There'll be lots of excitement then."

"Good lord!" I cried. "Can't you see what's happening? Those creatures are hunting a man."

I didn't hear her answer. I was too much absorbed in the chase that was now drawing nearer and nearer. The beasts had as yet gained little on their quarry, who, running, I am sure, as fast as any racehorse, kept a straight course towards the wall at the bottom of the slope. Like an arrow he flew across the open ground; like a boulder hurled by a giant he crashed through brake and scrub. Nothing could stop him, nor deflect his course by a handsbreadth. And after him, like a foaming river fretted by rocks, rushed the ravening horde of his enemies. Like great white wolves they seemed now, their faces barred with black, their savage teeth bared, as belly to earth they raced with an awful hungry intentness after their prey. On and on they tore, gaining little; but gaining. On and on came the man, still unflagging, still keeping straight in his course. With my splendid Rathean eyes I could see him, at a mile's distance, as clearly as across a few yards on earth. There wasn't a shade of anxiety or doubt on his face. He was running with perfect steadiness, fearlessly, almost exultingly, and evidently with reserves of power in hand. He inspired me with such confidence that I leaped to my feet on the wall and uttered a cheer.

Then, with appalling suddenness came a change. He must have struck his foot against a stone or something, for he stumbled, and though he recovered himself at once, and shot forward faster than ever, in the momentary halt his pursuers had swallowed up a third of the interval between them. Whatever had made him stumble had evidently hurt him too, for his spurt of speed did not last, and the full vigour went out of his pace. A patch of scrub that he would formerly have taken in a rush had now to be forced laboriously. He emerged from it in evident distress, the last shreds of his scarlet coat torn from him, his skin badly lacerated, fear dawning in his expression. Closer than ever raged the wolf-beasts. In his fancy their breath must have been at his very heels.

I began to wonder now whether, in the event of his reaching the wall, he would have enough strength left to climb it before his pursuers caught him. Tearing my attention for a moment from the chase I looked towards the point at which he was aiming, and so noticed for the first time that along the whole of the lower wall, at intervals of a dozen feet or so, was a series of step ladders, each with a pair of hand-rails. This cleared up now what had been a puzzle before—the reason why he made for that wall rather than for one of the others, which were a good deal nearer to him. He must have feared to be overtaken in the slow business of climbing.

But now the chase was coming ever nearer and nearer. When I looked at the hunted man again he was visibly approaching exhaustion. His breath came in agonised gasps, his face was drawn and pale, his body ran with blood from a hundred gashes. Still, spent as he was, he plugged on grimly, a wild reviving hope drawing him to a final spurt as he glimpsed the laddered wall now less than a quarter of a mile away.

But not fifty yards behind came the wolf-beasts, untiring, relentless, overwhelming, silent now for the last decisive effort. The broken man, staggering along on weakening knees, with arms waving feebly, seemed but a leaf driven onward by their whirlwind rush. Carried away by a wild desire to help I clutched at a loose stone of the coping of the wall, meaning to fling it in the teeth of the pack. But as I drew back my arm Ytteb laid hold of my wrist with a cry of anger.

"Spoil-sport!" she snarled.

I could scarcely believe my ears. Balked in my purpose I managed to shift the stone to my left hand and throw it, but quite uselessly. An instant afterward the hunted man's last effort was spent. A helpless swaying figure, with clutching fingers clawing piteously towards his goal, he fell forward, to be engulfed immediately by the howling torrent of beasts.

"O God!" I groaned, shutting out the awful sight, and sank on my knees on the wall, vainly endeavouring to shut my ears too with my hands. Then suddenly I gave a glance at Ytteb. She was still standing, bent down with hands on knees, gazing with fascinated interest at the horrible melee below. Her cheeks were flaming red. With a shameless thirst she licked her small red lips.

"Come down out of this," I said, disgusted.

"It *is* rather horrible, isn't it," she replied, still gloating.

"Come down," I repeated; and as I spoke a couple of the wolf-beasts, separating from the pack, came bounding towards the wall, and, leaping, snapped their hideous jaws just below our feet. Another made an attempt to scramble up the nearest ladder. At that Ytteb waited no longer, but slid to the ground beside me in an instant.

"I do believe you are shocked and horrified," she said chaffingly as we walked towards our bicycles.

"Very naturally," I replied. "The sight of a fellow-man torn to pieces ought to horrify anybody."

"Well, yes," the girl conceded. "It was a pity he didn't get away. But wasn't it a splendid run?"

"It was awful," I said, now utterly disgusted with the bloodthirsty little brute.

"Pooh!" she replied. "You're no sportsman. I simply love a good hunt."

I stood stock-still, staring at her mocking face.

"You don't call that a hunt, surely?" I said.

"What else should I call it?" she asked in reply. And then, seeing that I didn't understand, she rapidly explained.

Will you believe it, Mr. Gallagher? The sport of hunting in that world consists in being hunted. How it is done you can gather from the episode I have just described. The animals employed are a breed of wolf known as Xofs. The sight of anything red rouses them to fury. The Rathean sportsman therefore puts on a tunic of that colour, and flaunts it as near as is necessary to tempt them from their lair in the covert. If the pack is a young one, it will rush out at the first glimpse of the hated colour, and the sportsman has but a short run for safety. But an old and cunning pack will bide its time, refusing to budge until he comes within close range. Then tragedy often follows, as we had seen today. This explanation partly cleared Ytteb's personal character for me. I had imagined that what we had seen had been an accident, and so regarded her enjoyment of it as a piece of bloodthirstiness. That the incident was of common occurrence in a national sport rather mitigated things as far as Ytteb was concerned, but didn't tend to raise the Ratheans any

higher in my esteem. And I said so. I told Ytteb straight out that
their idea of sport was pure barbarism.

"What a deadly crank you are!" was her rejoinder. "What's
barbarous about it?"

"If the tearing of a man to pieces for amusement isn't barbarous," I said, "I should like to know what is."

"Stuff!" said the girl. "We must all die some time. Better to
die quick at the end of a glorious day's sport than to drag out
your last months in a sick bed."

"Racing across country with death at your heels isn't my
notion of sport," I said.

"It's the greatest of all sports," the girl insisted. "It appeals to
the finest and healthiest instincts of our race, and develops all
the best of those qualities which have made us what we are. If
the maudlin cranks and killjoys succeed in putting an end to it,
our greatness as a people will come to an end too."

"All that pleading leaves me unmoved," I said. "It's the most
barbarous pretence at sport I ever heard of."

"Is there no hunting in your world?" asked Ytteb.

"Yes," I said, "but of a very different sort;" and I told her all
that I knew (from stories and pictures) of a fox hunt. Ytteb listened with flushed cheeks and gleaming eyes. "How splendid!"
she cried at length in tones of admiration. "I guessed all along
that your tale about bravery was a joke. Why you're even more
cowardly than we are."

"Cowardly?" I exclaimed.

"Yes. Gathering all those dogs and men and horses together
to kill one unfortunate little animal—isn't that the very quin-
tessence of cowardice?"

"Maybe so," I said. "I don't go in for it myself, and never
could see much fun in it."

Ytteb looked disappointed. "I'm afraid you must be brave,
then," she said. 'That's why you cannot appreciate our hunting
either. One must be a coward to experience the full thrill of
being chased."

I saw that it was useless to argue the matter further, so I let it drop, and questioned her instead about their other sports. They were all equally savage. First there was shooting. Two parties of sportsmen would meet together and draw lots for which was to shoot the other. The actual method of playing varied. Sometimes the men to be shot were allowed to scatter over a moor, and the others had to hunt them out and shoot them before they could get away to a certain base. Another way was for the shooting side to wait in butts, while their prey was driven towards them by beaters with whips and dogs; but this wasn't considered quite so sporting as the other way. Then there was bullfighting: which meant a single-handed fight between a man, with his bare fists, and a bull. The Ratheans were tremendously strong, and often a man would succeed in breaking the bull's neck with a twist, or stunning him with a blow; but usually the bull came off best. There was also a sport called trapping.

A man would set a lot of traps and snares in a field and offer a prize to anyone who could get across without being caught. There were more limbs lost than prizes won in this game. Pleasant little pastimes weren't they? I asked Ytteb if women took part in them, and she said not very often. They didn't go in for bullfighting or hunting at all, except as spectators. They occasionally did a little shooting, but were usually content to load the guns for their menfolk: being of a softer nature.

In justice to the Ratheans I must here record, what I learnt later on, that only a small minority of them indulge in these sports, and that in many of the more civilised tribes they have been prohibited by law. The learned Camino and the athletic Ianda expressed the most unmitigated contempt for them, and for the so-called sportsmen who indulged in them, and they laughed poor Ytteb's defence to scorn. "As for hunting developing the finest qualities of the race," Camino scoffed, "in my opinion it develops the worst. And how could the habits of a few have made the race what it is?" "The race is made what it is—such as it is—" said Ianda, "by the cowardly sports of the majority: running, jumping and swimming." On the question of suppressing the rougher sports, however, I found that there was less agreement. Some people said that the being-hunted instinct was one which had been deeply rooted in man's nature as a result of his early history, and that it could be outgrown (as indeed most of the race had already outgrown it) but could not be eradicated by legislation. Others objected on humanitarian grounds. They said that the Xofs could eat nothing but human flesh, and therefore to suppress hunting was to condemn them to extermination. But I think the general view was that it was advisable to leave some outlet for the primitive instincts of the more lowly-evolved members of the community, and that it was better that they should slaughter each other than some unoffending animal as in my world. Opinions of this sort, joined with that of those who took part in the sports, had been sufficient to prevent action being taken. I was given to understand, however, that the happy results of suppression in other tribes had weakened the opposition considerably, and that Bulnid was likely to follow the general example at an early date. I must add that few of the people to whom I mentioned the matter shared Ytteb's admiration for our method of fox-hunting on earth. In fact it was generally condemned as a rather stupid form of cowardice—what they call by a world in their language which may be translated *fool-cowardliness.*

Before leaving this subject I think I ought to say a word about what Ianda called "the cowardly sports of the majority." Besides athletics they go in for two games, one a kind of football, and the other a kind of hurling. But they aren't very sporting in their notions. They all play, so there's nobody to look on. They also go in for horse-racing, but their ideas on that subject are a scream. Instead of big millionaire sportsmen owning proper stables and hundreds of horses, they have clubs of perhaps a dozen members owning one horse, which they all help to train, and take it in turns to ride. And instead of ten-thousand-guinea prizes, there's nothing but a cup, or a wreath!

God help the poor idiots! Here I leave this subject, and return to my adventures with Ytteb.

CHAPTER XII

Solar Phenomena

EVENING WAS NOW FALLING, so we flew back to the city, and, after returning our bicycles to their shed, walked home to the palace. As we strolled up the avenue the sight of the setting sun recalled to my memory the mystery of its rising that morning; and sure enough there it was sinking again toward that same horizon. Ytteb laughed when I questioned her about it. "What else would you expect it to do?" she asked in reply. When I told her of its behaviour on earth she was astonished, but she had no explanation to offer for its eccentricity in Rathé. "Of course," she added, "I learned the exploded old drivel of the astronomical textbooks at school, but I've never bothered about the subject since. You'd better ask Ianda. She knows all these things."

"I must go and find her," I said. We had reached the house by this time and paused on the verandah.

"What's the hurry?" asked Ytteb, a strange note in her voice. No, not a note: a special sort of softness that I'd heard in a woman's voice only once before—in a scene in a play.

I could say nothing.

"What's the hurry?" said the girl again. "Is twilight no more than an astronomical phenomenon?"

"O bother astronomy!" I said, and—well we'll draw the curtain.

All the same I remained curious enough to question Ianda on the subject next day. Ever since my revelations about the human eye that young lady had been very stand-offish towards me, which made conversation rather difficult. Instead of answering my question she asked me another: how did the sun behave in my world?

I told her.

"You know why, of course?" she asked doubtfully, adding: "your world rotates on its axis—"

"Once in twenty-four hours," I took her up, remembering my geography, "thus producing day and night."

"Exactly," said Ianda approvingly, as if I was a schoolboy. "And in some longer period it revolves around the sun—"

"Three hundred and sixty-five days," I said.

"Yours is a younger world than this, you see. Rathé did the same in some forgotten age, but its motion has slowed down, so that now it rotates on its axis in the same time as it takes to revolve in its orbit, and thus always turns the same face towards the sun. This would mean that half the world would enjoy perpetual daylight, and the other half perpetual night, but for two other factors which come into play. Would you care to hear of them?"

"I'm tremendously interested," I said.

"The first is that the path of our planet round the sun is not circular, but a long ellipse; and the second, that its equator is inclined at an angle to the plane of its orbit. The effect is that certain areas are turned to and from the sun alternately, as if the sphere were oscillating on its axis."

Ianda went on to tell me that it was from these circumstances that the various Zones into which the planet was divided took their names. The territory where there was perpetual daylight was known as the Sunny zone. On each side of it were the Eastern and Western Shady Zones, which had days and nights something like ours, except that the days were immensely lnger and the nights somewhat shorter. Beyond these were the Twilight Zones, which at one edge had widely separated visits from a sun low down on the horizon; and at the other oscillated between a dull gloaming and the long black night in which the last zone—the Dark Zone—was plunged eternally.

She told me also that these variations of climate had a profound effect on the nature and customs of the people. Those who lived in the Sunny Zone, she said, were naturally the most civilised. Both spiritually and physically they had evolved several degrees higher than the most highly-evolved types elsewhere. Their institutions, though not different in theory from those prevailing in the Shady Zones, worked better in practice owing to the higher morale of the people. In the Twilight Zones, on the other hand, the population was comparatively uncivilised. Their organisations and institutions were imperfect; their morality lax; their health not good; and their manners bad. On the farther fringes of the zones the few inhabitants were almost barbarous.

"What about the Dark Zone?" I asked.

Ianda shuddered visibly, and, in a low and warning tone, said: "Better not enquire. The less said about that subject the better."

This only whetted my curiosity and later I made many attempts to obtain—from her and others—some further information on this point. But it was useless. The subject seemed to be a universal taboo, the mere mention of which would strike a whole assembly pale and silent. That silence, however, made one thing certain. Those last black spaces at the back of the world were not empty. Out in that cold dark continent dwelt some awful, hair-raising, nightmarish Something.

CHAPTER XIII

He observes the Home Life of the Ratheans; and
comes to a Momentous Decision

WELL, MR. GALLAGHER, THAT'S the story of my first couple of
days in Rathé, told exactly as it happened. But I won't waste time
retracing all the misadventures and mystifications of the next
few days while I found my feet and learned to feel at home in
this mad world. Instead I'll try and give you an idea of Rathean
life as it is, without bothering much about my personal doings
until the time comes to tell of the wild and weird adventures that
brought my stay to a close.

You'll be thinking that I must have created something of a
sensation in the planet, dropping in, as I did, out of nowhere. If
a fellow turned up on Earth with a story like mine—supposing
he could get people to believe him, which, of course, wouldn't be
easy—you can imagine what a fuss there'd be: the seething mobs
of people choking up the streets outside his hotel and fighting
each other in the doorways; the journalists clambering in at
the windows or slithering down the chimneys, and pestering
him for exclusive interviews, or bringing articles ready written
for him to sign; the cinema producers rolling up in airplanes
with billion-dollar contracts, and all the rest of it. I may tell
you that I confidently expected some such publicity for myself,
and was actually figuring out what sort of terms I'd ask, when
one of the Chief's secretaries came up and asked me if I would
care to give an interview to a reporter of a local paper who had
just called. *A* reporter of the *Local* paper! and I had been thirty-
six hours in the place. But the whole planet was like that. No

push: no pep: no enterprise. I remember a story I heard once of a young reporter who happened to be on the spot when the MacWhelahan's agent was shot dead in College Green. In ten minutes he was at the man's house and was asking the window for his photograph. "But what you do want it for?" says she. "Because he's just been murdered," says he, and whipping out his camera, he snaps her as she faints. A live-wire, eh? That man's earning three thousand a year on Cumbersome's papers now. But you don't get pep like that in Rathé. The privacy of the person is regarded there as the most sacred of human rights, and time a matter of no consideration whatever. The young man to whom I gave my first interview came back with it three days later, all nicely written up, to know if I would care to make any alterations before it appeared next week; and when it actually did appear the other papers were content to copy it at intervals during the following month.

After my description of the streets and buildings of Bulnid you'll picture me established in the Chieftan's palace as in the very lap of princely luxury. But no such thing. The Ratheans, both chiefs and people, are, as a matter of fact, amazingly simple in their domestic habits. The palace itself, though so tastefully designed both inside and out, was rather a bare and comfortless abode. There were no carpets nor curtains nor upholstery. What little furniture there was was of the lightest description, giving a sort of Japanesy effect. A few cushions scattered about; a shelf of books; a palm or two, or some growing flowers, or perhaps a statue on a pedestal: that was considered enough for most rooms; though, of course, there was a splendid piano in the large drawing-room, and writing-desks and tolerably comfortable cane chairs in the library. I must add, too, that on the walls of every room, big and little, were fine pictures, real oil paintings like you see in the National Gallery on Merrion Square. Art, you observe, came a long way before comfort with these people—being cracked, I suppose. Still, queer as they were, I wasn't long in getting accustomed to their ways of living. The Chief himself was so busy always that I saw very little of him; but his wife—My Lady, as everyone called her—was most kind and affable, showing me a thousand and one little snags on which I might have tripped, and all with the greatest tact imaginable. "A great souled being from your starry altitudes must smile at these trifles," she would say, "but perhaps you wouldn't mind doing so-and-so." Nicely put, wasn't it? "So-and-so" meant such little details as putting the bathroom in order after one had finished with it. You'd have thought that in a great Chief's house that sort of thing would have been done by servants; but there were no servants in Rathé. Everyone had to tidy up his own bedroom and do such like services for himself, which I'm bound to say was no great hardship, the rooms being handy to keep clean, and each one having its little cupboard with brushes and things stowed in it. Any heavy work (there wasn't much) was carried out by a firm of Domestic Contractors, who sent their workers once a week or so and did the job with wonderful speed and thoroughness.

The one thing that was really difficult to get used to in the new life was the absence of meals. Not that I was starved. To my astonishment I soon found that I didn't feel the least bit hungry. On my first morning, you may remember, I had started out with the idea of getting hold of Ensulas and hunting up some breakfast. I had been diverted from the search however, and had spent the whole day in the open air without experiencing the smallest pang of hunger. By the end of the second day, as I wasn't feeling even peckish, I had come to the conclusion that the Rathean constitution must be radically different from our own, and would have worried no more about the matter if I hadn't been kept guessing by all the mystery that had been made about it. But you know how largely food and everything connected with it figures in our lives on earth, with our kitchens and our dining-rooms, our pots and pans, our crockery and cutlery, our cooking and washing up, our breakfasts and dinners and teas and suppers. Don't we spend a third of our lives in bed? Well, I bet we spend another third in eating. And if you're rich enough to pay other people to do the cleaning up job, don't you just take all the longer over the meal itself? I remember a young lady attendant at a restaurant that I once used to walk out with, telling me that one day it had suddenly struck her that she spent her whole life serving other people with their meals, and most of what she earned by it in paying for her own. "And what's it all for?" says she, impatient like, which she'd no business to be, seeing that if people didn't eat there'd have been no employment for herself or me and thousands of others in similar avocations. Anyway, as I was saying, when you know what a big place eating holds in our lives, and how conveniently the routine of meals breaks up the day, you can imagine how difficult it was at first to get used to going without them. However, practice makes perfect, and I did it in time.

My curiosity, however, remained, and the only person I dared ask to gratify it was Ensalus. Unfortunately he was seldom at home, and when there did his best to avoid me. His attitude towards me was that of a confederate in some disgraceful crime, of whose loyalty or discretion he was in doubt. He would creep up behind me to whisper mysterious cautions in my ear, and dodge away before I could turn round; or he would wink at me in a knowing sort of way across a roomful of people; but generally, as I have said, he avoided me altogether. At last one day I succeeded in cornering him and demanded an explanation of the mystery. "What mystery?" he asked. "This guilty secret about food," I said. "In the world I come from we eat what we like when we like. What are the rules here?" instead of answering he goggled at me with amazed, eagerly curious eyes. "Whatever you like!" he gasped. "And whenever you like! Do you mean to say you can eat eggs?" "Yes!" "And meat?" "Yes." "And sugar?" "Yes, yes, yes," I said savagely. "Any mortal thing we like down to candle-ends and tin tacks, and any old time we like, from sunrise to sunset. Now tell me what's the rule here?" But he wouldn't answer. "What a world!" he exclaimed enviously. "O *what* a world! How I wish I could go there!" and away he went in a kind of ecstatic dream, smiling idiotically and hungrily licking his lips.

You must not allow these last remarks, or any others that I have previously made, to give you a bad impression of Ensulas, who was really a thoroughly sensible and decent fellow, and without exception the finest man in the whole of Rathé: a man whom I am proud to have called my friend, and to whose memory I unhesitatingly take off my hat. I am afraid that I have shown him so far in a rather unpleasant light, because I have been relating things just as they happened, and on first acquaintance I admit I misjudged him badly. That wasn't my fault, for his appearance was certainly against him. To a superficial observer his pimply complexion and corpulent figure were decidedly unattractive; and he had a queer sidling sort of walk, which, coupled with his furtive way of looking at you, and his hesitating, almost whispering voice, was hardly calculated to inspire immediate confidence. A certain slobberiness about the lips, due to his tongue being too large for his mouth, was also likely to mislead those who judge a book by the cover. He had moreover a weak, somewhat irritating giggle, and a whole heap of nervous mannerisms (among which I remember chiefly a trick of starting guiltily when one came on him unawares) so that altogether one would have had to look very deep indeed for any sign of those magnificent characteristics which raised him far above all other Ratheans and were eventually to make us close friends and partners in the most colossal enterprise that ever shook the universe.

There was never in any world or any time a person whose looks so utterly belied his true character as Ensulas. He had all the qualities that make for success and endear a man to his fellows. His quickness of apprehension was astonishing; his determination to get on amazing. He had initiative, enterprise, and boundless energy. His ready tact and understanding were remarkable; his judgment shrewd and unerring. Sturdy independence and sound common sense were planted deep in his nature, and he had nothing but contempt for the silly ideas of the ordinary Ratheans. To his loyalty to tried friends I can personally testify; while his unselfish patriotism and wholehearted devotion to duty will, I hope, be brought out in my coming narrative so fully as to place them beyond the reach of calumnies of Rathean historians. Placed in any world where his abilities and merits would have been recognised and awarded the opportunity which was their due, he would inevitably have got on and done well for himself; but among the narrow-minded and short-sighted Ratheans he had been neglected, thwarted, and suppressed, and was generally regarded as a hopeless failure. He had actually been disinherited by his father. Ordinarily the chieftainship of a tribe was hereditary, but succession was subject to the passing of certain tests of physical and mental fitness, and to the approval of Chief and people, in all of which Ensulas had failed, his place being taken by a cousin, a pompous and priggish young man, who was now taking out a course in political economy at the University. Poor Ensulas had thus been compelled to enter a trade, and having tried a great many and been judged (according to Rathean standards) to have no aptitude for them, had been at length reduced to accepting a post as a scavenger. Thus unjustly treated and relegated to obscurity, it was no wonder that his mind should have become embittered and his manner have taken on something of the hangdog; and that in the circumstance I should have been some time in finding out his true worth.

So much for Ensulas. Let me now go on to complete the family picture by sketching in the girls.

Camino, the eldest, had at first struck me as a very charming young lady, but I had soon altered my opinion. She was devilish dignified, you know, and her conversation was dreadfully bor-ing. She was interested in Education, of all subjects, and used to bother me with questions about Education on Earth until she found I knew nothing about it, when she lost interest in me. She was a shareholder in a dye works, but was going to retire shortly in order to get married: for the Ratheans, though quite advanced in regard to women's rights and all that rot, believe that marriage and the care of children are a whole time job.

Ianda I had never taken to at all, nor she to me. She was a frightfully uppish person, with the eyes of a queen and a voice like a steel spring. She was an athlete, as strong as a bull and as swift as a deer, and her profession was director of a gymnastic institute. At home she spend most of her time training her son to run and box. I presumed her to be a widow, since there was no sign of a husband. She must have frozen the poor devil to death I thought.

What a contrast to these two was little Ytteb. She and I got on like a house on fire—pish! That's nothing; like a blazing celluloid factory sprayed with petrol. We were inseparable. I got used to her beastly eyes after a while, and found that in many ways she was quite like an earth-girl—game, you know, for a bit of fun and all that. O boy, what times we had! But I'm not going to be telling. She worked in a draper's shop, which is quite the thing in Rathé even for a chieftain's daughter, because they think one job's as good as another so long as it's done right, and you have to take the job you're fitted for, and can't be loosed on the public as a doctor because your father can pay the fees, or jobbed on the city as an electrical engineer because you've got a cousin in the Corporation. About Ytteb, though. We got on, as I have said, tremendously, and I was beginning to think of popping the question, being only held back by doubts as to how I stood, having no job, and she being a chieftain's daughter, and so on, when one day my Lady asked me to come to her boudoir for a chat.

"I see that you have made friends with my little Ytteb," she began.

"The young lady honours me with her acquaintanceship," I replied cautiously.

My lady sighed. "Ah yes," she said. "Ytteb is an attractive little girl, but I am surprised you hold her acquaintance an honour. Considering the starry altitudes from which you have come, the honour is surely the other way."

I murmured something modest and polite, but my Lady cut me short with a gesture. "Yes, yes. Of course she is an amiable little creature, and very popular with young men in her own stage of evolution. —By the way, I hope she hasn't been bothering you with erotic advances?"

"O no," I said. "Not at all."

"Doubtless the influence of your higher nature has kept her in check. Her instincts are rather primitive in that respect—so unlike her sisters, who are civilised to their finger-tips. Camino, you know, is to be married next week. As for Ianda, she is above that kind of thing altogether."

"I thought she was a widow," I said.

"O, dear, no. Ianda has never been married. She has too austere a nature."

"Then the child—" I suggested.

"I don't know. Some friend, I suppose, was willing to oblige."

She said it with such perfect innocence that I had no idea that the friend's obligingness went any further than letting her adopt a superfluous child of his (or her) own. I hadn't yet fathomed the depths of these people's immorality. But to return to our conversation.

"Either of these," said my Lady, "would have been competent to guide you around our world. I can't understand why you should have chosen Ytteb, who is little more than a barbarian, and quite beneath the notice of a person of any evolution in this world, to say nothing of a Being from Beyond."

Well, I stood up for little Ytteb; but as I wanted to preserve my reputation as a superior being, and was anxious to learn as much as possible about Rathean life and customs, I took care from this time to ask other members of the family to be my guides occasionally, which rather slowed down my affair de coor.

My Lady herself very graciously took me to call on some of her friends in their houses, which, I observed with surprise, were in no way inferior, except in point of size, to her own palace; and I noticed everywhere the same tendency to put art before comfort. I didn't see an upholstered chair in the whole of Bulnid, but every house was hung all over with pictures. Now I don't pretend to be an authority on arty matters, like those expert fellows who go into fits about a picture because it's supposed to have been painted by some big johnny—Velasky or someone—and wouldn't give a thraneen for it if they found he hadn't done it at all. But surely to goodness anybody with two eyes in his head knows a good picture when he sees it. Anyway, I get just as big a kick out of a first-rate bit of work as any of your connoisseurs: and you may take it from me that the pictures I saw hanging in ordinary folks' houses in Rathé were the real thing—none of your furniture-shop stuff, but genuine oil paintings like you see in the National Gallery, the sort of thing that millionaires pay a hundred thousand pounds for. There are no picture galleries in Rathé, and I couldn't get people to see the object of them. They said that pictures were obviously meant to beautify people's houses, and that it was absurd to store them in special buildings where they would be put to trouble to see them. Besides, a whole building cluttered up with pictures would be dreadfully boring. That, I think, was the first sensible thing I had heard since I came to Rathé. I once wasted a Saturday afternoon at the National Gallery, staring like a stuck pig at acres of coloured canvas till I was bored stiff. Never again, said I when I left: and I never will. But I'd have been delighted to have a few to hang in my room, and I can't see why they should be so dear that a respectable man who works hard for his living can't buy them. I know a man has to have a special gift to be able to paint. But isn't the gift itself worth having—its own reward, so to speak—without asking to have thousands of pounds thrown in? And isn't it better fun to sit in your own studio painting as the fancy takes you than to stand behind someone else's counter parcelling sugar?—not that I wish to complain, Mr. Gallagher, and don't think I'm getting above myself—but if a weeks' grocering can't pay for a week's painting, well, where do we get off?

Anyway, that's the Rathean notion about art: an old master and a few moderns in every home; and you needn't think it leads to any dog-in-the-mangerishness either. A Rathean who has got hold of a really good thing is only too pleased to invite the whole neighbourhood to come in and envy his luck or his taste. They also have an arrangement by which the Chief of the tribe has a first claim on all works of exceptional quality or interest, so that these can be hung in public buildings—railway stations, post offices, and so on—for the general enjoyment.

While I'm on the subject of Art I had better mention one rather queer custom of the Ratheans. They call it the Decennial Sacrifice. Every tenth year the tribal Academy of Arts collects a heap of famous pictures or statues in some public place and sets them on fire in presence of the whole tribe. Or perhaps instead they'll choose some historic building and blow it up. They told me they did this to prevent themselves attaching an exaggerated importance to art, and as an encouragement to artists to seek inspiration from the future instead of sponging on the past. Whether this is a sensible idea or not isn't for me to say, but it must be great sport to watch, and I was sorry that there was no festival of the kind during my stay.

But to return to the houses. Each stands in its own garden; and the garden opens into another much larger one which it shares with eight or ten neighbouring houses—a sort of semi-private park with little groves of trees in it, and perhaps a meadow, or a wild bit of a hill where the children of all the houses can play. The Ratheans seem to have no sense of urban land values. Think of those vast acres, which might have brought in millions in rent, lying waste under grass and trees. Think of the priceless opportunities for the speculator in real estate, and not one solitary Rathean with the grip or enterprise to take advantage of them. Well, said I to myself, here's my chance for you, my son. Just give me time to find my feet and learn a little of their ways, and I'll be top dog in this planet. Damn me, I said, I'll be Goshawk to these birds.

CHAPTER XIV

The Inefficient Schools of the Ratheans

FOLLOWING UP MY LADY'S hint, I asked Camino one day to show me over a school, and so at last I came to understand why the Ratheans were so ignorant and unprogressive. The building itself was all you could desire—airy and lightsome and cheerful, and as different as could be from the barracks they clap us into on earth. The playgrounds were the finest I had ever seen; and there were grand big recreation rooms, and gymnasiums, and a first-rate theatre. So far so good. But just imagine a school where there are no lessons and no punishments; where the boys can decide for themselves what they'll learn; and where there's no compulsion on them to do any work at all if they don't like. Lord, what a time I'd have had if I'd been sent there in my young days! I'd never have opened a book. I'd have broken every window in the building; cut my name on every chair and table; squirted ink all over the place; put gum and drawing pins on the teachers' chairs; and generally had a high old time of it. Is that the way with these Rathean boys? Not likely, the mugs! Caning would be wasted on them. They do their work without it.

The teachers in the Rathean schools are the servants of the boys rather than their masters. They aren't even called teachers, but a word which means, as far as I can translate it, helpers. The staff of a school consists generally of four or five upper teachers called Supervisors, and perhaps a dozen lower teachers called Librarians. The principle on which the system works is this. When a boy comes to school he puts himself under the wing of one of the Supervisors, who from then on has to make a study of his needs, tastes, and capacities, advise what courses he should follow, and in general act the part of guide, philosopher, and friend—with the additional attraction of being liable to be held to account if the lad should turn out wrong. You know how in our world schoolmasters always brag of the successes they turn out, though they never say anything about the failures. Well in Rathé it's the other way round. A man's success is held to be due to himself, and his failure to his schooling. Altogether then the Supervisors' job is a tough one, and a thankless, yet any I spoke to seemed contented and interested enough. There was one, I remember, whose speciality it was to help on the stupid. He told me it was an entrancing and altogether exhilarating occupation. There was another—a harassed-looking poor devil with prematurely lined face—whose main concern was to keep the ambitious from overworking themselves; and yet another whose whole function was to prevent superficially clever chaps from getting through their courses without really learning anything.

The Librarians on the other hand are specialists on particular subjects; their classrooms being really libraries to which the boys come to read up the courses suggested by the Supervisors. They don't give or hear lessons, or set exercises, but merely go about from one boy to another giving what help they are asked for, which may mean explaining a difficulty, suggesting a book, or even correcting an exercise which a fellow may have been fool enough to do on his own account. They have no authority whatever over their charges. In fact the authority is the other way round, the boys ordering the masters about as if they were dogs. "Quick! quick! quick!" you'd hear one say. "Am I to wait all day for that answer?" or "Attention please, Mr. Teop: you're dreaming again. Keep your mind on your work please"; or "Rubbish, Mr. Ibbleplaus. That's only your opinion. I want the facts, please"; or "Really, Mr. Soupmop, you ought to be ashamed to offer me such a mass of meaningless verbiage as an

answer to my very simple question. You needn't flatter yourself
that you can conceal your ignorance from me by such shuffling.
If you can't make up your mind to pay proper attention to your
work I shall have to leave the school." But I think the praise of
these young shavers must have been even harder to endure. I'm
pretty certain that I saw murder in the eye of one grey-bearded
etymologist who was being patted on the back by a patronising
brat who "believed that the school would be a credit to him
yet."

But the worst is still to come. Would you believe it, Mr.
Gallagher? in one classroom we looked into I saw an unfortunate master cocked up across a desk while one of his pupils
lashed him with a cane. It is in fact the regular practice. I was
told by Camino that teachers were flogged not only for unpunc-
tuality and other breaches of discipline, but for failure to make
their pupils understand the difficulties for which they consulted
them. Apart from the general absurdity of the whole business,
this seemed to me particularly unjust, because the fault was just
as likely to be the boy's as the teacher's. Camino admitted that
this was so, and that many masters had to suffer severely for
the stupidity of their pupils. Some particularly stupid boys, she
said, never had the cane out of their hands: indeed she knew
personally of one flagrant case where a learned historian had
been caned every day for a whole term by a young fool who
could not be got to understand an extremely simple question:
"but," she said, "hard cases, as you know, make bad law." She
also knew of instances where clever boys had caned their masters for explanations which they could easily have understood
by taking a little trouble. But in spite of these drawbacks she
warmly defended the system on the grounds that those who
took to the teaching profession were naturally of so dogmatic
and conceited a temperament that it did them good to be so
humiliated occasionally; that the fear of such treatment was a
most valuable check to the inborn ambition of all teachers to

mould the minds of their charges; that the art of teaching was
so difficult and thankless that the use of some such spur was
absolutely necessary to prevent wholesale shirking and sloven-
liness; that without some such corrective discipline could never
be maintained; that an occasional walloping was good for the
character; that the teachers themselves preferred a caning to the
alternative of taking tasks in their spare time; that there was religious warrant for the practice in the well-known saying "spare
the rod and spoil the teacher"; and finally that only the most
hopeless and unpractical cranks were against it. As the wretched
pedagogue tamely resumed his breeches and made shift to better the explanation for failing in which he had been punished, it
occurred to me to remark that such degradation was unlikely to
make the poor devil any fonder of his task, or to foster pleasant
feelings between him and his pupils; but these objections were
waved aside as of no account. I then went on to suggest that
the effect on the boy who administered the punishment might
be even worse than the effect on the master who endured it,
but that puzzled Camino completely and made her ask what I
meant.

"Well," said I, "some fellows might enjoy thrashing a man
out of mere devilment, and others might go out of their way to
thrash a man they had a spite against."

At this the girl became downright angry. "That is a revolt-
ingly cynical observation," said she, "and a gross libel on the
character of our youth. No Rathean boy would dream of so
misusing a sacred trust."

Well, I didn't want to hurt Camino's feelings, so I said no
more on that point. But I wonder. I know that if *I* had a Rathean boy's chances—

I discussed the subject afterwards with many other persons,
and found them all of much the same opinion. Even the teachers
themselves were staunch upholders of the system. One or two
people were inclined to agree with me that the infliction of the

punishment on a particular part of the body was an unnecessary degradation, but the majority pooh-poohed the objection.
Learning came out of the mouth, they said, and, if propulsion
were needed it must obviously be applied at the other end.
Apart however from this trifling difference on a mere detail,
there is no subject on which the Ratheans are so unanimous as
on this: that the advancement and propagation of learning are
inseparable from the frequent lambasting of teachers.

There was a third kind of master I haven't mentioned yet,
one of whom was attached to every Librarian for no better
purpose, as far as I could see, than to make his task as hard as
possible and undo any little good which the system allowed him
to do. They were called Questioners; their job being to question
any direct or unqualified statements made by the Librarians,
and to uphold the opposite point of view to theirs whenever
any controversial matters arose.

"But that must mean chaos," I objected to Camino.

"Why?" said she. "What sort of chaos?"

"I mean perpetual argument and contradiction."

"Not at all," said the girl, "It only makes the Librarians
careful what they say. If there was no one to contradict them
you'd find them trotting out their own misconceptions as facts,
their own ideas as accepted truth, their own predilections and
prejudices as right and wrong. That would produce the worst
possible chaos: chaos in the minds of the children."

"That sounds all very well in theory," said I. "But in
practice—"

"What!" said Camino incredulously. "Have you no
Questioners in your schools on Earth?" I said, "No." "What a
dreadful lot of lies and nonsense you must learn there," she said.

I was afraid I was losing caste in her eyes, so I stood up in
defence of the old world. "We don't go in for cranky ideas and
faddy schemes," I said. "We believe in a good sound practical

education, and you can't get that without discipline. What happens under your precious system when a boy refuses to work?"

"He remains ignorant, of course. What happens under yours?"

"We make him work."

"Indeed? Then are there no ignorant people in your world?"

It's hard enough to lie and look straight with ordinary human eyes; but what can you do with eyes as big as footballs which you haven't yet learnt the control of? I'm sorry to say that I had to blow the gaff on the old spheroid.

CHAPTER XV

The Singular Gastronomical Customs of the Ratheans

ON THE FIFTH DAY of my residence in Rathé I began to feel hungry. During the interval I hadn't felt a prick of that sensation, and what with the full life I was leading and the number of new things there were to see and hear about, I had quite forgotten that there was such a thing as food. Now with the first fresh pangs of emptiness beginning to trouble me I was disagreeably reminded of the difficulty of satisfying them in this idiotic world. Whiffs of that horrible meal in the underground eating-house blew like an unsavoury wind over my memory, almost sickening me as I gazed gloomily out of a window of the drawing-room at the wet roofs of the city under a drizzling rain. Ugh! I could never face that again. But oh! what a hunger was on me.

I was called out of my musings by the voice of my Lady, who had entered the room unheard.

"Daydreaming again, Mr. O'Kennedy!" she chaffed me. "I think I know what's the matter with you."

"O, do you?" I said ungraciously.

She wagged a playful finger at me. "Isn't there something tasty, now, that's caught your fancy?" she teased.

I stared at her blankly.

"Confess now," she smiled archly.

"Well, to tell you the truth, ma'am," said I, "and I hope I won't offend against your rules of etiquette if I say so—but I could do with a bite of something."

Blest if I hadn't done it again. There was her ladyship staring at me with the same old horror that I was so tired of, her cheeks going red and white alternately as she gasped some incoherent protest. But this time I wasn't going to be put off. "Look here, my Lady," I said. "Not knowing your ways, I mean no offence that I seem to have given. In my world if a chap wants a feed he says so, and he gets it, and no fuss about it at all. What the ceremonies are in Rathé I don't know, but I take it that you do eat, and that you know what it is to be hungry. That's my case at the present moment. I'm starving; and I appeal to you, as a wife and mother, to take pity on me and give me a meal, and if there's any palaver to be gone through first, you've only got to tell me and I'll do it."

All through this speech her Ladyship stood averted from me, the very picture of embarrassment. When I had finished she considered a moment; then said: "This situation is quite beyond me. Wait here a moment and I'll send a Professor of Mathematics to have a talk with you."

Off she went, leaving me to my hunger-pains and to wonder what the deuce a professor of mathematics could do to allay them. About twenty minutes later there came into the room a smooth-faced person in a purple dress with a manner expressing the most perfect self-assurance and certitude about everything. He spoke in a rich throaty voice. "My dear young friend, what can I do for you?"

"I want something to eat," I said.

The Professor coughed modestly into his hand. "Hm, yes. The cravings of our weaker nature. Hm. But no doubt you are determined to overcome them."

I gave the fellow a look.

"Come, come," he encouraged me. "You may talk to me in perfect confidence. I am a Professor of Mathematics, you know. Juicewit is my name: Professor Juicewit. You are Mr. O

'Kennedy, from the stars, I am told. So now we understand one another perfectly, don't we?"

"Like a table of logarithms," I said. "Honest to goodness, Mr. Juicewit, I haven't the slightest idea what you're driving at. I understood you were sent here to teach me table-manners and take me to a meal—"

The Professor stopped me with upraised hand. "Pray, pray, my son, do not speak so coarsely. If you have an earnest and scientific desire for nutriment, and are ready to submit its gratification to the laws of mathematics, tell me so, and I shall get the ceremonies performed as speedily as possible. Otherwise I am afraid I can do nothing for you."

"Look here," I said. "It seems that this is a case where the longest way round is going to be the shortest way home. Treat me as a child that doesn't know its ABC, and teach me your dining room etiquette from the very beginning. Tell me what on earth the laws of mathematics have to do with it."

Mr. Juicewit gave me a quick glance of surprise. "I fear, my son, that you come from a barbarous and licentious sphere. When a young Rathean finds himself in need of sustenance, he discreetly and scientifically seeks out a fruit which will be agreeable to his palate, conformable to his digestion, and so chemically constituted as to fulfil his physiological requirements. Having made his choice, he obtains a license from a professor of mathematics, and is then entitled to the comfort and nutriment of that fruit for the remainder of his life."

"I see," said I. "Well, I'm not in a mood to be very particular at the moment, so you might make me out a license for half a dozen of your most popular varieties, and let me get going at them at once."

Mr. Juicewit clapped a hand to his brow and collapsed on the nearest chair. I rushed to his assistance, but he waved me off. "I'll be all right in a moment," he said. "Pray excuse me. Shock. I hadn't realised—" He pulled himself together with an effort and went on: "I'm afraid I haven't made myself clear. You can only obtain a license for one fruit."

"Very well," I said. "There's no need to make a fuss about that. Give me a license for one of those big yellow things."

"Certainly, if you wish it. But I am afraid you are making rather a hasty choice. Have you good grounds for believing that they are the most suitable sustenance for your mind and body?"

"My dear sir," said I, "I don't even know whether I shall like the taste of them till I try. What does it matter anyway? You can give me a license for something else if I don't."

"I never dreamed," said the Professor solemnly, "that so uncalculating a mind could be found anywhere in the universe. Young man, you must try and realise the importance of what you are doing. The fruit which you now choose must be your constant diet for the rest of your life, and no other will be permitted to you."

"Heavenly bananas!" I exclaimed. "Why?"

"That," said the Professor, "is one of the fundamental laws of mathematics."

"Get along," I said. "What have the laws of mathematics got to do with it?"

Professor Juicewit looked at me sharply. "Surely," he said, "our lives must be altogether ruled by mathematics."

That was the first I had ever heard of the idea, but I assented for the sake of argument.

"Very well, then," said the Professor. "Since a man has but one mouth, one tongue, one throat, one gullet, and one stomach, it follows that he must eat but one species of fruit."

"It doesn't follow at all," I said. "You might as well say that because I have only ten fingers and ten toes I can only walk ten miles."

"No, my son," said the Professor condescendingly. "There is no analogy whatever between the two arguments. Your untrained mind has fallen into the common fallacy known

as Casuistical Pseudorefutation. As for this question of monophagous alimentation, it has been the law and custom of mankind from time immemorial, and is indisputably prescribed by
Scientific Ordinance.

"O very well," I said, wearily. "Have it your own way. I suppose that what's good enough for the rest of the world must be
good enough for me. Let's have up a few samples and I'll make
my choice pretty quick."

The Professor nearly did another faint at this suggestion—"this
monstrous suggestion" as he called it. "Such conduct could not
possibly be permitted," he said.

"But I thought I had to choose a fruit that would be conformable to my stomach, and all the rest of it," said I.

"Certainly."

"Well, how can I find out all that without sampling it?" I
asked.

"O, tush, tush!" said Mr. Juicewit decidedly. "Of course you
can. Everybody does."

"But how?" I persisted.

The Professor gathered himself together as if for a cold plunge.

"By what is known, in plain language as—appetite. Nature
has planted in the skin of every fruit a—what shall I call it?—a
faculty of stimulating the palate of those persons to whose nutriment its pulp is particularly suited."

"O it does, does it?" said I. "But even an appetite changes, you
know. What's to happen if in a few years' time I get so tired of the
fruit that I can't stand it any more?"

"You must exercise your self-control," said Professoer Juicewit.
"After all, a solemn promise is not to be broken at the dictates of
errant fancy."

"Exactly," I said. "That's why I'm against making such a promise. And what if the fruit disagrees with me and makes me ill?
Can I swop it for another then?"

"Certainly not, my son. But bearing all these possibilities in mind you must realise that it behoves you to make a prudent choice, and not allow yourself to be carried away by mere animal hunger."

"That seems to be all the more reason for sampling well beforehand," I protested.

"No, sir," said the Professor sternly. "No legitimate reason can support such licentiousness. It is a reason for developing the calculating faculty, and as such I cannot commend it to you too strongly. However unscientific people may be in the world you have come from, and however lax in their gastronomic customs, you will be expected, so long as you remain in this world, to conform to its laws."

"I suppose I must try," I said resignedly. "Do you people find that this curious arrangement works out fairly comfortably?"

"There is nothing curious about it," said Mr. Juicewit, annoyed. "It works out *perfectly* comfortably. Perfectly comfortably. And even if it didn't, it is absolutely prescribed by the laws of Science, and essential to the health and happiness of mankind. Perfect digestive harmony, you know, can only be obtained by perfect harmony of diet. The digestive juice of each individual is a nicely compounded mixture of acids, ferments, enzymes, and other chemicals, accurately adapted to the absorption and assimilation of one particular fruit, and to that fruit only. Admit one grain of unaccustomed matter to this delicate and complicated machinery, and a disturbing process is begun which will inevitably end in complete stomach disruption." There was more jawbreaking stuff in this style, and then off he soared into a full-throated rhapsody about the beauty, the harmony, the wonder, and the delightfulness of the union of one man with one fruit, which at last brought him to a stop from sheer lack of breath. It was the most puling eyewash imaginable.

"Hold hard," I said at length. "If all this is true—I mean if the union of one man with one fruit is so natural and so delightful—why is it necessary to make a law about it."

"Because, unfortunately, human nature is always prone to error and laxity," replied Mr. Juicewit suavely.

"O come," I said. "That argument won't hold water. Let's be logical. Either this monophagous idea is natural and pleasant, or it isn't. If it is natural and pleasant, these laws are unnecessary: if the laws are necessary, then all this luscious oratory of yours is humbug."

"That is not an argument," said the Professor, with a frown. "It's mere poetico-religious raving. It is a plea for dietetic promiscuity. — Tell me, sir: what is the law in your own world?"

"We have none," I said.

"What? No law whatever?"

"None whatever," I repeated.

"Do you mean that you are polyphagous?—that you can eat as many fruits as you like?"

"We can eat any mortal thing we please," I said. "And we make no concealment of it either. We do it as naturally as—well—putting on our boots."

The Professor threw up his hands in horror. "What a dreadful state of affairs! What hideous debauchery!" he cried. "Your life must be one long orgy of gluttonous enjoyment. You must sit guzzling and stuffing yourselves all day and all night. You must be always cramming yourselves with the vilest substances. You must be eternally munching soap and sawdust, and revelling in clay and chalk, cockroaches and cottonwool."

"Give us a chance," I said. "What would we be doing that for?"

"Why not?" he asked.

"Because we don't want to, of course," I said.

"Don't want to?" he cried incredulously.

"No," I said. "Would you?"

The Professor flushed angrily. "We are not discussing *my* gastronomy," he said, "but the customs prevalent in your world.

You say that you don't do any of these things we have mentioned. What is there to prevent you?"

"Nothing. We just don't want to."

"O come!" he protested. "Don't tell me that without any
mathematical formulae to guide you, you live naturally according to science."

"I know nothing about science," I said. "But we've no taste
for chalk or sawdust, and we find it convenient to eat at regular
hours."

Mr. Juicewit shook his head.

"That is mere empiricism," he said. "Human nature is essentially stupid and ignorant, and the guidance of our own wills
and appetites must inevitably lead us astray."

"O yes," I said. "Now and then it does. And then we get
indigestion."

"Ah!" said Mr. Juicewit triumphantly. "That *proves* my
point."

I didn't know what to say to that, and wished to goodness
I hadn't let the fellow draw me into an argument, because I'm
really rather a bags at the game. You see, I knew he was talking
through his hat, but didn't quite know how to catch him, if you
understand. Seeing he had me hasped, he went on jawing for all
he was worth. Alimentation, he said, was too important and too
complicated a function to be left to the individual judgment
of our weak and perverse minds. The numerous and delicate
chemical, physical, and psychological reactions and processes
involved must be subjected to mathematical guidance. The
fact, which I had admitted, that we Earthfolk imposed certain
voluntary restraints on ourselves proved that: and the fact that
we were subject to indigestion proved that those restraints were
insufficient.

Here I managed to get in a word. I suggested that what was
true for Rathé might not hold true for every world. It would
certainly be impossible to restrict our people to a fruit diet, let

alone to a single fruit. But perhaps the Ratheans were made differently—

At that the Professor cut me short with a magnificent gesture. Truth, he said, was absolute, and could not be qualified by time or place. Neither could the calculating faculty be subordinated to the gross appetites of our animal nature. "Let me counsel you therefore," he concluded, "to subdue these inordinate and unnatural cravings of yours, and seek solace in one of our wholesome and nutritious fruits. Be in no hurry, but spend the next few days looking out for such fare as may suit you, and as soon as you have found it I will give you a license." Then, with a kindly invitation to me to call on him some day soon and chat over my "scientific troubles" (whatever they might be) he left me to myself.

Of course I had no intention of following his advice, having already decided what to do while he had been talking. There was a wood near the house where on a previous occasion, when I had had no use for it, I had noticed some wild fruit, rather like a small apricot, growing in great profusion. There I repaired at once and feasted full. Later on, however, I came to the conclusion that it would be both more convenient and more respectable to fall in with the custom of the place; so I took out a license for those melonish things that had attracted me on my first arrival, and remained as constant to them as anyone had a right to expect.

CHAPTER XVI

Remarkable Mentality of a Monophagous Civilisation

DURING THE FOLLOWING DAYS I took great pains to observe the working of the food-law and its effect on the daily life of the people. I also had several conversations with Professor Juicewit, who discussed the subject with me with a frankness which I am sure was unusual. I am therefore in a position to give you a pretty complete account of the matter, though there are some points on which I am still in the dark myself on account of the extraordinary reticence shown by the people on this topic.

It will, of course, have occurred to you to remark that the Ratheans must be constituted very differently from us if they can live on such a limited diet. And so they are. They have no inwards, so to speak, beyond a sort of stomach, all the space which with us is taken up with liver and guts and things being occupied in their case by nervous tissue, which is a sort of extension of the brain. As I have already remarked, their jaws and teeth are a great deal smaller than ours, so that on the whole they are constructed for a very attenuated diet. Their natural habit is to consume a meal of fruit once every five or six days. This is apparently stored in the stomach, through the walls of which it is gradually absorbed, leaving no residue to be evacuated. In the intervals they keep going on wine and water.

I dare say you will also have been wondering about the children. What do they live on up to the time when they are old enough to choose a fruit for themselves? Well, the fact is that the Rathean young don't eat at all, but draw their nourishment from a reserve of fat stored in the abdominal cavity, which is gradually absorbed as they grow older, giving place to the downward prolongation of the brain which I have described. At seven years of age, when they are fully grown, this process is complete, and the youth experiences the first sensations of hunger and begins to take an interest in the fruit trees around him. Up to this point the facts about eating have been carefully concealed from him, but he is now discreetly initiated into the mystery. He then wanders around from grove to orchard until he finds a tree whose colour and shape please him; whereupon he applies to a professor of mathematics for a license. The professor asks the lad (or girl, as the case may be) if he (or she) will promise to stick to this fruit, whether it be good for him or bad for him, whether he likes it or dislikes it, for the rest of his life. The youth by this time is in a mood to promise anything, and does so. And the comedy is over.

Quaint, isn't it? These physical facts, however, do make the law seem a little less unreasonable than it had appeared to me at first sight, and I think that if it were merely a custom instead of a law it would have been as natural to the Ratheans as the breakfast-dinner-tea habit is to us. On the other hand, it isn't the beautiful and harmonious arrangement that Juicewit pretended either.

I dare say that many Ratheans—perhaps even a majority—find it tolerably comfortable; but it's jolly hard on the rest, as you may imagine. Some people make mistakes in their selection. The fruit of their choice may turn out to disagree with them, or they may tire of its flavour. There are some also with changeable appetites who dislike being tied down in this manner. In many tribes these facts are recognised, though somewhat inadequately; a change being permitted when it can be definitely proved that the disagreement is bad enough to produce chronic dyspepsia. Some tribes, however, including that of Bulnid, which is dominated by a singularly narrow and bigoted school of mathematicians, will not allow even this alleviation;

while nowhere is any consideration given to the poor beggars with capricious appetites, who are regarded by the respectable as the most abandoned of criminals. These, and of course a host of others—young people not yet licensed, people who have been refused a decree of tmesis (as a license for change of diet is called), sensitive people who are unwilling to face the ordeal of a tmesis trial, with the humiliation involved of making a public revelation of the most intimate details of their digestive arrangements—all these have either to suffer in patience or else break the law. Of course most of them break it. Some poach on their neighbours' gardens. Others go out into the woods after wild fruit. Others indulge themselves irregularly at illicit eating-houses, ruining their constitutions with the corrupt and unnatural food supplied there. From the number of these houses, and from the prominence given in jest, song, and story to the theme of dietetic infidelity. I imagine that disobedience to the law must be very common indeed; and I have a shrewd suspicion that without this safety valve there would long ago have accumulated a power of hatred and contempt sufficient to blow the whole institution to pieces. In short, the law only survives at all because it is so frequently broken.

On all this I dilated at length to Professor Juicewit, but he was not to be moved. First he took a high-handed tone. Were depraved gluttons to be allowed to do what they liked? I said: never mind the depraved gluttons. They weren't going to be stopped by any law. I was thinking of the numbers of decent people whose health and happiness were being wrecked by the law. He admitted that it bore hard on some, but insisted that hard cases were bad law, and that mathematics could not legislate for exceptions. There were a great many exceptions, I said. Mr. Juicewit replied that he was aware of that, but it was all due to the bad example of those lax tribes which had modified the law. He would tolerate no such laxity in Bulnid. So that was that. Fresh collapse of your humble servant.

The business had its comic side too. These asinine restrictions had driven the unfortunate Ratheans clean dotty on the subject of food. It was quite the most important thing in their lives. It seemed as if they could think and talk and write about nothing else. Not, of course, that they talked about it crudely and openly as we do on earth. They never mentioned the word Hunger, for instance, but the word Taste was never out of their mouths; and though they were always going into ecstasies about the beauty of fruit trees, and eternally discussing their habits, one was left with the impression that they regarded them purely as ornaments. Newspapers and books used the same ciphers, and oh! the unmitigated slush that rolled in this form all day from tongue and pen. The sensation of hunger—I beg its pardon, the Emotion of Taste—is universally agreed to be the dominant impulse of human nature. It is the noblest of all sentiments. It is fixed, unchanging, immortal. It is the mainspring of man's highest activities. Its gratification is the supreme joy, and sufficient reward for all endeavours. The world and all else are well lost for Taste. And so on, till you're sick of it. I once ventured to object to some enthusiast that perhaps other emotions also had their share of importance. Love, for instance. "Sex!" cried the enthusiast, coarsely and contemptuously. "That feeble, fitful, mutable, inconstant passion! Why, it's but a seasonal and incalculable whim compared with the deep, abiding, changeless, and insatiable emotion of Taste." And she proceeded to quote some poetry to the effect that

> Man's love is of man's life a thing apart:
> Hunger's his whole existence.

The number of these asses who told me that Taste was immortal and unchangeable was simply countless; and every one of them, without exception, when I pointed to some concrete example imputing the contrary, had the same answer

ready for me. "O that," they would say, "couldn't have been
real Taste." No age seemed exempt from these fatuous illusions.
"There's no finer inspiration to a youth's ambition," one ancient
wiseacre told me, "than a healthy taste." And another: "All that's
best in a lad or girl is brought out by an honest attachment
to a pure fruit." Then the news- papers. Maybe you think I'm
trying to pull your leg all this time, Mr. Gallagher, but just you
listen now, and if I tell you a word of lie, may I be kicked with
spiked boots from here to Kamschatka and put to bed there on
a mattress of cactuses. On my solemn oath you couldn't open
a newspaper in Rathé without finding some futile article on
Whether Taste can Perish, or Whether it can Change, or alter-
natively on the problem of preserving it or the best methods
of keeping it constant. There was endless chatter in them too
on the possibility of having a taste for two fruits at once; and
there were occasional mild queries on the propriety of smelling
the flowers of a fruit tree before taking out a license. It was all
inconceivably childish and silly.

As for Rathean literature, it has been reduced by this habit
of mind to sheer drivelling imbecility. One of their novels still
lingers in my memory. It was a jolly fine story by a man called
Sneckid, full of exciting adventures, comic situations, vivid
descriptions, and the most lifelike character drawing: and all
this wealth of workmanship was lavished on a trumpery little
incident of a woman who has eaten a wild strawberry in her
childhood, and whose whole life is made miserable by the fear
of the iniquity becoming known. When finally she is betrayed
she goes out into the night to die rather than endure the shame
which would have followed. Most of the books written up to
twenty years or so before my arrival in the planet were of this
type; but I was told that a modern school of writers had sprung
up who dealt with the subject in more realistic and outspoken
fashion. One such work, which I was greatly pressed to read,
entitled the New Politician, by Mr. Slew, tells the story of a man

of brilliant talents but insatiable appetite, who, after a youth misspent in pursuit of the fruits of the field, at last settles down with a dainty cherry tree. Presently his fancy strays to pineapples, and for a time he manages to gratify his taste clandestinely. But eventually he has to choose between discovery (which would wreck his political career) and relinquishing the fruit he loves. With sobs and tears he makes his choice. Politics, home, and cherry tree are abandoned, and off he goes to feast on pineapple for ever after. Other books too I read, by still more modern writers, with still fruitier stories to tell. Frank books, Courageous books, they were called by their admirers; improper, immoral, or scandalous books by the respectable majority. To me they seemed even sillier than the old-fashioned romances. It was, perhaps, something in the authors' favour that they should see the absurdity of the food-law; but that made their acceptance of the absurdities which had grown out of it seem all the more childish. I mean the supposed importance of Taste, and all the other delusions which the mystifications of the law had thrown round it: because after all, it was the seriousness with which the subject was taken that made it so comical.

These novels, however, were just a little more like Rathean life as I observed it than were their predecessors, or, indeed, their contemporaries in the old tradition, to which the majority of novels still obstinately clung. In fact, anything less like life than these romances it would be impossible to conceive, and I can't understand how anybody knowing the truth, could be bothered reading such inanities at all. Take the case of the young—the lads and the girls whose pretty petulant yearnings are pictured with such sweetness and gusto by these drivelling novelists. Well, it is a sort of axiom among the elders that nobody ever feels hungry before seven years of age, and consequently people are not allowed a license before that. But it was obvious even to my unpractised eye that many of the young folk began to be hungry much earlier. Numbers of boys and girls have thus to undergo considerable suffering at a critical period of their lives, while their distress is accentuated by the fact that they don't know what is wrong with them, and, owing to their training, feel vaguely that it is something disgraceful. Occasionally one of these precocious youngsters, driven desperate with cravings, steals an apple from somebody's orchard; for which, if discovered, he is treated as a depraved monster, and mercilessly punished. If, on the other hand, he resists the temptation, he becomes peevish and irritable, a prey to morbid longings and curiosities, and develops unhealthy tastes, which may or may not be cured when finally he obtains his license.

Many Rathean authors have written books on this theme. One of them I still remember vividly. It was called *A Picture of My Youth*, and gave a horribly detailed description of the effect on a clever and imaginative boy of all this suppression, and thwarting, and confusion with guilt of a perfectly healthy appetite. It was a painful, and in places a disgusting, revelation, but, I have no doubt, quite true to life. I made an attempt to discuss it with Mr. Juicewit, but the mere mention of the book drove him into a fury. It was a foul and filthy concoction, he said: thoroughly morbid, and the product of a diseased mind. It ought to be burnt publicly in the market place. As for the notion that children suffered from hunger—pooh! he waved it aside with a comprehensive gesture. It was mere theorising, and morbid at that. Possibly a few precocious little gluttons might—but the average healthy child, no. "No, No," he said in the brisk robust voice of a man who takes a cold bath every morning. "Not a word of truth in it. Not a word."

I left the Professor to stew in his learned ignorance, and turned to try my ideas on the public, who proved to be equally stupid. The average Rathean, who is quite content to stick to one fruit all his life, cannot understand why the institution which suits him doesn't suit everybody, and thinks that those whom it doesn't suit ought to be forced to put up with it. With

a blindness or hypocrisy which is almost incredible, he pretends
not to know that unlicensed young folk sometimes feel hungry, or that such things as eating houses exist; or, if he admits
their existence, he declares that the people who use them do
so out of sheer wickedness and depravity. My attacks on the
law distressed people like this intensely. They were unable to
regard the question as open to discussion; and so the more telling the arguments I used, the more convinced they became of
my wickedness. Their silly noddles were jammed tight with two
absolutely contradictory ideas: that the restriction of a person
to one fruit was perfectly natural and ideally comfortable; and
that if the smallest relaxation were allowed, everybody would
immediately start devouring anything and everything. A curious thing was that the people who showed most fear of these
terrible results were those who had the most sentimental views
about the beauty and the undying power of taste. I noticed
too that their fear was always for what "others" would do: for
whenever I tried to pin them down by demanding point-blank
whether it was only respect for the law that kept them faithful
to their own diet, they always flew into a frantic rage and called
me grossly insulting. So if I were to judge the question merely
from these conversations I would have to conclude that nobody
had the slightest desire to break the law, but that everybody else
would go to the devil entirely if they had the chance. This dab
of pharisaism gives a very pretty finishing touch, I think, to the
picture.

I soon found that the Ratheans were utterly incapable of
using their reason on this topic. Before I could get out half a
dozen words they were all in a panic with the idea that my object
was to abolish all restraints on eating and inaugurate a reign of
universal gluttony and depravity; and I simply could not get
the asses to see that the whole point of my argument was that if
the law were abolished the people whom it suited would go on
just as before, the people who were injured by it would obtain

a remedy, and the gluttons would continue to be gluttons just as at present, with the difference that they would no longer be compelled to ruin their health in those underground food-dens.

On these lines I once wrote an article for the Press, thinking in my innocence that a dose of reason would be enough to rid the people of their nonsense. The first two papers that I sent it to refused to publish it on the ground that the subject was too unpleasant; the third offered to take it if I would make certain cuts, which I refused; the fourth printed it after I had agreed to soften certain expressions which the editor considered too outspoken. In this form it drew an immediate reply from a popular novelist. He said that it was all very well for a Being out of Space, in the shamelessness and fearlessness of a sweeter and nobler world, to demand the abolition of restrictions; but the sensible Rathean, aware of his own limitations, accepted them as inevitable. Admittedly they entailed hardships for some individuals, but were they on that account to put no restraints on the aberrations and caprices of human appetite? Ideally speaking, the principle of a man being faithful all his life to one fruit was supremely beautiful and ennobling—and endless bilge in the same strain. "I dare say," was my reply to this last futility. "But practically speaking it's tiresome and conducive to indigestion," and how, I asked, could people be ennobled compulsorily? The following day he denounced me as a cynic, and the paper was so flooded with the replies of other indignant correspondents that the editor had to close the controversy.

CHAPTER XVII

Astonishing Extravagances of the Advanced Movement

IT WAS THE PROUD boast of the Bulnidians that they were the most obedient to the institution of monophagy, and the most moderate in their eats, of all the peoples of Rathé. Indeed the laxity of the other tribes was a thing constantly deplored by the excellent folk. Their newspapers contained lurid accounts of "the wave of gluttony" which was sweeping over the rest of the world; of the "food-plays" and "appetising novels" with which the young generation were debauching themselves; and of the alarming increase of tmesis which was tending towards the destruction of all the laws of science. Worse still they deplored the abominable writings of so-called thinkers and self-styled teachers, which, unchecked by the salutary censorship which was in force in Bulnid, had had the inevitable effect of bringing the institution itself into such contempt that many people dispensed with licenses altogether. In short, Bulnid was the one bright spot in an abandoned world.

Naturally I thought it would be rather fun to get away from these paragons and see what life was like in Donlon, Israp, and other sinks of inequity. Another reason for going abroad was also presented to me at this moment. My newspaper article had been followed, as I have said, by a flood of indignant letters, which poured in day after day for weeks after. You can imagine my feelings, Mr. Gallagher, when I saw signed at the end of the most vicious of them—and it was a stinger—the name of Ensalus. The thing was so incredible that I was ready to believe it was another man of the same name until he came shambling into my room that night with an explanation.

"Had to be done, old chap," he said. "Must get a respectable reputation somehow if I'm ever to make another bid for the chieftainship. My model cousin, you see, is suspected to be a bit unorthodox on this point, which gives me a sort of glimmer of hope."

"If you had a grain of sense," I replied, "instead of making a sham attack on me, you'd help me to put an end to this ridiculous law. I should think that the man who promised to abolish it would drive every other candidate from the field."

"Nonsense," replied Ensalus. "He'd be stoned out of the field himself. The people would never stand for such a thing."

"Not openly, perhaps," I said. "But don't you know very well that they all detest the law in their hearts. They'd probably talk against you and howl against you for appearance sake; but they'd vote for you in secret. Just you make up your mind to face the music at the hustings, and the throne of Bulnid is yours for ever after."

Ensulas shook his head. "You don't know our people. You don't understand the position at all. The whole idea is absurd—impossible—unthinkable. I wouldn't stand for it myself."

"You mean you stand for the food-law?"

Ensalus reddened and stammered. "O well, you know," he managed to get out at last, "it's mathematics, you know, isn't it? And you can't get away from mathematics, can you?"

"It's the most tomfool mathematics ever I heard of," I said. "It's sheer blooming superstition and folly."

Ensalus looked positively frightened as I spoke these words. "O come now," he said. "You shouldn't talk like that. I don't profess to be much of a stickler in my own conduct, but after all, mathematics is mathematics. You can't get away from that."

"If you're so damned attached to the law," I said angrily, "it's a pity you don't keep it better. Why are you always dodging into eating-houses?"

"O well," said Ensalus, "that's only human nature. I don't defend it. A man can't help giving way to temptation now and then, but that doesn't shake his belief in mathematics."

I saw clearly that Ensulas was useless for my purpose, and was about to let him go in despair when I remembered something he had said earlier. "You told me just now," I remarked, "that this cousin of yours is a bit unorthodox on this question. What does that mean?"

"I'm not sure. There's a rumour that he's in favour of introducing tmesis. I suspect myself that he goes even further. Either way, if the rumour gains strength enough—and I mean to scatter it as broadly as possible—the hash of his candidature is settled. But don't you worry. While there's wild fruit in the forest and eating-houses in the city, the law can't keep your belly empty, can it? Good night, old chap."

After this information my course seemed fairly clear. Since Ensulas was apparently no good (it was astonishing how dark he kept those sterling qualities of his) I decided that the horse for me to back was his cousin, Yasint, as he was called. I thought that if I could put the future ruler of Bulnid under an obligation to me now, I would be able to make use of him later on for the furtherance of my own schemes: for, remember, I had made up my mind that I was going to be boss of the planet some day. I accordingly resolved to set out at once for Israp, where the heir apparent was studying at the University. After a tender farewell scene with Ytteb, with whom my affair had been going ahead in spite of all interruptions, I took the air mail and in due course presented myself at Yasint's rooms.

That gentleman was immersed in his studies when I arrived. He was a big grave man with the larges pair of eyes I had yet seen. He looked distinctly please when I announced who I was; but after a few minutes' conversation, for some reason or other he seemed to lose interest. This obliged me to push on to the subject of my visit as rapidly as possible. I began by sounding him, fairly discreetly, as I thought, on the food question, but he must have been a deuced clever fellow, for, before I knew where I was, he had all my cards out like dummy's on the table without allowing me as much as a squint at his own. I could see that I had put him wise to Ensulas's little game even before I had mentioned his name. still there was nothing else to do but play out the hand.

"Now our course," I went on, "is clear and straight. First we've got to squelch that rumour about your orthodoxy and build you a water-tight reputation between now and polling-day. At the same time we get the gaff blown on Ensulas's nocturnal adventures. Then, when you're seated on the throne, if you and I can't put our heads together and find a way to scupper this mass of superstition—well, I don't come from a higher sphere, and my name isn't O'Kennedy."

Mr. Yasint answered me in a voice as cold as a judge's on the bench. "Your very interesting views, Mr. O'Kennedy, are based on four misconceptions. In the first place, you think I want the Chieftainship."

"Well, don't you?" I asked.

"No. Only a fool would want it, and we don't put fools in such a position. The post will be thrust upon me, not because I want it, nor because the people want me, but because I am the right man for it. You would know that if you had taken the trouble to study our political constitution.

"In the second place," he went on, "you think that if I were Chief I could alter the law. I could not. I could only carry out the law made by the people. In the third place, you think it would be possible for me to deceive the people; which shows that you despise them, and are therefore stupid; and in the fourth place, you think it commendable to deceive them, which shows that you are something I will not be so rude as to mention. But never

mind. It is not for me to judge you; and, lest you think I do not
trust you, I will tell you something that would do me some
harm in Bulnid if you were to betray it. These rumours you
speak of are true. I do indeed condemn this food-law, though
what were best to put in its place I cannot tell you. Now, my
friend, come out with me and see this city of Israp, which is the
very jewel of Rathé, and more fitting to be the landing-place of
a being from the stars than the dull streets of homely Bulnid."

I saw now that Ensulas would have to be my man after
all, for Yasint was evidently a typical Rathean—dull, narrow
minded, unenterprising, and without the slightest ambition to
get on. And then that pious win-you-by-kindness back-chat in
the tail of his speech! Gosh, he was a puling muff.

He showed me round the city; but I can't be bothered with
any more descriptions. It was just ten times as fine as Bulnid,
and the very gem of the universe. I shook Yasint off as soon as I
could and had a very pleasant time there, after which I moved
on to the neighbouring city of Donlon, which was a little larger,
but not quite so fine, though still very fine indeed. Everywhere
in both towns I was received with the greatest affability, for the
news of my arrival in Rathé had at last penetrated to the more
enterprising newspapers. Again there was no fuss or lionising;
but invitations of the most cordial kind kept pouring in on me
so fast that for a month I didn't sleep twice in the same house.
To my intense disappointment I found that the gastronomic
laxity of these cities had been grotesquely exaggerated by the
smug Bulnidians. I had been led to believe that, as a result of
the introduction of tmesis, dietetic fidelity, outside Bulnid, was
a thing of the past. This was enormously untrue. Mind you, I
am trying to look at the matter from a Rathean point of view.
To my unmathematical mind it would not have seemed very
shocking if half the population had changed its diet every week;
but the fact was that only about one person in a hundred made
use of the tmesis courts at all, generally to rid themselves of a

diet which had been rendering their lives miserable for years. The average respectable Donlonian or Israpian still regarded all such procedures as disgraceful, and in deference to these prejudices the conditions under which a decree could be obtained had been made extremely stringent. Indeed, the law of tmesis was almost as ridiculous as the food-law itself. You couldn't change your fruit merely because you disliked it, or even because it disagreed with you. It had to disagree so badly as to make you sick in public. And not only that, but you must be able to prove that you really wanted to keep it, and that the fault was entirely on the fruit's side. Otherwise the court had no power to set you free. Needless to say there was much evasion of the law, a favourite dodge being to take an emetic and get sick in presence of a witness, thus securing a change of diet at the expense of honour and decency. But the law was vigilant to prevent such abuses. There was a special officer known as the Proctor whose duty it was to investigate evidence which fell under his suspicion, and if his report was adverse you lost your case. There was nothing, then, in the tmesis statistics to justify the horror expressed by the Bulnidians; and in general the dietetic standard in the bigger cities was much the same as in the smaller one. Transgressors were perhaps a shade less circumspect: but that was all. I found presently, however, that apart from the loose and the gluttonous there were considerable numbers of earnest thoughtful people who were in open revolt against the food law itself; who regarded it not as something right, to be got around, but as something wrong, to be got rid of. This movement had been only mentioned to me with bated breath in Bulnid. Its prophet was a certain dramatist, not long dead, called Senbi, who in a series of plays had made attack after attack, delivered from every possible angle, against the whole institution. One of his plays happened to be revived during my stay in Donlon, and I went one night to a performance of it. It was called *Phantoms*.

It is the story of a man with an enormous capacity and appetite for food, which he is driven to enjoy in illicit and underhand ways, with the usual results to his health and character. His wife, a model and austere woman, suffers all this in silence for the sake of her child. She manages his business for him, restrains his worst excesses, and shields his good name so successfully that few people suspect his misdemeanours. Finally she sends her son away from home, to be educated in a foreign city, so as to save him from contamination by his father's example. After many years the glutton dies, leaving his wife free to call the young man home and enjoy his companionship and gratitude in her declining days. Unfortunately the son, Waldos, inherits his father's appetite; but for his mother's sake he does his best at first to conceal it. The dullness of her country house, however, soon defeats his resolution, and she discovers his depravity. What should be her conduct now? That was the problem with which Senbi faced the smug respectability of Rathé. To her husband she had behaved exactly as a model woman should, shrinking from him as a scoundrel, whilst carrying out her duties in a spirit of moral superiority. But then she had not loved her husband, whereas she does love the son. She thus sees her course clear at once. Instead of recoiling from him, or trying to force impossible restraints on him, she will leave him free to live his own life, and make it as happy for him as possible. But the law is not to be baulked so easily of its victim. Waldos now reveals to his mother that he is afflicted with a disease which he has inherited as a result of his father's misbehaviour, and that he carries poison in his pocket against the time when its pain be- comes unendurable. The same night that moment comes, and the mother has to face the terrible ordeal of helping him to end his life and his suffering together.

The moral of this play would seem obvious enough to you and me, but the Ratheans could not see it for their disgust at the theme. On the first production, some fifty years before, a perfect storm of abuse had burst over Senbi's head. The crit-

ics strove to outdo one another in foulness of language on the
subject. They called the play "naked loathsomeness", "literary
carrion", "garbage and offal", and other pleasant names, and its
author "a gloomy ghoul, bent on groping for horrors by night,
and blinking like a stupid old owl when the warm sunlight of
the best of life danced under his wrinkled eyes." The public,
already shocked, was soon lashed into such a fury that Senbi had
to fly from his native town. In time, however, the storm blew
itself out. When I arrived in Rathé Senbi had been dead many
years. He had become a classic; and the odour of his reputation
as an artist had drowned the stink of his message of revolt. I
have actually heard people say that they read Senbi for his style.

Still, the seed he had sown had quietly germinated. Other
writers, following in his footsteps, launched ever fiercer attacks
on the law. Tears, wrath, and laughter in turn were mobilised
against it. It was astonishing how much wit and energy were
used to undermine this molehill, and with how little effect—
comparatively. For the law was still the law, and the respectable
majority—a unanimous mob of ascetics and gluttons, faithful
and faithless, wise and foolish, honest and dishonest, believers
and unbelievers, cynics and sentimentalists—supported it tooth
and nail. But in every part of the world numbers of young people had been stirred to revolt. The unhealthy reticence which
had overlaid the subject like green scum on a stagnant pond
was rent and scattered as by an explosion of marsh gas, and
rampant discussion raged like a wind among the rank vegetation. The law was no longer broken only by sneaking gluttons
and unprincipled scallawags, nor by conscience-smitten yield-
ers to temptation, but bravely and deliberately by serious and
high-minded young theorists, who faced the consequent igno-
miny with the zeal of martyrs in a noble cause. Not that they
took to gluttony, or to habits like ours on earth, or even to a
moderately varied fruitarian diet. Perhaps some did. But the
majority were content to scrap their unsuitable fruit, if already
licensed, or, if not, to dispense with that formality; and in either

case they remained far more faithful to the monotonous diet of their choice than most respectable folk.

In these revolutionary circles I was hailed as a messenger of light. The young folk hung on my words like children round a storyteller. I was frequently urged to put myself at the head of the advanced movement, as it was called, and for a while I played with the idea, but discarded it in the end as unlikely to lead to anything. For one thing the revolutionaries themselves were of more than one mind as to what should be done. Indeed they were of fifty minds, if not fifty thousand. Some merely wanted a reform of the tmesis laws; others wanted tmesis to be granted simply on request. Others wanted licenses to be granted on trial. More demanded that they should be given for limited periods. In the heel of the hunt came the extremists clamouring for the abolition of the license altogether—or Free Eats, as they called it. The leadership of such a hopelessly divided mob would have been an utterly impossible position. But there was another reason, equally strong, for my declining it. The Ratheans could never do even a sensible thing in a sensible way, and on this food question they were more than usually idiotic. I suppose that the instincts of these "advanced" gentry had become so warped and cramped by generations of suppression that they couldn't take their new freedom naturally. Anyway they were so self-conscious, so intense, so infernally joyless, and at times so sentimental, that I positively split my sides laughing at them. The old-fashioned moralists who thought eating shameful were bad enough; but it was too much for me altogether to hear these ardent innovationers calling it beautiful and spiritually ennobling. "Well God help you," I said to them, "you wouldn't think it beautiful if you saw me tucking into tripe and onions or sausages and mashed." This annoyed them frightfully, and one superior blighter said: "I suppose you think it shameful and disgusting, then, like the mathematicians." "Not at all," I replied. "There's nothing in it either way. It's neither beautiful nor ugly, but jolly pleasant." This point of view was described by some as "narrow-minded" and by others as "paradoxical" but plainly none of them could see the sense of it.

They had another idea of the matter which was sillier still. The orthodox view was that eating was a horrible practice whose only justification was that it gave nutriment to the body; while many went so far as to say that nothing should be eaten without the deliberate intention of manufacturing it into tissue and energy. As a reaction to this the advanced crowd talked and acted as if eating had nothing to do with nutriment at all—as if it was just a pleasurable process unrelated to any purpose whatsoever. Out of this notion and the other there had developed a nasty habit which I must be excused for referring to. People who believed that eating was beautiful and spiritual and the rest of it, naturally came to deduce in time that the more one could ennoble oneself the better. But this tended to develop the corporation, which is regarded as the greatest disgrace that can happen to a Rathean. So a practice had grown up of taking emetics after a meal, as I'm told the ancient Romans used to do, and thus making room for a second or third bout of ennoblement.

Now it was an article of faith with all advanced people that this pretty practice was not only justifiable but necessary, and not only necessary but highly meritorious. They were absolutely cocksure about that: and they looked down with the perkiest disdain on anyone who doubted it. A person who disapproved of the practice they regarded as too worthless to be argued with. He was a fool or a knave, and there was an end of him. Indeed, Food Control, as they called it, had become for them an essential part of the scheme of things. It was simply taken for granted. Well, I couldn't stand for nonsense of that sort, but told them flat that the thing was disgusting and indecent, to say nothing of the danger to their health. Dear me, you should have seen the storm I loosed on myself by that simple opinion. It shocked the advanced folk even worse than my attack on the food-law had shocked the respectable. I was denounced as a reactionary, a bigot, an obscurantist, a hidebound mathematician, an enemy of light and beauty, and goodness knows what else. I wasn't even allowed to state my case. It was invented for me by my opponents, who then proceeded to demolish it with arguments of elaborate texture and subtle irony. One reason, which was declared to hold great weight with me, was that food-control interfered with the desire of Science to convert the largest possible number of carbohydrate molecules into living tissue. That was the first I had ever heard of this ridiculous view, which I now know was not even held by the Bulnidian mathematicians, but it was no use my denying it. The advanced folk insisted that it was the mainstay of my case, and, when I protested, I was simply shouted down.

One such scene—the last—still lingers in my memory. It was at a social gathering in Donlon, at which half the emancipated people in the town were present. Some young lady had been handing out the beauty dope in helpings that at last drove me to protest violently. "God help you," I said, "this cant of beauty makes me sicker than the old-fashioned cant of shame. For heaven's sake let's try and keep our sanity and not let our brains run to slush." A murmur of protest went through all the groups within earshot, which at once began to drift in my direction. I was the lion of the evening, you understand. "Feeding is a mighty enjoyable occupation," I said. "I'd be the last to deny that. Over beyond in Bulnid, when they told me it was shameful, I told them to go to hell. But when you people tell me it's ennobling and beautiful—well, all I can say is, don't make me laugh: I've a split lip. You know, you Ratheans, advanced or backward, think too much about your eats. That's what's the matter with you; and I'm not sure that you advanced blighters aren't worse in that respect than the others. Why can't you just take the thing easy and natural? Most of you are best suited by a monophagous diet, and I think the lot of you are healthier when you stick to one fruit at a time. Well, why not recognise that and stop worrying about the subject? You know all this advanced humbug about free eats and the rest of it is only possible if you go in for this food-control business, and that you must know, if you've any sense of delicacy at all, to be a very nasty practice—"

Well, before I could say another word, my voice was drowned by indignant remonstrances coming from all sides. A dozen champions had already sprung to the defence, but as they all insisted on talking together their arguments were not very lucid. Presently, however, one master mind succeeded in quelling its allies, and the field was held by a single voice. This was the voice of Slops, one of the most eminent of the advanced novelists. He had been accorded the post of danger on the strength, I suppose, of his reputation, for his arguments didn't amount to much. They consisted principally in the usual string of words like narrow-minded, hide-bound, bigoted, and so on, hurled at me, and a larding of syrupy dope, flavoured with revolutionary spicing, basted over food-control. He went on to tell me that I was a foul-minded fanatic who regarded the loveliest side of life as something disgraceful; an ignorant pedant who would forbid all pleasure that had not some scientific end; a maundering sentimentalist with vague yearnings after a carbohydrate apotheosis; and lots more that I can't remember. The man's command of language was astonishing. It overwhelmed me. When he had finished I hadn't a kick left in me. All I could say was this:

"Well," I said, "if you think vomiting a pretty operation, go on vomiting. But for heaven's sake don't get sentimental about it."

That little episode finished my chances of leading the great revolt against the food-law. But what did I care for the food-law? I could always break it.

CHATPER XVIII

Afterthought of Mr. Yasint

THE LAST WORD ON this topic I shall leave to Mr. Yasint, beside whom I found myself in the train on my return journey to Bulnid. He was on vacation, he told me, and expected to be nominated as successor to the Chief within a few weeks. He laughed when I related my adventures among the advanced people.

"It's the antics of these idiots," he said, "that prevent me from attacking the law myself. I have often raged inwardly against its cruelty and stupidity; sometimes I do so still; but more often now I hesitate. The law I begin to see as a blundering step in the right direction, while the advanced people are just slithering off in a wrong direction. The mathematicians are all wrong in their defence of the law. It isn't natural or pleasant. Quite the reverse. But how has man evolved himself out of bestiality but by forcing him to do unnatural and unpleasant things.

"I fancy sometimes," he went on, "that our ancestors were in too much of a hurry over this particular step upwards, and that the race overstrained itself in consequence. That's why we're so apt to relapse. You don't find us dropping on all fours, or barking, or yielding to panic. Only a very odd person gives way to anger. We breed, on the whole, rationally. That is probably because these steps in evolution were taken slowly and almost unconsciously. But with eating we seem to have leaped blindly and violently, reaching for a height beyond our strength, so that it is still doubtful whether we shall attain it or fall back.

"Of course the effort has been worth making," he said with a sudden spasm of energy, as if in answer to my unspoken thought. "Consider what strides we have taken in evolution as a result of it. Compare our interiors with those of our cousins the submen and the apes, to say nothing of the lower animals. Why, their carcases are little more than containers for their digestive apparatus. Mere hogsheads of guts. Whole areas of their brains and nervous systems are specialised for the control of this monstrous system. Their eyes, ears, and noses are deflected to its service from their proper functions. (I wish your advanced friends could be brought to realise how little their refinements in this respect differ from the grossness of brutes.) their days are almost wholly devoted to the stuffing of this receptacle. When they have filled it they are forced to rest, since in that state they cannot carry it around; and when energy returns it must be spent on filling the thing again. Pah! This belly more rules than serves them.

"So then, if what you say is true, and the men of your world eat as our animals do, your guts must be as their guts, and if your brains are better—as your power of speaking leads me to believe they must be—why, at any rate, they are not as good as they might be, since you can have little room for them."

"We don't eat like animals," I protested.

"Perhaps you do it cleanlier," said Yasint. "But how much of your time and labour is devoted to the process?"

I did a swift calculation, and gave him the result, somewhat toned down. He made no reply, but turned to watch the landscape flying past the window.

That's enough of this topic. I'm going round the corner for a spot of lunch.

CHAPTER XIX

The Shocking Immorality of the Ratheans

LITTLE YTTEB WELCOMED ME home with a hearty embrace and a heap of kisses. I may tell you that I was by this time head over heels in love with her. The aspersions cast on her character by her mother had made me pause for a moment; but it was impossible to look at the girl's pretty face, or hear her happy laughter, and think ill of her. Fully believing that she was worthy of me, I had gone on with my wooing, and when we had parted on the eve of my journey to Israp there had been a tacit understanding between us. How happy I was at that moment! As good as engaged to a really charming girl, who also, by sheer luck, was a most eligible match, and the finest possible asset to my career, the world of Rathé seemed to lie at my feet. But alas for human ambition, the frailty of woman, and fortune's fickle smiles. Fate had other things in store, and there's many a slip 'twixt the cup and the lip.

I had no such forebodings as this, however, as I clasped my lovely girl in my arms and ardently returned her kisses. Later in the day, after I had paid my respects to the Chief and my Lady, we went off for a favourite stroll down a leafy lane beyond the city, and so into a field of marigolds, where we made love to our hearts' content. We were happily playful at first, I weaving flower garlands about her, and calling her a thousand pretty names that came to me out of nowhere, and she answering with smiles and fleeting caresses. Then we fell a-kissing. Ytteb was made for kisses. She had a dimple on each cheek, from which I drew them like honey from a rose. There were warmly thrilling ones to be found lurking in the little hollows under her ears. The white expanse of her neck was like a scented meadow to pick them in: the sunny slope to a valley where for one bold moment I ventured also. Up and down her arms, too, it was delightful to wander. But as for her lips: I won't call them simply heavenly: they *were* heaven.

At last, in a blissful pause, I asked her to marry me. She was leaning on my shoulder at the time, her dreaming eyes half closed; but my question opened them to startled life. "Marry you?" She smiled, and shook her head. "O no, thanks."

Perfectly friendly was her tone, but perfectly decided. It was evident that the idea had never entered her head. I was struck dumb for a moment: not that I had expected her to jump at me as soon as I opened my mouth, but after the way she'd led me on I wasn't prepared for a flat refusal.

"Ytteb!" I said, recovering slowly. "Do you mean that?"

"Of course I mean it," she replied. "I really wouldn't care to be married."

"But my dearest," I protested. "After all our lovely times together! And all the things you've said to me. And our kisses. Have you not cared for my kisses after all?"

"They've been heavenly," she said, her eyes lighting up again. "Give me some more."

She held out her arms to me, with her head a little sideways, as tenderly as ever. "Come," she said as I hesitated. But I sat tight. "Then why won't you marry me?" I asked.

"Just because," she answered, dropping her arms. I had never seen her look so tantalisingly adorable.

"'Because,' is no reason," I said grimly. "Tell my why."

"Why should I have a reason?" returned Ytteb. "I don't want to: that's all."

"I thought you loved me," I said miserably.

"Why, so I do," said Ytteb. "Haven't I kissed you a thousand times?"

"Yes. But I don't want it to stop at that."

"Well, it needn't stop at that," said the girl.

"Why do you tease so?" I said, not understanding. "Come. Tell me seriously. Will you marry me?"

"No. I won't marry anybody. I don't want to be tied."

"And yet you love me?"

"I do. I'll go for a honeymoon if you like."

Quite simply she said it, neither boldly nor coquettishly, you know, but just sweetly inviting. It came from her so naturally that for a moment I was unconscious of anything wrong in the affair. It was mere disappointment at being offered less than I wanted that moved me to remonstrate: "But my dearest—"

"Now that's all you'll get," she said, very prettily adamant. "I simply can't be bothered with marriage. It's too exacting and serious for me altogether. You know I'm quite, *quite* lowly-evolved."

"I'm afraid you don't love me very much, then," I said. My moral sense wasn't yet quite awake.

"How can you say that?" she protested. "Hasn't every kiss I've given you been packed with love? Can't you see I'm simply longing for you? Look now—" putting one soft arm around my neck, she pointed with the other—"Over there between those hills there's a valley, and little quiet cottages in it, perched beside tumbling waterfalls—such music they make in the evenings!—a very paradise for lovers. I'll go with you there this very night, if you ask me."

Gosh! It was an awful temptation for a fellow, wasn't it? But I resisted. Mind you, I don't set up to be a saint, but you see there were no priests in Rathé—or at any rate none that would be of any use, as I'll explain presently—so there was no way of getting the sin wiped out, and maybe I'd have to die with it still on my soul. It was a cruel dilemma. There on the one side was Ytteb, the very flower of a man's desire: and on the other the eternal flames of hell. I won't say I didn't waver, but in the end virtue triumphed.

"Tut-tut," I said. "What would your mother say?"

"I don't see what business it is of my mother's," the girl replied. "However, you've lost your chance now. I'm going home."

A sort of chill seemed to come into the air as she rose to her feet, shaking the wilted marigolds from her in the act. All along the leafy way homeward I was awkward and silent; but Ytteb was just her old self, laughing and chatting as if nothing had happened. And that evening didn't she trot out the whole thing to the family in the drawing-room.

"Just imagine, Daddy," she said. "Mr. O'Kennedy has asked me to marry him, and he won't be content with a honeymoon."

There was general laughter, during which I felt myself flushing up to the eyes. Then the Chief patted me kindly on the shoulder, saying: "No use pressing her, my boy. Take what you can get. She isn't fit for marriage."

"You should have known that," added her Ladyship. "Didn't I tell you so myself?"

"It wasn't a fair thing to ask the girl," said Camino indignantly. "She's too lowly-evolved."

"Might as well expect her to lift a two-hundred pound weight," put in Ianda.

"Speak for yourself," Ytteb interposed. "I'm just as fit for marriage as anybody, only I don't care about it. A honeymoon would be more fun."

I was really shocked now. "You seem to think," I said, "that the choice is of no more importance than if you were choosing between two frocks."

"Well, isn't it rather important to choose the right sort of frock?" replied Ytteb.

This was too much for me altogether. "Good lord!" I cried. "Have you people no morality at all?"

"Morality!" cried Ytteb.

"Morality!" echoed Camino and Ianda.

"What has morality got to do with it?" asked the Chief.

I looked at him hard. He wasn't joking, or trying to be smart, but genuinely surprised. Looking round the circle of faces I saw the same expression in all.

"What ails you, boy?" asked my Lady impatiently. "If you love the girl, can't you go off with her and have done with it?"

"No, thank you," snapped Ytteb. "He can keep his love. I don't want it now." And off she strode out of the room.

"Well, I suppose that settles it," said the Chief. "You see, young man, you should have taken my advice while the chance was open."

The subject was then dropped as of no further interest. But next day Mr. Yasint came to me, saying that he had observed my bewilderment, and offering to explain matters. Well, to cut a long story short, I found they were like this. The Ratheans have no moral code, and no such institution as marriage. The word which I have thus translated is only the name given to a union which is intended to be permanent; but there's no ceremony attached to it, and it can be broken off at any time by either party. Moreover any other kind of union is equally legitimate, and equally respectable.

Why then, you'll ask, does anybody marry at all? Well, so did I, and got a nice telling-off from Yasint in consequence. He put it to me that marriage is a healthy and very agreeable habit which had gradually grown up and been found generally suitable to human needs. Was it not a pleasant thing to have a lifelong comrade bound to one by ties of affection, loyalty, and common interests? to know that there was one person in whose thoughts one was always first, who listened for one's step, from whom a look won a smile, to whom one could always turn in confidence for tenderness and understanding? To put it on a higher plane, was not this subordination of an animal appetite to spiritual and social ends an important step in evolution?

You'd have thought from the way he spoke that I was the

opponent of marriage and he the defender. It's a way the
Ratheans have in argument. It shows how crooked their minds
are. I tried to set him right on the point, but he swept on with
his sermon, regardless. The real clue to the business, I found,
was Evolution. The Ratheans are quite mad on this subject. I
don't mean that they're particularly keen on tracing their descent
from monkeys. Their ascent to some higher being is more their
concern they regard evolution as a process of improvement
which is always going on, and in which it's their job to assist.
Grades of evolution with them take the place of our class dis-
tinctions: they soar in the scale according to the number of
human desires they raise themselves above. Evolution has also
practically taken the place of morals. They judge conduct not
by standards of right and wrong, but by its evolutionary value.
Thus irregular sexual unions are considered lowly-evolved, as
relapsing towards animal conditions. A well-evolved Rathean
would not stoop to one himself, but he considers them quite
respectable, and very suitable to low-scale folk who hunt and
shoot. He smiles indulgently on such lovers, as one does on a
child for preferring sweets to meat and potatoes, deeming them
beneath the dignity, and too weak for the stress of marriage,
but not holding them blameworthy for that. On the other
hand, some few at the opposite end of the scale—the more
than usually highly-evolved—are supposed to be above marriage. Like Ianda, they have one or two children while they are
young, but live afterwards in strenuous chastity. The great bulk
of the people, however—the moderately-evolved, as you might
say—marry, and, I will do them the justice to add, are faithful
to one another and quite happy. Not only that, but strange to
say there's very little chopping and changing, though there's
nothing to prevent them. The great majority of people remain
united for life to their first choice, and hardly any go beyond
their second. I can't understand why. Yasint put it that affection,
common interests, and children were three very strong bonds,

but of course that's all nonsense and takes no account of human nature. Those are the facts anyway, and you can explain them as you like.

I'll say another thing in the Ratheans' favour. They are entirely devoid of jealousy. Men and women, whether married or single, form friendships freely, regardless of sex. A married women might spend a whole day in the company of a male friend, and it would never occur to her husband to worry, nor would he have any cause; our assumption that a man and woman cannot be alone together for five minutes without misbehaving themselves being quite outside the Rathean imagination. I gather that on the whole they think much less about this love business than we do. Certainly they don't talk much about it (though they can make love very prettily when so disposed) and it figures very small in their novels.

There is one more aspect of the question to be dealt with, and not a very pleasant one I'm afraid, but perhaps you'll excuse me. It is a recognized and perfectly respectable profession for a girl to become a courtesan. It is, of course, the most lowly-evolved of all occupations, but that is the worst these depraved people think of it, and if you'll believe me, Mr. Gallagher, no parent ever raises an objection to daughter joining it. I must admit however that the conditions are more attractive than on earth. The girls are not degraded, but generally pretty and possessed of some such accomplishment as music or dancing. They own their houses, which they decorate tastefully and cheerfully, and they take only such lovers as please them—these again being persons of the most lowly-evolved sort.

Having listened thus far to Mr. Yasint's exposition, I conceived it to be more than my duty to express my disapproval of such wholesale immorality, and to speak up for the holy institution of matrimony, which was ordained for the propagation of the race and a remedy against sin, and has bestowed such blessings and happiness among mankind. I preached quite a little sermon on the subject, to which Mr. Yasint paid such close attention that I thought I had made a convert, until he began questioning me in that nasty cunning way of his. Did none of us, he asked, ever engage in love outside those holy bonds? I had to admit that a good number did: not that I wanted to let down our race's reputation, but because, as I have explained before, it was impossible to tell anything but the truth in Rathé. Mr. Yasint went on. Were our people always happy within those holy bonds? I was afraid not. Were they always faithful to them? Again, no. Then on went the catechism until he had dragged it out of me that great numbers of our married people never had any children; that most countries had been forced to institute divorce laws, and that these were so stupid that divorce could only be obtained through such disgrace and debauchery that we had to censor the reports of the cases out of our papers; and finally that profligacy was so common that thousands of wretched women—most of them unwillingly—made a living by ministering to it.

"Well, then," said Yasint, when he had lugged the last unfortunate fact into the light, "I cannot see the need for these vows and indissoluble contracts of yours. Apparently the people who don't like them break them, and those who keep them would do so in any case."

"O no," I said. "Lots of people who detest each other are held together by them."

"And what," sneered Yasint, "is the good of that?"

"That's morality," I said.

Here Yasint positively howled with laughter. "What about your thousands of courtesans?" he demanded. "We have less than a dozen in Bulnid. How does that strike your moralityship?"

"That's only because you're too immoral to need them," I retorted. And there, having got the better of the argument, I left him.

I saw now that Ytteb wasn't to blame for her immoral ideas,

so I sought her out to make amends for my behavior. Coming upon her in the garden soon after, I found her quite friendly, but cool. There was no response to my handclasp, and she wouldn't let me kiss her. "What's the good?" she asked when I protested. "Kisses make a very sweet prelude to a honeymoon, but by themselves they're unsatisfying."

I then set to work to convert her, but I might as well have tried to kiss her by force. The obstinate little beggar simply couldn't be got to see that there was any good in marriage or any harm in the other thing. Worse still, I found that my own faith and morals were beginning to weaken under the strain. Lying awake that night I was tormented with worse temptations than St. Anthony ever had to put up with.

"After all," whispered the Devil in my ear, "what you want to do is perfectly right in Rathé."

"For a Rathean, perhaps," I answered.

"Well, aren't you a Rathean now?"

"Only in body," I answered.

"Well, isn't it your body that will enjoy her?"

"Yes. But it's my soul that will be judged for it."

"Very true," said the Devil. "But have you considered this point? At the Last Day soul and body are re-united, to be rewarded or damned together. Your soul therefore cannot be punished without your innocent body suffering along with it; and this would be contrary to divine justice."

"But surely," I said, "it would be an easy matter to punish my soul separately?"

"Young man," said the Devil, "are you so conceited as to think that an article of the creed would be scrapped for your sake?"

"Well, perhaps not," I said. "But if my soul can't be punished, it can't be rewarded either."

"O," said the Devil, offended. "I'm wasting my time on you. If you don't think a pretty girl's bosom more alluring than a harp in a cloud, well, please yourself."

"Don't go," I said. "Maybe I'll consider it."

"Maybe you will," said the Devil, "when it's too late."

"How too late?" I asked.

"She's losing interest in you already," said the devil. "Women have no use for laggards."

"Get away," I said.

"'Struth," said the Devil. "I was watching her undressing just now—Satan has his privileges, you know—and though your photograph was on her table she never once looked at it."

I groaned.

"Got you there, my boy! Eh?" says the Devil, swiping his tail around in triumph. But that was the saving of me; for he flicked a drop of brimstone right into my eye, and that was an object lesson of the very first water.

CHAPTER XX

The Plot Thickens

NEXT MORNING I FOUND myself the subject of no small amusement in the Palace. Ytteb and Yasint had both been retailing what I had told them to the others, from whom I had to stand a fire of criticism in consequence. What the Chief and her Ladyship said I forget. Camino was pityingly tolerant. As for Ianda, she outdid her usual cynicism. The Earthfolk, she said, were probably such repulsive creatures that only some very strong constraint could keep a pair of us together long enough for breeding purposes. Ensulas said nothing in front of the others, but having got hold of me later on in private, he said: "Look here, old chap, I rather like this idea of yours, and I think that if we put our heads together we should be able to put it in force."

I clasped his hand and told him to command me to the last drop of my blood. He then proceeded to take me completely into his confidence. He had been married, he told me, about a year ago, and his wife had left him inside a week on finding that his love for her wasn't spiritual enough. "Maybe she was right," he said. "I'm a full-blooded man without much room for soul in my composition. I wasn't to be put off with poetry when my pulse was up. So she left me. Ran away like a frightened hare. And now I hear she's going to someone else. He shan't get her though. She's mine, and I mean to have her."

I expressed my sympathy.

"What you have been saying," he went on, "strikes true to me, every word. A woman should belong to her man and feed the appetite she rouses. Shouldn't she? Isn't that only justice? Well, I'll have her. Body and soul I'll have her."

He smote his fist on the table and sat brooding a while. "And another thing," he said presently. "Perhaps you don't know they've a notion here that after a certain age a person ought to have risen above bodily appetites and to wish to turn to higher things. They then retire into monasteries and give themselves to religious contemplation preparatory to leaving the body. Now I don't care a damn about higher things, and I've no desire to rise above my appetites; but into a monastery some fine day I'll have to go: for, though it isn't compulsory, still, everybody does it, and a fellow who didn't would be rather out of countenance, so I think there's a lot to be said for this till-death-do-us-part idea, and I'll help you all I can to put it in force."

On that we shook hands. Ensulas then propounded his plan. The great majority of the Ratheans, he pointed out, were married, and clove to their partners for life. Only let a messenger from the stars put the idea into their heads that the arrangement which they found so comfortable was also of moral obligation, and at once it became imperative upon them to enforce it on the remainder. The plan was magnificent in its simplicity. It stamped Ensulas once and for all as a great man.

Unfortunately I wasn't quite the person to carry it out. I think I've mentioned before that I'm rather a bags when it comes to writing and speechifying. And mind you, the task I had before me was no easy one, so I don't think it any discredit to me to have failed. On the details of my defeat I need not linger. Enough to say that it was complete. Imagine a man on earth undertaking a mission in favour of compulsory vegetarianism. That was my position. I wasn't argued with. I was simply laughed at. The only person who took me seriously was a novelist named Colleb, a devout believer in the food-law, but a most doughty champion of free love. He tackled me very strenuously indeed as an enemy of liberty and all that made life worth living.

But no other literary man seemed to think me worth powder and shot; and the degraded and immoral populace, as I have said, took me as a joke.

The episode, however, marked an important epoch in Rathean history. Ensulas and I were now sworn allies, united in our determination to uplift and civilise that dark and degraded planet. We lay low, awaiting our opportunity, which was not to be long denied us.

CHAPTER XXI

The Unpractical Economic Ideas of the Ratheans

SOMEBODY OR OTHER ONCE wrote in some book or other that all wars and all revolutions have an economic basis. Our revolution in Rathé was no exception. It was among the people who were discontented with the economic system there that Ensulas and I enlisted our first allies. I will therefore try and give you some idea of it, though it must necessarily be rather a sketchy one, as I didn't altogether get the hang of it myself.

I think I have already mentioned that I never saw any signs of class distinction in Rathé. All the people seemed equally healthy and prosperous, and—apart from the mere peculiarities of individual taste—equally well dressed. I had often wondered over this, but found it difficult to make inquiries, owing to some curious lack of economic words in the language. However, an opportunity to acquire information indirectly occurred one day. I had been paying a round of calls with my Lady, and as we left the last house on our list she happened to mention that the gentleman who lived there was a remarkably brilliant plumber. I said "O!" having never known an earthly plumber, however brilliant, to be housed so elegantly. Then, by questioning my Lady, I learned that the other people we had visited were a railway-director, a university professor, and a bricklayer: whereupon I remarked that it was curious that they should all have such similar houses.

"Why?" asked her Ladyship. The Ratheans were like a lot of babies with their whys.

"O, well, because—" I began and floundered hopelessly in the bog of their lingo. "In our world," I managed at last, "a plumber would live in a house of three rooms, and a railway-director in one of thirty."

"Indeed?" said her Ladyship. "Are your railway-directors so prolific?"

"O no," I said. "If it comes to that it's the plumbers that produce the families. But railway-directors are—oh, bother this language of yours—they're—well—more high-up and import-ant sort of people than plumbers."

"Are they?" said her Ladyship, looking puzzled.

"Well, aren't they?" I answered.

"I don't know what you mean," said her Ladyship stupidly. "Surely all people are equally important?"

"I suppose they are here," I said. "But on Earth a railway-director is thought more highly of."

"So is he here," said her Ladyship. "He has a more diffi-cult task, which develops a more highly-evolved brain, than a plumber. But what has that to do with the size of their houses?"

"Well," I said, "we think that a man in a highly specialised job ought to have rather better accommodation than an ordi-nary manual worker."

"I see," said her Ladyship brightly. "So you fix the size of a person's house according to his value to the community?"

"That's about it," I said.

"What unpractical dreamers you must be," smiled her Ladyship. "Idealists, of course, I admit, but how utterly unprac-tical! How can you possibly estimate with any sort of accuracy the comparative values of each and every trade? And after that, how are you to proportion the houses? Why, my dear boy"— with an impatient shrug of the shoulders—"the whole thing is fantastically Utopian and impossible. It could never work out in practice."

"But it does," I said, "in a rough and ready sort of way."

"Rather a rough way, I think," said her Ladyship. "Surely you don't think a sterile railway-director worth ten prolific plumbers? Besides, thirty rooms are too much for anybody, and three are too few. It would be far more sensible and practical for you to strike an average and build all your houses accordingly."

Of course here I should have said that a plumber couldn't afford such a house, but again the Rathean language baulked me. So instead I suggested that a railway-director mightn't be content with such small accommodation.

"Are your plumbers content with theirs?" asked her Ladyship. I said, "No." "Then why are you so tender for the comfort of railway-directors?" she asked. "Is a whole community to be put to inconvenience to oblige a handful?"

I saw it was useless to continue arguing with a mind so deluded; but her Ladyship went on. "You see, this ambition of yours to give each person absolute justice is quite impracticable. It may be perfect in theory, but it doesn't work. Here we take the ordinary, commonsense, workaday view. After all, you can't judge between man and man: but it's safe to say that what's good enough for one is good enough for all, and what isn't is good enough for none. So we content ourselves with a general equality, and muddle along in tolerable comfort."

There we let the subject drop, and amid the discoveries of the next few weeks, which I have already described, I never thought of returning to it. I very quickly found, however, that the reason why I had never seen any money passed in the various taverns and other shops which I visited with the family, was that there was no such thing in the place: not a note nor a coin had they, nor banks, nor nothing. All you had to do when you wanted anything was to walk into the appropriate shop and ask for it. When I heard that, I began to sit up and take notice, feeling for the first time that this was a world worth living in, and for a while I didn't dare rub my eyes for fear of waking up and finding it all a dream. At last, after some hesitation, I decided that, as Ydenneko's clothes were beginning to look a bit shabby, I might as well get myself a new rig-out. So one day I walked rather shyly into a classy tailoring establishment in the Street of Azaleas to get fitted. Such a reception as I got! Two assistants (I beg their pardons: I should say share- holders) came forward with welcoming smiles, turned out hundreds of stuffs for me to choose from, showed me a dozen models of style, and in general gave me as much help and attention as if I was a millionaire and they were to get handsome commissions for securing my custom. Jove, they made me feel so devilish import- ant and benignant that I forgot myself so far as to fish in my wallet for tips. The same procedure took place at a shoemaker's which I visited next, only more so; for this was a one-man shop, and the fellow took himself very seriously, refusing to let me go until he had measured my feet in twenty-three different direc- tions, and forced me to look at nearly a hundred models. After having a free drink at the nearest wine-shop, I proceeded to a watchmaker's and asked for a magnificent gold repeater which I had noticed in the window. But here came a snag. The assistant asked me where my own was, and, without thinking, showed him Ydenneko's silver one.

"Anything wrong with it?" asked the assistant. I said, "No." "Well, then, you don't want another," said the assistant. "Besides, that repeater's too good for a young fellow like you. Come back in another twenty years and we'll see about it."

This experience should have warned me not to be too rapa- cious: but a few doors further on I spied the loveliest little two- seater car, which, with Ytteb in my mind (for our love-affair was then in full swing), I simply couldn't resist. So in I went to lodge my claim. You should have seen the withering smile of the shopman. "Celebrating your thirty-sixth birthday, tomorrow, sonny?" says he. I blushed. "Well, then," says he, "aren't the public buses good enough for you? Be off out of that." I learned subsequently that the legal age for private car-ownership in

Bulnid was thirty-six: and though I felt a bit aggrieved I had to admit that it was a jolly good thing really; for, if there's one thing that sickens me on earth, it's to see some damned young pup, who happens to have a wealthy father, driving off for a joy ride while nice old gentlemen tramp to work in his dust.

I began now to realise that the moneyless system wasn't quite such a give-away affair as I had imagined; but being absorbed, as I have said, in other more interesting discoveries, I made no further inquiries until the subject was brought to my notice again by Mr. Yasint's asking about our system on earth. The fellow was such an intolerable bore that I tried at first to fend him off, telling him that he wouldn't be able to understand the system, as it was based on money. But that only sharpened his curiosity.

"How interesting," says he. "We have often been urged by Utopian dreamers to adopt some such device as a remedy for the defects of our own system. Do you find that it works?"

"Of course it works," I said.

"Indeed," said Yasint. "Tell me then, how do you prevent wealth from accumulating in the hands of a few?"

"We don't," I said.

"Then you must have some people living in luxury, and others with insufficient means to be healthy and happy?"

"Well, naturally," I said. "That can't be helped."

"In that case, then," said Yasint, "your system doesn't work."

"Well, I like that," said I, laughing outright. "Doesn't work, indeed! Say, boy, you ought to travel around a bit and broaden your mind. It's time you had the corners rubbed off you and learnt not to judge everything by the narrow standards of this little star. It really is. Of course, if a fellow has never seen the universe, he can't help being a bit prejudiced in favour of his own world, so I don't blame you. But when I think of the progress we've made on earth in machinery and transport and commerce and the rest of it, and compare it with the backward state of this one-horse planet, and then hear you say our economic system doesn't work, well it just makes me laugh."

"I do not fully understand all that you have said," answered Yasint stupidly, "nor does it seem apposite to the question in hand. No doubt you have better machinery than we have, but we are not discussing machinery. The function of an economic system is not the production of machinery, but the sustenance of mankind. Any system which fails to do that stands condemned as unfit for human use."

"It all depends on your point of view," I said. "If you insist on looking on the dark side of things, you'll never find anything to satisfy you. Our system mayn't be perfect: nobody denies that it inflicts a good deal of hardship here and there: but on the other hand, look at the opportunities it offers to people to make a fortune. Why, I've read of fellows who started life without a bean, and by their industry and enterprise ended as millionaires."

"Millionaires!" said Yasint. "What a stupendous word. A millionaire, I presume, is a person who owns a million men's properties?"

"More or less," I said.

"Your system fails even more egregiously than I had imagined," said Yasint.

"If you call that failure," said I.

"Let us leave that question open for the moment," said Yasint. "I should like to understand your system better before criticising it. Pray give me a full account of it."

Well, Mr. Gallagher, I tried; but of course I know no more of finance or commerce than the man in the moon, so I soon got stuck. Yasint, however, was not to be denied, but kept at me perseveringly with question after question, all barbed, in the nasty Rathean way, so as to draw out answers which either showed me up as an ignorant fool, or represented conditions on earth in the worst possible light. For instance, when we were discussing publicity and advertising, which he couldn't see the value of, I said that they were absolutely necessary to secure a wide distribution for the enormous output of goods turned out by mass production. "Why have mass production, then?" says he. I said it was absolutely necessary to satisfy the enormous demands of our massed population. "But you said just now," says he, "that the demand was artificially created by advertising. Don't you see that you are arguing in a vicious circle?" Silly, wasn't it? What's a vicious circle anyhow?

In the same muddle-headed way he attacked the profession of salesmanship, which, as everybody knows, is the most progressive of all professions, and offers the finest opportunities to a young fellow who wants to get on. It was only with the greatest difficulty that I could get him to understand the object of the profession, which he then forced me to admit, by most unscrupulous reasoning, was simply to artificially increase consumption. And what, he asked, was the good of inducing those who already consumed as much as they wanted, to consume more, when there were other people who did not get enough for their ordinary needs? He was equally stupid when I tried to get him to understand the splendid system of tariffs by which each nation protects itself from being swamped by a flood of cheap goods from its neighbours.

"Is a plentiful supply of cheap goods a disadvantage?" says he.

"Of course it is," I replied. "It throws people out of employment."

"Naturally," said he. "But isn't that an advantage?"

"Far from it," said I (speaking from experience).

"Is leisure a calamity too?"

"What?" cries Yasint.

"It is, if you're poor," said I. "Only in that case you don't call it leisure. Unemployment, my dear sir, is the great problem of our times, and no Government so far has been able to solve it."

"I don't understand you," said Yasint stupidly. "Surely unemployment and poverty cannot exist together?"

"Get along," says I. "How do you make that out?"

"They are mutually exclusive," says he. "If a portion of the community is unemployed, it can only mean that everybody's wants are satisfied. If any portion is in want, it means that there is so much work to be done as will satisfy it."

"That sounds very clever," I said, "and may be quite true in theory; but the fact is that we have thousands of people unemployed, and even more living in poverty."

"I cannot believe it," said Yasint. "If your earth were unfruitful, you would all have to work very hard, and might yet remain poor; or if your earth were exceptionally fertile you might do no work at all and yet be rich. But the other position is impossible."

"It's a fact all the same," I said.

"Very well then," said Yasint. "Let us get the situation clear. You have, I suppose, a number of unemployed shoemakers, lacking bread, coats, houses, and newspapers?"

"You may put it that way," I said.

"Then you have a number of unemployed bakers, lacking coats, houses, newspapers, and shoes?"

"I suppose so."

"And a number of unemployed builders, lacking newspapers, shoes, bread, and coats?"

"Quite right," I said. "And unemployed journalists walking the streets with nothing at all. What of it?"

"Well," said Yasint, "what is to prevent them all supplying one another?"

"They have no money," I said.

"That's no reason," said Yasint. "Money doesn't create goods. It's only a means of exchanging goods already created."

"Still," I said, "you must have money to start an industry."

"On the contrary," said Yasint. "The whole object of industry in your foolish world is to make money. You don't seem to have the remotest idea of the meaning of cause and effect. What do you think is the cause of this unnatural state of affairs?"

"Well," I said, "some people say it's because too many people are getting born."

"Nonsense," said Yasint. "Even from your point of view, the more people who are born the better, because they have to be clothed and fed and housed and therefore, in your foolish phrase, create employment. And in very fact every human being is an asset, because each can produce more than he consumes."

"You may be right," I said. "Other people say that the cause of unemployment is the decrease of prosperity due to the war."

"That's nonsense too," said Yasint. "If you are less prosperous than you were there ought to be more work to do instead of less."

"More to *do*, perhaps," I said. 'But it can't be done until prosperity returns."

"I don't understand you," said Yasint. "You seem to imply that prosperity is the cause of work."

"Well, isn't it?" I said.

"In that case," returned Yasint, "what is the cause of prosperity?"

"O—well—it has lots of causes," I said.

"Yes. But what's the chief cause? the really indispensable cause?—Out with it."

"Work," I had to say.

"Then you have been arguing in a circle again," said Yasint severely. "If work is the cause of prosperity, how can prosperity be the cause of work? You made the same mistake a minute ago when you said that the reason for so many of your people being unemployed was your lack of prosperity. Surely it is obvious that the reason for your lack of prosperity is that these people are not working."

"Maybe so," I said. "But what practical difference does that make?"

"A most important one," said Yasint. "You opened this

discussion by saying that the greatest evil in your world was unemployment, and the most important task for your statesmen was the creation of employment. Well, that isn't true, for the simple reason that unemployment isn't an evil. There is plenty of unemployment in Rathé, for instance. It arises every time an industry produces more goods than the community can consume, and it is regarded as a sign that that industry has worked well and deserves a rest until the balance is restored. So far from its being regarded as a calamity, the hope of earning a spell of it is one of the greatest incentives to production that we have. If it were a calamity, the greatest blessing that could happen to you would be an earthquake. That would create employment enough, wouldn't it? On the same principle, the existence of a large number of idle people with wasteful and luxurious habits would be an asset to a community, since the remainder would have to work harder in order to satisfy them. So it isn't unemployment you are suffering from, and if your statesmen are trying to solve your difficulties by creating employment they are wasting their time. The best way to do that would be to set all your cities on fire and start rebuilding them. Your common sense, you will say, would prevent such a course. Why then does it not tell you that the economic philosophy which could lead to such an absurd conclusion must itself be absurd? There is indeed no end to the absurdities in which it must involve you. Nay, from something you said just now about a superfluity of babies, it would seem that you have already sounded the gamut of folly. For if your economic science is correct, it would be a benefit to society for a diseased millionaire to beget large numbers of idle and diseased children, who by their extravagant wants and silly pleasures, yes, by their very diseases, would give employment to many: and on the other hand, for a pair of healthy young workers to have many children would be a nuisance to society, as there would be difficulty in finding employment for them all. This proposition is perfectly sound earthly economics; but it is contrary to nature, to ethics, and to common sense. Can your economics withstand such foes?"

You see how difficult it was to deal with the fellow?

At last one day, smarting under his sarcasm, I turned on him suddenly and demanded that before criticising our system any further he should give me an account of theirs.

"That is a most reasonable request," he replied, "and I shall try to make my explanation a little clearer than yours. To start with first principles: our system is founded on the necessity of private property."

"So is ours," I retorted.

"But you told me just now that you yourself have no property on earth, and that the majority of your people have none either."

"True. But if I had any, the law would maintain my right to it."

"I am afraid you have misunderstood me," said Yasint. "I said nothing about a *right* of property. Our law is not concerned with rights. Nobody has any rights to anything that society does not give him. When we are born we possess nothing; we owe everything to love; and we could never possess anything that we could not hold by force unless society so arranged. What I said was that our system was based on the *necessity* of private property. We consider that the possession of a certain amount of property by each of its members is a necessity both to the individual and to society. We therefore provide every person, as soon as he comes of age, with the tools of a craft, the instruments of a profession, or a share in an industry; and every young couple with a house and grounds. These properties," he went on to explain, were assigned only for life: on the death of the owner they reverted again to the tribe. There was no such thing as inheritance, except in regard to minor personal objects, though in actual practice, a dead man's property was often handed back once more to his son or

daughter. Nor could property be passed from one individual
to another. Anything that the owner had no use for had to be
surrendered to the tribe.

The Rathean tribe is a collection of from 30,000 to 50,000
people inhabiting a city and the surrounding territory, and
ruled over by an hereditary Chief. It forms an economic unit:
that is to say it carries on trade with other tribes, but the members do not trade with one another. Each citizen works at his
own trade without pay, and takes out what he wants without
payment. The tribe thus resembles a family the members of
which pay in all their wages to the mother, who boards the lot
irrespective of each one's contribution. The surplus produce is
exchanged by the merchants, acting on behalf of the tribe, with
the surplus of other tribes, and the imported goods are shared
out in the same way. Every member of the tribe, high and low,
is equally entitled to take what he wants from the common
stock, within certain limits. A census of the tribe's production
is made every quarter and the individual s share calculated
from it. The figure thus arrived at is called the Noitar, and is
published in the press for the information of shops and customers. An article which is manufactured in insufficient quantity to go round is subject to further limitations according to
circumstances. In the case of motor cars, for instance, there is,
as you have seen, an age limit, varying according to the wealth
of the tribe. In the case of pianos, some proof of musical talent
is required; and so on. Articles of lesser importance are often
balloted for.

"Well," I said when I had heard the lecture out, "of all the
clumsy, stupid, unpractical, and intolerable systems I ever
heard of, this takes the bun. What's to prevent you all sitting
down quietly and helping yourselves to what you like without
doing any work?"

"If we did that," replied Yasint, "there'd be nothing to help
ourselves to."

"Well, what if a few people here and there did it?"

"Public opinion is generally strong enough to prevent such behaviour. If it isn't, the offender is liable to be prosecuted for theft. If that doesn't bring him to his senses, we banish him to Tiger's Island, which is a sort of asylum for persons who do not like our institutions."

"I suppose that gets over the difficulty to a certain extent," I said. "But I bet there's the devil of a rush for the soft jobs."

"I don't quite understand your point of view," said Yasint. "I suppose that under any system the indolent and unambitious will take up the easiest trades. But what of that? Are they not the most suitable persons for them? But all these objections you have been putting simply mark you—and I suppose the whole race you belong to—as of inferior mind and character. No ordinary Rathean wants to shirk his due proportion of work. His common sense and his education have taught him that the common prosperity in which he shares is the product of the labour to which he contributes: so that ethics and self-interest alike urge him to do his best. If they don't, he is simply stamped as an inferior; whom we get rid of in the way I have told you."

I saw that there was nothing to be scored on that point, so I let fly with a real knockout blow. "How do you get anybody to do the dirty and unpleasant tasks?" I demanded triumphantly.

"Quite easily," said Mr. Yasint. "We just conscript as many as are required and work them in chains."

"Oho!" I said sarcastically. "A nice state of civilisation indeed! And after all your cant about freedom, equality, and the rest of it! I knew there'd be a catch somewhere, but I didn't think it would be quite as bad as this. Slavery, begob! well that's a thing which even we benighted earthfolk have grown out of. O my eye! Maybe you'll come off your pedestal now, Mr. Hightalk."

"I take it then," said Yasint, "that you disapprove of this course."

"O not at all," said I. "Don't mention it. I only hope the chains are heavy enough. Why not put spiked collars on them as well, and use the lash to keep them from slacking?"

"We do not find it necessary," said Yasint. "But am I to understand that you regard such compulsory toil as an infringement of liberty?"

"I should just think so," I said.

"How then do you get people to undertake the unpleasant tasks in your world?"

"O, they just have to," I said. "There aren't enough jobs to go round, so people must take what they can get and be thankful for it."

"You mean they would have to starve unless they took this work?"

"Well, that's what it comes to," I admitted.

"Why, you wretched, fog-bound little shallow-pate," cries Yasint suddenly, "is not that a sterner compulsion than any chains? I told you that story just to make a fool of you, and force you to condemn your civilisation out of your own mouth. We compel no man to do unsavoury work."

"How do you get it done then?" I asked, still hoping to stump him.

"In the first place we reduce such work to a minimum by means of machinery. We do not employ machinery, like you, to pile up luxuries for the few, to rush aimlessly from one part of the world to another, to wipe out handicrafts, and plank a million identical flower vases on a million identical tables, while continuing to clean our streets and sewers by hand, and to dig coal out of the earth with pickaxes. We are quite content to travel at twenty miles an hour instead of a hundred, have no desire to slaughter one another in thousands by pressing a button, and prefer to make shoes and pottery by hand instead of by turning a crank; but we ask no man to spend his days under- ground in order that the rest of us may have coal."

"Do you do without coal, then?" I asked.

"Not altogether. Though we are gradually superseding it by water power, we still find it indispensable for some purposes, but instead of burrowing for it like you, we rip the whole surface from above by means of machines, and so work the mine in the light of day."

"But that must be frightfully expensive," I said.

Yasint gave an exclamation of disgust. "What could be more expensive than employing a man for such mole-work as you put him to? Would you use a racehorse to haul a dray, or break stones with a razor? You seem utterly destitute of any sense of values." He stood glowering at me a moment, and then broke out hotter than ever. "I cannot follow the working of your mind at all. First you told me that in your world people will do the heaviest and dirtiest work for the smallest reward. Then you doubted that they would do such work here for a fair one. Now you wonder at us for sparing ourselves such work."

I let all this blather drift by me on the breeze and asked to be shown one of their coalmines, which I thought would be more interesting than his economics. Yasint was quite willing; and in an hour or so we were jogging by railway over the border of the neighbouring tribe of Diffrac. A short run brought us to the edge of the coalfield. This was the nearest thing to an industrial area in our sense that I had yet seen on the planet. Two gigantic buildings like factories could be seen looming up against the skyline, each with the tallest chimney alongside that ever was built. Only one was smoking. Yasint told me that these were the power-houses which had formerly worked the stripping-machines, and which still worked the diggers. We were now running among a number of parallel tracks on some of which were long trains of full and empty coal waggons, and in a few minutes we had stopped in the station. we alighted, passed through a gate, and found ourselves standing on the very lip of the pit. What a sight that was! I saw an immense, enormous crater, goodness knows how many miles across, with sheer black walls, and down in the depths of it, a mile or more beneath us, dozens of huge machines boring and digging for all they were worth. They were shaped something like crabs, with the same sort of jointed legs, the boring instruments taking the place of the front claws. As fast as these dug up the coal the lumps were seized by a flexible steel tentacle and flung with perfect accuracy into a waiting truck, which, as soon as it was full, rushed towards a hoist at the side of the pit, while another took its place. The hoist at once whirled the truck to the top, where it was emptied into a railway waggon by a machine which looked for all the world like a steel monkey come to life. All these contrivances, said Yasint, were worked from a switch-board in an office. There were few men to be seen about the workings, and all they had to do, apparently, was to oil a joint or fiddle with a plug here and there.

"I take back anything I ever said about your machinery," said I handsomely: but magnanimity was thrown away on Yasint. In cocky silence the blighter led the way back to the railway station. he began, as we steamed Donlonwards.

"In the second place—"

"In what second place?" I asked.

"Can you not remember even your own questions for an hour or two?" he snapped. "When you made that idiotic inquiry about unpleasant work, I said that in the first place we eliminated as much as possible in such ways as I have shown you. In the second place, the more people there are in these trades, the less work there is for each, and therefore the more holidays, which is a great attraction to the lowly-evolved. Have you any other objections to make to our economic system?"

"Well," I said, "it doesn't offer any incentive to enterprise or exceptional ability."

"How do you mean?"

"Doesn't everybody, from the Chief to the labourer, get the same share of the tribal income?"

"Certainly."

"Well, that's the point. Why should anybody do his best if

he's going to be no better off than his neighbours at the end of it?"

Yasint looked at me with a queer grin on his face. "Why should one want to be better off than one's neighbours?"

"Good lord!" I cried. "If you can't understand that, there's no use talking to you."

"But you told me," said Yasint, "that your religion commands you to love your neighbour as yourself. How can you do that, and deny him anything you yourself desire?"

"Now, don't drag religion into it," I said. "We're talking economics."

"I see," said Yasint. "Well, will you tell me how you distribute the general income in your world?"

"We pay people according to their value," I said.

"Indeed? But you told me you knew a man who made a fortune by selling quack medicine."

"That was just a fluke," I said.

"You also told me of a person who made a fortune by buying a cargo of wheat and selling it again over the telephone."

"Legitimate speculation," I said.

"You also told me of a person who got a fortune through the death of a cousin in America."

"Lucky chap!" I said.

"You also told me that the men who mine coal get some trifling weekly wage; that those who organise and manage the mine get perhaps twenty to fifty times as much; and that the man who owns the land on top gets more still."

"That's an anomaly," I said.

"You also told me of a man who invented some machine from which the whole world benefited, but who nearly starved until somebody discovered him by chance, and who eventually died poor while others made fortunes out of hisinvention."

"He had no business instinct," I said.

"You also told me that poets are not paid anything at all,

unless, apparently, they write something stupid enough to please a king."

"O well," I said, "who cares about poetry?"

"Clearly you don't," said Yasint. "But even more clearly, you do not pay people according to their value."

"You've been quoting exceptional cases," I said. "Roughly our system works out so that a man gets what he's worth. If he's industrious and means to get on, given ordinary good luck, he'll prosper: if a man fails it's general his own fault."

"What does it matter whether it is his fault or not?" asked Yasint. "You are not commanded to love your virtuous neighbour, or your efficient neighbour, but your neighbour simply. Property and income are not a kind of lollipop, to be awarded as a prize for cleverness and good conduct. They are essentials of human existence, like the brain and the members. To let a man fall into the degradation of poverty because he is idle or inefficient solves nothing, but rather creates fresh problems. You should enrich him for your own credit, and the credit of the race, no matter what his deserts. But what's the use of talking to you?" he broke off. "Every objection you have made to our institutions simply demonstrates the silliness and malignity of the race from which you spring. The only difficulties you have seen in their working are such as would not arise unless we were all as worthless as yourselves. We do not need to be starved or bullied into working; we do not need to be bribed into good behaviour; we do not desire to rise on one another's misfortunes; we do not permit ugliness or dirt or suffering or ignorance to exist in our midst. Yet you, coming out of a world where these things flourish, have dared, with your little nasty mess of a brain, to criticise us in our wisdom. Pff! I blame myself for listening to you so long."

"Well, you're a puling sentimentalist anyway," I said. "How does all this bolstering up of the weak and inefficient agree with your theories of evolution? I think evolution's all my eye myself, but there's more chance for it under our system than under yours. Ours makes for the survival of the fittest."

"Of the fittest what?" retorted Yasint. "The fittest combatants in a selfish struggle for sustenance; in other words, the fittest animal. Do you think life has no greater purpose than to develop an omnivorous belly served by an omnirapient claw?"

"I never suggested any such thing," I said.

"If you didn't mean that," said Yasint, "you didn't mean anything. Now listen and learn. The struggle for existence is over, and man has won. He has established himself as the dominant animal. Hence- forward his evolution must be towards some higher goal: and such an evolution is impossible if the old struggle between the species is continued between man and man, because in that contest the higher qualities are not only of no avail, but are a positive handicap. We recognised that long ago. By transferring the burden of getting subsistence from the individual to the community we set the individual free to develop his higher faculties; to seek wider interests than his own; to follow some nobler ambition than the satisfaction of his personal needs. The scramble of individuals after money, with its individual successes and failures, which constitutes your system, has no vital purpose at all. It is as meaningless as the scramble of individuals after beatitude which constitutes your religion."

Of course it was no use discussing finance with a fellow who talked such a mixture of twaddle and blasphemy as that. I went away thinking furiously. It was obvious that however silly and unpractical the Rathean economic system was, the people were quite prosperous in spite of it, so that if sound business methods were introduced there must be lots of fortunes to be made. If we could sweep away all those footling little handicrafts, what a magnificent market for mass production there would be in a world where everyone was well off! If only I could induce the idiots to adopt a currency! I knew better than to undertake another propaganda campaign, having finally realised that the Ratheans were quite impervious to new ideas. The game would have to be played a lot more subtly this time. I would have to spy around for individuals who were dissatisfied with the existing system. There must be lots of them. Every man who had built up a really successful business must be more or less discontented at getting no more out of it than the bunglers and failures. Everyone with a spark of initiative must be resentful of being held back to accommodate the slowcoaches. If these people could be got together, and adopted a common policy, they should be able to carry any proposition against the general ruck of duds.

I decided to take Ensulas into my confidence at once. He didn't take too kindly to the idea at first, being disheartened by our previous failure to make any impression on the people, and having rather lost faith in me as an ally in consequence. Moreover he didn't believe in trying to change things. The Rathean system, he said, was certainly imperfect, but it worked. What was the use of playing about with theories that would probably turn out to be quite impracticable?

"But, my dear fellow," I said, "this isn't a theory. It's the actual state of affairs in the world I come from."

"O yes, no doubt," says he sceptically. "It's a perfect Utopia, that world of yours. But these beautiful ideals won't make any appeal to our practical Rathean economists."

However, I kept at him, and gradually he began to see daylight. When at last the full beauty of our system dawned on him, and he began to appreciate the glorious opportunities it held for him, he pricked up his ears like a terrier scenting rats. All at once he became a different man. He had discovered his true self. He gripped on to the essentials of finance with marvellous quickness, questioning me, whenever he was in doubt, with a keenness and understanding that were very refreshing after Yasint's cloudy subtleties. He became, in short, an immediate and whole-hearted convert to earthly ideas. He agreed with me also as to the course to be taken; adding the information that I should have a splendid opportunity of meeting the principal industrialists at the coming quarterly meeting of the tribe.

CHAPTER XXII

The Political System of the Ratheans

THE RATHEANS HAVE VIRTUALLY no politics. "Our method of government," Yasint told me, "is a poet's dream made real." It appears that in the days when the world went round (which is their way of saying in prehistoric times) the primitive tribes did actually fall under the spell of an ancient poem, and organised themselves after the fashion described in it. The tribe, with its hereditary chieftain and sense of kinship, remained as the sole political unit. Within it the Assembly of the People was the source of all authority; and the only external power above it was the Supreme World Court, a purely judicial body which decided all disputes between tribes.

The tribe, as I have said, consists of about thirty thousand people, who nearly all dwell in the capital city. There are no small towns or villages, and hardly anybody lives in the country, so that it is quite easy for everyone to attend the meetings of the Assembly. Not that the Assembly has much to do. There are no political parties, and, in our sense, no government. If a person gets a bright idea for a reform, he writes a book or a poem about it, and if sufficient people are interested in it they form a committee to push it. In course of time, if they make sufficient converts, they bring the matter up before the Assembly, and if two-thirds of that body vote for it it's referred to a committee of experts to put into legal shape. Then, if the Chief passes it, it becomes law. However, their constitution is (in their opinion) so perfect, that no such alterations have occurred to anyone for a long time. The Assembly therefore has nothing but routine business to attend to. A funny thing about its procedure is this. They always open their sittings with music and the recitation of poems, in order, as they say, to purify and exalt their minds for what discussion may arise. If there is nothing to be done, as often happens, the meeting resolves itself into a concert.

I said just now that in our sense—by which I meant a political sense—the Ratheans have no government. The work of administration is carried out by a committee of ministers chosen by lot from amongst those citizens who have taken an honours degree in political and economic science at a University. They hold offce for three years, but if a man shows exceptional ability the Chief may retain him for a longer period.

I could tell you more on this subject only it's very dull and boring.

CHAPTER XXIII

He discovers the Subtle Secrets of the Rathean Woman

IT OCCURRED TO ME one day that if ever I got back to earth I would surely be bothered by droves of asses wanting to know about the position of women in Rathé. So I asked Yasint to tell me about it.

"It all depends," said he. "Those that are on their feet are standing up; others, by bending the hams and applying the hindquarters to a chair, are sitting down."

"I don't mean that," I said. "I mean, what is the attitude of the men towards women?"

"That depends also," he said. "If we dislike a woman we avoid her; if we like her we seek her company; if we love her we take her on our knees and kiss her."

"I don't mean that either," I said. "I mean, how are they affected by things in general?"

"Much as men are, of course. The sun warms them, the wind chills them, wine cheers them, dull conversation bores them, they like to be caressed by the opposite sex—"

Well, I dropped the inquiry at that point. But from subsequent investigation I can report that the position of women in Rathé is the same as the position of men. They are not regarded as a special subject, or as being of any special interest. You never hear any bilge there about Woman with a capital letter; or about Woman's Point of View, or Woman's This or Woman's That: still less any drivel about the Rathean girl. Women there are regarded as men's equals, but they are expected to act up to their position and take it in earnest, not grabbing the smooth and dodging the rough as they do on earth. They are expected to behave as decorously as men, and are absolutely forbidden to ply their flirtatious tricks (or procreative stimuli, as they call them there) except in private on their lovers. They have no legal remedy if their fiancés get tired of them (in fact a man's right to change his mind is considered at least as good as a woman's) and they can shuffe none of their responsibilities on to their husbands. They are liable to exactly the same penalties at law as men.

At first sight you would imagine that they had an inferior status. They don't attend the Assembly, for instance; but that is only because their right to do so has never been disputed, and they have found by experience that they aren't much use there. Neither do they enter men's professions, for the same reason. But in their own sphere they are accorded a supremacy like nothing on our earth. Motherhood is recognised not only as the greatest profession for women, but the most important of all professions, and the whole Rathean social and economic code is arranged accordingly. The home is always the property of the woman, not of the man, who, whether husband or lover, is only there on sufferance. A woman who is about to become a mother can command the services of any young girls she may require to attend on her; and no girl can get married until she has served a year of such apprentice- ship. The children are entirely under the mother's jurisdiction, not only when young, but until they come of age, the father having no say in their upbringing unless he is asked for advice.

The Ratheans marry very young, there being no economic obstacles, as I have shown, to hinder them. Their families are of moderate size, not limited to two children like the English and French, nor going to the length of a dozen of whom ten die in infancy, like in holy Ireland, but averaging from five to eight. This they manage without any artificial methods because, in spite of all their immorality, they are rather austere in their habits. They think lovemaking is beautiful only in the young, and beneath the dignity of older men and women, so they generally cease all marital relationship when their families are large enough, and take up other interests. In fact the more high-ly-evolved couples often separate after having had one or two children, and betake themselves to what they call the Higher Life, whatever that may mean.

That's all I can tell you about women in Rathé, except that they have nicer figures than those on earth, better tempers, bet-ter manners, and less conceit.

CHAPTER XXIV

Enter Bhos Kwashog

QUARTER-DAY IN RATHÉ WAS the queerest sort of mixture of business, politics, and festival. The Assembly was to open at ten o'clock in the morning, and for an hour before that time the great square before the palace was a scene of colourful animation as the citizens came pouring in. I noticed that the older men carried campstools, but the others were content to stand throughout the proceedings. When the hour struck, the Chief led the way to a platform which had been erected in front of the main gate, where he advanced to the front to deliver his speech, while the rest of us stood or sat in the background.

The speech was a simple and homely one which any fool could understand: not like those marvellous learned annual statements of the bankers on earth, which I never could read more than ten lines of, and would have been Double Dutch to the poor Ratheans. He told the tribe that the quarter had been, on the whole, a good one. The noitar had been sustained at its accustomed level, and production had exceeded consumption by the usual margin. But there were one or two features of the balance sheet which required comment. The production of shoes had again fallen several points, with the result that in this commodity the noitar for the next quarter would be at the rate of only two pairs per annum. Against this the only commodities which showed an increase were fountain- pens and houses. The increase in fountain-pens, however, was negligible, and that in houses was of no immediate use, as there was more than a sufficiency of these already and the surplus could not be exported.

The Committee of the Chamber of Commerce had therefore decided to recommend a further shortening of hours in the building trade, and to make investigations into the conduct of the shoe industry. One other complaint had to be made. A certain carpet manufacturer, whom it would not be necessary to name as yet, had included in his export consignment a quantity of goods of such inferior quality that they had purchased barely three-quarters of the usual supply of pianos. The age for pianos would therefore have to be raised by two years. This case would also be investigated by the Chamber of Commerce.

The Chamber of Commerce, I must mention, was a body consisting of the heads of all firms which produced a surplus of goods for export. The Committee was composed of a dozen or so of the biggest producers, with representatives of the shipping and transport companies, under the nominal presidency of the Chief. Its job was to organise the marketing of the whole surplus produce of the tribe, which was thrown into a common pool, against the produce of other tribes: and its members got no personal profit out of these transactions at all, beyond the honour and glory and the right to the title of Bhos.

But to return to the meeting. When the Chief had finished speaking, a man in the body of the Assembly went up on to one of the platforms which had been erected here and there about the square, and moved that the Balance Sheet be handed over for examination by a committee of the Assembly chosen by lot from those present, and that the Assembly meet again in three days' time to receive their report. This, which I learned was a routine resolution, was carried unanimously. One of the Chief's secretaries then came out from the Palace carrying a large book, which I recognised as the muster-roll of the tribe. He walked up to the nearest citizen, and handed him an ivory paper knife, with which the latter "cut" the book like in a game. The secretary then read out the first six names on the left-hand page, and thus the committee was constituted. When this childish performance was over the meeting proceeded to the next business. This was the distribution of prizes won at the Annual Industrial Fair, which had been held a few days before my arrival on the planet. You can imagine that I pricked up my ears on hearing the announcement, for it seemed to make an end of old Yasint's high falute about the Ratheans working without any incentive. But I found he was right after all, because the prizes were of no value whatever, being only silver and bronze medals and paper certificates. Gosh, it did make me smile to see those captains of industry trotting up to the platform steps, and strutting back to their places as proud as peacocks of the few penny worth of metal round their necks, never dreaming of the fortunes they were being robbed of by the system they lived under. Suddenly, when the ceremony was half over, a bright idea struck me. Darting into the palace I grabbed a pencil and some paper; and then, standing un- obtrusively in the background, I wrote down the name of every prize-winner as it was called, with a few that I still remembered of the earlier ones. This gave me a list of the most ambitious and efficient men of the tribe, who, I felt sure, would only need a judicious hint to realise how their energy and enterprise were being exploited by their unprogressive neighbours. When the prize-giving was concluded, the Chief once more addressed the Assembly.

"I have now to announce," he said, "that the five years term of office of the capable and energetic Vice-President of the Chamber of Commerce expires tonight. Bhos Kwashog has served the tribe well and faithfully during that period. Largely as a result of his policy the noitar has risen eleven points, and fifteen new tribes have been enrolled among our customers, to the increase not only of our bodily comforts, but of our intellectual and artistic possessions. The consciousness of good work well done is, of course, sufficient reward for any man, but the tribe feels that some lasting token of recognition should be accorded to a citizen whose services have been of exceptional

value. We have therefore decided to present to Bhos Kwashog
the masterpiece of one of the greatest painters of the last generation: Toroc's Dancing Nymphs."

Here another secretary came forward carrying a jolly nice
picture; and at the same time a man advanced from the crowd
and began to mount the steps of the platform. I was struck
at once by something vaguely familiar about this man's face.
It was altogether different in expression from any other I had
seen in Rathé. There was no sloppy philosophy in it; no indifference to realities. It was the face of a man who knew his way
about and meant to get on. At the moment it expressed complete contempt for everything the Chief had said, for the silly
cheering crowds behind, and for the great painter's masterpiece
in front. Its owner, however, put a tactful smile on it, as, with
a few becoming words, he accepted the gift of the tribe. Then,
in a moment, he was gone, and the Assembly was breaking up.

That evening the Chief gave an entertainment to the principal prize-winners, during which I found myself sitting beside
one of them, a man named Sniknej, director of the largest
match-factory in the tribe. Here was my opportunity to sound
the views of a leading industrialist. I got into conversation with
him, and presently, after a few tactful preliminaries ventured on
a leading question.

"Do you find commercial success a very satisfying achievement?" I asked.

"Not at all," he replied. "Once I thought it would be the
summit of my ambitions. Now that I have reached it I find it
profitless: quite profitless."

This was better than I had dared to hope for. "But it needn't
be," I said encouragingly.

Mr. Sniknej shook his head. "O yes, it must," he said. "After
all, the potentialities of any industry are limited."

"No, no," I said. "For a man who knows his business the
limit of what he can get out of it is incalculable."

Sniknej shook his head again. "So I thought when I was your age. But now I know better. There is a limit to the perfectibility of matches, and I have reached it. There is a limit to the practical possibilities of marketing them, and I have reached that. I can now extract no more profit from such exercises than an adult man from a child's dumb-bell."

"It was another sort of profit that I was thinking of—"

I began to explain: but he cut me short.

"So am I. Tomorrow I give up my share in the match-works to younger hands and start work in a scientific laboratory. There, in the unaccustomed exercise of pure research, I shall develop new powers and new faculties."

"It'll be like starting life all over again from the beginning," I objected.

"Yes," said he. "Isn't that splendid? I shall have youth, and hope, and ambition once more. A new life for an old one."

"It doesn't pay to change businesses like that," I said. "Unsteadies you, you know. I can show you how to make a profit out of your old business."

"O nonsense," said the fellow. "Besides I don't want to. There is far greater profit to be gained from Science."

"O no!" I said. "Even in my world there's nothing to be got out of science unless you discover something really wonderful."

"Well," he replied, "if I do not find anything wonderful in myself, I shall at least be reconciled to the Long Sleep."

"Never say die!" I rallied him. "But it wasn't a discovery about yourself I meant—"

"So much the better," says he. "Hush! Miss Camino is going to play."

Well, I wasted no more time putting spurs to that limpet. During Camino's song I looked round the room searching for a more likely-looking recipient of new ideas, and at last pitched upon a prominent coal- merchant named Tonhei. He proved to be an even more perfect dud than Sniknej. He hadn't even the politeness to give me a proper hearing. As soon as I mentioned the word "money" he burst into a laugh.

"The pet idea of all the crazy cranks in the world!" he cried. "It's pure humbug. Couldn't possibly work. The wildest bit of Utopian tomfoolery that ever was invented. Don't try it on me, my lad," and so on.

I wandered away from him and again searched the room, but every face seemed to wear the same sort of dead-head expression, until suddenly my attention was caught by the scornful face of Bhos Kwashog away in a distant corner. As soon as the song was over I started towards him; but to my dismay I got buttonholed by an inquiring old dowager who held me all the rest of the evening by her side while she pumped me circumspectly about our eating customs on earth. By the time I had got rid of her Kwashog had taken his leave: and next morning all Bulnid was ringing with the news of his arrest.

CHAPTER XXV

The Perverted Notions of the Ratheans concerning Justice

THE ARREST OF KWASHOG marks the beginning of a new series of adventures; so before I recount them let me briefly finish off my description of the manners and customs of the Ratheans. I will first deal with their judicial system.

I paid a visit to the Law Courts one day in company with Camino. As you may guess, the procedure there was very different from ours. There are no judges, since the Ratheans hold that no man has a right to judge his fellow. Neither are there juries, barristers, nor solicitors. The Court consists of a sort of committee of experts (varying in number according to the importance of the case) who are called Gogaleths, or, as nearly as I can translate it, Truth-finders. They are men of the most highly-evolved type, who have risen above all human weaknesses, and have undergone a prolonged training, not only in Law and Philosophy, but in Psychology, Medicine, Science, and the art of Detection; so that each of them is judge, jury, counsel, expert witness, criminologist, detective, and court missionary rolled into one. Their business is to hear each side of a case in turn, question all parties and witnesses, and then, after consultation among them- selves, pronounce their decision. Camino said this was a much better system than ours, which I had described to her, because it was designed specially to elicit the truth. With each party paying a barrister to bamboozle a judge and jury, the verdict might well go to the side that hired the cleverest speechifier. That sounded plausible enough: but wait till you hear some of the verdicts of these courts!

When Camino and I entered, the trial of an idler was just coming to an end, and we heard the President's summing up.

"After a most careful reckoning," he was saying "the Court has come to the conclusion that in the past six months you have consumed one hundred and eighty calories more than you have produced. We are glad to notice by the expression of your countenance, that some preliminary recognition of the seriousness of this offence is beginning to dawn upon your mind; and we accordingly recommend you to acquire a full understanding of it by studying a primer of political economy. In such a work you will learn, what should have been obvious to the meanest intelligence, that whatever an idler consumes must have been produced by somebody else; that he is therefore not only useless, but a parasite; not only a sluggard, but a thief; and that, as he adds to the toil and trouble of others, thereby injuring their health and shortening their lives, he is something akin to a murderer. However, as this is your first offence, and as it is quite plain to us that you have erred in ignorance of the implications we have outlined, we shall not on this occasion deprive you of your belt of citizenship. Our sentence is that in the course of the next six weeks you shall produce in your spare time the full measure of calories of which you have defrauded the tribe."

The young man humbly thanked the Court for its Clemency and its good counsel. He realised now, he said, the enormity of his offence and was deeply grateful for the opportunity of atoning for it offered by the Court's decision. Then he bowed and went out with a most chastened air.

The second case was that of a witness in the previous trial, who had already condemned himself out of his own mouth. He was the schoolmaster from whom the idler should have learnt the elementary principles of political economy; and he had admitted that the young man's failure to understand the subject was partially his fault. He was directed to assist his reparation to the extent of fifty calories, and was warned to be more careful in future.

The next case was another idler, and one who already wore the white belt. The trial was brief and purely formal, the records of the Court showing that the belt had been conferred on him exactly a year ago, and that he had made no application for its removal in the interval. The President addressed him in tones of genuine sorrow.

"It is but too evident," he said "that your idleness is incorrigible. For the full twelve months that the law allows. you have been consuming in idleness without remorse or shame. It is therefore my duty to inform you now that whereas the Law of Rathé recognises the right of every man to live his own life; and whereas the tribe of Bulnid will not suffer an idle man to consume the fruits of its labour; and whereas by not consuming a man falls into ill-health and becomes a burden and a source of infection to the tribe: therefore the tribe of Bulnid will neither interfere with your rights nor retain you in its membership, and you shall betake yourself to Tigers' Island forthwith."

The defendant thanked the Court and said that he thought he would be happier there.

The fourth case was a young girl who was accused of riding a bicycle at night without a light. She admitted the fact, but pleaded that she had done it intentionally with the object of running down someone she disliked. The Court took a very serious view of the case, which was adjourned for the purpose of obtaining evidence of motive. I learned subsequently that the girl lost her case, it being proved to the satisfaction of the Court that she was not spiteful by nature; that she had no grudge against the person named; and that that person could not have been on that road at that particular time. Prisoner was accordingly found guilty of gross carelessness, she was forbidden ever to ride a bicycle again, and informed that on a second offence she would be condemned to death.

But this is anticipation.

The last trial we saw that day was of a girl who was accused of attempting to obtain more than the noitar of jewels by practising sexual wiles against a jeweller. There was no defence. In regard to the first part of the charge no sentence was pronounced, as the attempt had failed, but the defendant was warned to practise control of the acquisitive instinct and if necessary to take a course at a College of Moral Training. In regard to the second part, she was sentenced to wear a velvet mask for six months, and warned that further abuse of her procreative functions might necessitate her removal to Tigers' Island.

"What sort of place is this Tigers' Island?" I asked Camino as we left the Court.

She replied that it was a sort of asylum for hopeless cases. People were sent there who made nuisances of themselves by persistently breaking the law, and yet were not dangerous enough to justify their execution.

"A sort of penal settlement," I suggested.

"O no," replied Camino. "There's nothing penal about it. How often shall I have to tell you that we do not punish in Rathé? If people do not like our ways we simply get rid of them, and this island is set aside as a place where they can follow their own inclinations."

"What sort of life do they lead there?" I asked.

"I don't know," said Camino indifferently. "Rather bestial and uncomfortable I should think."

"Where is it?" I asked.

"Some seventy miles away, in the Citnalta Ocean. But why bother about such unpleasant subjects?"

"It would be rather interesting to know how they get on," I said. "Is there anybody who could tell me?"

"Nobody that I know," answered Camino. "But I daresay some criminologist might help you. Now let's talk of something else."

CHAPTER XXVI

*Concerning the Dearth of Policeman in Rathé: with a
note on the traffic directions, their inefficiency, and a
uggestion as to the cause of it.*

THERE ARE NO POLICEMAN in Rathé. Everybody does what seems
right in his own eyes. Why they aren't always killing and robbing
each other I can't imagine.

Of course they have traffic directors in the streets; but as the
traffic is not great, and what there is is quite orderly, they don't
get much practice; so they aren't very efficient.

CHAPTER XXVII

Why, nevertheless, there is very little Crime in Rathé

THE REAL DETERRENT FROM crime in Rathé (where I will admit that it is so rare that the Law Courts are nearly always closed) is the influence of the theatre and the comic press. Don't smile, Mr. Gallagher: I mean it. You can gain some idea of the big part comedy plays in the lives of these people when I tell you that in the town of Bulnid, which though nearly as large as Dublin in area, has less than thirty thousand inhabitants, there are nine theatres. These are quite small, but they are much better designed both for comfort and for seeing and hearing than any theatres in our world; and the roofs, and portion of the walls, are moveable, so that daylight performances, which are more usual than night ones, are held practically in the open air. Each theatre is owned by a company consisting generally of three or four playwrights, a few scene painters, and a troupe of actors.

The license accorded to these theatres is something awful. That old philosopher chap who gave me the kick off into this funny world said when I told him of it that it reminded him of the days of aristophonies—whoever *they* were. There is no law of libel in Rathé. You can say or write anything you like about anybody—so long as it's true (if you tell a lie you are liable to prosecution as well as an action for damages by the victim)— and the dramatists there make full use of their opportunities. There's never a wrong done, high or low, but they'll expose it; never a bit of humbug or hypocrisy but they'll tear it to tatters; never a mean action but they'll make the perpetrator wish he had never been born. For fear of that searching ray of ridicule, clever people try to be humble, and stupid people try to be sensible; public men try to mean what they say, and journalists try to say what they mean; professors and teachers dogmatise as little as possible; and their pupils try to learn something; writers take care to have something to say, and athletes and actresses keep their opinions to themselves; fathers learn to curb their tempers and sons their impatience; and even women dare not show that they think themselves the most important subject in the world. In fact, Mr. Gallagher, you may take it from me,as from one not unduly prejudiced in favour of Rathean customs, that a good comedy stage (with which I would couple a good comic press) is a jolly powerful preservative of order and decency.

All the same, as I remarked to Camino, there are some types of criminal on whom it would have little effect. Take for instance the sort of man who makes a living by marrying one woman after another and murdering them. Camino gave me a look of horror. "There is no such profession in Rathé," said she. "What a dreadful world yours must be."

CHAPTER XXVIII

Tigers' Island

CAMINO'S RETICENCE ON THE subject of Tigers' Island only increased my curiosity about it; but I was saved the necessity of bothering a criminologist by Ianda, who was by no means so squeamish as her sister. She told me that the condition of the islanders was horribly barbarous. "They live," she said, "in a state of disorder, dirt, disease, and misery impossible to conceive. Remember that for thousands of years we have been dumping there the refuse of our civilisation: the selfish, the avaricious, the quarrelsome, the spiteful, and the lazy; and that they have bred and multiplied and degenerated from generation to generation."

"So after all your fine talk," I said, "you punish the children for the faults of their parents."

"We punish nobody," said Ianda stiffly. "The misery of the islanders is of their own making. As for those who are born there, they are at liberty to leave at any time, and any who do are taken, on probation, into the tribe to which their family originally belonged. But very few avail themselves of this freedom, for it is rare for any of them to escape the degenerative process. The enormous majority of them, in fact, are quite contented with their state, and, I am told, actually prefer the appalling conditions to which they are accustomed to the civilisation which we enjoy here."

I said it would be amusing to pay these savages a visit; whereupon Ianda offered to run me over there in her yacht. I didn't quite relish the prospect of a long spell of Ianda's company, but,

as I had never been on a yacht in my life before, I jumped at
the opportunity. Accordingly, one fine day we went down to
the harbour together, and rowed out to one of a score of very
handsome boats which lay at anchor in the section reserved
for pleasure craft. It was about thirty feet long, and had two
masts, one a great deal smaller than the other—what is called
ketch rig, as Ianda informed me. There were two little triangular
sails before the front mast, and a great big one at the back of
it, with a middle-sized one on the mast behind. "Best rig for
single-handed cruising," Ianda said as she hoisted them. "I've
sailed half round the world in this little lass." Then she chucked
off the anchor chain, did a twiddle at the steering gear, and we
were off.

There was a pretty stiff breeze blowing, and the sea was a
nasty hard-looking green. The yacht bent over until the deck
was awash, and as we cleared the harbour the crested waves
came hurrying to meet us, crunching against our sides, lashing us with spray, and setting the boat bounding like a young
horse. It was a thrilling experience, and I couldn't help thinking
it strange that with the sea almost at my doors in Dublin I had
had to come billions of miles to taste it. But I wasn't left long
to my thoughts. Ianda, looking like a sea goddess in her wind
blown tunic, ordered me about like a colour sergeant. She kept
me moving, I can tell you, hauling in here, letting out there,
and in general doing all the work of the ship, while she took
her ease at the helm. As the day advanced, however, navigation
became less difficult. Towards midday the sun shone out at its
warmest, the breeze slackened, and the sea became blue and
almost playful. It was then that I caught my first glimpse of
Tigers' Island, as a long low bluish bank showing dimly on the
horizon. For a couple of hours I watched it growing steadily
nearer and clearer, but by the middle of the afternoon the breeze
had so fallen away that we were merely creeping along on an
even keel.

"No hope of reaching it before nightfall now," declared Ianda. "May as well heave to." She brought the boat to a standstill by some arrangement of the sails and steering gear. Then, diving below, she fetched up a bottle of wine and a pair of glasses. Over these, for lack of a better subject, we began to discuss what we should find on Tigers' Island whenever we got there.

"Are they really utter savages?" I asked. "Do they paint their faces and go on the warpath?"

"They do," said Ianda.

"Do they slaughter women and children?"

"Yes. But only when a very powerful tribe attacks a very weak one which can't retaliate."

"Do they burn and torture their prisoners?"

"Yes."

"Do they worship idols?"

"They do worse. They believe in charms, omens, mascots, fortune-tellers, and other superstitious fooleries. They submit to the most horrible mutilations at the hands of medicine-men, in the hope of warding off diseases. And they are the helpless dupes of anyone who pretends to have magical powers."

"Are they very simple-minded?" I asked.

"Very. They believe any lie that is told them with a solemn countenance."

"I suppose they're very licentious," I said.

"Disgustingly so. The most important part of life in their eyes is sexual gratification."

"Are they hostile to strangers?" I asked. "Shall we be in any danger?"

"O, you needn't think *I'm* going to land there," said Ianda. "No civilised person could endure the place. But of course that doesn't apply to you."

The prospect of going alone amongst the savages rather alarmed me; so, ignoring her insult, I repeated my question.

"One is always in danger," said Ianda contemptuously.

"Would they kill me, I mean?"

"They might. They are always slaughtering one another on the most trifling provocation. But as the moment they are recovering from a more than usually sanguinary period, and so may be in a peaceful mood. In any case you will be in far greater danger of catching one of their loathsome diseases than of being murdered."

"I'll risk it," I said, thinking, in a forgetful moment, to impress her.

"That is very stupid of you," she said indifferently. "However, suit yourself."

By nightfall there was almost a flat calm. Beginning to feel sleepy, I stole a look at Ianda to see if she realised the impropriety of our position. But she was quite unembarrassed. "You can go below," she said. "I prefer to sleep in the open air." I found a comfortable place on a heap of sail bags, and with my head on a life belt, lulled by the lap-lap of the water on the planking, I fell into the deepest sleep of my life.

When I awoke a sunbeam was shining down the cockpit, and the yacht seemed to be moving. Hurrying up on deck, I found that we were no longer at sea. We were gliding slowly up a broad river that ran through the heart of a splendid city.

"Sleepy-head!" cried Ianda from the helm. "We have been sailing since dawn."

"Why didn't you wake me?" I demanded.

"I thought you would need all the sleep you could get to strengthen you for the horrors to come."

"But surely this isn't Tigers' Island?" I said.

"Most certainly," she replied. "but you must not let the inhabitants hear you call it that. We gave it that name because the instincts of the ape and tiger are stronger in these people than the human. But the natives call it some high-sounding name which I have forgotten, and believe themselves highly civilised."

Here Ianda brought the yacht close up against a flight of
steps leading down from one of the quays. "Skip along now," she
said. "I'll anchor near here and expect you back this evening."

Reluctantly, but feeling that there was no help for it, I set
foot on the dripping lowest step of the flight. "One moment,"
said Ianda. "I'd forgotten. If you get into any trouble and the
savages look dangerous, use this on them." She thrust a small
but heavy leathern bag into my hand as she spoke, then added
a cheery "good luck," and, letting the wind into her sails again,
stood off towards the centre of the river, leaving me to face the
unknown world before me as best I might.

Dropping Ianda's weapon into my sporran, I climbed the
slippery steps, and, hearing voices and the sounds of many feet
close by, crept softly towards an opening in the quay wall, and
warily peeped out. Mr. Gallagher, what do you think I saw?
Redskins and cannibals, tomahawks and knobkerry clubs? No
sir. Before my eyes—you'll never believe it, and I don't blame
you, because for nearly five minutes I stood like a stuck pig
unable to believe It myself—before my eyes, as I was saying,
was a teeming street such as you might see in any city on earth.
There were buses and trams and lorries and taxis and delivery
vans all rushing along in the homeliest manner. There were
bustling people on the sidewalk dressed in proper breeches
and skirts like ourselves. There were ten-storeyed houses, and
smoking chimneys, and advertisement hoardings, and yelling
newsboys, and policemen, and loud speakers and skysigns, and
a millionaire in his car, and a group of unemployed at the corner, and all the other signs of a progressive community. For a
moment I thought that I had awakened from some enormous
nightmare and that maybe I had walked in my sleep into some
street on the South Side that I didn't know. But almost immediately I saw that I was wrong, for these people had the beastly
eyes of Ratheans. Anyway there was nothing to be frightened
of now, so I stood up on the landing and had a good look at

everything. It was all so absolutely earthly that I felt quite at home, and before I knew where I was I was winking at a nice little colleen that went tripping by. Pretty she was, with eyes no bigger than cricket balls, and distinct traces of hair on the back of her head. This was interesting. I looked at the other passers-by, and saw that on the whole their eyes were smaller than those of the people on the mainland, while quite a number of them approximated to the earthly type. What rot Ianda had been talking! These people weren't savages. They were almost as civilised as we are.

Suddenly I became conscious that I was being stared at. People were slackening their steps, even standing still, to look at me. Some boy uttered a rude remark. I realised at once what was the matter. My costume to these people was as conspicuous and strange as it would have been to a crowd on earth, and here I was posing for them on an eminence like a bally street acrobat. It was even worse than that. With a frightful shock I realised that I was almost naked. Blushing from my waist up, I tore the brooch out of my cloak, and amid a howl of derisive laughter, wrapped its ample folds around my body. Then, feeling my position still a little too prominent, I stepped down on to the pathway. At once a respectful silence fell on the onlookers, and for a most excellent reason. I stood a full head and shoulders taller than the biggest man present. They were all the puniest midgets beside me. I had never appreciated before the magnificent physique which Ydenneko had handed over to me. Now I thrilled with delight at the sensation of power and majesty it gave me. I took a step towards the sniggering little wretches, who in an instant were all scuttling about their businesses.

Plucking up courage I now started to walk down the I had not gone fifty yards when I saw a ragged street man leaning against the quay wall. He had a wooden leg and a shade over one eye, with a placard hung on his breast announcing that he was a wounded soldier. In a plaintive voice he asked me to buy a box of matches. A little further on I saw a white-faced woman in clean but threadbare clothes selling bootlaces on the kerb. She had a label also: "Widow. Three Children."

A little further on I saw a consumptive poor devil playing a fiddle of his own construction.

A little further on, as I was crossing the street, I was nearly run over by a thousand-guinea motor car full of sable-coated rich folk. It was the narrowest shave you ever saw, but my own fault entirely, being moonstruck by the sight of that poor widow's white face and the fiddler's eyes. Quite morbid they'd made me. "Come now," says I to myself. "Pull yourself together. You're in a civilised country now, and you can't have progress without waste products. If they were any good they wouldn't be what they are. Get on or get under's the motto—By Jingo!"

Here I had come out into the full blaze of the most wonder-ful thoroughfare that ever was. O'Connell Street's a back lane compared with it. Such shops! Such traffic! Such women! There was no being morbid in that atmosphere. I strolled along as happy as a skylark, positively revelling in the looks of wonder and admiration that were thrown at me.

Presently, among the flashing shop-signs ahead of me I saw dancing aloft the welcomest of all words to the traveller: Restaurant. Little white tables under an awning gleamed invit-ingly in the sun. A waiter, bowing obsequiously, tendered a chair. I dropped into it without thinking, and ordered a meal.

Shall I tell you about that meal? It was such a meal as I suppose you get in a classy restaurant on earth, and after several weeks of fruit juice you may bet I walked into it. There were a lot of sardiney-tomatoey things to start with. Then soup, lovely clear brown stuff with a winey taste to it. Then a bit of fish that melted in your mouth, with a sort of yellowish sauce that made your tongue ready for a couple of stone of it. Then a wing of chicken tenderer than a baby's cheek. Then some asparagus. Boys-o-boys, to think that greens could taste like that! Then a creamy-fruity I-don't-know-what, sweeter than a kiss scented with lily of the valley. Lastly a cup of coffee and a cigar to make you dream. If ever I was happy in all my life it was when I blew the fifth long puff of it to the breeze and sank back into my chair for a real good laze. For a moment I believe I closed my eyes.

When I opened them again they nearly started out of my head with sudden horror. On a plate in front of me lay something white and flat, whose menacing appearance held my gaze with fascinated dread, while a cold sickly despair came over me. What do you think it was, Mr. Gallagher? It was the bill. In my long stay in that backward world I had forgotten that such things existed, and of course I had nothing to pay it with. What the deuce was to be done? I gave a cautious glance around, wondering should I risk a bunk. The coast seemed to be clear, so, rapidly making up my mind, I rose noiselessly to my feet and did a side-step towards the exit. It was no go. Where he sprang from I've no idea, but before I was well clear of my table, there was the waiter kowtowing at my elbow.

Bluff was the only game left. I reached over languidly for the bill, and, after a glance into my sporran, said: "I'm afraid I must ask you to take my cheque. I've no small change about me."

"We do not take checks, sir," said the waiter respectfully, but, O, ever so grimly."

"By Jove," I said. "That's deuced awkward. Now what do you think I ought to do?"

"I'm sure I don't know, sir," said the waiter indifferently.

"Suppose I slip off home and send my man along at once with the cash? How would that do?"

"Wouldn't work at all, sir, I'm afraid," said the fellow with the most intense conviction.

"It looks as if you didn't quite trust me," I said.

"O not at all, sir, not at all." The protest was politeness itself, but nothing more helpful followed. I was at my wits' ends what to do. Hope seemed to be vanishing like water down a sink, and not a sign of a plug to stop it, when suddenly, at the very last swirl, so to speak, I remembered Ianda's last words and the mysterious weapon she had given me. It might be a hand-grenade. It might be a smoke signal. Either way it should provoke a diversion.

"Let's see. I might have some change that I overlooked," I said, diving a hand into my sporran. I fetched up the little leather bag and tore it open. It was full of golden coins.

I flatter myself that I showed no signs of shock, though it was all I could do to prevent my hands and voice from trembling. "How easy it is to forget such a trifle," I said gaily, flicking a few of the coins on to the plate. "Thanks, boy. You may keep the change."

It was a glorious exit.

I spent the next couple of hours exploring the town, but I shan't bore you with any more descriptions. When I was tired I returned to the quays and signalled Ianda to come and take me off. In a few minutes we were scuddling downstream before a freshening breeze. For obvious reasons I was disinclined to tell Ianda about my adventures, nor did she ask me to do so. But presently it occurred to me that I should return her the bag of money.

"Did it save you any trouble?" she inquired as a placed it in her hand.

I said yes, but volunteered no further information.

"You can do anything with savages by throwing them baksheesh," said Ianda, as with a careless gesture she tossed the gold overboard.

CHAPTER XXIX

The Abominable Religion of the Ratheans

As to their religion, the Ratheans are, I regret to say, Devil Worshippers. They believe in one Devil, whom they call Darkness who alone exists of himself, who is infinite and eternal, and who will put an end to all things; for which reason he is also called the Destroyer. He is the enemy of Life, and particularly hates mankind, whom he would willingly annihilate, but spares on account of the evil they do. The Ratheans believe that it is the highest duty of man to honour and worship this Devil, to propitiate him with evil deeds, to make life as short and barren as possible by hatred and distrust of one another, and to subdue the cravings of the spirit by the pursuit of material ends. In return for this service he has promised that after death he will blot them painlessly out of existence, whilst those who offend him will be condemned to everlasting life. This they regard as the most dreadful of calamities, for they have no conception of an after-life of eternal bliss, but imagine that life in the spirit must necessarily be more intense than life in the flesh, and must therefore involve more intensity of learning, being, and suffering as well as of happiness.

Now Darkness has an enemy whom they call Light, or God (the two words are again the same) whom he created as a kind of foil to himself, so that he might become more conscious of himself, as it were, by the existence of his opposite. Light's purpose is to snare men from the service of Darkness, tempting them to develop their souls, to live more abundantly, and to fill the great emptiness of space with life. There is thus an eternal warfare between these two, in which, as the Ratheans represent it, the odds seem to be all on Darkness. He is infinite: Light is finite. He exists of himself, without effort; Light exists only by perpetual exertion. He wants nothing; Light wants to live, to see, to grow, to understand. Light may perish; can only continue at the price of travail and suffering; and has no certitude that continuance is worth the struggle. Darkness will be for ever in any case.

Did you ever hear such a blasphemous abomination labelled as a religion before? The moment I under- stood it, I got up on my hind legs and told them so, straight. Well, you should have seen how surprised they were. The blighters had no idea that their obfuscated notions weren't the religion of the whole universe. They absolutely refused to listen to me, and said that my conversion to the faith must be taken in hand at once, for which purpose they appointed one of their most learned theologians—diabologians I should rather say—to be my instructor. This gentleman presented me with a beautifully bound copy of their Great Book, as it is called, which is a sort of history and textbook of the faith. I can't pretend to have read it very thoroughly, but I skimmed through enough of it to give you a fair idea of the sense of it. It's written in a sort of sing-song that sticks well in my memory; so here goes.

THE GREAT BOOK OF THE RATHEANS

In the beginning was Darkness; and Darkness was everywhere; and all was Darkness.

And a Light shone in the Darkness; and Darkness said: Let be.

And Light made matter out of his own forces; and of the matter he made stars and moons. And Darkness was not well pleased.

Then Light made Rathé; and he set Rathé in the middle of the universe and caused the stars and the moons to encircle it, giving it light and heat. And Rathé was beautiful to look upon;

Having mountains and valleys, seas and lakes and rivers, and being clothed with flowers and verdure.

And Darkness was angered by the beauty of Rathé; and he smote Rathé with his might, leaving it ugly and awry as it is to this day.

But Light went on making; and he made animals and Man. And Man fell upon his knees and worshipped Light, and served him.

And Darkness said: ye shall not worship Light, nor serve him. I am your master, the Devil, who will destroy Light and all things. Therefore worship me.

So Man turned away from Light and worshipped Darkness. But Darkness hated him.

And seeing that man grew and increased by loving, Darkness was exceedingly angered, and laid further commands upon him, namely:

To worship Darkness and turn altogether from Light; and to set up Ideals and Institutions and render them service.

To misuse the language Light had given him, and to curse and to lie;

To consecrate certain days to Darkness, and to do no work nor play thereon;

To train their children to the service of Darkness;

To kill the trees and the flowers and the animals and one another for a sacrifice to Darkness;

To mate without love and to deny themselves offspring;

To make money and accumulate it;

To speak ill of one another;

To seek pleasure above all things, both in the body and in the soul.

And Darkness made a covenant with man that to
all who obeyed his commands he would give peace and
death; and to those who would not he gave the torment
and the trouble of living.

Men therefore built temples and churches and tab-
ernacles to the worship of Darkness; and they prayed
on their knees to Darkness, and his name was ever
on their lips. But they obeyed not the commands of
Darkness, but increased and multiplied and loved one
another, and recreated the beauty of Rathé.

Now after many generations Darkness saw that Man
walked not in his ways in anything, but was altogether
turned to the service of Light. And he resolved to go
himself among men and teach them the way of Darkness.

And the spirit of Darkness descended upon one
Procrustes; and Procrustes went forth preaching the
word of Darkness by precept and example.

He was proud and overbearing, and very cruel, and
a liar, and he would not suffer children in his presence.
But the people knew him not for a son of Darkness,
and would not hearken to his words. Then Procrustes
took a fine handsome buxom wench and a strong
lusty youth, her lover; and he mated them, and spoke
certain words over them. And the girl conceived not.
And by that miracle the people knew that the spirit of
Darkness was in Procrustes, and they hearkened to his
words. And gathering the people round him Procrustes
spoke as follows:

"Blessed are the proud, and the fierce, and the hard
of heart. Blessed are the unjust, and the merciless.
Blessed are the voluptuous and the quarrelsome and
the unforgiving.

"You were commanded of old to kill the trees and the animals and one another: but I tell you to mow down the forests and extirpate the animals and slaughter one another in thousands.

"You were commanded of old to mate without love: but I tell you not to mate at all; or if you must mate, render your seed barren;

"For mating is an obscenity invented by God, and children are an abomination in the eye of Darkness.

"You were commanded of old to curse and to lie to one another; but I tell you never to speak but with an oath, and to lie to yourselves.

"You were commanded of old to take an eye for an eye, and a tooth for a tooth, and a life for a life: but I tell you to take two eyes for an eye, and ten lives for a life.

"Give nothing except there be a subscription list published; and lend only at good interest.

"Blow thy trumpet in every street, and have thy name upon the hoardings.

"Lay yourselves up treasures in banks, and be merciless to robbers. Serve Mammon faithfully, and thereby you serve Darkness.

"Take much thought for the morrow that your capital may be increased. Insufficient for the day is the income thereof.

"Judge all sinners and punish them severely.

"And if there be a beam in thine eye, hasten to cast the mote out of thy brother's eye; that thy beam may not be observed.

"You were commanded of old to make money and accumulate it: but I tell you to value all things in money, and to strive always after money, and to do nothing except for money, and to accumulate as much money as you can;

"And compete with thy neighbour that thy profits may be greater than his.

"This is the fulness of wisdom, to adapt thyself to thy environment: the soul to the body, the body to the raiment, and the raiment to economic laws.

"Fret not against facts, and accommodate thyself to circumstance. As thy bed has been made, so must thou lie: inexorable are the laws of political economy.

"Therefore, if thy body be straitened, straiten thy soul also,

"That thou mayest rest secure in eternal darkness."

This, if you'll believe me, is the stuff that passes for religion with these benighted people. Not that there isn't a good deal of commonsense scattered through it, like, for instance, the advice to make money and save it, and that about the stimulus of competition. But commonsense isn't religion, and the rest of his talk is sheer wickedness. The book records that Procrustes went about everywhere preaching this villainy to tremendous crowds, and working the most abominable miracles. He rewarded people who believed in him by ridding them of their children, or making them sterile; and he punished doubters by giving them diseases. He brought out a crop of sores on the face of one man who railed at him, and then, when the fellow repented, cured him by rubbing the sores with pus from a cow which he had previously smitten for daring to low in his presence.

Procrustes used to preach a good deal in the form of parables; and of these I will give one sample.

THE PARABLE OF THE LABOURERS

"A certain man went out early in the morning to hire labourers for his factory: and having agreed with some for a noitar a day he sent them into his factory.

"And going out about midday he saw others standing about the market place, and sent them also into his factory, saying that he would give them what should be just.

"But towards the end of the day he found others still unemployed, and hired them in like manner.

"And in the evening he called the labourers together to pay them their hire: and to those that had come in first he gave each man one noitar.

"But when those that had been hired at midday came he gave them only half a noitar; and to those who had worked for the last hour he gave one-fifth of a noitar.

"And receiving it they murmured, saying that their needs were as great as the needs of the others.

"But the master said: You are worth less to me.

"And they replied: We cannot live on less than a noitar.

"But the master said: That has nothing to do with me: neither would it be fair to those others to reward you equally with them for less work. I am a just man and a practical: therefore must the first be first, and the middle midmost and the last last; and so it ever shall be."

Compared with all the wicked nonsense Procrustes usually talked this parable seems to me to be very sound sense; and I marvel that, with such clear instructions set down for them in black and white in their Great Book, the Ratheans still cling to their absurd economic system. But to return to Procrustes' own story. After he had preached up and down the country for several years, the authorities were at last frightened into taking action against him. He was arrested accordingly and put on trial. In his defence however he made so masterly a statement of his doctrines that everybody—judges, accusers, witnesses, and all—became converted on the spot. He left the Court apparently master of the world. A triumphal procession escorted him to his house. He delivered a final oration from the balcony to a throng numbering hundreds of thousands. Then he went indoors, and was never seen again. The legend was that he was spirited away to his infernal progenitor, but my own belief is that someone in authority, acting on the sound notion that if the people could be got to worship his person they could be trusted to forget his teachings, quietly did him in in the watches of the night. Anyway, there his story ends. From that day the Ratheans called themselves Procrusteans, and their faith Procrusteanity.

Over this monstrous conglomeration of absurdities I fell fast asleep. Next day I received an early visit from the Diabologian, who, greeting me with a joyous face, asked if I was ready to be instructed in the faith. Not wishing to hurt the poor beggar—for his smile was rather touching, and made me quite forget that he was a Devil worshipper—I said I was afraid I was still a bit of an unbeliever.

"What is your difficulty, my son?" he asked, evidently quite confident that, whatever it was, he could sweep it away with infallible ease.

"There's no particular difficulty at all," I said. "It's the whole blessed creed that beats me."

"The whole *damned* creed," he corrected me gravely. "Do you mean to say, my son, that you are an adiabolist?"

"I suppose I must be," I said.

"O come, come!" the Diabologian remonstrated. "Is it possible that you can survey this universe with a seeing eye and not observe in its every aspect the trace of a destroying mind? Consider the recurrent phenomenon of death—the dreadful fact that no life can survive without destroying other lives. Consider the ever present occurrence of pain and sorrow. Consider man himself—the finest living creature that we are aware of—how weak he is in mind and body, how ill-designed, how short-lived. Have you not on every hand testimony to the feeble efforts of a limited creative force eternally thwarted by a malevolent destroying power?"

"That sounds very plausible," I replied. "But don't you think that a really omnipotent devil, who really hated us intensely, could torment us a good deal more severely than your Devil does? After all, we knock out a fairly comfortable time here on the whole."

"Ah," said the Diabologian, "the inscrutable ways of Darkness are not for our feeble minds to fathom."

"That," I said indignantly, "is mere dodgery. You say that all the evidence points to an omnipotent Devil, and as soon as I give you a piece that points the other way you take refuge in evasion. Well, here's another nut for you to dodge. You say Darkness commands us to take ten lives for a life. Why then does he let off his own enemies so mildly as you pretend he does?"

The Diabologian seemed to take thought for a moment or two. Then, throwing off his paternal air, he assumed one of brisk intellectual efficiency.

Let us waste no more time fencing over minor aspects of the question," he said. "We must get right down to bedrock. You will perhaps admit to start with that everything must be destroyed?"

"Not at all," I said; which was an answer he obviously hadn't expected.

"O come!" he said.

"Surely things can't go on existing for ever?"

"I don't see why not," I said.

The Diabologian looked as if he'd like to bludgeon me, but he constrained himself with an effort.

"Is it not your experience," he said, "that things all tend to get worn out or to be broken?"

I agreed to that.

"Nothing is indestructible in fact."

I agreed again.

"Then the world and the rest of the universe are also indestructible."

"Quite right."

"They must therefore be destroyed by somebody."

"O no," I said. "They might be destroyed by our natural forces, or they might just wear out."

"Fortuitous dispersal of atoms?" said the Diabologian with a sneer of pious superiority.

"I don't know what that means," I said. "What I said was plain enough."

"I had better fall back on a homely and rather hackneyed illustration," said the Diabologian with a pitying smile. "Suppose that a savage, wandering in the wilderness, were suddenly to come upon a broken watch, what conclusion do you think he would come to?"

"That it couldn't tell him the time," I said.

"Do not be flippant," said the Diabologian. "He would surely come to the conclusion that *someone had broken it.* Wouldn't he?"

"Very likely," I said.

"Very well," said the Diabologian. "Now the universe is an infinitely more complicated thing than the most ingenious watch ever invented. Therefore it can only be destroyed by an omnipotent devil."

"That sounds very clever," I said, "and leaves me without a leg to stand on, so far as argument goes. But all the same, I know it's wrong."

"That," said the Diabologian, "shows that reason alone is not enough to guide us in these matters. One cannot believe without the will to believe, and the will to believe can only be obtained by prayer. I will therefore leave you for the present,

earnestly counselling you to *pray hard* to the Evil One to grant
you that gift. Remember that, my son. Pray hard, and I too will
pray for you. Good-bye." So saying he pressed my hand and departed. We had many diabological wrangles thereafter, which I
won't bore you with. But needless to say he couldn't convert me.

CHAPTER XXX

The Religion of the Ratheans (continued); with
the Sermon of the Priest of Beelzebub

THE RATHEANS FIRMLY AND profoundly believe in their religion;
but they do not practise it. They dislike the Devil intensely, but
they are tremendously afraid of him, and always speak of him
in terms of love and reverence, though how they imagine this
will benefit them I don't know, since they believe that he is everywhere and knows their most secret thoughts. They attend at
some hideous mummery once a week in their tomb-like churches, and perform occasional little deeds of meanness or cruelty
in a perfunctory way that shows that their hearts aren't really in
them; but otherwise every act of their individual and collective
lives is a direct violation of the precepts of Procrustes, while
anyone who really tries to follow them is consigned sooner or
later to Tigers' Island. In fact, judged by their own standards, the
Ratheans are a lot of thoroughgoing hypocrites.

I'll just give you one example to prove it. When a dispute
of any kind arises between two tribes it is always referred to the
World Court for judgment. While the case is in progress services
are held daily in all churches of both tribes, at which priests and
people pray earnestly, not that they may gain the verdict, but
that justice may prevail; and when everything is over they hold
thanksgiving services, at which they thank the Devil for having
prevented strife between them. As for the priests, well, to see
them skipping along in the gaudiest of clothes at the head of a
birth procession, you'd certainly never take them for ministers
of Death and Darkness.

The Ratheans seem to be quite unconscious of this inconsistency between their principles and their conduct. When I
remarked on it to my instructor, the Diabologian, he looked
extremely shocked, and said I was quite wrong: Procrusteanity
was the basis of the entire legal, political, social, and domestic
system of the world, and the guide and inspiration of the private lives of the people. I received exactly the same reply from
everybody else to whom I spoke on the subject. One old priest
however admitted that there was some justice in what I said,
and attempted a weak sort of apology, saying that many of
Procrustes' teachings were counsels of perfection; and for the
rest, that man was naturally weak and liable to be led astray by
the promptings of God. At last one day I made the acquaintance
of a genial middle-aged man named Yccni who frankly declared
that I was right; that very few Ratheans made any real attempt
to practise Procrusteanity; that this was perhaps regrettable; but
that, men being what they were, it was inevitable.

"Of course," he said, "we all know that Procrustes was the
Devil incarnate, and as such we worship him and honour his
words as being those of Darkness himself. But ask yourself candidly if those words are applicable to practical everyday life. Do
you really think his precepts would work? Take that one, for
instance, about making money and each man devoting his life
to getting as much of it as possible. Very noble and inspiring as
an ideal, of course, and the sort Of thing a medieval saint might
have attempted. But as an everyday working proposition—why,
it's impracticable. Once coin money and it will soon cease to
be a token and acquire a fictitious value. And if everybody tries
to get as much of it as he can, well, since men are not equal,
either in brain power, body power, or acquisitive instinct, some
people would soon have far too much, and others far too little.
As time went on you'd have some people with more clothes
and houses and motors than they knew what to do with, and
growing idle and proud in consequence; and others with too

little, and becoming unhealthy and degraded. In fact, if you follow Procrustes' teachings to their logical conclusion, civilisation would become impossible and society would lapse into chaos.

"Then take his advice to slaughter the animals and massacre one another in thousands. Admittedly it's a pious deed to put an end to lives which are detestable to Darkness. But after all we're human and want to make the most of what short lives we have; and few of us are cast in such virtuous mould as to relish the killing of animals. On the whole then I think that if we attend to our ordinary religious duties, say our prayers, and don't sin too flagrantly, Darkness won't expect from us any heroic virtues, but, taking us for what we are, poor weak erring mortals, will still find it in his heart to grant us obliteration."

"But," I objected, "if Darkness hates you so much, why on earth should he reward you?—and for all eternity too."

"Oh," replied Mr. Yccni, "I never care to probe these questions too deeply."

Mr. Yccni's views—though I never again heard them so candidly expressed—were those on which the majority of the people acted. They passed their lives in a state of indifference and virtue punctuated by churchgoing, and on their deathbeds would perhaps kill a flower or beat a child in token of repentance, and pass away in full confidence of final obliteration. A more complete system of hypocrisy and superstition I cannot imagine.

I cannot show this difference between their principles and their practice better than by retailing you a sermon I heard in one of their churches. Being curious to know what Devil-worship was like I asked my Lady's permission one day to accompany the family to a service (meaning, of course, to take no part in it, but only to watch what was going on). She very gladly consented, so the following Sabbath (if I may so call it) saw me duly installed in the family pew. The Church was not inky dark as on weekdays, but was dimly lit by a ghastly green luminosity diffused from the roof, the effect of which was if possible even more creepy. In what one might call the sanctuary there stood an altar consisting of a solid block of black marble, on which rested an immense cube of ice. Otherwise the church was absolutely bare of symbols, ornaments, or furniture except for a pulpit. Shivering with cold, or dread, or a mixture of both, I waited anxiously for the coming deviltry to begin. What I expected I don't know. Some Satanic dance, perhaps, with the priests hacking their bodies with knives. Perhaps a human sacrifice. Perhaps I looked for some awful manifestation of Beelzebub himself on that block of ice which glimmered in such ghostly fashion in the gloom of the apse. Presently, as I watched in tense anticipation, out of the vestry crept a grim and hideous figure: a semi-bestial form clothed in black, with swishing tail, goats' horns, and evil leprous face: the priest of the devil, if not the devil himself. Pausing before the altar, it made a bow, and began a droning invocation in tones too low for me to distinguish any words. After a few sentences the congregation murmured a response. Then the diabolical figure intoned again; then again the congregation; and so they prayed in alternate solo and chorus of mumbles, for nearly half an hour. By that time my feelings of awe were beginning to give place to boredom. But now came a pause and a prolonged silence. The minister of Beelzebub prostrated himself in mute adoration before the cold symbol of his lord. There was something absolutely corpse-like in his perfect immobility. All around me in the black and sickly twilight seemed frozen into an equal stillness. New expectations arose in me during that deathly pause, which sent fresh shudderings up my spine. I believe that for a while I really stopped breathing. The long moment spun itself out to the utmost limit of endurance. Then just as I was about to cry aloud in anguish, the minister arose and turned to face the congregation. The spell snapped. There was a stir and shuffle of feet. I knew instinctively that nothing was going to happen after all—and oddly enough I felt disappointed, because when you're all strung up to endure something frightful you get rather a jar if it doesn't come off.

As the priest stood with outstretched arms, two little imp-like creatures came sneaking out of the background and stood behind him. Instantly his diabolical costume, tail and all, dropped off, leaving him in a plain black tunic. Next he raised a hand to his chin and peeled off his hideous mask, revealing a face which even in the green twilight looked healthy and reas-suring. Then, as the two imps scurried off to the vestry with his disguise, the priest ascended the steps of the pulpit.

I settled myself comfortably in my seat, prepared to be deli-ciously shocked by a perfect orgy of blasphemy. The sermon of the priest of the Devil was no more, however, than this:

"*Keep thine eye open, lest an opportunity pass thee by.*

"There is a duty, ladies and gentlemen, which is laid upon every man and woman who is born into this world: the duty—I need hardly name it—of getting on. It is not however my inten-tion today to develop simple and obvious a theme as this. It is the first lesson that every child learns at its mother's knee; the last admonishment which every lad hears from his anxious pedagogue as, fresh with the enthusiasm of budding manhood, he goes out into the world from the shelter of his beloved alma mater. The vision of that goal is the spur which like the distant light seen by the lonely traveller, beckons the aspiring youth onward through the days of toil and struggle, and warms his heart with the promise of rest and reward. And the attainment of that pinnacle is the crowning glory which each successful servant of Mammon carries with him to the grave as his passport to final oblivion. Neither, ladies and gentlemen, need I remind you of the terrible punishments which our infernal master Procrustes has decreed for those who fail to perform this duty. The dread sentence is familiar to every ear. 'Get On—or get Out.' O sub-lime and awful malediction! Get on, or get out. Out, mark you.

Out of what? Out of credit; out of the march of success; out of the city; out of everything. Out into obscurity; out into the wilderness; out into penury, poverty, and impecuniosity. Such is the well-deserved fate of the inefficient. And not of the inefficient only. In spite of this terrible warning there are people who make no attempt whatever to get on—who deliberately dare to flout success: dabblers in poetry, scholarship, and science; hot-headed young folk who marry for love and produce untimely children; restless spirits who wander about the world in profitless exploration. All these must get out. There are some, too, who fondly imagine in their worldly cynicism that getting on is a co-operative business; who regard other men not as competitors, but as partners; who presumptuously dare to dispense with their competitive instinct. O, ladies and gentlemen, let me warn you against such folly as this. Without the stimulus of competition—without the desire to rise above our rival-men—we are no good. And of what value is the success that is shared by another? Therefore regard every man as your rival, and do unto him as you know he will do unto you. Show any weakness in this regard, and inevitably you will go to the wall.

"But, ladies and gentlemen, as I have already said, my purpose today is not to urge upon you the necessity of getting on. It is rather to suggest to your minds the most efficient methods of getting on, and to utter a few words of warning in regard to the obstacles which lie like pitfalls to trap the feet and dazzle the eyes of the unwary and the inexperienced. Thus, ladies and gentlemen, I hope to impart to you a lesson which each and every one of you, as you leave this edifice, will feel deep down in your hearts to have been full value for the contributions which I have heard rattling so generously into the collection box.

"There is one virtue, ladies and gentlemen, which is of supreme importance to everyone who sets out upon the road to success, and which it behoves us all to cultivate, for nobody can make good without it. What is its name? It is indicated in these wonderfully cute words of our master Procrustes which serve for my text today: 'Keep thine eye open, lest an opportunity pass thee by.' In one word, Slickness! With slickness alone, even unassisted by any other virtue, we may do much. Without it, though dowered with every other quality that adorns a profiteer, our chances are but small. For remember, opportunities are all around us. If they were few and far between, if they lurked in the shadows and waste places of the world, then luck, or cunning, or perseverance would be required to find them. But they are everywhere, and consequently, if *you* don't grab them, some other fellow will. Remember that man is a creature with an infinitude of needs, and that the satisfying of any one of them should be the means of making a fortune for somebody. Therefore keep your eyes skinned and your mind void of any but the single purpose of recognising an opportunity and following it up. The money-making instinct is a big thing and leaves no room in your head for any other idea. So don't allow yourself to get distracted by notions of art, or amusement (except, of course, as much as is necessary to keep you in physical form); and above all, don't go messing about helping people who are less efficient than yourself. A man must make his own way or be prepared to knuckle under.

"And now, ladies and gentlemen, what is the obstacle that lies in the path to hinder our progress towards success? What else, my friends, but sin. And of all the sins those are most to be dreaded by the aspirant to success which are known as the seven deadly sins. First, Pride. Ah, my friends, there have been far, far more promising careers wrecked upon this rock of pride than upon the shoals of inefficiency itself. The proud man goes about with his nose in the air, and thus he lets opportunity pass him by. O, ladies and gentlemen, be humble. Remember that opportunity often comes in so lowly a disguise that only the eye of the humble can pierce it. If, for instance a shabby undistinguished-looking old man should ask you to help him across the street, do not scorn his piping voice or repulse the appeal in his rheumy eye, but offer him your arm and guide his tottering steps to the security of the sidewalk. Remember that he may be a millionaire, who will be capable of rewarding you a thousandfold.

"Secondly, there is covetousness. The covetous man expects to receive without giving; or at any rate, strives to get as much as possible in return for as little as possible, and thereby ruins his chances. Remember that those above you have their eye on you, and that those who never do any more than they get paid for never get paid for any more than they do. Remember too, that in the contest for success it is almost as dangerous to overreach oneself as not to grab hard enough. So much depends on bamboozling your rivals that it is often better to keep your ambition dark, let the small early prizes fall to the boobs who fall for them, and reserve your own energy for the big things later on. Therefore cultivate a large outlook, and don't be grasping. It doesn't pay in the end.

"Thirdly, ladies and gentlemen, comes lust. On that unpleasant topic I will be as brief as possible. Ah, how many an eye for opportunity has been distracted by the swish of a petticoat or the lascivious lips of Vice. Nay, I have known some of the most promising young men to marry for love and devote to the propagation of a family the energies which should be consecrated to Mammon. Cut all that out, my friends. Don't have a family till you can afford it, and don't imagine you can afford it until you've a bigger bank balance than is ever likely to come your way.

"Fourthly comes the hideous sin of anger, and oh, my friends, let me counsel you to beware of its onslaught. If you have a bad temper, keep it under. If you feel hatred for any man, don't show it. If you are insulted, swallow it. Remember that your time will come, but above all things don't quarrel with your bread and butter. Better eat any sort of humble pie rather than that.

"Fifthly there is gluttony, but there again is a subject on which I prefer not to dwell. Enough to say that no man worth his salt will allow his appetite for nutriment to diminish his appetite for profit. Therefore, save all you can. If you earn but a penny a day, see that you live upon a halfpenny; and if you earn but a halfpenny a day make what shift you can upon a farthing.

"Sixthly comes envy—a sin, ladies and gentlemen, on which it is incumbent upon me to dwell at some little length, as it is one of the greatest of all obstacles to getting on, and the easiest of all vices to fall into unawares. For this insidious and detestable sin is—alas! too frequently—confused in the mind of the unwary with the noble virtue of emulation which produces that spirit of competition on which all progress depends. Oh, my friends, let me warn you to be on your guard against making such a disastrous error. Envy and emulation are as the poles apart. Envy renders a man impotent; emulation makes him strong. The envious man, consumed with hatred of a more successful rival, learns nothing from him, and is soon left further behind than ever; while the man who is inspired by the noble spirit of emulation keeps his feelings in check, watches his rival's little games, and, biding his time, eventually rises in triumph above him and sees him sink into the ruck of the failures. Therefore, my friends, do not envy those who have made good. Pal up with them, and learn their methods.

"And lastly comes sloth. One word on that, and I have done. Laziness, my friends, is the mother of lost opportunities. No matter how sharp be your eye; no matter how keen your nose; if you haven't the pep to follow up their discoveries, you are lost. Therefore, keep moving. Get a hustle on. And that's that."

Well, I did feel let down I can tell you. I had been expecting a bloodthirsty harangue on the duty of murder, or an exhortation to practise the virtue of thieving, or perhaps a glorious canticle about wine and women, and here I was fobbed off with some quite excellent advice on how to succeed, mixed up with some of the most old-fashioned goody-goody jaw that ever I'd listened to. One thing about the sermon puzzled me extremely, and that was the occurrence of words and ideas which I had come to regard as quite outside the comprehension of the Ratheans. For instance, that remark about the contributions rattling into the collection box, which, besides being inconsistent with the Rathean economic system, was actually untrue. Not a soul in the congregation had possessed a coin, and there was no collection-box to rattle them in. Camino explained the matter to me. It was an archaic phrase, she said, which still survived in religious usage, though it had long lost all significance.

"Out of date and meaningless, like the Church itself," sneered Yasint, who had not been at the service, but had met us afterwards.

"Now, now," my Lady warned him. "Don't shake the faith of others, even if you don't believe yourself."

Lord, what a people!

CHAPTER XXXI

The Londicean Mentality of the Ratheans

PROCRUSTEANITY IS THE ONLY religion known in Rathé, but it takes several forms. These however have not crystallised into separate churches, but are merely shades of difference in belief which cannot be classified except in the roughest fashion. The great majority of the people may be said to accept the creed as I have just described it, believing in a personal devil and attending the services of the church with more or less regularity. The more highly-evolved classes, however, regard the Great Book as being figuratively, rather than literally, true, and hold varying views as to the nature of the Devil. On the whole they incline to deny his personality, while accepting his existence as an intangible force—what they call the Death Force, or, more scientifically, the force of Negation, against which Life, or the Positive Force, has to struggle for existence. Those who take this view may be divided into the Negationists, who believe that the struggle is hopeless, and therefore maintain that men should make the best of this life as there is none to follow; and the Positivists, who hope for an ultimate triumph of Life and urge men to fit themselves for the after-existence by subordinating the flesh to the spirit.

All these, as I say, accept the faith, each according to his own interpretation. The most highly-evolved classes, however, have no religion at all. As far as I could understand it, their view is that virtue and strength should be cultivated for their own sake, as being better than vice and weakness, irrespective of what powers may be above us, or whether there be any such powers at all. As to these questions they keep an open mind, professing that, even should they prove to be soluble, their conduct would be the same whatever the answer.

In a sense the Ratheans are all agnostics, for even the most convinced adherents of Procrusteanity do not go so far as to declare that it is the true religion. Perhaps I should except the class in the lowest stage of evolution—the hunters, shooters, and so on—who are both devoted and bigoted in their worship of Procrustes. But these are a negligible minority of the population. The rest, as I say, do not maintain that their religion is the true one. It is simply the religion in which they believe. They claim that it is a valid interpretation of known facts, but they are not so unimaginative as to think that no other interpretation is possible. They therefore keep an open mind on the subject, encouraging religious speculation in every possible way, in the hope that some day their faith may be either confuted or confirmed. They particularly encourage it in the young, believing that their fresh unprejudiced minds must be especially receptive to truth. Indeed they push their open-mindedness so far that they give their children no religious instruction at all, but urge them to observe the phenomena of life for themselves and draw what conclusions they can from them. They say that it is an abuse of a parent's position, and a betrayal of the trust of a child, to take advantage of its innocence to foist on it a conception of things which may be only the product of one's own ignorance, stupidity, fear, or prejudice. They therefore keep their beliefs in the background, and encourage every sign of original and independent thinking on the child's part, only throwing in an occasional tentative suggestion where an idea seems to conflict with fact. In spite of all this, they tell me, the great majority of the young folk are driven sooner or later into the old faith by the remorseless logic of things as they are.

"With this cracker of scepticism," Mr. Yasint once said to me, "we crunch the shells of the nuts of knowledge," and he bade me contrast the vast range of natural and supernatural discovery achieved by the free play of imagination and intellect among poets and religious thinkers with the hopelessly backward condition of science, whose professors were hidebound by their adherence to rules and formulate which they obstinately clung to as unchangeable.

That sounds funny doesn't it? Well, here's the sense of it.

CHAPTER XXXII

The Extraordinary Scientific Notions of the Ratheans

ON SECOND THOUGHTS I hardly like to deal with this question of science at all. You see, I know absolutely nothing about it, whereas the Ratheans are tremendously keen on the subject. They all call themselves scientists; their whole lives are conducted on scientific principles; they are always talking about science; and the books they have written about science would fill the Phoenix Park. So what right have I to criticise them? None at all, I quite admit. At the same time I have a sort of notion that there's something wrong with their scientific ideas somewhere. What it is, or where it is, I, in my hopeless ignorance, do not like to say. If I wasn't afraid of putting my foot in it and making some frightful blunder, I would be half inclined to suggest that it might possibly be their incapacity for simple arithmetic. As I say, I don't know, and I would like to be corrected if I am wrong, but that's my idea. It is a fact, anyway, that the Ratheans are pretty bad at arithmetic. It's a sort of natural deficiency with them: like not having an ear for music. They reminded me of a fellow I was at school with, who was a regular dab at composition and things, and afterwards made good as an advertising specialist, but when it came to sums couldn't add two and two together. The Ratheans are all like that, the only difference being that while my friend was well aware of his inability, and only too glad to be offered a helping hand, the Ratheans thought themselves first-rate mathematicians, and used to be frightfully insulted if I tried to set their bunglings right. Not only that, but if I ever came near convincing any of them they'd run away in a panic, saying that they had been foolish to listen to me at all, as my perverted cleverness was capable of proving wrong right and right wrong.

I remember one time in the early part of my stay, coming upon a young lady in some difficulty about the arrangement of plants in a flower bed. What the difficulty was I couldn't exactly make out, but when she had dug them all up the fourth time and was reduced almost to tears, I went up to her and asked if I could be of any assistance.

"Why, yes," she replied, brightening. "I'm terribly puzzled what to do here. I have forty-five of these plants, and I want to arrange them in six equal rows. That's seven to a row, of course. But somehow it doesn't work out right. I always seem to have three over."

"No wonder," I said. "Six sevens are forty-two."

"O, no," she replied. "I know my tables better than that. Six sixes are thirty-eight, and six sevens are forty-five."

I couldn't help smiling at this, and, not having any tables handy, I tried to convince her by working the thing out practically. But she was too stupid to under- stand, and at last told me to go away, remarking with some sharpness that I might find something better to do than undermining a girl's mathematical convictions. Then she set to work again, uprooting and shifting the plants this way and that, getting redder and more exasperated every instant, till at last she said: "I must have more plants than I thought," and after fixing her six rows of sevens, she threw the three plants left over among the scufflings.

At the time I wasn't a bit surprised at this and other displays of ignorance, for I put it all down to their ridiculous system of education. But a new complexion was put on the matter when one day a young fellow produced a book of arithmetic to prove his mistake right, and I found at a glance that the multiplication tables were all wrong. Rashly perhaps, I said so, and next day down on me swooped my old friend Professor Juicewit, as fierce as a mother hen, to demand what I meant by undermining the mathematics of the young.

"I'm not undermining them," I said. "I'm propping them up. Your tables are all wrong."

"O, indeed," says the Professor with a fine irony.

"All wrong, are they? And on what authority do you make that pronouncement?"

"On my own common sense," I said. "I can prove it to you in half a minute."

"Your common sense, forsooth," says the Professor.

"Do you set up your feeble common sense against the science of mathematics?"

"No," I said. "I say that you people have the wrong notion of mathematics."

"That is quibbling," said the Professor. "You have said that the mathematical tables are wrong, and that is an attack upon the science of mathematics itself."

"Well, if it is, I can't help it," I said. "They are wrong, anyway, and I'm prepared to prove it."

"That is rather a fundamental question to begin with," said Professor Juicewit. "Let us first deal with some simpler aspects of science. What are your views on Differential Calculus?"

"None," I said.

"Well, have you any theory as to the causation of Allotropism?"

"No."

"Or the relationship of valency to atomicity?"

"None whatever."

"What do you know of Karyokinesis?"

"Never heard of him."

"Can you calculate the precession of the equinoxes?"

"Not very accurately."

"Have you even achieved perpetuum mobile?"

"Not yet."

Professor Juicewit's voice began to tire.

"Have you ever read any scientific work?" he said. "The *Summum Scientificum* for instance?"

I shook my head.

"Under the circumstances," said the Professor, "does it not seem rather presumptuous on your part to question the very basis of mathematical truth?"

Put that way it did seem so, but I still feel that there's something wrong with Rathean science somewhere, so I'll set the facts before you and let you judge for yourself.

The attitude of the Ratheans to science is this. They do not regard it as the pursuit of systematic knowledge of natural phenomena by the observation of facts, experiment, and deduction, but as a collection of conclusions already immutably fixed, with which facts must be squared, or in obedience to which they must be explained away. To put it in another way, mathematics, physics, biology, and so on are not branches of knowledge to be studied and developed, but jumbles of rules and legends to be accepted on faith. Apparently in some far distant time a bunch of early experimenters wrote down all they could find out about these subjects in a book, which has been accepted as authoritative ever since. Unfortunately the book is so obscure and confused that nobody can be quite sure of its meaning, with the result that the whole population of Rathé is divided into scientific factions, about five hundred and seventy in number, each with its own view of the subject, its own schools (which are different from the ordinary schools I have described), its own teachers, its own books, and its own rules and theories, all differing in greater or less degree from one another. You never saw such a muddle. These factions have nothing to do with the general division of the people into tribes and continents. They cut across all other divisions whatsoever. They are known as Colleges. Every Rathean as soon as he is born is enrolled by his parents in the one to which they themselves belong and is trained in its curriculum from thenceforward, and carefully kept from contamination by any other College. The liberal notions which the Ratheans hold on religion and other subjects don't seem to apply at all in this case. A Rathean parent would not dream of allowing his children to be taught a different scientific theory from his own and it is considered a frightful thing for a man to change at any time from one College to another; though, by some strange inconsistency which I do not profess to understand, every College is delighted to welcome such traitors into its membership.

How did this extraordinary state of affairs arise? This is a difficult question to answer, for the Ratheans themselves are hopelessly divided on it. However, I went to a good deal of trouble to get at the truth, and I don't think I am very far wrong in the account which I shall now set down.

At one time apparently there was only one College which was known simply as the College of Science and which held almost undisputed sway until about five hundred years ago. Its professors taught a simple rather limited, and wholly materialistic curriculum laying down as absolute truth that there was no Devil and no God; that the universe had arisen from fortuitous concurrence of atoms; that all matter was composed of earth, air, fire, and water; and that the sun and stars revolved round Rathé at a distance of four thousand and four miles. As to the origin of man they solemnly declared it to have occurred literally and actually as follows.

In the prehistoric times when the Fabulosaurus and the Gigantotherium and the Lantern-jawed Tiger ranged over the world, the ancestors of man were a race of baboonish creatures going on all fours who inhabited the murky depths of the primeval forest. Timid and feeble, they led a precarious existence, constantly harried and hunted by the great carnivores, and in particular by the lantern-jawed tiger. To escape this ferocious enemy they used to seek refuge in the tree tops—or, to put it more scientifically, they developed an automatic arborascensal reflex. Naturally the quickest and strongest beasts were the most likely to get away, while the slower fell victims to the pursuer. The monkey race in consequence increased steadily in strength and agility, and developed an upright posture, while the tiger, by being fobbed off with inferior sustenance, degenerated into a weaker and slower-footed animal. But the monkeys had yet further selective circumstances to mould them. The agile individuals who escaped the tiger had no sooner reached the tops of the trees than down from the sky swooped that grisly bird the Teratopteryx, to carry them off in its talons to its eyrie in the mountains. Placed thus between two seemingly inescapable enemies, the race appeared doomed to extinction, the teratopteryx eliminating the strong as surely as the tiger eliminated the weaklings. It happened, however, that the trees were of exactly such a height that those monkeys which had just sufficient strength to escape by an inch or so from the snap of the tiger s jaws would, by an equally narrow margin, miss exposing themselves to the swoop of the teratopteryx. A premium was thus placed on mediocrity as against superfluity or deficiency of strength. So small too was the margin of safety that those who benefited by it invariably left their tails between the teeth of the tiger. Moreover, those monkeys which possessed short tails originally had the best chance of escape. Taillessness thus acquired a strong survival value; the tailless members had the choice of the finest mates and the best food; and so, after billions of millenniums, the lantern-jawed tiger having meanwhile been driven back on a vegetable diet and evolved into a bullock, and the teratopteryx having dwindled by starvation into a sparrow, a tailless mediocrity walked erect as master of the world.

The College of Science, as I have said, taught this drivel as literal fact through the whole period of their dominance over Rathean thought. Now that the legend has been blown upon by poets and religious thinkers they deny this, and say that they only upheld it as figuratively true. Such dodgery may perhaps deceive the simple-minded Ratheans; but it doesn't go down with me. All the evidence I have examined shows that the College of Science not only insisted that this tale was the literal fact, but that they actually put people to death for refusing to accept it as such. However, I haven't time to argue the point here. The College was equally dogmatic and equally limited on every other subject.

Now, as time went on, some of the more enterprising of the Ratheans, both teachers and others, began to make new scientific discoveries, and to find out mistakes in the accepted curriculum. The Professors didn't like this at all. They tried to stop it by forbidding unauthorised persons to undertake experiments, and prohibiting the people from reading the discoverers' books. When that failed they tried imprisoning the discoverers, torturing them, and burning them at the stake. One of the earliest speculators questioned that part of the Evolution story which attributes the survival of man to the mere chance of a certain number having just the requisite strength to evade the tiger without falling foul of the teratopteryx. He suggested that mere chance alone would have been insufficient, and that some element of skill or calculation on the monkeys' part must have entered into it. This view the College declared to be a Fallacy, contrary to the laws of causation and to scientific truth; and at the same time laid it down as an axiom that all vital phenomena were the product of the blind force of material circumstance. The champion of brains, however, refused to recant, and, after being racked and flogged, was sent along with a number of his followers to the stake. Nor was it only scientific thinkers who suffered in this way. In those days the College claimed jurisdiction over every field of thought, and in particular over religion, whose advocates they seemed to regard with a mixture of fear and hatred as younger rivals destined eventually to supplant

them. Religious thinkers therefore found themselves persecuted in the same fashion, believers in the human soul being
racked until they recanted, and then consigned to the flames.
But all this was to no purpose. New theories and discoveries
kept springing up on all sides, and whole cities, tribes, and
continents adopted them. Indeed the modern Ratheans, keen
as they are on science, admit to some amazement at the zeal
of their ancestors. Such questions as the Magnitude of Points,
the reality of Recurring Decimals, whether Arithmetic, Algebra,
and Geometry were one Science or three, whether muscle was
designed to move bone or bone to support muscle, whether the
egg came before the hen or vice versa, what would happen if
the Irresistible met the Impenetrable—all these questions and
a hundred others of lesser importance were bandied about in
arguments of such incredible bitterness as often to lead to war.
A large and populous country which adopted what was known
as the Balbigensian Fallacy (a denial of the indestructibility of
matter, the Law of Inverse Squares, and some other theories)
was utterly laid waste and its whole population butchered by
order of the College of Science. A controversy as to whether
Geometry proceeded from Algebra or Arithmetic or both on
another occasion rent the greater part of a continent with strife;
and a most savage and intensive struggle was waged over the
question whether there should be a c in isosceles.

But all these controversies related only to individual points in
the scientific course. They did not affect it as a whole, nor were
their results lasting. The present divisions date back no further
than five centuries, originating in the revolt of a young teacher
named Thelru, who repudiated the authority of the Professors
and set up a College of his own. As to the rights and wrongs of
that quarrel I shall say nothing, as they are still the subject of
dispute in Rathé, and having heard— or at least having listened
to—an absolute inferno of argument on both sides, I am still no
wiser than I was at the beginning. The people who back Thelru

say that what first disgusted him with the College of Science was the faking of experiments by the Professors, while the defenders of the College say that there was no faking, that the faking was due to excess of zeal on the part of a few minor lecturers only, that even if there had been faking this was insufficient reason for revolting from the College, and that anyway Thelru was no better than he might have been. However, believe which story you please, the revolt took place. Great numbers of the people followed him, and once again Rathé was rent with wars and racked with persecutions. Wherever either faction had the majority it persecuted its opponents. Whole communities were convinced, or extirpated, by the sword. The people of Bulnid, for instance, who remained true to the College, were for centuries persecuted by the Donlonians, followers of Thelru, who deprived them of self-government, confiscated their property, and forbade them to keep schools or universities. Again, in the city of Israp the adherents of the College rose up one night against their Thelruvian fellow citizens and butchered them in thousands. To add to the confusion and horror, the first great cleavage was followed by others among the Thelruvians themselves, who broke up into a variety of schools teaching all sorts of new-fangled and conflicting stuff, and fought and persecuted one another with equal ferocity. It is difficult to follow the exact course of events during this period, for the Ratheans themselves regard it with horror and shame, and have kept all but the mere mention of it out of their records. Eventually however the turmoil subsided, and I understand that for some centuries there has been scientific peace.

But the cleavage—or rather cleavages—remain permanent to this day. On the one hand stands the Old College, exactly where it has always stood, affirming itself as the sole depositary of scientific truth, condemning all other factions as being in a state of error, and forbidding its adherents to enter their schools and universities or to read their text-books. On the other hand are the Objecting Colleges, so called because they *object* to the errors of the Old College. They believe in private judgment on scientific questions, and maintain that science speaks directly to the individual intellect. Each therefore has its own idea of its laws, which gives a pleasant spice of variety to their calculations. To describe each of these Colleges fully would be a tax on my memory and your patience, so I refrain. It is enough to say that there was at one end of the scale a college which would have neither lecturers nor teachers, axioms nor postulates, nor so much as a blackboard in their schoolrooms; and at the other a college which differed from the Old College only on such questions as the colour of the bindings and the style of printing to be used in text-books. Between these two extremes there was every variety of curriculum that the imagination of a lunatic could invent.

Now, hopelessly unscientific as you know me to be, I don't think you'll say I'm wrong in holding that under these cir-cumstances it was no wonder that science in Rathé was in a backward condition, or that I am over bold in attributing the muddle to a wrong conception of what science is. I put the blame in the first instance, if I may venture to say so, on the Old College. As I said to Professor Juicewit, if you're going to rely for ever on a dubiously worded book written thousands of years ago, and to suppress discussion of everything that appears to contradict it, what chance is there for scientific discovery? And what do you think he replied? He said there was no need for scientific discovery, as the whole of science was already to be found in the teachings of the Old College. "But that entails absolute stagnation," I said. "Not at all," he replied. "Quite the contrary. The College is always ready to put the seal of its approval on well-founded theories which are not in conflict with already accepted truth. Quite a number of such theories have in fact been defined as axioms within recent times—as for instance, the hypothesis that the apple which fell upon the head of Tonwen, and thus demonstrated the truth of gravitation, was a pippin and not (as Objectors erroneously hold) a russet; and the consoling revelation that when Medesarchi entered the bath in which he discovered specific gravity he was perfectly clean."

How far science is advanced by these remarkable discoveries (in consequence of which, by the way, the College lost a number of adherents) I leave to the judgement of more scientific minds than mine. Having expressed my opinion in regard to the Old College, I conceded to Juicewit that the establishment of five hundred other Colleges with a fresh supply of axioms had not done anything to improve matters; which hugely pleased the old chap, who reminded me promptly that the Old College had done its best to prevent that.

"You mean by those bloodthirsty persecutions?" I said.

"They were an unfortunate necessity," said the Professor. "But scientific error is so calamitous a thing that any method of eradicating it is justifiable."

"But persecution didn't eradicate it," I pointed out.

"I agree. And it was for that very reason that the College, in its wisdom, abandoned it."

Let's be thankful for small mercies, thought I to myself. But I'd better get on with my story. As I have said, the factions no longer persecute each other. Indeed the modern Ratheans are rather fond of preening themselves on the "Scientific Toleration" of the age. Occasional reminders of the old-time bitterness do, however, make their appearance. In the tribe of Fastelb, for instance, scientific differences are so acute that Collegians and Objectors avoid as far as possible any social or business dealings with one another, while their political life is a scientific battleground. This, at any rate, was the state of affairs until very recently. I have been assured, however, by more than one prominent member of the tribe that a better spirit has lately been in evidence, and that the more broadminded followers of the opposing schools occasionally nod to one another. Again, in Donlon, which is generally held to be a very advanced city, there is a law that the Chief must belong to the Donlonian College, of which he is declared to be the head; and in the still more advanced tribe of Acirem, though there is no actual law about it, a follower of the Old College would have no chance of being elected chief. Toleration, however, is, as I have said, the ordinary rule of life, and in general the factions manage to rub along together fairly peace-ably. Of recent years there has been developing a movement towards what is called Scientific Reunion. This takes the form of meetings of the representatives of the various factions for the purpose of reconciling differences and arriving at a common curriculum. Quite an intelligent idea if their object was to combine in an effort to discover what the facts of science really are. But instead of that they just sit about in an atmosphere of amiability, chatting about the niceness of unity, and trying to arrive at a compromise by what they call mutual concessions and understandings—one faction offering, for instance, to drop the theorem of Pythagoras if another will modify its law of gaseous diffusion—just like diplomatists arranging a treaty. Last year they actually discussed a composite multiplication table designed to meet the views of all parties. The Old College, of course, refuses to take any part in these confabulations, for which it is condemned as narrow-minded and unconciliatory by the other Colleges. But this seems to me extremely inconsistent on their part. After all, their principal quarrel with the Old College is that it dogmatises to its followers instead of letting them think for themselves. How then can they expect it to turn round and order them to change some of their beliefs in order to oblige another College? The Old College, as a matter of fact, does not accept the principle of toleration at all. As recently as seventy years ago its Chief Professor actually issued a circular letter on the subject, definitely condemning what he described as "the absurd and erroneous doctrine—or rather raving—in favour and in defence of liberty of experiment," and only a short time before my arrival one of its most eminent authorities declared that "he doctrine of scientific liberty, though convenient for Collegians who have to do with Objecting governments is one which is not, never has been, and never will be approved by the College of Science." In my own presence Professor Juicewit went so far as to say that the Collegians would be bound to take repressive measures against the Objectors if ever they should become powerful enough to make them effective. Now it happened that a few minutes earlier he had been complaining, with what seemed to me unnecessary heat, of some trifling act of intolerance against Collegians in the neighbouring tribe of Donlon. I reminded him of this, suggesting that what was sauce for the goose was sauce for the gander. "Not at all," says he. "The Objectors have no right to persecute, because they are in the wrong; whereas with us persecution is a duty, because we are in the right. Besides," he added ingeniously, "in demanding toleration from Objectors we are appealing to *their* principles, not to ours." Which appears to me somewhat equivocal, though whether it is scientific or not I am too ignorant to say. I must however add, in common fairness, that the ordinary follower of the Old College has no idea that it holds these principles, and is quite as tolerant a man as the average Objector. Indeed any to whom I spoke on the matter refused to believe me, and insisted that the quotations which I showed them were malicious fabrications of Objecting propagandists. Anyway, I don't think there is the smallest danger of the Old College ever being in a position to institute another persecution; nor does it matter a thraneen whether the other Colleges come to an agreement or not; for between the burnings and battlings of yesterday, and the futilities of today, they've lost most of their influence. Many Ratheans reject science altogether. Many others say that there may be some truth in it but that it is impossible to find it; which, all things considered, is, I think, the most sensible conclusion for people in their case.

By this time I suppose it will have occurred to you, Mr. Gallagher, to object: "But if these people were such idiots at science, how could they have made the scientific discoveries and carried out the engineering feats you have described?" Well, the answer is simple. In every generation there have always been a few men who were exceptions to the general rule and were actually first class scientists. The ordinary Ratheans have, of course, always disliked and distrusted them, and refused to listen to their ideas or to allow them to corrupt their children. But very sensibly they have recognised that the things made by these people are good, and have profited by them accordingly. You might imagine that it would possibly occur to an intelligent being that a man who could invent electrical motors or bridge a great river might conceivably know something about simple arithmetic. But not your Rathean infallible. He's right and you're wrong; and if you invented a new contraption every day of your life you'd still have a lot to learn from Mr Knowall. I've been fairly staggered sometimes when some whipper-snapper of a fellow who couldn't add three and three together has told me that some distinguished inventor was "Unscientific" or had "queer ideas about mathematics," or when some solemn humbug has assured me that "deeply as he admired So-and So's really brilliant achievements, he could not help thinking that his view of science was perverse and distorted." But the most delicious remark that I ever heard was from a dear old lady on the airmail from Bulnid to Donlon. "Wonderful things, these airplanes, aren't they!" she said. "And to think," she added reflectively, "that the man who invented them didn't believe in mechanics."

You will now be in a position to understand the drift of Mr Yasint's remark. While the professors of science, in the intervals between burning and abusing one another, had been poking aimlessly about with their inefficient telescopes and microscopes, in a fog of foregone conclusions, the poets and philosophers had been using their brains and imaginations to make discoveries. As a general rule, Mr Gallagher, I haven't an awful lot of use for poets. But the poets of Rathé are cute birds, and I take off my hat to them. They can discover things by just sitting still and thinking about them. That was the way one of them discovered the theory of electrons. Before his time the Rathean scientists, as I think I have mentioned, taught that all matter was made up of earth, air, fire, and water. This poet fellow wasn't satisfied with this prescription and seems to have spent quite a slice of his life worrying about it. At last one day, when he was deep in his speculations, his gaze became fixed on a speck of light reflected in the gold ring on his finger. Gradually he fell into a kind of trance, and in that condition it seemed to him that the ring began to grow larger. Slowly and steadily it swelled up, rising in front of him like a great yellow wall, and blotting out all other objects. Then, by some strange transition, it had become a vast plain of gold, over which he seemed to be hovering. The surface of the plain was covered with pits and excrescences, and these rapidly grew till they became valleys and hills spread over a miniature landscape. This golden world presently filled all his vision. It continued still to grow, until soon he found himself at the bottom of one of the valleys, which was huger than any valley he had known in Rathé, and whose overtopping heights were already passing away into immeasurable distance. And now as he gazed upon the floor of the valley its texture seemed to change. It was no longer an unbroken surface, but a pattern made of tiny contangent discs, which in their turn were transformed into rapidly spinning spheres revolving round one another. Swiftly the spheres swelled in size, until one alone monopolised his attention. It grew and grew, and lo! it was a microcosm in space, a group of four spindle-shaped bodies whirling round one another like elves in a ring. And these bodies grew in their turn. They were like four tall pillars of flame, writhing spirally as they roared in their courses. And the pillars grew, and their courses lengthened, and there was the poet alone in the black universe, and one elemental flaming giant bearing down upon him. Nearer it came. He was caught in the current of an irresistible force and borne into the heart of the monstrous whirl. He was one of a myriad particles dancing madly in a vortex round a central fire. The fire was of a dazzling white unalloyed purity; it was imperturbable, changeless. Into it passed the spent particles from the focus of the whirl to be fused and remodelled; out of it came the new ones with the impetuosity of worlds unleashed that had never known birth before. Down to that great white heart of life the soul of the poet rushed in its turn. Down, down, down, down, drawn by remorseless force. He braced himself for the shock of dissolution.

And then, like a call from some infinite distance, came the thought that he had told nobody of his experience. Followed instantly the realisation that he must tell it (which is the impulse of poetry). And so, with an effort like the reversing of the engines of a car running at racing speed, he wrenched himself back from the hypnotic glare of the white light. Cataclysmal vibrations shook his being. A wild desolation overwhelmed him. And there he was in the light of common day sitting in his chair, blinking at the ring on his finger.

The poet at once made a song out of this experience; and if you notice any bits of my description that look like fine writing, it's because I read the song and stuck them in here from memory. Its publication caused no little stir in Rathé. The College of Science condemned it as contrary to revealed scientific truth. Religious thinkers on the other hand welcomed it as confirming the universal creed by suggesting that even in the apparent stasis of inert matter the cosmic struggle between light and darkness was waged unceasingly. Meanwhile a young scientist of independent views had been so fascinated by the idea of the poem that he set to work on a series of experiments to find out if it was true. After many years he succeeded in doing so, but the College deprived him of his degree and refused to admit his book to the schools, so that as far as the general public are concerned the theory is unknown to this day.

And while scientific discovery has thus been left almost entirely to religious thinkers, the alleged scientists, not content with keeping their own subject as backward as possible, have done their best to interfere with the progress of religion as well. No longer in a position to use the rack and the stake, they nevertheless oppose every fresh advance of religious knowledge with all the denunciations and all the remaining powers at their command. Each discovery in turn has been met with three successive lines of defence. First of all they denounce it as a malignant attack on Science and an attempt to dethrone Matter from its place in the universe. Then as the idea begins to make headway, they change their tone. They say that it may possibly be true, but that even so it does not contradict the truths of Science. Finally, when it becomes firmly fixed in the popular mind, they claim that it is fully in accord with their own teachings, and that they never condemned it, but merely opposed its premature revelation to the simple- minded before it had been authoritatively affirmed. This dodgery has saved their faces up till now, but I think that in the end it will undermine their whole position. Take the origin of man for example. Their original teaching, absurd as it was, was at least clear and comprehensible; but I defy anyone to make head or tail of what they mean since their admission that it's only symbolical. "What the dickens is it symbolical of?" I asked Professor Juicewit. But I could get nothing out of him: nothing but shifts and evasions that might mean anything at all.

Now I am all for giving fair play to both sides in a controversy; so, having given you Yasint's version, I feel bound to state that the professors of science indignantly repudiate every word of it. They say that the scientific history which I have related to you is a grossly garbled travesty of the facts and they gave me an account from their own point of view, which, however, was so long and so complicated that I cannot remember it. They were particularly insistent on repudiating the allegation that the College of Science is hostile to religious research. They declare that it never interfered with Religion in its own sphere, but only when its so-called discoveries were employed to cast doubt upon scientific truth. Well, they may be right for all I can tell. It isn't for me to pronounce judgment in a quarrel between devil worshipping priests and monkey worshipping scientists.

CHAPTER XXXLLL

A Chat with the Chief

ONE DAY ABOUT THE beginning of the fourth month of my stay in Rathé, one of the Chief's secretaries came to me with a courteous message from his master, regretting that pressure of public business had hitherto deprived him of the pleasure and profit of my conversation, and intimating that he was now free and would see me at any hour I might name. I named an hour, and looked him up accordingly.

The Chief's apartment was a biggish room, absolutely lined with books, and furnished like a business office, with letter-files, a couple of typewriters, and a roll-top desk. The Chief himself was sitting at a table with writing materials before him. At the opposite side of it was a vacant chair in which he signed to me to sit. I did so, feeling beastly uncomfortable, because he was rather an overwhelming personality, and I couldn't make out from his expression what his mood was. His eyes gazed solemnly into mine for what may have been two or three minutes but seemed an age to me. It was a most embarrassing stare. At last I had to speak or go mad.

"It's a fine day, your lordship," I said.

"Thank you, sir," he replied gravely. "I have received the weather report." So I had to grit my teeth and endure another silence.

"Mr. O'Kennedy," said the Chief presently, "you have now spent some considerable time on our planet, and have been afforded, I hope, every opportunity of studying our laws, customs, and ways of living and thinking."

I felt greatly relieved by this opening, and assured him that I had been met with every kindness and attention.

"Tell me then," said the Chief, "what you think of our ways. I should like to hear them judged in the light of the wisdom of other worlds."

This request, as you can imagine, bucked me up no end. But, not being sure where he might be leading me, I decided to take a cautious line for the present.

"Are you not satisfied with them yourself?" I asked.

"Satisfied is a big word," replied the Chief. "No human institution is exempt from doubt."

"Well, what's your doubt?" I asked, determined not to commit myself till I saw how the land lay.

"This mainly," said the Chief. "Are we evolving fast enough?"

I was on the top gear of my confidence at once. "Don't you worry, old chap," I said. "There's a good deal of good in this little old world, and with me at your elbow we'll head it straight on the road of progress in no time."

"Your pardon, sir," said the Chief, "but your thoughts move too fast for my slower wits. What is your meaning?"

"You'll learn that in time," I said. "Just put your trust in your uncle, and all will go swimmingly."

"You surely aren't going to suggest," gasps the old guy, "that we should revert to amphibianism?"

"Not on your life!" I replied. "I was only talking metaphysically, so to speak. But, to get right down to brass tacks: do I take it that you're with me for a forward policy in evolution?"

"There is, of course, no question of that," says the Chief. "My doubt is whether our course is fast enough. This world of ours is, as you know, an old one. Its retardation is perceptible, and is increasing. At what time it will fall back into the sun from which it sprang we have no means of knowing, but it is evidently nearer to its consummation than to its beginning. So here's the point. Are we so speeding our evolution as to be able to dispense with it when that catastrophe occurs?"

"Well," said I, "there's nothing like foresight, but it's early to worry about the colour of the winning post before you've put your gee in training. Why, my dear sir, you haven't started evolving yet, and at the present rate you never will. Your life here is too easy altogether. It offers no stimulus to the ambitious, and does nothing to eliminate the inefficient. A man could no more evolve in Rathé than a goldfish in a glass bowl."

"Why?" asked the Chief, looking at me sharply.

"Well," I said, pitying his ignorance, "I thought everybody knew that evolution is caused by the struggle for existence." (Of course I was only codding the fellow, because I know that evolution is contrary to faith and we aren't allowed to believe it whether it's right or wrong.)

The Chief looked as if a wasp had stung him. "Is that the idea of evolution that prevails in your world?" says he.

"Sure," says I. "Circumstantial selection, you know—the Missing Link—survival of the fittest, and all that sort of thing."

The Chief sighed, and says he: "I had hoped for more wisdom from the stars."

That remark gave me a jolt. "What!" says I.

"Don't you believe in evolution? I thought you were all dead keen on it hereabouts."

"We do not believe that it is caused by circumstantial selection," says the Chief.

"O come, governor," says I. "You'll agree that if a specie is chased and has to run for it, the fellows that can run best will have the biggest chance of surviving, and—er—carrying on the race, and all that?"

"Certainly," says the Chief.

"And if a specie lives in a cold climate, the fellows with the thickest coats will have the best chance, won't they?" (Queer

position, wasn't it, for a Christian lad to be de ending evolution
against a benighted heathen.)

"I agree," says the Chief.

"Well, there you are," I said. "The struggle for existence
means the survival of the fittest. Q.E.D. Now all you need is to
dig a few bones out of a strata, and the proof's complete."

"My dear young friend," says the Chief, smiling, "all you
mean by those remarks is that circumstantial selection occurs, a
thing which I have not denied. But so far from being the cause
of evolution, it is an obstacle to it."

Well, Mr Gallagher, all through this scientific discussion I
had been feeling rather like a fellow who's taken a hand at poker
without knowing the game against a gang that does, and now I
was stumped entirely. The Chief's remark showed me too that
even if I could carry my point there was nothing to gain by
it, so, in a thoroughly fed-up mood, I threw in my hand. The
Chief, however, was in no hurry to call off his dog, but went
banging away at the subject like a steam-hammer cracking nuts.

"Maybe you aren't aware," says he, "that this whole subject
was thrashed out long ago between our scientists and religious
thinkers. The scientists told some ridiculous tale about tigers
and teratopteryges which perhaps you have heard." I nodded.
"Well, they were compelled, after a stiff controversy, to drop it,
and I believe that they now pretend that they only held it to be
a piece of symbolism, though what it can possibly symbolise,
in the light of modern knowledge, I don't know. However, as
nobody wants to destroy the precarious hold which our people
have on science, we don't press that point. What matters is that
circumstantial selection as a sufficient explanation of human
origins is exploded. The struggle for existence has no more to
do with evolution than the circumstances of your upbringing
had to do with your growth. Undoubtedly those circumstances
affected your growth considerably, and to judge from your
mental development," says he, with a sort of dignified nastiness,

"very unfavourably. But I do not imagine that even you would think that they were the cause of it. In the same way, circumstances may affect the course of evolution, also generally unfavourably, by diverting it from the end at which the will is aiming. They may, for instance, have forced the limpet to develop a shell; but only by sacrificing its mobility. They may have forced the rabbit to develop its limbs, but at the expense of its brain and courage. In no case could they have done anything if the faculty to respond—in other words, the will to overcome the obstacle—had not been already present. If that were absent, circumstance could only kill—as it grinds the stones of the seashore to sand.

"What then can circumstance do for man?" he demanded. "Being material, it can select only material qualities, as cunning, audacity, greed, ruthlessness, selfishness; sacrificing to them all those things that truly become a man. That is the whole tale of existence. Look around you, and everywhere you will see life seeking after power, power seeking after wisdom, wisdom seeking after the spirit, and everywhere circumstance barring the way. Even still it bars our upward course, and our souls' development is stayed by It was for this that I sought your compromise with it. advice, unfortunately in vain."

"Well," I said, "I'm no great authority on soul matters, but it'll do you no harm to talk it over with someone, anyhow—sort of relieve your feelings, you know."

"Thank you, sir," said the Chief. "I need no such relief. But I will satisfy your curiosity. I sometimes wonder whether the development of mechanical resources which the hard conditions of our environment forced on us, is not as great an impediment to our further progress as is its protecting shell to the limpet."

"In what way?" I asked.

"By becoming indispensable to us. By making us dependent upon it instead of upon ourselves."

"I dare say there's a lot in that," I said. "But what else could you have done?"

"We could have developed our own powers instead of creating machines as substitutes. We could have become runners instead of motorists. We could have flown instead of inventing airplanes."

I wasn't so rude as to say what I thought in reply to this remark. But I must have looked it; for the Chief said: "Incredulous young man, the thing has been done."

"Where?"

"Upon this very planet. Have you not been told about the Lands of the Sun?"

I replied that I had heard mention of them from time to time, from which I had gathered that they were a highly desirable residential locality, but so far had received no very definite specification of their attractions.

"That must be remedied instantly," said the Chief, "for there grows the fine flower of our people, the most highly-evolved race in Rathé. To spend one day in their society is a liberal education."

"But I don't want to go to school again," I said. "I finished my education years ago."

The Chief smiled. "You will be all the more welcome, then," he said. "They are always ready to learn."

"But say," I said. "Is this serious? Can these people really fly without machines? Have they wings?"

"Certainly."

"And can they run as fast as a motor car?"

"Very nearly."

"I suppose they can tell the time by looking at their wrists?" I said jokingly.

"They don't bother about the time."

"Bit awkward if they had to catch a train," said I. "But I suppose they haven't any trains."

"They have no machinery of any sort."

"Sounds a bit backward" I said. 'Didn't you tell me that these people were slap-up civilised?"

"Certainly. They are even more superior to us than we are to the people of the Black Lands."

This was the first time I had heard the Black Lands mentioned spontaneously by Rathean lips, so I seized the opportunity to inquire about them.

"You shall visit them also," said the Chief, "if you desire it, and thus observe for yourself the effects of circumstantial selection on human evolution. But first you must see the Lands of the Sun."

CHAPTER XXXIV

The Isles of the Blest

NEXT DAY WE STARTED on our journey. We did the first part of the trip by airplane, crossing narrow seas and broad continents dotted with cities, and arrived at the end of a week at the port from which we were to sail for the Isles of the Blest—for the Sunny Zone was not, as I had supposed, a continent, but an archipelago set in the middle of a vast ocean. We had to wait two days for a ship, as there was little traffic with the islands, so I had the opportunity to observe that the nights were now very short, little more than an hour intervening between sunset and sunrise. The heat, however, except at midday, was not oppressive, whether because the Rathean sun is not so powerful as ours, or because it is further away, I never thought of asking. At last we learned that our steamer was ready; and a poor little craft she was, though sufficient for anything she had to do; for she had no cargo to carry, and only about a dozen passengers, dry old blighters going, as each of them told me, "to study wisdom at its source."

The voyage lasted ten days. The heat increased as we proceeded, and the sea took on an intensely deep blue colour, like you sometimes see in pictures. At noon it would be as calm as a pond in a park, but in the morning it would be ruffled by breezes, which were very refreshing. The nights grew steadily shorter till on the sixth day the sun ceased to set, merely dipping its edge for a few minutes into the sea. After that there were no more mornings or evenings, but only a continuous day, with the sun travelling backwards and forwards across the sky,

standing right over our heads at noon, and at midnight falling
to the position ours occupies late on a summer afternoon. We
found it convenient to change our habits accordingly, taking
the few hours of sleep we required during the midday heat. At
last, coming on deck one evening, I saw quite close on our right
hand side the prettiest little island you could possibly imagine, with a dazzling white beach, and tall trees, and flowering
shrubs, and green slopes stretching away up the sides of a gentle hill. We passed on, and sighted others, and soon we were
threading our way through a crowd of them, each prettier than
the last. The sea was like a blue cloth in a jeweller's window
strewn with emeralds set in silver. Gosh, it was lovely! And you
should have seen the birds that went darting about among the
trees, or came soaring over our mast-heads—the colours and
the shapes of them, and their extraordinary cries; and the queer
sea-creatures that lolled about lazily in the water near the shore,
or basked on the weedy rocks; and the wild goats, or whatever
they were, grazing on the green slopes of the hillside. By Jove,
I almost wish now that I had stayed there for good, the peace
there is such a restful memory here among the traffic.

An hour later we were gliding slowly up the channel between
two much larger islands, one of which the Chief had pointed
out as our destination. As we approached nearer to it I looked
out eagerly for signs of habitation, but it seemed to be as wild as
the islets we had left behind us. I couldn't see a house, let alone
a town of any sort. There wasn't even a road in sight. Wherever
I looked there was nothing but trees and shrubs and wide
stretches of rolling grass land. Then suddenly a movement near
the shore caught my attention, and a great white bird flashed
into view, soaring towards us. At least I thought it was a bird
for a moment, but almost at once I saw that I was wrong. The
Chief was no romancer. The creature that with beating wings
was mounting rapidly into the air was a man. I watched him
balance himself like a gull fifty feet or more above our deck,

then slowly glide across the channel, to alight, as I judged, in the interior of the farther island. Well, sir, I tell you it was a pretty sight, and many's the time since I've imagined myself doing it in my dreams.

I was still staring after him when there came a jingle of bells and the shudder of reversed engines. We must be in port, I thought, and went back to the other rail. But there was no sign of a port: nothing but a wretched apology of a pier, a derelict stone structure, green with moss, and with weeds growing in every crevice, which jutted out from the fringe of the forest into the sea. There wasn't a building, nor as much as a shed, on or near it. There wasn't a human figure anywhere in sight: not a boatman, nor a ticket-collector, nor a solitary lounger. It was a most desolate spectacle. Our ship, having to carry her other passengers to some further destination, did not go alongside, but a boat was lowered to put me and the Chief ashore. It left us at the foot of a flight of slimy steps, up which we climbed with difficulty to the top of the pier. We struck out at once along that moss-tufted causeway towards the silent forest—I with a regretful glance backward at the ship, for I had had rather a jolly time with the lowly-evolved members of the crew, and naturally felt a bit lonely at leaving such snug quarters for this wilderness. I saw the boat hoisted aboard, and then turned to follow the Chief.

The forest wasn't a bit like those on the outer islets, which rather resembled those tropical ones you see sometimes on the films. I mean there was no tangle of undergrowth, and the trees were well spaced out though not by any means regularly disposed, as if they had been artificially planted with an eye to a natural effect. The soft springy turf beneath made walking easy, so that altogether our progress was as good as if we had been on a road. Presently I asked the Chief how far off was the capital. "There is no capital," he replied. "Well, where are we making for?" says I. "I haven't the slightest idea," says he. "Where do

you expect to find the people then?" says I. "Nowhere in particular," says he, "and that's where I'm aiming for."

After that asinine remark I held my tongue. We walked on
for an hour or so in the cool shade of the trees, in a silence
broken at rarer and rarer intervals by the calls and songs of the
birds. It had been altogether unbroken for quite a long time
when a new faint sound came stealing into my ears out of the
far distance ahead—the dim, but soon unmistakeable sound
of human singing. I saw that the Chief had heard it too. As we
pushed forward it increased in volume, and presently I could
discern two voices, a man's and a woman's, now separately, now
in unison. A few moments later we sighted the singers, and
stopped instinctively. There they stood in the centre of an open
space, singing to one another in a lovers' embrace, for all the
world like a couple of actors in an opera. They had the same
sort of eyes as the other Ratheans, only a little larger perhaps.
They were also somewhat taller; and from their arms to their
feet hung a sort of loose white leathery arrangement which I
guessed must be their wings. And there, quite unconscious of
us, they sang to one another, pouring out music rapturously,
spontaneously, like birds at sundown. The woman's notes came
low and tremulous now, perturbed with questions; and full and
firm came the answers of the man in a rising tenor. Followed a
burst of harmony, pulsing with passion, the two voices soaring
into some region beyond the range of thought, then sinking
into a tender crooning with the singers cheek to cheek.

My amusement at this scene was interrupted by a touch on
the elbow, and I looked up to see the Chief, with a finger to his
lips, motioning me to follow him. So we skirted the glade in
silence and went our way, while the song gradually hushed in
the distance behind us.

"Were those guys rehearsing for an opera?" I asked when I
was sure we were out of earshot.

"No, no. Making love, of course," answered the Chief.

"O, so these superior folk do condescend to make love?" I remarked.

"In their extreme youth," said the Chief. "But they deem it a shameful weakness in one who is fully adult to yield to such desires, and they abhor our marriages as orgies of selfish sensuality."

Soon afterwards we emerged from the forest, but still there was no sign of road or town. Before us lay what might have been a neglected garden, or wild ground partly reclaimed: I couldn't tell which. There were trees laden with variegated fruits, shrubs blazing with blossoms of every shape and colour, banks of gorgeous flowers perfuming the air, and all the ground between carpeted with a close short grass of the richest green. Paradise itself could not have been more beautiful. Several times I saw people flying high above us, and once I observed a couple perched in the upper branches of a very tall tree—making love I dare say, for they took no notice of us. Then a little further on, we came upon a single gentleman on terra firma. He was standing facing us, right in our path, in a peculiarly rigid attitude, and even when we were close up to him he made no move. He was a full head taller than the Chief, who was himself taller than I. He was evidently quite unaware of our presence: must be both blind and deaf, I thought. A half notion that he was a statue vanished when I saw the movement of his breathing. But that was all the movement that he made. As we walked round him his great eyes didn't as much as flicker. Something about him gave the effect of age. It wasn't his bodily appearance, for he was as fit as an athlete in his prime. Perhaps it was the expression of his face, smooth and unlined though it was. But whatever betrayed it, age was as clearly written upon him as youth upon the pair of lovers in the forest. It was only in a last look as we went on our way that I observed that the wings which lay in folds under and around his arms were brownish and crinkled. When I drew the Chief's attention to this, he said:

"Yes. They cease to fly after a certain age: lose interest in it, I suppose: and their wings shrivel from disuse."

"But what was that beggar up to?" I asked. "Why didn't he notice us?"

"I suppose he was thinking of something more interesting." said the Chief. "They do little else but think after they cease to fly."

Well, on we went, the ground rising steadily all the way, till presently I saw that in front of us it fell away quite suddenly. We were coming, in fact, to the brim of a valley, which in another moment lay smiling beneath our feet. It was just such another paradise as we had passed through, with a river winding down it, and purple hills on the further side. Right in the middle, on the bank of the river, was a collection of huts, with white figures among them, and here there and everywhere the winged men were flying. As we strode down the slope, one of these alighted near us, and gave me an opportunity to study the construction of his wings. They were more like a bat's than a bird's, consisting of a leathery membrane attached to the under side of the hands and arms, along the body and legs, and terminating on the outside of the foot. They were much bigger proportionately than they would be on us, for I noticed that the great height of these people was due to their length of leg, their bodies being actually smaller than ours. The wings were worked by complicated motions of the arms and legs resembling the motions of swimming. When the man alighted and dropped his arms, they fell around him in graceful folds like a cloak. This particular blighter was young, and, having no girl to attend to, gave us a friendly smile; but he showed no further interest in us, flopping down on the grass for a rest without as much as bidding us good morrow. So we went on till we came to the village.

A regular bunch of native huts this was: quite a cinema scene. Beehive shaped things built of wicker and straw, they were grouped in a ring round a central space, in the middle of which was one long low erection consisting of a thatched roof supported by wooden poles several feet apart. Standing at a little distance from all this savagery, on an eminence by itself, was one civilised house of the ordinary Rathean sort. I took it for the residence of the Governor or somebody, but the Chief said it was a hostel for strangers, and led the way in that direction. We passed right through the village without any of the people who were standing or strolling about paying us the slightest attention, and reaching the house walked in through the open door. It was a most inhospitable sort of hostel. There wasn't a stick of furniture in the place. In one room there was a pile of books on the floor, and most of the walls had pictures—and very good pictures I should think— painted on them. Otherwise the house was empty from top to bottom. I felt horribly let down, but the Chief wasn't a bit disturbed. When, a few hours later, we decided to go to bed, he just curled up on the floor without a word and went to sleep, while I lay in my room sweltering and squirming through the baking hours of noon.

This, however, is anticipating. When we had chosen our rooms we turned out to have another look at the village. I had previously noticed that many of the inhabitants were lying about on the grass reading out of large yellow-leaved books, and now I pointed this out to the Chief, remarking that with all their simple habits these people must have printing presses.

"Not at all," he replied. "An author here writes out his books by hand, and people who like them copy them in the same way."

"And what about the paper?" I asked.

"That is hand-made by people who like that craft."

"Their literary output must be pretty small," I observed.

"All the better. How many of the books produced by us in a year are worthy of the time and energy spent in printing them? Besides, these people hope some day to dispense with books."

"How?"

"By being born wise."

"I suppose that even now their babies are more advanced than yours," I observed.

"Of course," said the Chief. "They are born able to read and write. Some of the exceptional ones are even capable of abstract concepts."

I suppose I must have looked incredulous, for the Chief said: "Why do you find that hard to believe? You saw no difficulty in their being born with wings. You know that our babies are born able to talk. You know that your own babies, undeveloped as they are, know how to breathe, see and hear."

"That's different," I said.

"Not a whit. Man, as a poet named Hwas has said, is only an amoeba with acquirements. At one time we were born as specks of protoplasm; and all our limbs and organs, all our powers and faculties are merely accretions to that speck, gained by willing. When acquired they become habits in the race, and are transmitted by heredity and used unconsciously. As soon as that occurs the will and the consciousness are set free to make further acquirements. That is the whole process of evolution. So you see that while your children are tediously learning how to walk and talk, and ours trying to read and write, these are already acquiring whatever knowledge and wisdom can be got from books. At two years of age they are fully grown, mentally and physically. By seven or eight they know as much as the previous generation. In course of time that knowledge will be transmitted at conception and developed in the womb. Then there will be no more need of books."

I began to wish that our ancestors on earth had taken to this evolution stunt. It would be grand to have all your lessons done with before you were born and never be bothered learning anything for yourself.

"Well," I said to the Chief, "what do these johnnies do with the remainder of their lives?—after seven years old I mean. You say they don't do any more sweet- hearting, or read any more books. Do they work?"

"A little," said the Chief.

"That's evident," I said, for really there wasn't a thing in the place that would have been any trouble to make except the books. "Do they go to the theatre?" I continued.

"O no. All the situations that could possibly occur are stale to them."

"Do they go in for politics?"

"Of course not. They settled all political problems ten thousand years ago."

"Then what do they do?"

"They discuss philosophy, think, and pray."

"Good lord!" I cried.

"Praying is not an unpleasant function," said the Chief.

"O," I said, "I didn't mean any disrespect to religion, but all the same—One can't be always praying, can one?"

"One can if one is strong enough."

"Do they pray to the Devil?" I asked.

"O no. They pray to God. They are devoted to his service and believe that they can make him strong enough to overcome the Devil."

"And what reward do they expect for that?" I asked.

"Reward?" says the Chief looking queer at me. "They look for no reward."

"Well, then, what the dickens do they do all this praying for? In our world we believe that if we say our prayers and lead a good life we'll get an eternal reward for it, and if we don't we'll get an eternal punishment."

"You mean that without such hope and fear you would lead wicked lives?"

"Well, why wouldn't we?"

"Then you dislike virtue?"

"No, not exactly. But—well—there must be some incentive, you know."

"Why?"

"Well, after all, we're only human."

"You must be sub-human," said the Chief. "Suppose you were offered the choice of a good and handsome tunic or a bad and ugly one, would you require a bribe or a whipping to induce you to choose the former?"

"Well, no," I said.

"Then why do you need such incentives to help you choose between a fine and an ugly soul? Do you dare call such a mixture of bribery and threats a religion?"

"I'm not answerable to you for my religion," says I, flaring up.

"Quite true," says the Chief. "You are answerable only to yourself, and if you are satisfied, well, you are satisfied, and there's an end of it. But these people never think of reward or punishment. As they prefer life to death, and light to darkness, they prefer good to evil, and God to the Devil."

"This is all very well," I said. "But where do the beggars think they get off? What are they aiming at?"

"Eternal life," said the Chief.

"Aha!" I said. "Just the same as my low-down race. I knew right well they wouldn't be good for nothing."

"You misunderstand," said the Chief. "They don't seek an eternity of bliss for themselves, but an eternity of life, which may very well be the reverse of blissful, for their species. Their hope is that when this world perishes, as some day it must, their life may be able to continue independent of it. To that end each generation strives for greater power of mind and fuller freedom from matter, so that even now many of them become strong enough to dispense with the body before it decays, and to leave it for a spiritual existence of greater or less duration."

Weren't they just beggars for preaching, these heathens? We had reached the village by this time, and the Chief stopped a young woman who was passing and introduced me to her as a stranger from the stars. She was all smiles and affability at once.

The Chief went off, to find some duller company, I suppose, and left us together.

"Tell me about your world, stranger," says the girl immediately.

"O," says I, "we are a lowly-evolved lot of scuts hardly fit to live. We have wretched little eyes set under our foreheads like monkeys, hair on our heads, and big clumsy jaws, but no tails. Most of our habits are too disgusting to mention, we are rotten with money, and our religion is a base mixture of bribery and terror. There now, you have us in a nutshell. Let's talk of something pleasanter."

"You have at least the merit of knowing your deficiencies," said the girl. "There is hope in that."

"O, don't think that's *my* opinion of us," I said. "That's just a list of the pretty things you'd say about us if I was to answer your question. You see I have it all off by heart, for repetition will impress things on the poorest memory."

"The Bulnidians have evidently taken some pains to speak kindly to you," said the girl.

"Here," I said. "Just let's drop these parallaxes and talk sensible. I didn't come a million miles to listen to chaff," says I, "or at least not that kind of chaff, because I'm ready as anyone for a bit of fun with a girl. And between you and me and the wall, miss," I said, "I wouldn't be a bit surprised to find you were game for something more than the local pi-jaw yourself."

"I don't understand you," says the girl.

"O come. Don't you find the life here a bit slow at times?"

"Yes indeed. Sometimes I am tempted in my impatience to discard my body before I have utilised it to the full."

"What do you mean?"

"I have not yet mastered it. Some of its passions still command me instead of obeying. I know therefore that if I were to leave it I should not be strong enough to maintain myself, yet the necessity of dragging it around becomes every day more repellent."

"You shouldn't give way to fancies like that," I said, "a fine handsome girl like you!"

But even a neat little compliment like that couldn't cure her collywobbles. "Look here," I said, "you know, you people don't give yourselves a chance. Talk of the dullness of country life! Why a Meath village is a giddy whirl compared with this place. You haven't a thing to make life worth living."

"We don't need it," replied the girl. 'Life is worth living of itself."

Sounds a bit inconsistent, doesn't it? and I think the girl was rather a humbug, because I saw her later on talking with another girl and the two of them were in fits of laughing. I saw I was going to have a dull time in this paradise, so I asked the Chief when we were turning in how long we were going to stay. He said he didn't know, but a boat might call again in a week or two. Actually we remained ten days, and they were a bore. Of course it was pleasant to watch the people flying around like great swans—till you got tired of it; and we had very nice concerts in the evening sometimes, all song and simple wind instruments, and some of the tunes were quite pretty, though not sufficiently catchy for my taste. But conversation with the people was simply impossible, and I soon gave up trying any. You can guess what it was like from the conversation with the girl which I've just quoted. The men were just as bad. I remember one fellow consulting me about a doubt he had. He said he'd achieved some new and original faculty or other and was anxious to transmit it to future generations. But to yield again, at his time of life, to the pleasures of the senses would be a grave set back to his spiritual advancement. According to his own version he was struggling to overcome his selfish spirituality in the interest of his descendants; but I ask you, Mr. Gallagher— well, I ask you! Anyway, I wasn't any help to him, and after a few more encounters with other such holy Joes I gave myself up to moping around the island and keeping an eye out for a ship.

One of my last days, however, I encountered a damned nice little girl who cheered me up a little. It was quite romantic the way we met. Just as I was abandoning my daily look-out I saw her come flying across the Channel from the opposite island. In a few seconds she was volplaning down towards me. She made a slightly faulty landing, and apparently hurt her foot on something, for she gave a stagger and fell. I was beside her in an instant, but her hurt was nothing. It was enough, however, to make us friends. We sat talking for a while, and I found her really agreeable, almost human, in fact. She told me she was almost three years of age. We larked about very pleasantly, and then she offered to teach me to fly. I said that wouldn't be any use as I hadn't any wings. "Well, don't you wish to evolve them?" says she. "It's too late," I said. "Evolution takes generations." "Yes," says she, "but if you develop the will to fly in yourself, it will develop wings in your great-great-grand-descendants."

Well, I wasn't interested in my descendants, but I thought it would be nice to learn flying with her hand under my chin. And it was. We chose a place where there was a long clear run, with a drop at the end of about a dozen feet on to soft sand. Just before reaching the edge she'd say: "Now will to rise! Will to rise!" and I'd feel her bearing me up with one hand as we went over, she light as a feather, and I with a flop like a sack of potatoes. After an hour of this exercise I was a mass of bruises and as stiff as a poker, but she rubbed me with some sort of ointment which had me as fit as a fiddle against next day, and ready for another lesson. You wouldn't believe it, Mr. Gallagher, but after a few days I really felt I was throwing less and less of my weight on her. She changed her slogan, too, from "Will to rise" to "Now you *are* rising," and I felt that a sort of new power was coming into my brain, and that it was this which sustained me. I began to achieve quite a respectable imitation of a flutter, at last managing to perform the descent with a grace not markedly inferior to that of a barndoor fowl, to the immense delight of my instructress, whose smiles and praises bucked me no end. O, I was having a perfectly gorgeous time. And then I must needs go and put my foot in it. It was this way. We were sitting together resting after a lesson, and while she was enthusing over some project for developing my will power a little further she put her hand (absentmindedly I suppose) on mine. Well, you know, I'd been getting sentimental about her already, and this finished me. Turning, I caught her in my arms, and gave her one hug and a kiss. But lord, you never know where you are with women. At that kiss—and mind you, I'll swear there wasn't a lot in it: just a good smack on the lips like you might give in fun—she went all faint and shaky, so I laid her on the grass in an awful funk.

"O!" she gasped, coming to herself. "You musn't do that again."

"I'm sorry," I said. "I didn't think you'd mind—being so friendly like."

"I didn't mind," she said. "That's the worst of it. I liked it. You stirred something animal in the depths of me. Even my lover has never kissed me like that."

"Your what?"

"My lover. O, you must never do it again. You know I can never breed with you."

Well, that did feed me up. You know we'd been getting on splendidly up to this, and I was beginning to think for the first time, from the way she put things, that there really might be something in this evolution business after all. You see she didn't talk in the high-flown way of the others—with paradiddles and awkward questions that fetched the wrong answers out of you, and so on—but fairly ordinary, like a knowledgeable person on earth, such as you yourself, Mr. Gallagher. And now she must come out with this brutal indelicacy, though I assure you my intentions were as honourable as the babe unicorn. Anyway, what right had a girl that on her own admission had a lover in

the offing (and mind you there was no question what she meant
by that word) to be so squeamish? Well, I dropped her, though
with genuine regret, and next day the steamer showed up.

CHAPTER XXXV

Weird Expectations: with the Important Story of Inac and Lirg

A FEW DAYS AFTER our return to Bulnid I reminded the Chief of his promise to take me to see the Black Lands.

"You shall certainly go if you desire it," replied the Chief. "But I give you fair warning that you will see there such horrors as will haunt your dreams for the remainder of your life."

Remembering how I had been let down over the horrors of Tigers' Island I wasn't impressed by this admonition, so I said I'd risk it.

"Very well," said the Chief. "We'll see what can be done. But first, by way of preparation, I will tell you a story.

"There was a poet in the ancient times who pondered long over the strange division of our race into two fractions so totally opposite in their characteristics. After many years' contemplation there came to him an inspiration which he set down in a poem in the form of an allegory in order that it might be the better understood. He told how when God first made man in opposition to the will of Darkness, he set him in a garden where there were flowers and fruit trees, and commanded him to cultivate it and to eat of its produce whatsoever he pleased. And the Devil, hating the work of God, placed in the garden a heap of gold, telling the Man that by this means he might reap what he had not sown, and gather what he had not scattered, and accumulate until himself power and riches. And the Woman urged the Man to utilise the Devil's gift. But the Man sought counsel of the God that made him. And God said: touch it not; for in the day whereon thou reapest one grain thou has not sown, thou shalt be a slave and the slave of slaves, thou and thy children after thee. So the Man touched not the gold, and commanded his wife to keep away from it. And in the fullness of time, when he had sons and daughters, he commanded them likewise.

"Now the Man and the Woman had one son of the name of Inac, who cared not for toil and often cast longing eyes upon the heap of gold. And one day, approaching nearer than was his wont, he perceived a serpent coiled about it. And the serpent said to him: Inac, why dost thou not take of this gold that I have given thee? And Inac replied: Because the God of our father has told us that in the day whereon we touch it we shall become slaves. But the serpent answered: Not so; for he that hath possession of this gold shall be the master of all mankind. And as Inac doubted what he should do, there came to him saying his wife Lirg, who had been listening hard by, saying: Take thou what is offered thee, and ask no more questions. We shall not better ourselves if we labour for ever. So Inac was persuaded, and laid hold upon the gold.

"Then God stretched forth his hand to protect mankind. And with his finger he stopped the rotation of Rathé, so that one half thereof was turned away from the sun. And Inac and Lirg, seeing the Darkness, loved it: because of the gold they had taken. And going forth into the darkness they built a city and dwelt there, they and their children after them. But the rest of mankind lived in the sunlight, toiling and sharing even as in the beginning.

"Now, sir," said the Chief, "is not the meaning of that poem obvious even to your simple intelligence? It is a suggestive proposition that at some remote period a part of the human race took a step downward from the evolutionary path trodden by the remainder; that that step was the adoption of an economic polity hitherto regarded by the race as iniquitous; and that in consequence of its adoption, when the rotation of the world ceased, the descendants of these people, being tied down to their economic machinery, were unable to leave the darkness for the other side of the globe. It is, even at first sight, a most plausible theory, and the closer it is examined in the light of the facts the more convincing does it become. Of course it was at once attacked by the scientists, who, unable to think except in their own terms, assumed that it was a foregone conclusion which the poet intended to establish in order to overthrow science; and demanded that he should produce the bones of Inac and other proofs of the actuality of the tale. It was in vain for the poet to protest that there had never been such a person as Inac, and that the tale was only a theory to which a study of the facts had led him. They insisted that it must be either true or false. But the curious thing is that while their own story of the lantern-jawed tiger, which they endeavoured to ram down people's throats as true, has been long since discredited, this poem, put forward as an allegory, is now everywhere accepted as being philosophically true."

"Well, assuming that that is so," I said, "what sort of people are their descendants today?"

"That," said the Chief, "I will leave to your imagination. The poet deduced their origin from their circumstances. To deduce their circumstances from their origin should be an easier task. If you cannot accomplish it, you may read it up in my library. Meanwhile I shall ask someone skilled in such matters to devise a means of making the journey."

This was a straight hint to me to be off, which I took. Little did either of us guess what tremendous things were to happen before we spoke to one another again.

CHAPTER XXXVI

The Hatching of Revolution: with some
account of the Land of Nightmares

You haven't forgotten Bhos Kwashog all this time I hope?—
the ex-Vice-President of the Chamber of Commerce whom the
Bulnidians had showered with honours that one day, and thrown
into prison the next. At least that's an exaggeration, because he
wasn't really put in gaol but only presented with a summons to
come up for trial at a certain date. The trial, I found, was to be
held the day after the conversation I have just set down, and,
having nothing else to do, I sauntered down to the Courts to
hear it. I was disappointed to find that it was already practically
over, but I heard the President's summing up, which was more
or less on the following lines:

"Bhos Kwashog, having heard all the evidence on both sides
of the case, and having devoted our most earnest consideration
to its every aspect, my colleagues and I have come to the unanimous conclusion that the charge of acquisitiveness which has
been brought against you is proven. You have used the position of
power and responsibility, in which you were placed by the trust
of your fellow-citizens, as a means to your own aggrandisement,
thereby showing that you consider that what is good enough for
your fellow-citizens is not good enough for you. That opinion
may be perfectly justified for all we know. It may be that you
are intrinsically more valuable than ten other men. It may be
that your services to the tribe deserve twenty times the reward
assigned to those which less gifted citizens can contribute. This
is not the time nor the place to argue such questions. Whether

your opinion be right or wrong, it is certain that the holding of it renders you an enemy of those principles and institutions upon which our civilisation is founded and upon whose stability it depends. We use the word enemy without any implication of censure, for we do not hold any human institution to be sacrosanct from inquiry, criticism, emendation, or condemnation. But, such as they are, mankind has chosen to abide by these institutions, and is resolved to defend their integrity. Therefore, without malice or desire for vengeance, without justification of ourselves or condemnation of you, we now order that within fourteen days from this date you do withdraw yourself, with all your moveable property, out of the territories of the tribe of Bulnid, and beyond the precincts of civilisation, and that you betake yourself to Tigers' Island, there to remain for the rest of your natural life."

Bhos Kwashog, standing in an easy attitude in the dock, heard this harangue with a sneer on his masterful face. When it was over he bowed carelessly and walked out of the court. As I moved out slowly among the crowd I felt a tug at my tunic, and there was Ensulas grinning at my side. "Let's slip off to a wineshop," he whispered. "I've something to say to you."

Over our drinks a few minutes later, he told me that, while I had been away, he had sounded Kwashog about some of my ideas, and that the latter was impressed by them and would like to meet me. "Now," said Ensulas in a low voice, "are you game—supposing we can come to an agreement—are you game for a bold stroke?—something big, with a dash of risk in it, but a good chance of success." I said I was. "Well then, come on," says Ensulas, and finishing our drinks we stepped out into the street.

In a few minutes I was shaking hands with Kwashog himself in his own house, and hearing from his own lips the story of how he had got into trouble.

"I can see no harm whatever in what I did," he told me.

"You know, we merchants have the job of marketing the surplus produce of the tribe against the surplus of other tribes. Well, as a general rule one knows exactly what one can get in return for so much of any commodity. Values do fluctuate in accordance with the ratio of supply and demand, but normally only between fairly narrow margins. I found, however, that in various little ways which I needn't describe it was sometimes possible to create an artificial demand for what I had to offer, or, more rarely, to produce an artificial scarcity. By either or both of these means I have succeeded from time to time in getting more for our goods than they were really worth, and as this profit was attributable entirely to my own cuteness, and not to the tribe, I thought that I was entitled to reap the benefit of it."

"And rightly so," I put in.

"The difficulty," went on Kwashog, "was how to manage it. It's impossible to accumulate stocks of commodities without being found out, and useless too, for what could one do with them? After much thought, I hit on what I imagined was a brilliantly original idea, though I have since learnt from Mr. Ensulas that it is the basis of the whole economic system of the world from which you, Mr. O'Kennedy, have come. I simply converted my profits into bars of gold, which can be stored easily, and exchanged these in turn for the control of real property in some of the more needy parts of the Twilight Zone where the laws are less stringently administered than here. Thus, by the exercise of shrewdness, enterprise, providence and thrift, I had in the course of years laid up for myself reassures which only the narrow laws of our so-called civilisation prevented me from enjoying. Unluckily the officers of the law were put on my track by the stupid bungling of a subordinate, and I now find myself a banished criminal, forced to start life anew in a land where everyone else has the start of me."

"Mr. Kwashog," I said, brimful of sympathy, "you are an ill-used man, and the victim of disgusting injustice. In a properly constituted social system your industry and enterprise and services to the community would be recognised and honoured and meet with their due reward." Then I proceeded to give him as good an account as I could manage of the way we run things on earth. Jove, it was a treat to see him take it in, and more agreeable still to be allowed to talk away without the asinine interruptions I had been accustomed to. Instead of the usual sneers, I saw interest and appreciation lighting up his commonsense countenance, till at last he could contain himself no longer but burst out with an exclamation. "By Procrustes! It's just a perfect system. Perfect! My only doubt is whether it would work. It sounds too good to be practicable."

"Man!" I said. "I tell you it does work."

"Boy," says he. "You've got conviction behind you. Very well. Now let's think out ways and means."

Can you picture me, Mr. Gallagher, sitting at the table with those two high and influential men, plotting how to overturn a whole civilisation and make ourselves masters of a world? Well, strange as it sounds, there I was; but I know my place, and you needn't be afraid I'll be a bit above myself on the head of it. Anyway, we thought out dozens of schemes, and the one we decided on at last was the rouse the people of the Twilight Zone to conquer their more fortunate neighbours. The Twilight Zone is that broad belt of the world where the days are less than six hours long. Naturally it is less fertile than the sunnier parts, and the people are poorer and less civilised. Only half of the Zone is populated; the remoter part, where the days only last two hours or less, like the still more dismal Dusky zone beyond, is desolate of all but the lowest forms of life. The civilisation of the Twilighters, though based on the same principles obtaining elsewhere in Rathé, is less highly developed; and the people, as a result of their perpetual struggle against adverse conditions, are hardy and resolute. Kwashog believed that they were sufficiently discontented with their lot to be ready for revolt if given a lead and supplied with the necessary weapons. Fortunately every tribe kept a small standing army of riflemen—varying from a dozen to perhaps a hundred—to deal with the hordes of apes and sub-men which frequently raided them from the darker wilderness. These would form the nucleus of an army. The question was how to equip the remainder. Firearms were not manufactured in the Twilight Zone. Those they had were imported from more advanced regions, and it would be impossible to ask for a large consignment without exciting suspicion. There remained one other possible source.

Here Kwashog paused and looked at Ensulas. Ensulas stared back, evidently at a loss.

"What about Harpaxe?" said Kwashog in a low voice. Eunsulas went pale and visibly shuddered.

"Harpaxe!" he gasped.

"Yes. Harpaxe. What's the matter with you?"

Ensulas was unable to answer. He could only stare idiotically and gasp again: "Harpaxe!"

"What is this Harpaxe?" I demanded of Kwashog, feeling frightfully thrilled by this display.

"The capital of the Black Lands," he replied. "The region of perpetual night at the back of the world."

"We daren't do it, Kwashog," said Ensulas, almost gibbering. "They say the Devil walks the streets there, and those he looks at die where they stand."

"That's all superstition and nonsense," said Kwashog. "Besides, don't you profess to worship him?"

"Of course I worship him," said Ensulas loudly, as if anxious for someone to overhear him. "How do you know it's nonsense?"

"Because I've been there," said Kwashog.

"You've been there!" Ensulas's great eyes actually bulged with wonderment.

Here I broke in with a demand for information. "Is this black region really so awful?"

"Not at all," said Kwashog. "The finest people in the world live there."

"They are devoted servants of Darkness," put in Ensulas unctuously.

"And they obey the inexorable laws of economics," said Kwashog.

"This capital of theirs, Harpaxe—?" I began.

"The greatest city in the world," Kwashug enthused. "I have seen it with these eyes. I have walked its streets with these feet. There's no city like it. It stands out there in the wilderness, three hundred miles beyond the horizon over which the sun never rises, a vast hive of men, a blazing jewel in the dead of the night."

"The noblest city in the world," chorused Ensulas, and shivered again.

"Pah!" cried Kwashog. "You're just a mass of superstition: all faith and no works. I don't believe in Devil or God, and because I practise the religion which the rest of you profess to be devoted to, I'm treated as a criminal. Pull yourself together, man. We'll meet no Devil. And if we do, won't he be delighted to see you acting up to your convictions at last."

I must say I wasn't altogether pleased to find the devil counted amongst our allies. However, Kwashog's breeziness was reassuring, and the die was no cast. Kwashog's idea was that he and I should go to Harpaxe with gold to buy the guns, while Ensulas and some other merchants, who had also been sounded and would be brought into the plot, were to rouse the Twilight people. I wondered how on earth we were going to cross those three hundred black and icy miles of fear-haunted wilderness, and shuddered at the thought of the difficulties and dangers that must lie in the way, and of that mysterious city at the end of it, whose very name people dreaded to mention; but Kwashog bundled us off before I could ask any questions, saying that he had a lot to do and begging us to keep away from him until all was ready so as not to arouse suspicion. Ensulas knew nothing;

had never believed that the journey was feasible; but pointed out that it must be so since Kwashog had already done it. I had to be content with that, and spent the next few days in the library, reading all there was to read about our mysterious destination. That wasn't much; for apparently few Ratheans had ever penetrated to those regions, and these had done so at such distant intervals that comparison of their narratives was little help. However, the general effect of what I gathered was this.

As a whole the Dark Hemisphere is entirely empty of life. It is also believed to be devoid of water, the oceans having been drawn to the other side of the world by the attraction of the sun. whatever seas or lakes remain are of course in a frozen state. In one narrow strip, however, on the western edge of the hemisphere the continuance of life has been made possible by the presence of a number of warm mineral springs, in the marshes formed by which grows a plant of fungoid character which is capable of giving sustenance to both men and animals. By the side of these marshes human settlements have existed for an unknown period. Whether they date from before or after the cessation of the diurnal motion of the world is a subject of dispute among Rathean authorities. Some maintain that during the transition period there was a great migration of the inhabitants of the Dark Zone towards the sun, and that the population of this favoured spot remained behind by choice. Others say that when the earlier hordes of emigrants had occupied the sunny lands they must have resisted the further encroachments of their kindred, and that these on their repulse would have settled by the springs as the only alternative. A third opinion is that there was no migration at all, and that the inhabitants of this warmer region survived when the rest of the race had gradually perished of the increasing cold. Anyway, whatever their origin, there the settlements are. Before complete darkness set in the people must have had time to adapt themselves to the coming conditions. Their cities had been walled in and roofed over, and a comprehensive mechanical system of lighting and heating installed, the source of power being the currents of air perpetually flowing between the warm and the cold hemispheres. Doubtless they had also walled in their precious marshes on which their existence depended, either for protection against poaching by their neighbour cities, or to reduce to a minimum the necessity of venturing out of their strongholds into the bitter outer atmosphere. And so, as generation succeeded generation, they fortified themselves more and more securely against the darkness that was creeping toward them, so that when the sun peeped for the last time over their horizon it looked upon a race that had no regret for his passing.

But all this is ancient history. When we come to times of which written records still survive we find that one city, Harpaxe, dominates the whole country, while the others have sunk into mere villages dependant on it, and their inhabitants into something little different from serfs. Even this hardly expresses the case. The latest traveller to visit the country described the villages as "no better than collections of huts clustered round the engine or factory in which the people toil for their Harpaxean overlords." How this change came about nobody knows, but the cause of it is plain enough. Today there is but one source of the fungus on which the people subsist, and that is the marsh girded by the walls of Harpaxe. It seems to be certain that the marshes on which the other cities depended were smaller, and one by one they must have dried up or been exhausted. What happened then? In the absence of records we can only use our imaginations. I suppose that the first cities whose supplies ran short would have traded with Harpaxe for the stuff. Quite voluntarily they would have increased their output of manufacturers to pay for it. Then, as city after city came into the market, keen competition must have sprung up between them, one outbidding the other, while the Harpaxeans screwed the last possible ounce out of the lot of them. So much of their fetters was of their own forging that I imagine they must have scarcely noticed the transition from trading to servitude. But of course I may be wrong. Perhaps they may have put up a fight for liberty. Was there a general revolt against the tyrant city? Did besieging armies fling themselves desperately against its walls in a vain endeavour to break through before the cold of the surrounding wilderness overwhelmed them? Who can tell? Anyway, fight or no fight, there stands Harpaxe today, mistress of the plain, paying in meagre doles of fungus for the labour of serfs who are seemingly as patient as tinkers' asses.

Does this plain tale disappoint your appetite for horror, sharpened by the intimations of dreadful mysteries which I have dropped by the way? Well, wait a little and you'll taste enough of it to keep you in nightmares for a lifetime. But for the moment I must go on disappointing you. You will probably be thinking that the Harpaxeans practise frightful cruelties on the Outlanders (as they are called): floggings and shootings, perhaps. But not a bit of it. On the contrary, I learnt that the Harpaxeans are most considerate masters, supplying their serfs with medical attention, keeping their houses and drains in repair, and in general doing for their comfort all those things which they are too ignorant or too busy to do for themselves. They only thing in the nature of cruelty that I could discover is their habit of sterilising every man who has had two children; but even this is done painlessly. What horrified visitors from the Bright Side seems to rather to have been a sort of dispassionate indifference shown by the Harpaxeans to the feelings of the Outlanders. The writer I have already quoted says that they regard the latter as hard worked, but on the whole, comfortably situated people who ought to feel very grateful for having masters to give them sewga (as the fungus is called) in return for their labour. He complains more of their lack of imagination than of their cupidity, and he gives one very striking example of this characteristic. It appears that wilderness surrounding the city is infested by hordes of horrible carnivorous beasts called Showps, which lie in wait for the Outlanders when they go to the city to be fed. As a protection against these brutes the Harpaxeans furnish their serfs with little flappers made of cardboard, which are of course quite useless for the purpose, so that scores of the poor devils are killed and eaten every day. The writer says that when he mentioned this to some Harpaxeans he found that they were quite aware of it and honestly regretted it, but assured him it was inevitable. They appeared, he adds, really to think that to be eaten by a showp is no great inconvenience to an Outlander—or at any rate far less so than to one of themselves.

The same writer says that the differences, both mental and physical between the two races, both sprung as they are from the same stock, are a valuable testimony to the power of circumstantial selection. On the one hand he describes the Harpaxians: tall, comely, urbane, masterful, dispassionate, and entirely devoid of imagination. On the other the Outlanders: short, ungainly, muscular (yet without reserves of stamina) irresponsible, devoid of self-reliance, quarrelsome, peevish, fickle, and utterly lacking in initiative. He also describes them as morose, lethargical, and incapable of enjoyment; but in this he conflicts with the testimony of visitors in earlier times, who record that on their rare holidays the Outlanders used to deck themselves with gaily coloured ribbons and indulge in much discordant singing and jangling of rattles. No doubt, says my authority, these demonstrations were the vestigia of the natural human love of colour and music which succeeding centuries of further degradation have now eliminated.

So much for what I learned of the Dark Country out of books. Now for what I saw for myself.

CHAPTER XXXVII

The Night Journey

OUR ARRANGEMENTS WERE THAT Kwashog was to leave Bulnid openly in his car (which he could do quite safely, being entitled under the law to use his days of grace as he pleased), while, to avert any possible suspicion, I was to travel separately to the neighbouring city of Fastelb, where he would pick me up. Everything worked without a hitch, and in due course we were speeding eastwards along the great white transcontinental roads. We crossed the Middle Zone in eleven days: days that steadily grew shorter and colder as they flew by, so that before long I had to get myself a warmer tunic. It was a curious experience, this rapid passage from glorious midsummer into October, and to mark the change in human habits that accompanied it: houses becoming more solid, costumes evolving towards decency and warmth, and so on. But throughout the zone the Rathean civil-isation remained unaltered in its main features. Everywhere there were the same splendid cities, the same glorious roads, and the same absurd customs. Right up to the frontier, where the days were only six hours long, these things persisted: and there, though it was marked only by a low range of hills, they stopped abruptly. We came down the slope into November weather, to find ourselves in a different world and amongst a new race of men. The roads were macadamised like on earth, and in very poor repair. They wound anyhow through villages and small towns of mean and shabby appearance. We passed only one city of any size. The whole countryside was extremely bleak, and sleet was falling drearily. The people, compared with those we had left, were almost human, having eyes not much larger than cricket balls, hair on the backs of their heads, and mouths and jaws of a decent capacity. They were clothed much like the people you see in films of the Far North. One Rathean characteristic remained to them: their humdrum equality. But, whereas in Bulnid and elsewhere there were no poor, here there were no rich. There was just a general level of frugal comfort. So you see the Ratheans didn't push their equalitarian

principles to their logical conclusion. Equality between man and man they had: but they drew the line between tribe and tribe. Kwashog and I didn't delay, but pushed on deeper into the country, which became more and more desolate and thinly peopled as we proceeded, arriving at last on a snowy night at a house just outside a remote little town where the day was only two hours long: the last town, in fact, in daylight civilisation, beyond which lay the gloomy ape-haunted desert that separated it from the dark zone. This house and the surrounding lands, Kwashog told me, were his property, acquired as part of one of his illegal bargains which fortunately had not yet come to light. After a good sleep and a change Into yet warmer garments we went out to the garage to look at the car in which we were to make the rest of the journey. She was a regular snorter, built long and low, with a torpedo-shaped body, and beautifully sprung. The outside was studded all over with spikes, and fixed to each axle-end was a sharp two-edged steel blade—useful provisions against the possible attacks of showps. Standing in the draughty garage, with the snow driving past, Kwashog explained her points. The cosily upholstered interior was electrically Warmed and there was a snooty arrangement for passing the incoming air over heated wires. Alongside the speedometer was a compass, on which we must rely to find our way through the trackless wilderness.

"No need to bother about keeping the engine cool," remarked Kwashog. "The trouble is the other way round. Petrol would freeze out there, you know, and we couldn't carry enough of it either; so what do you think we're driving her with?"

I had no suggestion to make.

"What about hydrogen?" said Kwashog. "Compressed hydrogen, used on the same principle as steam in a steam engine."

He indicated a pipe which passed from the back of the car to a gasometer outside, remarking that the gas had been manufacturing while we slept, and that it was time to fill up. While the apparatus was working we occupied ourselves in transferring to the car the bars of gold we had brought with us. This was soon done, and when the gas tank was full we were ready to start.

I felt a return of the old thrills which the mysterious hints about the Dark Zone had always set going in me as we turned the nose of the car towards the gloomy eastern horizon. The snow had stopped, and the sun was up, struggling through banks of cloud, to shed a light which was about as strong as that of a late winter afternoon on earth, though it was midday in these god-forsaken latitudes. Before us lay miles and miles Of almost level plain, with one low melancholy-looking hill standing to one side of our course. Nothing else was to be seen except the grey sky deepening into blackness in the distance. At a steady pace we advanced resolutely into the unknown. Further and further behind us fell the sun, but with him also we left the clouds, so that when at last we burst with blazing headlights into the realm of night, we saw the rare stars shining in the sky with diamond brilliance. I thought to myself that maybe one of them was our own old earth, and could fancy some fellow lounging at a door in Stoneybatter looking up at this very star I was on, and wondering could it be true that they are inhabited. Then, as we drove ahead, more slowly now, a moon rose hard and clear to our right, and showed us a line of rocky mountains straight in our path. Kwashog wasn't a bit disconcerted, only altering our course by a hairsbreadth. We would go right through, he said, by a series of tunnels and cuttings, evidently the remains of a prehistoric railway, which he had discovered on his previous trip almost by accident after failing in an attempt to get round the chain at its southern end. The thought of negotiating such a passage rather chilled me, but of course it was useless to object. And it was just at this moment that the Smergs made their appearance.

They first became visible as a cloud of what might have been very large flies whirring in the glare of our headlights: but in an instant we were in the midst of them, and could hear their bodies plopping softly against our windows as if they were being pelted with overripe fruit. Disgusting looking creatures they were, with round flat bodies about the size of a farthing, and hundreds of legs. They were a bleached white in colour, and I saw no sign of wings, but that may have been because they moved so fast.

"Smergs," said Kwashog, without taking his eye from the ground ahead. "One of the plagues of the Outlanders. Look out, by the way. They can squeeze through the narrowest crack, and they're dangerous companions."

Sure enough two of them had already insinuated themselves between the door and the jamb, and I was only just in time to swot them with my glove. Then another showed its ugly snout at the edge of the window on Kwashog's side, and when I'd finished him I had to turn and deal with another on my own. So I was kept busy swiping around from right to left and from floor to ceiling to the accompaniment of encouraging remarks from Kwashog in this tune: "When these brutes get a footing in a village—look, down there in the corner: that's the stuff!—when they get their grip on a village—near the handle: quick!— they clear the inhabitants right out. Right out, you know. There's another. Lucky I had you with me or I was a goner. They didn't bother me last time." "Do they sting?" I asked, still swotting. "Do they kiss you?" said Kwashog ironically. "Quick! there's another near your foot. They get into your mouth and burrow down into your lungs and breed there. Then their progeny proceed to eat you alive."

For half an hour the work of massacre continued. Then we got clear of the swarm. By that time we had reached the entrance of the passage through the mountain, which I saw at once must be what Kwashog had suggested. It was just like the old abandoned railway round Bray Head, a succession of deep cuttings through the naked rock alternating with tunnels, and sometimes a mere shelf winding round the face of a cliff, with a sheer drop on one side into black abysses below. Here of course we had to go dead slow, and my heart was in my mouth the whole time, for Kwashog *would* steer as close to the edge as possible so as to avoid snapping off our axle-knives against the wall of rock. I trembled to think of what would happen if we found our progress barred by some fallen boulder. There would be nothing for it but to feel our way backwards, for the shelf was too narrow for turning. And what if the disturbance of our passing had brought down a landslide behind us? What, above all, if Kwashog lost his nerve under the strain continuously put on it? Four times we crept at a snail's pace past gaps where the edge of the track had crumbled away. Those were awful moments. On the last occasion I don't believe we had an inch to spare, and we had to sacrifice our sword tips to get even that. Once I really thought we were gone, and when the long moment of suspense was over I found my fingers clenched deep into the cushions of my seat, and my body running with sweat. After such an experience the plunge into a tunnel was positively a relief. So on and on we went, escaping I don't know how many disasters through miracles of adroitness on Kwashog's part, and at last found ourselves descending a broad safe incline to another plain.

I wish I could give you some idea of the desolate scene that now met our eyes. But it's hopeless. There's nothing on earth that has the smallest resemblance to it. Try and imagine a countryside absolutely bare of vegetation, without a sign of roads or rivers or houses, or anything to break the monotony but bare hillocks and jagged rocks. Imagine this under the light of a moon much larger than ours, shining out of a black sky almost empty of stars. Imagine every shadow black as ebony, and the whole ground so uneven as to be chequered with such shadows. That conveys something like the picture. Into that desert we now plunged. The going was so rough that in spite of our excellent springs we were most infernally jolted, and more than once I feared for our axles. But they went through it all unharmed. We skirted a lake whose waters had been frozen iron-hard for thousands of years. We passed the ruins of a city so long abandoned that its walls and houses had become mere shapeless mounds of dust. We lost our way for a time in the hopeless maze of a petrified forest. Then Kwashog found some landmark he recognised, and on we went again, chug—chug—chug through wild weird scenery of which I can remember nothing now but moonlight and inky shadows. I found it hard to believe that my companion really knew where we were going. To think that our safety depended on that little flickering needle! that if it failed us we might be left to wander for ever in this nightmarish country as for a dreadful hour I had feared we were doomed to wander in the forest. But Kwashog's face was serene and confident, and having reassured myself by looking at it I decided to shut my eyes to the disquieting sights outside. I actually slept for a bit, but was wakened presently by a jog from his elbow to hear him say: "No mistaking that landmark. We're right on the track."

Blinking wearily through the front glass of the car I nearly fell back with fright, for standing straight in our path was the figure of a giant, one of Jack-and-the- Beanstalk's own, an immense hulking brute about sixty feet high. Of course it was only a statue, but in the moonlight it looked horribly real. Kwashog laughed at my panic, and said: "Time for a rest now." Then running the car close up to the giant's enormous ankle, he stopped the engine, and began rearranging the seat in a way to provide beds for the two of us. In a very short time we were both fast asleep.

We awoke after a while, quite unrefreshed and with vile headaches owing to the close atmosphere of the car. We pushed on at once, jolting our way through the same dreary monotony of landscape hour after hour until I sank back in a sickly lethargy and looked from the windows no more. I don't know how long I had lain like that when I was again roused by the voice of Kwashog, now sharp with excitement:

"Quick, man! Look! The Showps!"

I looked. This time I really did cry out, and with reason. For loping out of the darkness came a pack of the most loathsome beasts I have ever seen in the most dreadful of nightmares. Their long slug-shaped bodies were naked, and of a dull dead white colour. I could imagine them cold and clammy to the touch. They had no recognisable heads, but each sinuous tapering neck terminated in a lipless sucker-like mouth, above which grew a waving horn like a snail's with a single eye at the end of it. Their fore-legs were considerably longer than their hind-legs, and they had enormous curved talons to their feet. They ran and leaped with most astonishing agility around the car, making horrid smacking noises with their slimy mouths and shooting their eye-horns in and out as if measuring the distance for a spring. Our lights seemed to bother them, for they kept out of their ray as much as possible, and when we maneuvered so as to cast it on them, they drew in their horns sharply just as a snail does when you touch it. Ghastly it was to see them there dodging about as they tried to make up their minds to attack. It was our speed that baulked them. Time and again I'd see one pause and gather himself together, then relax and look foolish, and then come racing after us for another attempt. If we could have kept up our pace we could have got clear away from the pack without mishap. But, as luck would have it, just then we struck some rising ground, and with a groan I heard Kwashog change gear. A second later one of the brutes sprang. I couldn't see exactly what happened, since it was on Kwashog's side, but. one of our knives must have got him, for he gave a scream of pain, and a jet of blood spattered on the windows. Kwashog at once swung the car sideways to the slope so as to put on speed, with the result that a second showp, which had already sprung, fell short and impaled itself on the broken blade of the rear wheel on my side of the car. There it stuck, letting out the most appalling screeches, while Kwashog, who had succeeded in his maneuver, changed again into high gear. The engine roared and shook like a live thing as the car shot forward; but almost at once we felt a check, and after a succession of h bumps we came to a standstill. Redoubled shrieks from the wounded showp told us what had happened. The brute had got caught in our wheel, and every pulse of the engine jammed him there more and more inextricably.

The instant we stopped another showp leaped on to our running board and began clawing furiously at the window within a few inches of my face. We were soon entirely surrounded by the detestable creatures, which seethed and roared about us like waves against a jagged rock. First there'd be a surge forward, then leaps and yells as those in front tasted our spikes, then a frantic attempt by these to back away, frustrated by the pressure of the mass behind, then a second onward surge, with the unfortunate vanguard struggling vainly against it, and more screeches as the spikes repeated their work. As the assault swayed in this manner, one of the brutes leaped upon the bonnet of the car, danced madly for a second on its bristling points, then hurled itself with a yell among the ravening pack below. Another succeeded in scrambling up to the roof, which was unprotected, and we heard it clawing with devastating effect above our heads. I looked in despair at Kwashog, who imperturbably applied the reverse gear. The car at once gave a violent jerk, and began to crunch its way slowly backwards through the clamorous horde, while shrieks of wrath and agony rose from the tortured flesh under our rear wheel. Back we went, a dozen yards or more, rocking and swaying under the furious assault of the showp on the roof and the other brute which still raged and tore at the window like a fiend out of hell. Every instant I expected the glass to cave in, and to feel that filthy mouth at my throat. As it was, one vicious blow cracked it from top to bottom. Breathless I awaited a second stroke. Then, all of a sudden I was knocked over by Kwashog's arm. A frightful crash followed, deafening and almost stunning me. The car lurched violently, flinging me from my seat and nearly cracking my skull against the board in front of me. I lay utterly helpless, too dazed even to be frightened. Then I heard the engine again, and we were running free, while I shuddered in the grip of the most intense cold that I have ever experienced. In another moment I had lost my senses.

When I came to I found myself stretched flat on the seat, with a delicious flavour of brandy in my mouth. Kwashog was looking down anxiously into my face.

"Feeling better, old chap?" he asked.

I nodded, and allowed myself to lie in dreamy silence for a while. But presently I was demanding what had happened.

"It was touch and go," Kwashog explained. "You saw the showp at the window? In another second it would have stove the glass in, and then it would have been all over with us. There was nothing to do but shoot. Of course there was the risk of breaking all the glass in the car, but I had to chance that. As you see, it's all cracked: but it held: that patent glass is wonderful stuff. Well, I fired, and got the brute so neatly that he fell into the jaws of his comrades. I think that's what saved us—no showp can resist fresh meat. Meanwhile the cold air came spurting through the hole in the window like a stream of needles out of a hose. However, I managed to bung it up with my glove. Then I let the car rip—I'd got her crosswise to the slope just before the jam—and away we went with a leap that flung off that fellow on the roof like a stone from a sling. So here we are. I had to go hell for leather for a couple of miles before I dared stop to attend to you. The worst if it is that we've been driven right out of our course, but if you're well enough to spare me the seat we'll soon set that right."

He'd the devil of a nerve, had Kwashog. There he was, at the end of an experience like that, as cool an oyster, and when he had his hand on the wheel again it was as steady as if we were just starting on a joy ride. As for me, I lay there, sick and shaken, with a racking headache and a bump the size of an apple under my eye, still shuddering over the thought of what we had escaped, and weakly wondering how many more of such adventures might be in store for us. When at last I roused myself to an interest in what we were doing, I saw that we were still climbing uphill, labouring heavily over very rough ground towards a crest a dozen miles away which cut the sky with a straight sharp line. As we neared the top, Kwashog turned to me with a look of exultation.

"Up there," he said, pointing, "you'll see something worth seeing."

And so we did. When we reached the crest, Kwashog stopped the engine, and in the ensuing silence we looked down upon an immense moonlit plain. Scattered all over its expanse was a large number of tall chimneys which belched out columns of smoke and flame high into the air. Each chimney seemed to spring from the middle of a low dark structure with a curving roof which reflected the moonlight and from which other smaller chimneys protruded. These things were in the foreground, and I guessed them at once to be the factories and dwellings of the Outlanders. Beyond, on the far edge of the plain, the domes and towers of Harpaxe itself stood black against the sky and the rising of the second moon.

CHAPTER XXXVIII

The Outsiders

THERE IT STOOD, THE Devil's own capital, and by jove it looked it. There was something about it— I don't know what—that affected me even more unpleasantly than the first view of the showps. At once a horrible thought occurred to me. What if its interior were like that of the Devil's temples which I had seen in Bulnid? If so—if such a climax were to come at the end of the ghastly experiences I had already been through—I should go stark mad. Then I remembered Kwashog's first description of the place: "a blazing jewel in the heart of the night," and felt reassured.

For a short while we remained still, gazing in awe at the spectacle before us. Then the car began to glide down the hillside, heading for the nearest of what I shall call for convenience the villages. From this point our progress was smooth and rapid, the ground having apparently been artificially levelled, though there was no sign of anything like a road. The rising of the second moon, which was larger and brighter than the first, was also a help to us. As we drew near to the village I took note of its appearance more exactly. I saw a circular stone wall enclosing a space perhaps half a mile in diameter, with a dome-shaped roof, from which rose the big chimney amid a forest of smaller shafts. I saw two doors in the wall situated widely apart. As we approached one of them Kwashog sounded the horn, whereupon the door flew open, and closed again behind us when we had passed through. For a moment we found ourselves shut up in a narrow dark passage; but almost immediately another

door in front opened, and we drove slowly into a quaint looking street lit up by rows of standard electric lamps. Kwashoy at
once stopped the car, and heaved a sigh of relief. "At last!" he
said. "Now we can stretch our legs and get a breath of air," and
with that he threw open the door, and we stepped out on to
the roadway. The air, enclosed as it was, seemed like mountain
breezes after the atmosphere of the car. And what a relief it was
to loosen up our cramped and battered limbs!

For a while we were too busy yawning and stretching to
pay any attention to our surroundings, but soon curiosity had
me looking around. The street was quite empty of people, and
silent. The whole town was silent save for a muffled thump-
thump-thump like distant machinery. But it was evidently not
asleep, for there were lights in nearly all the windows of the
houses. I was immediately struck by the extreme smallness of
these. Though they were all two-storeyed, they were not more
than twelve or fifteen feet high, and yet the doors and windows,
though small, were not small in proportion.

"Are these people dwarfs?" I asked of Kwashog.

He grinned. "Well, yes. I suppose you might call them
dwarfed," he said, and, lifting the bonnet of the car, began
tinkering with her engine.

Just then I heard the sound of footsteps, and in a moment
there came pouring out of a side street ahead of us a crowd
of the queerest and most grotesque looking people you could
imagine. Not one of them was over four feet high, and they
had an oddly misshapen appearance. Their bodies and heads
seemed to be too large, and their legs too small. Their legs in
fact were altogether wrong: too thick and too short, and hopelessly clumsy in movement. And their arms reached nearly to
the ground. As to their other features, their eyes, which were
about the size of golf balls, protruded so as to give them an
expression of vacuous stupidity; they had practically no noses:
only a pair of triangular holes like you see in a skull; while their

skins were of a dull pasty complexion and their faces broad and flat. They were all dressed alike in plain grey tunics and trousers. My Rathean authority was right in describing them as lethargic. Though mingling in a crowd evidently with a common purpose, they walked in silence. Not only that, but they never even glanced in our direction. It seemed incredible. Here was a motor car of a unique pattern, with swords on its wheels, splashed all over with mud and blood, and with a pair of, to them, absolutely unique beings standing beside it; yet it excited not a spark of curiosity in their minds. They passed on up the street and vanished from our sight.

Kwashog, emerging just then from the bonnet, was amused at my bewilderment. "What did you expect them to do?" he asked. "Lick your boots?"

"Not at all," I answered. "They might have shown some sort of interest though."

"Why? They've nothing to gain by learning anything."

He seated himself easily on the running board and began to lecture me.

"Life in these regions," he said "is based on common sense and economic facts, not on the romantic theories that flourish in the sunshine. Did you notice those people's legs? Not pretty, are they? Well, they weren't born like that. They get them shortened artificially by removing the shin bones in infancy."

"Whatever for?" I asked in astonishment.

"So as to adapt themselves to the size of their houses."

"I beg your pardon?" I said.

"To adapt themselves to the size of their houses," he repeated.

"I don't understand," I said.

"It's simple enough," said Kwashog. "Their houses are too small for them, so they cut themselves down to suit them."

"But why don't they build bigger houses?" I cried.

"Can't be done economically," said Kwashog coolly. "There aren't enough bricks and mortar to go round."

It was a good and complete answer, but somehow it didn't satisfy me. I had often been impressed by the argument that one must cut one's coat according to one's cloth, but it seemed a bit thick to expect people to cut their bodies according to their coats. I inquired whether the Outlanders submitted their children voluntarily to the operation, or whether it was necessary to compel them to do so.

"Not at all," said Kwashog. "No self-respecting Outland mother would dream of letting her child keep its tibias after six weeks old. You mustn't imagine that this operation is a piece of Harpaxean tyranny inflicted on helpless slaves. It was instituted at the request—the demand rather—of the Outlanders themselves. The Harpaxeans had been accustomed for generations to undergo all sorts of mutilations for the sake of appearance or fashion, and the Outlanders insisted, with some show of justice, that they should not be denied in their necessity a relief which Harpaxeans enjoyed as a luxury. The Outlandish women were particularly violent in their clamour, protesting on that it was a cruel injustice to expect them to go bearing children who were doomed to grow too big for the houses in which they were to dwell. The Harpaxeans at last gave way, and now the operation is performed free of charge on every Outland baby as soon as it is strong enough to bear it. This is regarded as the greatest step ever taken for the regeneration and advancement of the Outlandish race."

Kwashog went on to tell me that this was not the only mutilation practised by this deluded people. In obedience to the law of mass production all boots for adult Outlanders were made the same size and shape, and the feet of the people were trimmed to suit them. For the same reason the hips of the women were compressed so as to make them fit the standard breeches worn by both sexes. It was also customary to eradicate the hair and trim the nose and ears to minimise the danger of getting caught in the machinery. Altogether the Outlanders had shown a most reasonable spirit of compromise in grappling with the problems of a highly industrialised civilisation, and a praiseworthy readiness to adapt themselves to the conditions of the age which had produced them.

I thought it would be amusing to take a stroll amongst these extraordinary people before proceeding on our journey. Kwashog was quite agreeable; so, leaving the car where it was, we set off. There was little to see in the town, one street being exactly the same as another, and very few people being abroad. But as we walked the noise I have already described grew steadily louder, so I knew that we were approaching the factory which was the centre of the place. At last at the end of a street we came upon a large metal door in a wall which cut right across it. Kwashog pushed this open, letting out an ear-splitting clangour, and revealing an astonishing view to our gaze. In the white glare of a number of arc lamps I saw an immense and complicated maze of machinery such as I cannot possibly describe, a regular warren of working pistons, whirring wheels, racing belts, and spirting valves, that made the eyes ache with their unceasing motion. Each section of the mass seemed to be in charge of one or more of the truncated specimens of humanity I have depicted, who watched it with a strained attention which our presence did not for a moment distract. Kwashog and I made a circuit of the bobbing and gyrating puzzle of ironwork. At one point a number of the serfs were feeding flat pieces of metal into a slot. At another, on the opposite side of the room, there poured forth a stream of cutlery sets, complete with velvet-lined canteen, into which they had been transformed in the interim. It was a case of mass production with a vengeance. I couldn't help wondering how a single city could ever provide a market for such a vast output; but Kwashog explained that the Harpaxeans made it a point of honour to scrap their belongings and get new ones as often as possible, the richer classes going so far as to discard any article which had been used once. Thus production was stimulated and constant employment was assured to the Outlanders.

As I watched one of these silent serfs intently bent over his task, a horrible thing happened. Opening his mouth as if to yawn, he slowly stuck out a thin white tongue about six inches long, waved it about in the air for a moment, and then pushed it home again with his fingers. Maybe that doesn't sound very dreadful as I tell it, but it fairly gave me the creeps to see it. That snakish tongue, thin as a pencil and a nasty dead white in colour, was so utterly different from anything one would expect to issue from a human mouth. A little later another of the creatures repeated the performance; and in the next few minutes I saw half a dozen more do the same, and all, you know, in the most matter-of-fact way, and with perfect solemnity. It was the most disgusting sight. Then one fellow quite close to me did it, and you can imagine the start I gave when I saw that what I had taken for a tongue was no part of the man at all, but a live worm, an obscene-looking vermin which apparently lived in his mouth. Sickened, I gripped Kwashog by the arm. "Let's get out of this, quick," I said. "They've got some frightful disease." But Kwashog only laughed. That's not a disease," he said. "It's a prophylactic."

"What do you mean?" I asked.

"Those worms," said Kwashog, "are called Warderworms. They keep them in their stomachs as a protection against smergs. In fact they breed them there. The egg of the creature is put into their stomachs in infancy, and it hatches out there and grows up with them, so to speak. Then if any smergs come along it eats them up.

I gave an ejaculation of disgust.

"What a squeamish crank you are," said Kwashog. "This is one of the great scientific discoveries of the age."

"That doesn't make it seem any pleasanter to me," I said. "Doesn't the worm itself do any harm to its hosts?"

"Science is divided on that question," said Kwashog.

"But in any case, for the Outlanders it's a choice of two evils, and they choose the lesser."

At this moment a terrific bang like the blow of a hammer on a gong rang through the air. Instantly the machinery came to a stop, and with a precisely similar automaticness the serfs ceased their attentions and walked out of the factory. In less than a minute the whole place was empty but for Kwashog and myself. Smart, wasn't it? We followed at once, and emerging by a different door from that by which we had entered, came upon a bunch of the Outlanders in the street outside, who were silently reading a large white poster pasted on a wall. Kwashog and I had no difficulty in reading it over their heads. It ran, as well as I can remember, as follows:

THE TYRANNY OF THE LONG NECK

COMRADES!

What is the principal cause of the present downtrodden condition of the Outlanders?

The Answer Is

OUR NECKS

All the most advanced thinkers of the age have declared that without a shorter neck further economic progress for the people is impossible.

A MEETING

To support the Policy of

SHORTENING THE NECK

Will be held today in Central Square immediately after closing time.

Prominent Speakers will Speak.

NECK OR NOTHING!!

This was too good a thing to miss, so off the two of us went in the wake of the silently waddling Outlanders. We soon reached the Square, which was densely packed with people. Again no notice was taken of us by these misshapen beings, who kept their dull eyes on the platform, where four men were sitting. Three of them were Outlanders, but the fourth was a tall handsome chap who might have stepped out of our world, with ordinary human eyes and hair like us. I guessed at once that he must be a Harpaxean. A fifth man, also an Outlander, stood at the front of the platform, orating hard, in a debased version of the Rathean tongue which I had some difficulty in understanding.

"Our demand," he was saying "is based on the simplest and purest common sense, and I find it hard to understand how anybody who is not a congenital idiot or utterly blinded by prejudice can fail to see the justice of it. Our bodies are too large to be properly nourished by the miserable dole of sewga we receive in return for our toil. There is no getting away from that hard fact. Is it not then a very obvious remedy to reduce the size of our bodies? Here we have, between our heads and our shoulders, an entirely superfluous mass of bone and muscle which raises our heads to an inconvenient height above the ground, and intercepts the nourishment that ought to go to our brains and develop our intellects. I defy anyone to tell me a single use that that mass of tissue can be put to. The Harpaxeans themselves don't value it. If they did they'd grow theirs longer, because, if three inches of neck is a good thing, thirty inches must be ten times as good. But has anybody listening to me now ever seen a Harpaxean with a neck that length?"

The whole Outlandish audience answered with perfect seriousness: "No."

"Of course not," said the orator. "Why then do they foist these useless excrescences on us? Is it because they love us? Not likely. Why then? I'll tell you, my friends. They insist on us keeping our necks so that they may more easily keep their yoke on us. Away with them then, I say. Off with the neck, and we can no longer be compelled to bow the neck in servitude."

The speaker paused a moment for breath, and then resumed.

"I have proved, my friends, that the neck is a useless append-age. But it is more than that. It is a dangerous encumbrance. Who that has ever been attacked by showps has not wished that there had been less of him to act as a target for their savage teeth and claws? Ah! how many a life might have been saved if the victim had had no neck to be gripped by their rapacious fangs. Such horrible conditions must not, shall not be allowed to continue as an everlasting blot on our so-called civilisation. Science has provided the remedy—a simple commonsense remedy, whose application has been too long delayed in deference to hypocritical objections based on old-fashioned and out-worn doctrines of physical symmetry. What do such academic theories matter to us? What do we care about the symmetry of bodies too large to be properly nourished or effectively defended? To us the neck is a grim reality, an intol-erable burden under which we are crushed with ever increasing severity to the ground. It is a burden of which we must rid our-selves or perish, and all abstract questions must give way to that. I appeal to you therefore, men and women of the Outlands; to you, the toiling millions on whose labours other people batten and grow fat; to yield to this opposition no longer, but to arise in your might and, with no uncertain voice, lay claims to your rights."

Murmurs of approval from the crowd marked the conclusion of the speech. A second speaker then came forward: a woman, as I learned from her first few words, though there was nothing about her dress or appearance to tell me so. There was, in fact, hardly any distinction between the sexes in this extraordinary race. Speaking in a strained, nervous voice, the lady said that it was an outrageous tyranny that the latest scientific discoveries, which were freely accessible to the rich, should be denied to the poor. She strongly suspected that their opponents in this matter were secretly in favour of abolishing limb control altogether and restoring the old regime of long legs and bulging hips.

"It was not so very long ago," she continued "that a prominent Harpaxean woman underwent a far more radical treatment than that which we propose, merely in order to improve her appearance. I am told that before the operation she was a sight. She had a hooked nose, ears that stuck out, a long scraggy neck, thin calves, thick ankles, and fat buttocks. Well, the doctors got to work on her. They straightened her nose, flattened out her ears, shortened and unscragged her neck, fined down her ankles, transferred her buttocks to her calves, and in short made such a good job of her that the anaesthetist fell in love with her before she left the table. Now I ask you, is it not a crying shame that the same treatment should not be made available for us if we desire it?

"Remember that we do not ask that this operation should be made compulsory: not at any rate, until, as in the case of tibiectomy, it has proved its value by results. Though we on this platform hold the same opinions on this subject as those of all rational men and women, we have no intention of doing violence to the moral convictions of those who differ from us. We therefore do not propose compulsion. The one and only thing we demand is simply that doctors should be free to give the necessary surgical relief to Outlanders which is already available for the Harpaxeans."

The Chairman of the meeting now stood up and said it was his pleasant duty to introduce to the audience one whose name was already familiar to them as that of a protagonist of limb-control and a staunch friend of the Outlanders—the celebrated Harpaxean scientist, Professor Hoaxeye. He would say no more, but called upon Professor Hoaxeye to come forward. The gentleman I have already described at once strutted to the front of the platform. I noticed that his neck was a very short one, but this I think was natural, and not due to surgical interference. Clearing his throat he said that, being a scientist, he would rely entirely on facts and figures, not on legends and dogmas, to prove his case. What were the facts?

"I have here," he said, "a page from the book of one of those clinics to which those Outlanders go for treatment who have been wounded in conflict with showps. Let me read you a few typical entries:

> Mr. As, age 44 years: 12 wounds; 5 in the neck.
> Mrs. B., age 38 years: 9 wounds; 5 in the neck.
> Mr. C., age 24 years: 7 wounds; 4 in the neck.
> Miss D., age 22 years: 6 wounds; 3 in the neck.

"Adding up these figures you will see that out of a total of thirty-four wounds inflicted, seventeen were in the neck; from which I have calculated that if the neck were abolished the number of wounds which the toiling millions would have to endure would be reduced by exactly fifty per cent. But a still more significant fact is brought out by the same figures. Of all those thirty-four wounds, not a single one was found upon the leg. And why? For the simple reason that that part of the anatomy had been eradicated.

"Now, ladies and gentlemen," went on the Professor triumphantly, "in the face of those two facts, what possible case can be made for the retention of the neck? There exist, as far as I am aware, two kinds of argument against limb-control. The first is that it will gradually lead to a serious reduction in the size and strength of the race. The second is that man has no right to alter the length or number of the limbs assigned to him by Nature. With that type of argument an industrial civilisation need hardly feel itself called upon to contend; but in regard to the other I will say a few words. Within wide limits, a decrease in the number of limbs or organs is always compensated for by increased strength in the remainder. The choice therefore is between quantity of limbs and quality. Who can hesitate?

"There is another and more serious aspect of the situation. One of the most salient facts of the age is the general falling off of the physique of the human race. This has been very marked in the upper classes, but much less so in the lower. Its result, though certainly not so serious as writers like Bilge and others seem to think, is certainly dysgenic. The better elements in the population are deteriorating more rapidly than—er—hm!"

Here the speaker reddened and paused, and began fumbling at his notes in some confusion. I think he must have wandered by mistake into a speech intended for some other audience. Presently, however, he found his place, and resumed, though not quite so confidently as before.

"As I was saying, the arguments which have been advanced against limb-control are beneath contempt. The people who now heap obloquy upon this latest development are in exactly the same tradition with those whose antiquated and narrow-minded prejudices in favour of legginess roused them to denounce that great and beneficent reform which made it possible for an Outlander to stand upright in his own home and not bang his head against the lintel whenever he passed through a door. The same forces have opposed every other step which modern science has devised for the advancement and uplifting of the Outlanders. Happily their power to obstruct has not been equal to their will. Their tactics have failed before and will fail again. Old prejudices and superstitions die hard, but no man living can put back the hands of the clock nor stop the onward march of enlightenment. Three inches of bone and a few lumps of muscle: these alone bar the way to progress and prosperity. Away with them!"

When the fellow sat down I couldn't contain myself another instant. I had to speak or burst. So up I gets, and, "Well," says I, "that's my neck of a speech!" Boys-o-boys, you should have seen the commotion that followed. The Chairman sprang to his feet and began waving his arms and shouting "Put that man out!" Some of the crowd turned to obey him, but didn't seem to like the job, we being a pair of giants to them. Kwashog had a hold of me by the arm and was begging me to hold my tongue, but there was no silencing me. "You pack of tame lick-spittles," I cried. "Why can't you keep your manhood and use it to overthrow your tyrants?" Gosh, I was so mad I couldn't find words for what I had to say, and there was Kwashog hauling me off by the arm and saying "shut up you fool," and the crowd trying to make up its mind to go for me, and the Chairman fairly dancing with excitement on the platform. It was a great moment altogether, but too good to last. Kwashog, who had the strength of a lion-tamer, got me away by main force; the crowd was too lethargical to follow us up; and so we soon found ourselves back in the car and sailing off for Harpaxe. By jove, Kwashog was wild with me.

CHAPTER XXXIX

Harpaxe

ON WE DROVE ACROSS the moonlit plain, until presently, with feelings of dismal foreboding, I saw the huge walls of Harpaxe looming over us and sat waiting in their shadow while its ponderous iron gates rolled slowly open. Then, creeping past the loopholed and embrasured towers that flanked them, we halted in just such another dark passage as had received us in the Outland village while the outer gates were closed and the inner ones opened. What a picture then burst on our sight. I don't know how to describe it, there were so many things that hit the eye all at once. I saw a broad and brilliantly lighted street, thronged with traffic and swarming with people. The traffic was all private motors—thousand pounders every one—hurrying this way and that and hooting like hell. And the shop-fronts were big affairs of plate-glass and window displays. And there was a blare of jazz music that pervaded the atmosphere, and, as I presently discovered, went on unceasingly. As for the people, you can imagine how glad I was to see that like Professor Hoaxeye they closely resembled ourselves, with plain human eyes and hair growing on their heads. Indeed I was so delighted that I was ready to rush out and catch some of them by the hand; but before I had time to do anything so silly the impulse was frozen up. I can't say what it was exactly that repelled me. I just seemed to know instinctively that it wouldn't do. Perhaps it was the expression of their eyes, in which there was a placid coldness that held me off like an iron bar. Never in all my life had I seen eyes so empty of human sympathy, or faces so hard and unfriendly. Man and woman and boy and girl I watched them streaming by (Kwashog had pulled up to unscrew the sword-blades from our wheels) and though many were chattering and many laughing there wasn't a soul amongst them you could have borrowed a match off or asked the time of day; there wasn't a laughing face among them that knew how to smile: and when one stopped laughing, the laugh dropped off like a mask leaving no expression at I saw too that I was mistaken about all behind it. their having hair. Their heads were completely bald, but stained or tattooed in a way to suggest a close-cropped growth; and they had neither eyebrows nor eye lashes. I suppose these things had been evolved away by thousands of years of living indoors. Then their clothes. They were dressed in all the colours of the rainbow, and every possible shape of garment, each one, I dare say, according to his taste: but they gave you the impression of having had so much variety to choose from that they hadn't been able in the end to choose at all. Like the Outlanders these people paid us no attention whatever. There we were, travellers from another world, arrived in their midst in a scythed chariot soaked in the blood of battle, and they passed us by, incurious and indifferent.

Kwashog, having completed his work, now climbed back into the car and we joined the stream of traffic. We were making for the house of a man he had made friends with on his previous visit, for of course there were no hotels in Harpaxe, since no strangers ever came there. We alighted eventually at a carved and gilded door, on which, in the position where there would have been a bell or a knocker on earth, there was fixed a small brass horn like that of a gramophone. Kwashog put his mouth close to this and said: "Hello, Mr. Felp. Bhos Kwashog, from the Bright Side, speaking. Just arrived in my car. Are you at home?" A gramophonish voice at once answered: "No, sir. Mr. Felp went out half an hour ago, and is not expected to return till late." But immediately afterwards there came a genuine human shout: "Hi! Wait! Don't mind the machine. That was for ordinary callers. Come right in old chap." At the same time the door opened of its own accord, showing a courtyard in which two fine motor cars were standing. We drove in, and parked ours in a convenient corner. Then we crossed the court towards an open doorway in which a man awaited us. He was of middle age, dressed in a purple tunic reaching to his knees and an ermine-bordered cloak held by a gold chain across his breast. He received Kwashog, and me also when introduced, with an easy cordiality, and led us across a sumptuous hall into the room from which he had come. Then we dropped into capacious armchairs round an electric fire, while our host pressed a button by the chimney piece.

A moment later a young woman marched into the room with the regular step of an automaton, and stood to attention like a soldier beside Mr. Felp's chair. Her face was so perfectly expressionless that at first I thought she actually was an automaton. She was stark naked except for a loincloth. Her eyes looked straight ahead of her without as much as a flicker. Her hands hung plumb by her side, with the fingers extended. The only sign of life about her was the slight rise and fall of her breast.

"Drink," said Mr. Felp, giving her a cut with a dogwhip, which left a red weal across her body, already marked, as I now. perceived, with the scars of previous lashes in various stages of healing. The girl neither winced nor made any other sign of feeling, but marching out in the same mechanical fashion as before, brought in a trolley laden with glasses and decanters, and again stood to attention until dismissed with a second blow of the whip. I winced myself this time, and felt really annoyed by our host's unnecessary brutality to the docile girl, but thought it wiser not to interfere. He saw what I was thinking, however, and said with a laugh: "Don't worry, sir. The girl has no feelings. She's been pithed." Then, realising that I didn't understand, he went on to explain that she was an Outlander who had had the

higher centres of her brain removed during childhood in order
to adapt her to domestic service; that she was in consequence
virtually an automaton, devoid of emotion and reason, and re-
sponsive only to such stimuli as I had seen him apply; and that
she was, of course, perfectly insensitive to pain. By this process,
he said, they had at last solved the servant problem.

"But what about a drink?" he inquired pushing the trolley
towards us. In the decanters were liquids of various colours:
red, blue, several shades of yellow, and one colourless like water.
Kwashog helped himself from this, and suggested I should do
the same.

"It's the mildest," he said. "They don't run to wine in these
latitudes: only spirits, and they are rather potent."

They were. Even the innocent-looking one we had chosen
burned like an acid, but once swallowed it was certainly buck-
ing. Thus oiled, Kwashog got down to business straight off.
While he talked I took a view of the room. Though rather more
luxurious in its appointments than any on the Sunny Side,
it was laid out on similar labour-saving and dust-preventing
principles. Along one wall was a row of nickel-plated levers,
which I afterwards learned were the means of working various
mechanical substitutes for servants, pithed parlour maids being
somewhat of a novelty as yet, only found in the houses of the
very wealthy.

My attention was next caught by a curious device over the
mantelpiece. Standing on it, just like an ordinary photograph,
was a framed cinematographic picture of a street, with traffic
and people moving up and down, as it would look from the
doorway of a house in it. Beside it stood a small loud-speaker.
I watched the miniature cinema for a while, expecting something to happen, for I had at once jumped to the conclusion
that it was a sort of home-substitute for a picture-house. But
nothing did happen. The scene remained obstinately the same,
with the people and traffic buzzing by, and no sign of a hero

or heroine appearing, so that I was just turning away from it in despair when a man stepped out from the crowd and stood right in the foreground. Immediately there came a voice from the loud-speaker: "Mr. Felp at home?" and then the distant lie that had answered Kwashog and me. Mr. Felp, however, let this caller depart unenlightened. Tricky dodge, wasn't it?

It cannot have been long after this that I fell asleep. I was horribly tired, and my limbs were stiff and aching. I remember being dimly conscious of the talk of Felp and Kwashog coming as a wordless murmur through the comforting stupor produced by the spirit I had drunk. Then all was blank. When I awoke I found myself in bed in a strange room with Kwashog standing over me.

"Good morning," he said. "How are you feeling?"

I stretched myself with the abandon of a cat.

"Fine. How did I get here?"

"Felp and I carried you up yesterday after you'd fallen asleep in your chair. Do you know that you've slept thirty-six hours?"

"Great Satan! What's been happening meanwhile?"

"O, everything's settled. Four villages are working overtime on our stuff for double rations of sewga. We'll be able to start back for the Sunshine in a couple of days."

"What about yourself?" I asked. "Have you had any sleep?"

"O yes. I managed to snatch a wink or two between whiles. What about getting up and seeing something of the town?"

"Good idea," I said, flinging off the bedclothes. But somehow, in spite of the long rest I'd had, I felt none of the fine freshness of early morning that you get on earth. One couldn't in that atmosphere of electric light and artificial heat. As I dressed a sudden thought occurred to me.

"Say, Kwashog. What about that gold of ours? Was it safe to leave it down there in the car?"

"Why not?" asked Kwashog.

"Well, if these people are so devilish pious, mightn't they think it a sacred duty to steal it?"

"Undoubtedly," said Kwashog. "And, viewed from an absolute standpoint, it is their duty. We know, however, from the teachings of Procrustes, that there is a higher duty with which this would conflict: the supreme duty of getting on. Now, no business can be run successfully on dishonest lines, for if a man is once found out in lying or thieving, people will refuse to have any further dealings with him. We are thus driven to the paradoxical conclusion that dishonesty doesn't pay, and therefore that honesty is the best policy. So don't be afraid: our gold is safe."

Quite suddenly at that another and deeper fear caught hold of me. "Have they any higher duty," I asked, "to keep them from murdering us?"

"Murder," answered Kwashog, "is held here as a work of supererogation, and beyond the capacity of the ordinary man. It is practised only in some of the sterner monastic communities, and even there only on animals. One of these orders, however, did send round here yesterday to demand that you and I should be handed over to them."

A cold shiver ran up my spine. "What happened?" I asked.

"Our host showed them every deference, and said that he would willingly assist their pious purpose only that he was engaged in making money out of us."

"And did that satisfy them?"

"Perfectly. They said his zeal was most edifying, and departed with pious invocations. When they had gone, however, Felp told me he had no use for these monkish practices and wouldn't have given us up in any case." Kwashog seemed to think this very handsome on the part of our host, but you can imagine that I finished my dressing in rather a thoughtful mood.

Just as I was ready to go downstairs a loud harsh voice rang through the room. "Hello! Hello! Hello! Office of the *Hourly Shout* calling. Is that Mr. O'Kennedy from the stars?" Looking in the direction from which it came I perceived a loud-speaker standing on a table in a corner. "Hello! Hello! Hello!" the voice resumed. "Office of the *Hourly Shout* calling. Is that Mr. O'Kennedy from the stars?"

"Better answer," said Kwashog, "or they'll keep on all day."

"Hello! Hello! Hello!" brayed the trumpet again. "Offce of the *Hourly Shout* speaking. Is that Mr. O'Kennedy from the stars?"

"Yes," I said.

"Pleased to meet you, sir. Will you give us your views on the Modern Girl at four scugs a line?"

"Well," I said, "I haven't thought very much about the subject, but if—"

"Five scugs a line," cut in the voice.

"It's awfully kind of you," I said, "but the fact is that I haven't met any Harpzxean girls yet—"

"Six scugs a line," said the voice imperturbably, "You think her frank and free and boyish, don't you? Yes. And what about her jhash-smoking? Sign of emancipation, eh? Yes. And the exposure of the thighs? Makes for health and sanity and does away with prudishness, what? Good. And now about your ideas on Love. The greatest uplifting force in the world, of course. And no man is worthy of a good woman's affection, eh? And the determination to win the girl he loves is the finest possible inspiration to a young man to make good. Yes. And personally you owe all your success in life to its ennobling influence. And also of course to the homely lessons you learned at your dear old mammy's knee. Fine. And your religion—well, you have your views on that, but it is too sacred and personal a matter for cold print. Right, Mr. O'Kennedy. That's the stuff. A cheque will follow."

I hadn't been able to get in a solitary word all this time. But within a quarter of an hour a copy of the *Hourly Shout* was in my hands, with the interview, running to two columns, featured on the front page. And next day I received a cheque for twelve hundred scugs. The scug is the Harpaxean monetary standard, and is worth in our money £1 19s. 11¾d.

CHAPTER XL

Manners and Customs of the Harpaxeans

MR. FELP WAS AN eminent and highly respected citizen of Harpaxe, distinguished alike for his high character and his general good fortune. An excellent husband and father, his business career was without blemish. He had had eleven wives, and only one child, a daughter; and though born to great wealth he had not allowed that to blunt his appetite for more. Still, in spite of all these recommendations, I felt not a little uneasy on learning that, as Kwashog would be kept busy arranging for the convoy of our munitions, I was to spend the next few days entirely in his company. Suppose, I said to myself, that in a sudden burst of virtue he were to hand me over to some of those awful monks! All the same there was no way out of it, and as things turned out nothing of the sort happened. He very kindly offered to take me round the city to see the sights, and I found him a most agreeable and charming companion. He was also very broadminded. He told me that Kwashog had informed him of my religious views, and that I might feel quite at ease on that score. "Personally," he said "I believe in toleration for all religions, however mistaken. After all, it's not what a man *believes* that matters, but how he *behaves*. I dare say there's quite as much murder and money-getting practised in your world as in ours." I took these remarks in the spirit in which they were intended, and we proceeded with our exploration of the town. I don't propose to give you a detailed account of how we spent the day, but will set down instead a few flashlight impressions of things that struck me.

There was nothing very extraordinary about the city itself except the roof. Apart from that it was just like a big American city, of which I had often seen pictures, with perfectly straight streets and immense blocks of skyscraping buildings, mainly consisting of flats. The roof was composed of a succession of huge domes supported on concrete pillars, and occasionally pierced by tall ventilation shafts—the towers which I had noticed on my first distant view. The city was much bigger than those on the Sunny Side, and more sumptuous except in one particular: the lampposts were not made of gold, which was regarded there at its proper value—fortunately for us, since otherwise our ingots wouldn't have purchased many guns. I had expected to find Harpaxe well supplied with churches, devoted to some hellish ritual far different from the milk-and-water services I had seen in Bulnid. But I was mistaken. There were no churches there at all. "We have no need for them," Mr. Felp explained. "We believe in practical piety, not in ceremonies and lip-service. Isn't the Stock Exchange a perfect act of Mammon-worship, with human sacrifices and all? And didn't Procrustes himself say that wherever two or three economists were gathered together, there he would be in the midst of them?" There was, however, one shrine of Procrustes which he now thought it well to show me. It was a queerer erection even than the churches on the Sunny Side. It stood in the centre of the bustling market-place, between the Bank and the Stock Exchange, an immense black pillar rising sheer to the highest dome of the city. Entering by the only door, we found ourselves as it were at the bottom of a well. The only light in the place came from above, where the moon looked wanly down through the glass of the dome. In the centre of the floor, just now in the very path of her ray, stood a strange statue—a powerful stern-looking man gripping the rail of an ordinary iron bedstead.

"That's Procrustes," Mr. Felp whispered.

I asked what was the significance of the bed.

"Don't you know the story?" said Felp. "It's said that he used to invite people to stay at his house, and if they didn't fit his beds, he used to stretch them or shorten them as required."

"The beds?" I said.

"No. The guests, of course. It was this commonsense and economic practice that turned the Sunnysiders against him, and led to his downfall. — By the way, I hope you slept comfortably last night?"

"O perfectly, perfectly," I said, smiling agreeably in spite of a queer sinking sensation in my stomach.

"Bed nice and roomy, eh?" said Mr. Felp.

"O quite, quite," I assured him.

"Bit on the large side, perhaps?" he suggested, looking at my long limbs with a solicitous expression that fairly made my flesh creep.

"Not at all, I assure you," I said, edging towards the door. "I never was so comfortable in my life."

It was all I could do not to scream when the handle refused to budge. But that was only because I had tried to turn it the wrong way. When I reversed the movement it gave quite easily, and with a gasp of relief I found myself out of the darkness and in the midst of the hustling stock-brokers in the Square, who were bashing and tearing one another in the urgency of financial business. From that moment I never had an easy night's rest in Harpaxe; for, as a matter of fact, my bed *was* a bit on the short side, and whenever I fell asleep I used to dream that I was fastened to the bed of Procrustes, with Mr. Felp preparing to begin operations with a handsaw.

But to return to the manners and customs of the Harpaxeans. There was one thing in which Harpaxe resembled the other cities of Rathé. There were no advertisements there. But it was for a different reason. Mr. Felp told me that the art of advertising had reached its zenith some fifty years before, when every square inch of space had been pasted over, and it became impossible to tell which articles in a newspaper were news and which were advertisements or publicity puffs. It was then found that people had ceased to notice advertisements, and the whole business crashed.

The social system of Harpaxe was a very simple one. Every citizen owned a share of the Sewga marsh, and received dividends out of the produce wrung from the Outlanders in return for the fungus. These shares were not equal, so that though every Harpaxean was comfortably off, many of them were forced, in order to cut some sort of a figure in this luxurious world, to take up professions like medicine or teaching to supplement their incomes. There was more money to be made out of these professions in Harpaxe than on earth, because they were organised on thoroughly business-like lines. There was a Doctors' Trust, for instance, to regulate cures and fees—*i.e.*, to restrict the former and increase the latter. There was also a Scientific Research Combine. I'm told that on earth scientific research is mainly conducted by brainy fellows without any money-making instinct who work for the pure love of the thing without thought of reward, and often live in poverty while big capitalists scoop the profits of their discoveries. The Harpaxean scientists aren't such fools. There's a story told that once when the city was in the grip of a plague that wiped out nearly half of its inhabitants, a chemist who discovered a remedy to cure it refused to reveal it until he was handed over some colossal sum of money, on which he was able to retire and found a completely idle family. His name is regarded with the deepest veneration and his story related to children as an example of how to get on. A similar story is told of a general who commanded the army in a revolt of the Outlanders. When the enemy was at the gate he refused to take command until his price was paid; and, as he was the only general they had, they couldn't refuse him. He also has a shining name in the pages of their history, though personally I think this was pushing enterprise and initiative rather too far.

But in spite of their rather grasping character the Harpaxeans were, as my Rathean authority had remarked, extremely fond of the Outlanders. I met great numbers of them, when I was going around with Mr. Felp, in clubs, restaurants, and other places, and one and all spoke of their serfs in the kindliest manner, the ladies always referring to them as "the dear Outlanders" and the gentlemen as "the decent" or "the sturdy Outlanders." I was assured over and over again that the Outlander was the finest fellow of his type in the universe, and that if it were not for the machinations of agitators he would work even harder and take less in return for it than he did. This attitude encouraged me to put in a word or two suggesting that the policy of mutilating these excellent people might be abandoned. The first person I sounded on the subject was a lady who, I had been told, was a well-known supporter of all measures for elevating the condition of the Outlanders. "Ah, Mr. O'Kennedy," she said. "If only you had seen the dreadful homes these people live in you wouldn't make such a suggestion." Then I tackled a young man about it. "My dear sir," he exploded, "how the devil are the unfortunate people to fit into their homes if we don't keep 'em shortened? My opinion is that they aren't short enough, and I'm sending a subscription to help this agitation for shorter necks." The next person I tackled was a mild and elderly gentleman who answered sagely: "Ah, my young friend, if only you knew the conditions under which these miserable people lived before this great reform was introduced, you would change your opinion. I am old enough to remember the time when the operation was still voluntary, and I do assure you that the conditions were too shocking for words. The poor people couldn't stand up straight in their houses. Think of that!" Finally, when I had heard the same old argument, dished out in slightly different sauces, for about the twentieth time, I burst out in a great rage. "My God," I said, "are houses such unchangeable things? Is humanity to be cut and trimmed in the interests of bricks and mortar? Why can't you build houses to fit the men, instead of fitting the men to the houses?" "But, my dear sir," said the woman I was speaking to (the women were much the keenest supporters of the system), "there aren't enough bricks and mortar to go round." "Well then," I said, you must make them." "Ah yes," she said. "That's an ideal which of course we must aim at. But in the meantime we must pursue immediately practicable reforms." "Well," I said, "there's one practicable reform that requires no miracles of surgery to carry out," and after giving her an account of our terrible struggle with the showps, suggested that the Outlanders should be supplied with some better weapon than the wretched little fly-flappers they had. "Yes, yes," she said. "The showps are a terrible problem: a terrible problem, and one that is always with us. I should like to see strong measures taken to deal with them, and I am sure much could be done to lessen their depredations. But then on the other hand we must be careful lest, if we give these people too complete a security, we may undermine their self-reliance and discourage them from seeking a remedy for themselves."

The worst of it was that I think she sincerely meant this blurb. Mr. Felp however was of a different opinion. He told me he had been delighted by my attacks on his countrymen's most precious theories. "It's all a blessed piece of hypocrisy," he said. "The real reason why they want these beggars' limbs lopped is because they're afraid of them and want to keep them under. And quite right too, so why not be frank about it?"

In the course of our perambulations we passed a number of people who were accompanied by dogs of a most remarkable appearance. They walked erect, though somewhat unsteadily, on their hind legs, and were dressed like their owners. Many of them carried canes and smoked cigarettes, and I saw one or two of them actually smiling in unmistakeable human fashion. Nevertheless it was a distinct surprise to me when, on our stopping to chat with some ladies of Mr. Felp's acquaintance, their dogs joined in the conversation. They did, Mr. Gallagher, on my solemn oath. And mind you, it wasn't mere gabble like what parrots do, but genuine speech: such as "Topping day, what?" or "I brought down sixteen brace of rats yesterday," or "That's a pretty little bitch over there from the males," and "Isn't she a perfectly *odious* creature," and "What do you think he's worth, dear?" from the females. Not highly intelligent, perhaps, but when you consider that they were only dogs! More astonishing still, when we adjourned to a restaurant, where my host was giving a party in my honour, they all sat down to table with us, and gave their commands to the pithed attendants in the customary manner—with the whip. I noticed that they ate and drank, for the most part, very daintily, and that their manners were in no way inferior to those of the rest of the company. In one respect, indeed, they were a good deal better; for the human Harpaxeans indulged in a good deal of rather bold flirtation, with not a little suggestive banter, which I could not help contrasting unfavourably with the dignified decorum of their pets. When the party was over I asked Mr. Felp how these marvellous dogs were bred: to which he replied that they were a comparatively recent invention of an enterprising surgeon, who grafted into their brains the excised tissue obtained in the process of pithing servants. Afterwards they were sent to special schools, where no expense was spared to give them the best education procurable. Altogether, said Mr. Felp, this was an excellent example of the economic exploitation of the by-products of industry, such as would only be possible in a highly competitive civilisation.

CHAPTER XLI

Astonishing Opinions of a Lucky Dog

LATER ON IN THE course of my visit I managed to get one or two of these dogs by themselves and encouraged them to talk to me. On the whole they were a decent, well-behaved lot of creatures. They looked upon their masters more or less as gods, who had given them their brains and could take them away again if they pleased, and they worshipped them in consequence with a grotesque mixture of gratitude and apprehension. How exactly the brains had been conferred on them they had no idea (and I was warned by Mr. Felp, for reasons which he would not reveal, not to tell them); but they believed that it was done by a kind of miracle performed during a deep sleep into which they remembered having been cast.

There was one dog to whom I took a particular fancy—a nice black-coated creature of a sort of spaniel breed, who told me that by industry and thrift he had saved up enough money to buy his freedom, and that he was now his own master, earning his living as a rat-catcher in a small way. We had many interesting chats together, which gave me a remarkable insight into his outlook on life. He was really a most deserving brute, honest, hardworking, and respectable, with no ambition to push himself forward, but anxious nevertheless to better himself by steady attention to his business. This he had conducted with such success that already he had saved up a tidy little sum which he had invested in shares in the Sewga Marsh. He had an unqualified admiration for the economic system which made it possible for a mere dog to get on as he had done, purely by his own exertions. Indeed he was not a little bumptious about the fact that as a Sewga shareholder he was an employer of Outland labour, and a receiver of its tribute. I felt it my duty to administer a quiet snub at this point; for it did really seem too much of a good thing that a dog should be in a position to regard any sort of human beings as his inferiors, and I couldn't help feeling that the wretched Outlanders were, in a manner of speaking, my fellow-men, so that his estimate of them reflected to a certain extent on myself. The dog, however, at once fawned on me so humbly, and assured me so heartily that his remarks were intended in no spirit of presumption, that I presently relented and allowed him to continue his confidences. He protested that nothing was farther from his thoughts than to claim equality with human beings, but that thrift was entitled to its reward, and if the result of his saving was to give employment to men who, however high above him in other respects, were less provident than he, surely he was serving them in the most effective possible way.

He spoke with such a winning modesty and discretion, and his plea was so eminently reasonable, that I felt it only right to withdraw my censure, and, patting him on the head, encouraged him to speak on. So, with a little yelp of pleasure at my approbation, he proceeded.

"I am a practical dog," he said, "and I look upon life essentially as a practical proposition. I have no use for theories of any sort. Thinking may be a help to some people, but, personally, every lesson of real value that I have learnt has been taught me by experience. Anyway, in these go-ahead days one can't afford to waste time in thinking: one has to be up and doing. This may not be a very high view of life, but the proof of the pudding, after all, is in the eating. By acting on it I have made good and got on, while many human beings have remained where they were."

I was really impressed by the animal's sagacity and sense,

and listened with the deepest interest as his confidences became more intimate and personal. The new life, he confessed, was not altogether a bed of roses. Or at any rate there were thorns in it. "First there's the difficulty of dressing up to one's position. One simply must be more smartly turned out than the unfree dogs; but they have their masters to clothe them, so it's a bit of a struggle. I seem to be always in debt to my tailor.

"Then there's the perpetual strain of repressing one's animal instincts. Of course one no longer barks or bites, but one is apt to give oneself away in little things—" and rather pathetically he asked me if I could recommend him a remedy for tail-wagging. I was unable to do so, and down went that signal of his emotions, with a jerk, between his legs.

"Of course I could have it docked," he said, "but I'm afraid that would be rather presumptuous. It might be thought that I was trying to pass myself off as a man, and the humans would resent that. My pups have done it, but they are beginning to find out their mistake already."

Then, resuming the thread of his discourse, he said that the most unfortunate of all the results of his success was the social isolation that it involved. "You see, I have had to drop all my old canine friends. Not that I wish to appear snobbish or unkind, but it's only due to my position to keep my inferiors at a proper distance. You can have no idea what a wrench it has been, but one simply *must* draw the line.

"On the other paw," he went on, "I haven't yet been able to get a footing among human beings. They're very stand-offish towards manumitted dogs. Snobbish if you don't mind my saying so. I can't understand it, seeing that they're so fond of us as pets."

From this he turned to talk about his home life and family cares. His wife, I learned, though a dear good creature, did him no credit in his new position. "She still clings," he said, "to the habits of the days when we lived in the old kennel at our master's gate. Nothing will ever make her get a move on. — Not that I amn't fond of the old dear, but you know what I mean." His children, on the other hand (he had reared a son and daughter from their last litter) were too go-ahead altogether. "Going in for all this modern stuff—jazz and night-clubs and free love and so on—just as if they were human beings, and only getting snubbed for their pains."

At last, emboldened by my continued patronage, the dog came to me one day with a more than usually ingratiating air, and, after some preliminary shuffling and fawning, asked timidly if I would condescend to pay a visit to his humble home. The request was rather a stunner, as I think you'll agree; but after some hesitation I consented. The gratified brute, who had been awaiting my decision with bated breath, nearly went off his head for joy. Forgetting all his dignity, he gave three leaps into the air and frantically licked my hand. Then off he dashed down the street, stopping every few minutes to look back at me, while I followed, more than a little doubtful of the wisdom of what I was doing. After a longish walk we reached his house, which was situated in a lowly quarter on the outskirts of the town, mainly inhabited by artists, philosophers, and other failures. He lived above his place of business, for which he apologised. Over the shop was written J. TOWSER, RATTER, and on the window in white lettering: TOWSER, THE DEMON RATTER : FAMILIES WAITED ON. I was surprised to notice that on the door of the neighbouring private house there was a tarnished brass plate with the words: OMREH, POET. RATS CHARMED. The dog explained that the gentleman who resided there had formerly earned a living by luring rats to destruction by playing on a pipe, but that he had been practically driven out of business by his own more efficient methods. Then, as he drew out his latchkey, he begged me to grant him a favour.

"What is it?" I asked.

He lowered his voice. "Perhaps you wouldn't mind calling me *Mister* Towser when we get inside. I should be so pleased, and it would be a real gratification to the wife."

I promised; and a few minutes later I was sitting down to supper at the family table, watching Mrs. Towser clumsily angling with a ladle in a steaming pot, which for a moment I was afraid contained rats, but which really held an excellent stew of sewga. At the other end of the table sat her husband in a miserable state of nerves, keeping a wary eye on his pups, Dash and Flo, who were opposite to me. Two such comical specimens of doghood as these I have never seen. In order to humanise themselves they had shaved their faces and the backs of their forepaws, docked their tails, stained their lips red, and drenched themselves with some abominable perfume. Gee, what a pair of exhibits! It was all I could do not to burst out laughing whenever I looked at them. The son was too much overwhelmed by my presence to utter a word; but the daughter kept up an endless chatter about dances and night-clubs and humans, spiced with malicious tittle-tattle about acquaintances, all delivered with an accompaniment of giggles and sidelong glances at me to see what impression she was making.

"It's an awful nuisance," says she. "I've had to refuse an invitation to a dance tonight because I've nothing to wear."

"But, my dear," remonstrated her mother, you bought a new dress only last week."

"Yes, but I've worn it already," said Flo.

"Well, why not wear it again?"

"Don't be ridiculous, mother!" snapped Flo. "People would think I couldn't afford another."

"Neither can you," said her father. "At the rate you're going you'll have me bankrupt, and then you'll have to go and work for your living."

"Don't talk nonsense, father," replied the pup. "I'd sooner starve."

"Dad's right, though," said Dash, speaking for the first time. "If we don't pull in a bit he won't be able to save, and then how can he leave us independent?"

"I don't care," answered his sister.

"I'd rather have a good-time while I have the chance, even if I do have to pay for it afterwards."

Poor old Towser subsided with a sigh, while his mate threw up her paws in despair. Soon Flo was off on another grievance. "That little wretch Toto had the impertinence to smile at me in the street this morning," she whined. "When I was walking with a human, too."

"But you were at school together, dear," said her mother reprovingly.

"Well," said Flo. "That's no reason why she should disgrace me. She's not the sort of person I could *possibly* know now."

Inspired by his sister's brilliance, Dash now managed to overcome his shyness, and began to regale us with a long involved story of how he had got the better of some human greenhorn in a money transaction which was so shady that I lost my way entirely in its mazes. Long before he had finished I was bored stiff and told him to shut up; which sent him into sulks for the rest of the evening.

Whelps, weren't they? Mrs. Towser was a perfectly delicious contrast to them. She made no pretences of any sort. "It's no use an old body like me trying to pick up new tricks," she said. "I'd only make myself a laughing stock. You can't expect human heads on dogs' shoulders." Once or twice in a merry moment, she even forgot herself so far as to bark, to the acute embarrassment of her husband and children.

But the titbit of the entertainment came after the meal was over, when, the pups having sneaked away (to a night club, I suppose), and Mrs. Towser having gone to the kitchen to wash up, Towser and I settled down by the fire for a chat. With a sort of bashful pride he showed me a tattered primer of physics, saying that he had lately taken to the study of science, partly in order to improve his mind, but principally because he wanted to refute current scientific theories as to the origin of dogs. He said it was generally believed in Harpaxe that they were evolved from wolves, and he intended to devote his life to removing this stigma from the canine race.

"It is impossible," he declared, "that we could have sprung from ancestors so brutal and debased. Science has evidently been misled by certain external physical resemblances. I have an inner conviction, which I hope to develop into a certainty, that we are not a product of evolution at all, but a special creation, with some high eternal destiny before us. Surely we were intended for something better than the chasing of rats and the cracking of bones? And surely our fidelity, obedience, and other canine virtues are deserving of some reward hereafter? I perceive that you are sceptical," he remarked, for I had been trying ineffectually not to smile, "but this faith of mine is not without a rational foundation. The canine mind has an ardent desire for happiness, and an intense repugnance to the idea of eternal death. Such desire, and such repugnance could not have been implanted in us if existence really terminates with the decay of our bodies. It would be incredible. It would argue a fundamental cruelty in the scheme of things, and that is a possibility which no thinking mind could ever accept. I believe therefore in a future existence, which will be one long orgy among bones which need no cracking, and rats which need no chasing: in short, a life of eternal bliss."

I was so touched by the dog's faith that I bowed my head in silent assent. After all, what was the use of destroying the one illusion that made his life worth living? But it was awful cheek all the same.

CHAPTER XLII

Hell's Revels

I COULD TELL YOU lots more about Harpaxean customs, only I haven't time, and there's one night's jollification that I simply can't leave out. The evening after my visit to Towser, as Felp and I were sitting by the fireside, Kwashog being still away about our business, the door opened, and a young lady popped her head in.

"Good-night, dad," she said. "I'm off to the club."

She would have vanished at once but for a call from her father.

"Just a second, my dear," he said. "Let me introduce my friend Mr. O'Kennedy, a visitor from the Bright Side. Mr. O'Kennedy: my daughter Zip."

The girl, coming forward a few steps into the room, condescended to acknowledge my salutation with an air of languid boredom. She was pretty, but in a vampish, made-up sort of way. Her face was a dead white; her lips an artificial vermilion. She wore a dress of cloth of gold, cut very low in the bust, with the skirt reaching to her ankles, but slit at one side almost to her waist, so that every alternate step obtruded a crimson-stockinged leg with a golden garter, and some inches of bare thigh.

"Are you going out alone, my dear?" asked her father.

"Yes," she replied. "Ycrep is indulging in another bout of peevery."

"Well, why not take Mr. O'Kennedy with you," suggested Felp. "I'm sure he'd like to see a bit of life."

"Delighted," said the girl in a tone that implied complete indifference to the prospect. However, I accepted the invitation at its face value, and followed her out of the room. In the hall she said: "What do you say to a kick-off before we start?" and without waiting for an answer led me into another room, evidently a dining room, where there were more decanters and glasses ranged on a sideboard.

"Have an eaglesbeak?" said the girl, taking down one decanter containing a vivid green fluid of a most poisonous aspect.

"What's that?" I asked.

Zip became animated for the first time. She clapped a thin hand to her brow and gave me an astonished stare. "Almighty Satan!" says she. "Have you never tasted an eaglesbeak?"

"Never heard of it," I said.

"Impossible!"

"True all the same," I said.

"Then, how in Beelzebub's name have you managed to live? Come, you must have one quick, or you'll die on my hands."

"But what is it?" I insisted as she gripped the decanter by the neck.

"Why, hell and damnation, man! it's the spirit of life, the devil's own drink." (You mustn't think, by the way, that this strong language was spoken with any violence. Never once did the girl's voice rise above an even conversational tone. Oaths and curses flowed from her mouth as quietly and naturally as pious invocations from a nun's. She didn't seem to mean very much by them.) "Just look at the stuff," she said, holding the decanter up to my nose. "Look at the colour of it! Clap just a drop of that inside you, and you will experience the most voluptuous sensation, as if an eagle were tearing at your liver with beak and claw."

Here, with a feverish movement, she plucked out the stopper and filled two tumblers to the brim with the vitriolic-looking decoction.

"Now," she said. "Stuff that between your fangs and drink in the Devil's name."

A bit fearfully, though not taking her words as literal, I took a sip at the spirit. By jingo, she hadn't exaggerated one iota. I staggered as if I had been shot, while a rending pain gripped hold of my very vitals. For a moment I thought I was killed. Then, almost instantaneously the pain vanished, and a feeling of immense exhilaration took possession of me. I wanted to dance. I believe I did dance. Then with a spasm of bravado I gulped down nearly half of the diabolical fluid. Well, I nearly killed myself in earnest that time. The pains that followed were ten times as bad as before, and they were a much longer time in passing. I danced again, but it was in sheer agony. When at last they left me I sank on a sofa shaken and exhausted.

As I lay there I saw Zip toss off her own glass to the very drains without as much as winking. "How on earth do you manage it?" I asked in admiration.

"Pooh!" said she. "That's nothing. What puzzles me is how you've managed to exist without it. Personally I couldn't *live* without a glass every hour, and even with that I don't feel quite up to the mark. I'm frightfully modern you know. Frank, free, boyish, and all that. I'm always on the move, and I smoke jhash all days—That reminds me. I feel rather like a puff now."

Here she took out a jewel-studded case from some recess under her skirt and, springing it open, held it towards me. It contained a number of long thin cigarettes of various colours, which, after my experience with the eaglesbeak, I thought it better to decline. The girl, with a contemptuous snort, took one for herself and lighted it. Pff! what a stench it made! Something like medicine mixed with stale incense. Even Zip didn't seem to enjoy it very much. She scarcely inhaled at all, but produced a brave display of smoke by blowing outwards through the cigarette.

"How filthily old-fashioned you are," she said to me. "I adore jhash. I'm mentally deficient about it. Being so modern, you know. I'm the very last word. You've no idea how frank and free I am. I show more of my thighs than any other girl in Harpaxe! Isn't that modern! I've all the latest slang too—ripping and topping, and I gotta date with a trouser, and all the rest of it. And, oh girl, I'm so boyish!"

Here she threw away her cigarette and applied a fresh coat of paint to her lips. "Now I'm ready," she said. "Let's be off. I'm in a perfectly demoniac mood tonight."

She clutched me tightly by the arm, impelling me towards the hall-door. I was positively frightened by her strength and the feverish glitter of her eyes. Hurrying me across the courtyard she kept on urging: "Come on! Come on! We're going to have a fiendish good-time tonight. Life, eh? Ranting roaring tearing life. Blast that door. Come on!"

We got through the door without the assistance of dynamite, and hurried along the street amid a swarm of couples bent on similar amusement. "This is life!" I could hear them saying to one another. "O, aren't we modern! We'll have a tearing good-time tonight, won't we?" It was extraordinary to hear the same stereotyped ejaculation from every tongue, and to see the utterly joyless faces with which it was uttered. The infernal jazz band which had been playing when we entered the city was still hard at it, though where I couldn't say, and the revellers kept time to it with their feet and bodies with a tireless idiotic persistency. Zip, clinging to my arm, did the same. "Dance!" she kept urging in my ear. "Dance and enjoy life! Dance, blast you!" But it was no good. Full and all as I was of eaglesbeak, my sense of humour kept me quiet.

In a few minutes we arrived at the dancing club. There was no missing it. The whole face of it was lit up with millions of coloured lights, and round the arched entrance there were six brazen loud-speakers It was the most pouring out different dance tunes. discordant braying you ever heard, but it seemed quite acceptable to the Harpaxeans, whom it stimulated to even wilder jiggings. In we went into an enormous hall so brilliantly lighted that my unfortunate Rathean eyes were nearly blinded, and filled with a clangour fit to drive me mad. Will you believe it? there were twenty great horns fixed to the walls, and out of each of them came a different tune—all jazz time played by brass bands with supplementary drums and rattles. O what a pandemonium! What a dumfustitudilation! And to that racket, in an atmosphere foul with jhash smoke, the people were dancing like golliwogs on a drumhead.

"Don't stand staring," came Zip's voice at my elbow. "Come and dance, man. This is the Lousy Crawl, the very modernest thing out"; and she bustled me on to the swirling floor. Lord, what a dance that was. In spite of my encumbrance, Zip tossed her arms and legs about like flails, but her steps were tame compared with some of those I saw. Round and round with the jigging crowd we spun: round and round and round and round, with the music lashing us on like so many peg tops. I was deafened, blinded, sickened, stupefied.

"Look here, Zip," I said at last. "What's the sense of so many bands playing together?"

"What else would they do?" she asked.

"Well, one tune at a time would do for me."

"That would be a measly way of doing things," the girl scoffed. "Besides, we'd never have time to get through all the new tunes at that rate."

Here to my relief the music came to a pause, leaving us in the comparative silence of the distant city band and the six howlers at the door. The floor was at once emptied, the dancers trooping to the couches and the tables round the sides. Zip, securing a table, called for another eaglesbeak to one of the pithed waiters, who stood stiff and expressionless as door posts amid the revelry, and pressed me to take one too, but I refused.

"You don't know how to enjoy yourself," she said, tossing the stuff down her throat with the ease of continual practice. Then, crossing her long legs in a way that left nothing to the imagination, she lounged back in her chair murmuring: "Satan, but this is life. I *am* having a good-time."

All round the room people were posed in similar attitudes, some even more so. You never saw such indecent dresses as the Harpaxean women wore. The half-naked Ratheans were modesty itself compared with them. I noticed too that the women drank much more freely than the men, and more particularly favoured the eaglesbeak, frequent draughts of which seemed absolutely necessary to keep them going.

"Rather distinguished company here tonight," drawled Zip presently, gazing languidly round the room. "There's Twiddler the non-stop dance record-holder. He danced for four months last year, and had to have his toenails cut six times in the process. That's Piff, the long-distance piano-player, beside him. She's just finished playing the five-finger exercise a million times. Over there near the pillar is Toidi, who holds the record for standing on one leg with a pea in each ear and a clothespeg on his nose singing Titti-fol-lol-fol-lay. And beyond him is the Reverend Broadnut, who holds the record for sermons by preaching from Guzzlemas Day to Mammontide without blowing his nose. This club holds the record for record breakers. When the devil is the music going to start again? Those cursed Outlanders seem to be always resting: idle, worthless, good-for-nothing, discontented, loafers."

"O, are the musicians Outlanders?" I asked.

"Hell, no. There aren't any musicians anyhow. All that music is produced by machinery, and of course it's the Outlanders keep it going. I wish they'd start again: intervals are such a bore."

It started again, much too soon for my requirements.

"This is the Filthy Flop," cried Zip, "the modernest thing yet. Come along!" and off we went on the same old round, with my head nearly bursting and my body ready to drop from fatigue. This dance was even more vigorous than the last, and the high stepping even more outrageous. One or two of the more fanatical women actually managed in their ecstasy to get their legs curled round their necks, so that it was only with difficulty that they were rescued from strangulation. "Modern! Modern!" I heard people saying as they whirled. "O aren't we having a good-time!" and with hard set faces they'd fling themselves into the most abandoned contortions.

At the next interval Zip suggested supper. I said I wasn't hungry. "No matter," said she. "Neither am 1. But a couple of eaglesbeaks will soon give us an appetite, and then we'll have a rattling good feed to take it away."

Two eaglesbeaks appeared at once, and when I again refused mine Zip polished off both without turning a hair. Then she proceeded to put away several gallons of a sort of stew made of mushroomy things which I guessed to be Sewga. After that she had another eaglesbeak "to put her right," and was ready for the floor again.

"Do you often dance?" I inquired as we staggered around.

"Do I often breathe?" answered Zip contemptuously

"Far from it," said I gallantly.

"Then why do you ask such absurd questions? I've danced every night of my life except once for a few weeks when I was having a baby."

"O, are you married?" I asked.

"Not now," said Zip. "I've no use for that sort of husband. I divorced him at once, and got the custody of the child saddled on him too—he being the guilty party."

"I don't understand," I said. "Is a baby grounds for divorce in this country?"

"Of course: the best grounds of all."

"Well, if you'll excuse me asking," I said, "what do you get married for?"

"To have a good-time, of course. What do you think?"

"Then how does the race go on?" I asked.

"O, accidents will happen in the best regulated families. Besides, after they've had a good-time for ten or twelve years, people are often ready to settle. down and do the needful. But, look here, this conversation is getting devilish deep and serious. Let's have another eaglesbeak."

As the evening wore on I began to get seriously alarmed by Zip's behaviour. She was now swallowing an eaglesbeak every ten minutes or so. Each one strung her up to a higher pitch of excitement and activity: but each time the effect was less enduring, and the collapse that followed more pronounced. After the draught her eyes would be terribly bright, her voice high-keyed, her manner feverishly vivacious: then all of a sudden she would whimper like a tired child, and drop listlessly into a chair, making me hope that she would ask next to be taken home. But no. Each time her hand would creep to the bell-push, and a fresh bumper of the infernal potion would appear before her. At last I could stand the business no longer. After a dose which had kept her going even shorter than usual, I took the law into my own hands, and, having to carry her from the floor, I carried her right out of the building as well. She was too weak to resist: quite light too: so I carried her the whole distance to her father's house.

By the time I reached the door she had revived somewhat. "You are so warm and strong," she said, clinging to me. "Your touch has put new life into me." I put her down, and with a little assistance she was able to stand. She produced a latchkey from her garter. Inside the house, she made at once for the dining room, with obvious intent.

"No, you shan't," I said, catching her wrist. "Not another drop."

"O, but I must," she said weakly. "If I don't, I'll die in the night."

"If you take any more of that poison," I said, "you'll drop dead where you stand."

She broke into a desperate wail at that. "No, no, my dearest. Believe me. I must have it if I'm to live. I must."

I resisted her for a while, but, between the piteous pleading and a sort of idea that came to me that to cut the stuff right off might do more harm than good, I at last consented to allow her a quarter of a glass. I insisted on pouring it out myself though. The stuff bucked her up sufficiently to let her walk upstairs, but I went with her in case of accidents.

Above, she began to get faint again, and she was leaning heavily on me when we reached her door. There was nothing for it but to lead her into the room. I turned the electric switch, and instead of the usual glare there came a sunset glow from a cluster of rose-shaded lamps above the bed.

Zip sank wearily on a couch, murmuring something about a blazing good-time.

"Good-night," I said, moving away. "I hope you're all right now."

"Don't go," said the girl faintly. "I'm not quite myself yet."

I hesitated, thoroughly fed up with her, but not quite liking to leave her in case she might faint.

"Get me a little water," she said.

That seemed reasonable enough, so I went to the jade washing basin and drew some in a silver cup. She sipped a little of it distastefully, steadying the cup so as to bring her fingers in contact with mine.

"What cool hands you have," she said, smiling.

"Are you better now?" I asked.

"So anxious to get away from me?" she teased.

"I'm very tired," I said.

"Of me?"

"No. Just tired."

"Poor boy!" Her tone was as soft as she could make it, but that wasn't saying much. "Very well. You shall pop off to bed at once. But first, what about a candy?"

She produced a gaudy looking box from the drawer of a table behind her. In it were rows of things something like chocolates, but I suppose they were some sort of synthetic product. "Look. There's a nice one," she said. "Now do sit down for a moment, like a dear boy"—swinging her legs off the couch with the usual flash of provocative revelation.

I knew I mustn't do it or I was lost. You know, in that rosy glimmer she really did look devilish seductive, her sinuous body and long shapely legs making you forget the deathly face with its painted lips and lashless eyes. "Good-night," I said again, and turned to the door.

At the same moment there came a sound of footsteps in the passage outside. The girl's face took on an expression of alarm.

"Get behind that screen," she whispered. "Quick!"

With my heart beating guiltily I obeyed her, while she tiptoed to the still open door and noiselessly closed it. The footsteps came nearer, seemed to pause, and then retreated. Silence again fell on the house.

Once more I made ready to go, but Zip now barred my way, standing with her back to the door, a subtle smile on her face. Then suddenly her dress fell from her, leaving her with nothing on but her stockings and a wisp of a chemise.

Now I ask you, what could a fellow do? As you know I had resisted many a temptation in this abandoned planet. But in a case like this, what chance had I? Now I ask you—

It happened that next morning when I was sitting on the couch where Zip had rested, I began to fidget idly with a tassel that dangled from an arm of it. Unexpectedly it yielded to a pull, and at once there came a sound of footsteps along the passage outside.

CHAPTER XLIII

The Gathering of the Twilight Host

ON THE GREY EDGE of the dawn our convoy of loaded lorries met the fleet of empty ones which our colleagues had assembled. The journey to the frontier had been carried out without mishap, for Kwashog had obtained the help of a party of young Harpaxeans to reconnoitre a safer route than the railway cutting through the mountains, and the size of the expedition had been sufficient protection against the showps. In the border region Kwashog and I, ranging ahead over the plain, had sighted the lights of the car in which Ensulas was scouting for us. We had met and shaken hands. Then the two convoys were brought together and the work of shifting the munitions begun. Ensulas's little band of sturdy Twilighters, toiling like niggers under the languid gaze of the boxed-up Harpaxean drivers, soon had the job done. Then the queer assemblage broke up, and we turned our faces towards the day.

I needn't describe the rest of the journey, nor tell you how glad we were to see the sun again after all those days of darkness. When we reached the town from which we had started, the whole population came out to meet us with bands playing and flags flying, and gave us no end of a welcome. Later in the day the convoy was handed over to one of our colleagues, a chap called Tundra, who had been charged with the job of distribution, and while it proceeded on its way, Ensulas, Kwashog, and I gathered together at Kwashog's house to report progress and discuss plans. Ensulas told us that everything was going splendidly. The Twilighters had been living in a state of smothered discontent for generations, and only needed a hint to give it direction. "We knew that," he said, "before we had finished our preliminary feelers. But they're a cautious, cold-blooded people, and for a long time we couldn't get them to face the idea of battle. At that point, in fact, we'd have stuck to this day if it hadn't been for Snikmot."

Mr. Snikmot was one of our colleagues, a nice chatty sort of fellow whom I had taken quite a fancy to when we had been introduced in Bulnid. Ensulas was enthusiastic in his praise. He had shown himself to be a most eloquent and resourceful orator. While the rest of our mission, plain blunt business men as they were, had made no bones about our purpose and directed their arguments straight to the discontent and cupidity of their audiences, Snikmot had put things on a higher plane, appealing to their love of the Old Zone, and talking of the Twilight's Cause, the honour and glory of Twilight, and so on. It was he who had invented the flags we had seen—a form of decoration hitherto unknown in any part of Rathé. From the beginning he had gained more recruits than all the rest of his colleagues put together. Then a sudden flash of inspiration had come to him. He told the people that the Man from the Stars had come down to Rathé specially to help them, and that it was their sacred duty as Procrusteans to follow him against the enemy.

"That fetched them," Ensulas concluded. "They've been tumbling over one another ever since to sign on at the recruiting offices."

"Have the people of the Middle Zone taken alarm yet?" was our next question.

"Yes," said Ensulas. "They've sent a friendly remonstrance," and he lay back in his chair with a howl of laughter while Kwashog smiled grimly. For myself, though I had no very high opinion of the commonsense of these people, I was a bit surprised to find them quite so soft. However it was a very satisfactory thing to know.

Next day we drove to the town which had been chosen as
our headquarters, a place called Esab, about 160 miles from the
frontier. On the way we saw everywhere signs of the revolution:
people standing about in excited groups talking or reading the
posters stuck up on the walls, extemporised flags flying from
roofs and windows, business generally at a standstill, men drill-
ing and children imitating them. Wherever we went we were
cheered, being, of course, easily recognisable by our eyes. At
headquarters, which was the guest-house of the town, we found
our fellow conspirators assembled: six of them, including the
inspired Snikmot. With them were two of the Twilight leaders:
one young, earnest, and very much under Snikmot's influence;
the other middle-aged, and obviously a cod of the first water.
The two of them were introduced to me by Snikmot. The
younger man, whose name was Estern, looked up at me with
a sort of dog-like devotion in his eyes, and could hardly bring
himself to take the hand I offered him. He couldn't speak at all.
When he tried he choked, and blushed like a tomato. The cod,
on the other hand, was all over me, and his protestations of
readiness to die for me were beastly embarrassing. His name, if
I remember rightly, was Gubmuh.

These preliminaries over, we moved into another room,
where all was in readiness for a council of war: a table laid out
with paper, pens, ink, and maps, and eleven chairs standing to
attention around it. I am, as you are aware, a fellow that knows
his place and has no inclination to push himself forward, so
I was the last of the company to claim a chair. Judge then of
my dismay when I found that the only one left was the one
at the head of the table. I had no choice but to slip into it
as unostentatiously as possible. A dead silence followed. Then
Kwashog gave a brisk cough, and, turning to me, said: "Well,
Chief, what's the first item on the agenda?"

If he had banged me on the head with a ruler I couldn't have
been more stupefied.

"Say!" I managed to stammer at last. "I'm not the general of this campaign."

Kwashog looked very black at me. "Of course you are," he said. "You're the only person here who knows anything about war."

"Besides," put in Snikmot, "the people will insist on being led by the Man from the Stars."

"Hear, hear!" cried Mr. Gubmuh.

Jove, I did feel in a hole. But there was nothing to do but accept the job. After all, though I knew sweet damn all about military matters, there wasn't a man in the planet that didn't know less. To them I was a regular Napoleon. Besides, it was rather nice to be top dog in our enterprise. So I decided to shoulder the responsibility and get on with the work.

"Very well, gentlemen," I said impressively. "At your solicitation I accept this very onerous position, and will use what knowledge and abilities I possess to bring our expedition to a successful conclusion. (*Hear, hear!* from Gubmuh.) Now let us get to business. First of all, what's the news of the enemy?"

Here Mr. Gubmuh passed me up a copy of a note which had been received that day by the chief of every Twilight tribe from the World Court. It briefly pointed out that as the mandate of the Court had not been obeyed, trade relations with the rest of the world were suspended as from tomorrow.

"Well, that doesn't frighten us, gentlemen, does it?"

There was a unanimous murmur of No, with a laugh from Ensulas, and something about being ready to defy the tyrants from Gubmuh.

The next thing we dealt with was the formation of our men into an army. At the moment they were in training in their own districts, so we decided as a preliminary move to get them concentrated on the larger towns and there form them into army corps, each under a general. The young Twilighter Estern was assigned to me as a sort of Chief of Staff, and Tundra was to remain in charge of munitions. That left nine of us to take commands, and we were just about to distribute the districts between them when Snikmot stood up with a request for a hearing.

I knew what was coming as soon as I heard his discreet cough. There was, he said, a matter of some delicacy which he felt it to be his duty to mention. Briefly, our gallant Twilight allies—of whose excellent qualities there was no more sincere admirer than himself—permitted themselves certain laxities—or perhaps they might more agreeably be styled freedoms—in matters which in our more conventional land—etcetera, etcetera.

It shows how perfectly Ratheanised I had become that I had clean forgotten this question of commissariat. That, however, was soon rectified. It turned out that the Twilighters like their neighbours, were frugivorous, but were not bigoted about it. Their staple diet was a sort of sweet potato which grew freely in their not very kindly climate, and could be easily stored and transported. The job was at once entrusted to the excellent Snikmot, the number of generals available being thus reduced to eight. We made our arrangements accordingly. The whole bunch then set out for their respective headquarters, leaving me (with a touching faith in my military ability) to draw up a plan of campaign.

Alone in my glory, the self-confidence with which their presence had propped me up collapsed under me like a rickety chair. I don't suppose that anybody was ever thrust into such a responsible position at such short notice, and with so little qualification, before. Talk of Log Cabin to White House! Didn't I just wish I had had the energy to take one of those correspondence courses in Mind Training and Efficiency that you see advertised in the papers. However, there was no use wasting time in vain regrets, so I set to work to make the best of the situation. I tried to remember something of what I had read in the newspapers about the last war, but it wasn't much. Anyway, our war wasn't going to be conducted on modern lines, with air bombings and poison gas and disease-shells and supertanks, but with rifles and bayonets like long ago. Of course that made it a lot simpler, so I began to feel a bit more cheerful. I tried to recollect what I had learnt about old-fashioned war in the history books at school. They used to march along and capture towns, I remembered, and when the enemy came along the two sides formed up and fired at each other, and afterwards charged with the bayonet. Then they marched on and dictated terms of peace in the capital. Good, thought I: that's not so frightfully complicated when you come to think of it. All the advantages would be on our side. Though the enemy wouldn't be taken entirely by surprise, still they could never raise and equip an army as good as ours before we'd be on top of them; and, when it came to fighting, our sturdy Twilighters would make short work of such softies.

And now to get a move on, says I, quite bucked. I had a notion that the right thing to do would be to invade at several points at once. It would be more strategical, like. But I was afraid that I wouldn't be able to manage a lot of complicated maneuvers, or even keep the positions of the different armies in my head, so I decided to lump all my forces together into one army and keep it right to my hand. Then I'd just march straight forward and hit the enemy one smashing blow, wherever I could reach him. rolled the map and proceeded to take stock of it. At first it was like trying to solve one of those mazes or find-the-policeman puzzles. But presently things began to take some sort of shape. There was Esab my present head-quarters, clearly marked, in a most convenient position, right at the focus of the most densely inhabited part of the Zone, and about 160 miles from the frontier of the Middle Zone. All the other towns of any consequence were situated within three hundred miles of it, so that altogether it was the natural concentration point for our troops, and an excellent base from which to start the invasion. Next I cast my eye round for an objective.

There was a convenient enemy town called Yllab on the direct
road from Esab to Israp. It was just two hundred miles away,
and forty beyond the frontier. On second thoughts it occurred
to me that there was no point in giving our troops so long a
march as that, so, after hunting about, I decided to concentrate
them at another town called Nowt, nearly ninety miles further
west, instead of at Esab. That would reduce the march to 110
miles. Suppose the men would march four miles an hour for
eight hours a day: that would be thirty-two miles a day: we'd get
there on the fourth day. That would mean sleeping three nights
in the open—a bother if the weather was bad. However, armies
always had such discomforts to put up with. On the fourth
night we'd billet the troops at Yllab, and then we could await
developments. Altogether it seemed a jolly good plan of action,
and I felt distinctly proud of my achievement.

During the next few days reports kept coming in from my
generals, and at last, having learnt that their commands were
complete, and that a hundred thousand men stood ready to
march, I issued orders for the concentration on Nowt to begin.
The following evening one of the nearest corps was marching
through Esab on its way westwards, the men roaring war –
songs and cheering with enthusiastic loyalty as they passed my
headquarters. It was jolly thrilling I can tell you, and when I
thought of all those hundreds of columns everywhere moving
in obedience to my directions I was a very proud man.

But what a crash my pride came down with. For a while
everything seemed to be going smoothly, and each day the members of my staff would come in to report the steady approach of
marching hosts along every road. Then quite suddenly troubles
came crowding on me like sparrows round a crust. First came
a worried looking member of my staff wanting me to unravel a
tangle that had arisen on one of the northern roads. It appeared
that two army corps, marching by converging routes, had
reached a main road simultaneously. Neither being willing to
give way to the other, they had continued their march side by

side. This, of course, made the road impassable for traffic going in the opposite direction, and the result was that all the local vehicles, going about their ordinary business, had been turned back. The armies had thus marched on, sweeping an accumulating throng of reluctant traffic before them, until finally there had been a breakdown somewhere, and the whole mass had become jammed. What, asked the puzzled staff officer, was to be done?

"Do these infernal carters not realise that the Zone is at war?" I demanded. "Order them to clear off the roads and take their vehicles home."

"Half of them were trying to do that already," said the officer. "The armies have cut them off from their homes."

"Well, they'll just have to go back and get round some other way."

"What other way?" asked the officer patiently.

"Any other way," I snapped. "You don't want me to go and explore one for them, do you? If there's no way round, pitch them all into the field, and let the armies march on."

The officer was about to go off when two others came in and stood breathless before me.

"Well?" I said.

"There's a traffic block on the Elthil road, general," said number one.

"There's a traf—" began number two, but I cut him short in a rage.

"Flaming devils!" I said. "Has the commander in chief of eight armies nothing else to do but help the van drivers of the country to find their way home? Go and tell the generals that the Zone is at war, that the armies have got to get to the front, and that if civilians get in the way they're to be flung out of it."

When I had got rid of the fellows I called for my car, and drove out into a drizzling rain that had been falling all day to see if things were really as bad as they said. They were. I hadn't gone far before I found my way blocked by a barricade of smashed motor lorries which had somehow managed to pile themselves up on top of one another. A whole fleet of lorries was waiting patiently behind this obstruction, while a breakdown gang of soldiers laboured in the downpour to remove it. Questioning the officer in charge, I learned that this was an independent contingent from an outlying part of the Zone which had come in lorries to be sure of arriving in time. More haste less speed, eh, Mr. Gallagher? I turned back, and on approaching the town, found myself cut Off from it by another corps that was just marching in. I had to wait half an hour to let them pass.

They splashed along over the puddled road in weary silence, and I thought the men had a rather wolfish look. The column tailed off miserably in the rear, wider and wider intervals appearing between each unit. At last I slipped my car into one of these gaps and so reached the town. Here it seemed that discipline had completely broken down, for whole sections had dropped asleep by the wayside, a wine shop had been plundered, and a rabble of soldiers were singing drunkenly outside. Full of apprehension I hurried to headquarters. There was nobody there. Estern and all the staff were away, detained, no doubt, by other difficulties of the same kind.

I sat down and waited in the growing gloom in the company of thoughts more gloomy still. How was I to have calculated on this disorganisation? And how the deuce was it going to end? Not half our men were up yet, so what would the confusion be like when they all marched in? My mind simply refused to work, and I just sat there moping. Presently came a quick step, and in burst Snikmot, covered all over with mud, with his clothes in tatters, and a sorry tale to tell. His commissariat system was breaking down.

"What?" I cried, jumping to my feet. "Has the potato crop failed?"

"No," said he.

"It's a question of transport—"

"Commandeer every cart in the country," I said grandly.

"So I have," said he. "But of course they take time to arrive. The real difficulty is that the empty carts can't get back after delivering the stuff, because the roads are all choked up with soldiers. That's why I'm in my present state. I had to leave my car and foot it across country. There's nothing but soldiers everywhere, and nothing can get past them. All the carts I'd mobilised in the last week are now stuck in blind alleys or creeping back slowly along the hedges, while I've piles of stuff waiting to be distributed, and scores of units have been without food for forty-eight hours."

Our attempts to find a way out of this muddle involved us in a terrific wrangle, in the heat of which we were interrupted by the arrival of Kwashog.

"You here, Snikmot?" he said. "Commissariat broken down, I suppose? I thought as much. Not your fault though." Here he turned an aggrieved face on me. "Why the deuce, when you were ordering this concentration, didn't you settle the roads the different units were to take?"

"One must leave something to the intelligence of the lower command," I said stiffly.

"Certainly," said Kwashog. "But the intelligences of two independent commanders, in the absence of orders from above, are liable to pick the same route as the best one to the same place. Moreover, when so many bodies are making for one point there's apt to be a jam whenever two roads converge. That's what's happened anyway. What are you going to do about it?"

I acted with great presence of mind in this emergency. I made a dash at the map, and with the other two on each side of me began to study it hard. Of course I hadn't a notion in my head what I was going to do, but I hoped that if I could only gain time an inspiration might strike me, or perhaps one of the others might make a suggestion on which I could seize.

"If we could clear one road to begin with—" I hazarded after a long silence.

At that moment we were interrupted by the bursting in of an excited man in the same condition of dirt and disrepair as Snikmot.

"Are you the leaders?" he demanded. "I'm the Mayor of Nowt. My town is in a state of chaos, and I don't know what to do about it. Soldiers have been pouring in for the last week— thousands of them. I was told to billet them in the houses. I've done that: four to a house: and every house is full. And they keep *on* pouring in. The streets are choked with them.

"They're camping in the fields round about, and trampling down the hedges and the crops. And now the food supply has failed, and everyone is starving, townspeople, soldiers, and all. We're in a hopeless state. I sent you six messengers yesterday, but I suppose they couldn't get through. The road is completely blocked with soldiers and waggons. I had to come across country myself, and my car's a wreck in consequence. What are we going to do?"

"There's one thing we've got to do at once," said Kwashog decisively. "We must prevent any more bodies coming into the mess." He made a dash for the telephone, rang up three numbers in succession, and rattled off a string of orders to each of his hearers. "There," he said. "That'll keep the three hindmost corps back for the present. Now, Mr. Mayor, will you make the best of your way home and try and keep your people from getting into a panic. We ll send supplies up to you as soon as we can." Jove, it was wonderful the way that man could get himself obeyed. The Mayor was off like a shot, and then Kwashog turned on me.

"Now, look here," he said. "Had you any special object in concentrating all these armies on one town? And, if so, why did you choose a little bit of a place with only two roads leading to it?"

I couldn't answer. You see, I hadn't taken any notice of the number of roads. I felt just the biggest ass that ever was born outside a stable, and my one desire now was to get out of the position that had so addled me. Kwashog must have read my thought, for he suggested, not unkindly: "Perhaps you'd like to resign the job?"

"I couldn't put it into better hands than those into which it has fallen," I said gratefully. "You're a military genius, sir. I saw it the moment you went for that telephone."

"Stuff!" said Kwashog. "Mere common sense. You haven't had any practice in organisation, that's all. You'll have to command on the day of battle though. The people will insist on that. Besides, I shouldn't know what to do in that case."

"Quite right," put in Snikmot. "Kwashog will get us out of this tangle all right, but the Man from the Stars must lead us into battle."

Well, it was something to get even that respite, so I agreed. Kwashog at once took things in hand. I wondered how on earth he was going to straighten the mess out, for fresh trouble had been accumulating while we had been talking. Staff officers, commanders, messengers, even stray soldiers, kept coming to the door every few minutes with tales of calamity. Indeed, it seemed that the army was hopelessly banjaxed. But it was a treat to see Kwashog at work: to see him forcing his personality through the telephone to distant incompetents, to hear him directing twenty different people on twenty different tasks at once. It seemed that he could even command the weather, for before he had been long at work the rain stopped. The night wore away, and still he kept at it like an inexhaustible machine. Snikmot and I fell asleep where we sat, but he never bothered about us. We slept until daylight, and when we woke he was still there, a telephone receiver at his ear, and his pencil working furiously on a scribbling block. He threw down both while I stared at him, yawned, stretched himself, and said: "Well, that's done. I'm off for a rest. Call me in three hours' time."

CHAPTER XLIV

The Battle of the Plains of Yllab

NOW FOR THE CLASH of arms and the glory of war, the rattle of guns and the tramp of marching men.

The fruit of Kwashog's labour was that in a very short time our armies were massed at three separate bases, ready to advance in a concerted movement against three separate objectives. I was in command of the central force, which was to strike at Yllab; the right wing was led by Kwashog, and the left by Ensulas. At length the fateful moment struck, and the invasion began. Our reconnoitring parties had reported that there was no sign of any activity on the part of the enemy, so I drove with my staff and a small mounted escort in front of the column of troops. There was still no sign of opposition when we crossed the frontier hills, nor yet when we descended into the fertile plains beyond. The country in fact was ominously quiet, and seemed to have been deserted by the inhabitants. We camped for a night well within hostile territory, and resumed our march in the same fashion the following day. It was not until we were within a few miles of Yllab that even a show of resistance was made. And it was no more than a show. Approaching a cross-road I and my escort found ourselves confronted by two men in a car. Telling my men to hold themselves in readiness I drove forward to see if they had anything to say. One of them I knew by his dress to be a chief—probably the Chief of Yllab.

"Are you the leader of this plundering expedition?" he asked as I slowed down.

"The Commander-in-Chief, at your service," says I.

"Then it is my duty to request you to order your men to return home and to place yourself in my custody."

"Don't make me laugh," says I. "I've a split lip."

"Am I to understand that you decline?" says the Chief. "Very well. You have had your warning. Good afternoon." He turned his car and drove off: didn't believe in a faithful-unto-death policy apparently. I thought it would be a good idea to give the enemy a taste of our quality, so I ordered my escort to fire after him, but they missed.

What a true saying it is that if you want peace you must prepare for war. The Yllabians now had to pay the penalty for their failure to realise it. There lay their rich and well-ordered land at the mercy of our more enterprising allies, and not a solitary soldier ready to defend it. On we marched like conquering heroes, bands playing and colours flying, to enter their capital in triumph, while the frightened citizens sought shelter in their homes. It was the greatest moment of my life. Never till my dying day shall I forget the thrill of it. To think that I, with no advantages of birth or education, a mere nobody in my own land, should have come to this! By jove, it was stupendous.

Having made arrangements for billeting the men on the town I got into telephonic communication with Kwashog and Ensulas, who, I learned, had also attained their objectives without opposition. Satisfied with this intelligence I then proceeded to the palace, where I found the Chief all by himself.

"Got home safe, I see," said I, chaffing him. "I hope our bullets didn't frighten you yesterday."

The Chief said nothing, but handed me a letter. It was from a body calling itself the Supreme Defence Council of the Middle Zone, and briefly informed me that if the leaders of the rebellion, whom it named, would order their followers to go home, and submit their own persons for trial, the people of the Middle Zone would pardon the outrage which had been committed against them.

"They will in their necks," said I haughtily, and, crumpling the paper into a ball, I flung it in the Chief's face with a laugh of derision. I then ordered my guards to arrest him and lock him up. I occupied his own room that night, and I'm afraid the troops made rather free with the property of his tribesmen. However, they had only themselves to blame for their criminal unpreparedness.

My first task next day was to send out scouting parties and airplanes to watch for the approach of the enemy. Talking of airplanes, you may be wondering why we didn't use them to bomb the Rathean cities instead of attacking them with infantry. Well, in the first place, all the machines we had were light ones, only suitable for scouting, and we had no time to train the men as bombers. In the second place, we didn't want to make ourselves too unpopular with our new subjects. In the third place, two can play at that game, and we hoped that if we didn't start it the Sunshiners mightn't think of it. And in the fourth place, the Twilight Chiefs thought the idea too barbarous. Besides, we hadn't any bombs or any means of making them. But to return to my tale. About midday came word that a hostile army really was approaching at last. It was reported to be moving towards Yllab, and to number not more than twenty thousand men. I fairly chuckled with delight at the news, foreseeing an easy and glorious victory at the very start of our campaign, which would strike terror into the population and ensure that rapid conquest which is said to be the greatest blessing to a subjugated people. I telephoned the word at once to my colleagues, calling upon them to move their armies inward towards mine so that we might crush the enemy between overwhelming forces.

These operations were soon in progress, so that by nightfall our concentration was more than half accomplished. In the meantime the enemy's advance had continued, and at the close of the day he was bivouacked on the edge of the great plain that lay westward of the city, about a dozen miles from our outposts. Thus everything was in readiness for a great battle on the morrow.

I couldn't sleep that night, and the dawn saw me on the roof of the palace surveying the scene of action.

The battle-ground which the enemy had chosen was a perfectly ideal one from our point of view. A vast plain as level as a playing-field, it offered every advantage to our vastly superior numbers, and left not a chance of escape to the defeated army. Early as it was, developments had already taken place. watched through my glasses the preliminary maneuvers of each of the four units. At my feet were my own men mustering on the edge of the town, a long skirmishing line thrown out in front, the reserves massed in small striking forces behind. Far away to the right were Kwashog's men crawling over the plain in little mobile columns not yet deployed. Only the advanced scouts of our left wing were visible, feeling their way forward from the skirts of a wood which there bounded the plain. And miles off in the distance, still shrouded in the morning mist, were the dim lines of the enemy standing where they had halted when the outposts first came in contact. A few airplanes circled about overhead.

As soon as I saw that our forces were in touch with one another, I went down to put myself at the head of my men and lead them into action. I was in such a state of excitement that I caught up my umbrella instead of my sword as I rushed out of the palace, and never discovered my mistake until I was about to order the advance. Gosh, I did feel a fool. You see the weather in the Twilight Zone had been so bad that I had never dared go anywhere without it, and my hand had simply gripped it by force of habit. I dropped the beastly thing unobtrusively behind my back, hoping that no one would notice it, but an infernal well meaning ass of a soldier sprang from his place to retrieve it, and handed it back to me so nicely that I didn't like to hurt his feelings by refusing it. So with blazing ears I uttered the command "Forward!"

The atmosphere cleared rapidly as we advanced, and the rising sun shone out with a brilliance which was anything but an advantage to us. The long skirmishing line in front trudged stolidly forward, heads bent to avoid the glare. The spaced out columns followed, Estern and I leading the foremost. The whole host moved in a grim silence save for the muffled tread of feet on the grassy ground. The enemy awaited us silent also and motionless. My spirits began to recover somewhat as we proceeded, and a kind of before-the-battle exultation seized hold of me. I wish to heaven I'd had more sense than to let it. For, partly inspired by this, and partly with a desire to outface the shame of the umbrella incident, I threw my chest out and my head up in a valiant manner more suited to the parade ground than the battle-field. It was a silly thing to do, for a moment later, in descending a slight undulation of the ground, slippery with the previous days' rain, my feet shot from under me as suddenly as if I had trod on a banana peel. My hat! but I blush still when I think of that moment. The leading file of soldiers at once rushed to my rescue, and while two of them helped me to my feet, anxiously inquiring if I was hurt, a third set to work cleaning me down with great slaps of his hands, and another solicitously tendered me that cursed umbrella. The shock of that sit-down drove all the military spirit out of me, but of course I had to march on all the same, and beastly uncomfortable I felt too, with the twice-muddied umbrella gripped in my fist, and the soaked seat of my breeches clinging cold and clammy to my nether parts.

I thought the march would never end; but at last, rising from a depression that had hidden the enemy for a while from our sight, we saw him in full view not half a mile away. And in that instant I got a really nasty jar, for, spaced at regular intervals along the front of their lines, was a row of—what do you think—big guns? My heart stopped beating for a moment at the sight. How the devil could they have produced the things in the time? And what the blazes were we to do? At that range a few volleys would tear our ranks to tatters, and drive the survivors in panic from the field. Why hadn't they fired already? Probably their gunners were raw hands, only to be trusted at short range. We'd have a chance then. We could rush the remainder of the distance without heavy loss if only the men were game for it. Then our numbers would settle matters. That was our only hope anyhow. We must charge at once.

Sporadic shooting had already broken out from different portions of our line, and I actually saw some of the enemy drop. Still, however, no reply came from them. It was now or never. Half turning and waving my umbrella, I shouted, "Charge!"

Charging was no easy matter over that slippery ground, so our pace was not a fast one. Formations had already begun to loosen during the long advance over open country, and now they melted away entirely as the rearmost units closed up on the heels of their comrades in front and blended with them to form one long deep wave of panting rushing humanity. Only the skirmishers in front preserved their distinctiveness, running briskly ahead like the foaming wash that scurries before a breaker on the seashore. They were firing from the hip as they ran, but with little effect that I could see. And still there came no answer from the motionless lines of the enemy. As the distance between us lessened—oh, how slowly it seemed to do so—that confident steadfastness struck me with a kind of fear. I found myself wishing that they would fire those guns and break that ominous silence, for surely they would not dare to let us come so close if they had not something up their sleeve—some frightful resource more blasting than any artillery. But still they did nothing, and still we slogged and panted forward.

I was soon near enough to distinguish the features of the enemy soldiers. They were packed close, in a kneeling position, in shallow trenches which they had hastily dug, and they did not seem to be armed. By each of the big guns stood a crew of four men. At this close view I began to doubt if the things were guns after all. I stared hard at one which almost directly faced me. The barrel of the thing was very long, but, if I wasn't deceived by the distance, its material was quite thin—mere sheet-iron. And it was mounted on a light tripod like a camera-stand, with no visible mechanism. I saw all this in a glance, and up went my spirits to the skies again. They couldn't fire any missile to worry about from a thing like that.

I began to brace myself for the final rush, and at the same moment one of the gun-crew stepped to the breech of his weapon. Immediately after a warmish sickly-scented breeze seemed to sweep past me. Then came a second and stronger puff. I felt a tingling sensation in the throat, and a catch in my breath. I staggered slightly, and stopped running. I saw the skirmishers in front of me swaying and reeling. Good lord! I realised: invisible poison gas! Then I doubled up with a fit of coughing, and was down on my knees, gasping in agony for breath. In one wild glance around I saw that our whole army was breaking up into a helpless mob, racked by paroxysms like mine. Then my own torment re-absorbed me. I was enveloped in a tide of pungent vapour that grew steadily denser. Sight and hearing were leaving me. My breath came in vast shuddering sobs that seemed to rend my body asunder. There was a frightful throbbing in my head that grew louder and louder and louder, and louder and louder and louder. Then silence and a black mist swallowed up the world.

CHAPTER XLV

He departs from Rathé

I AWAKENED OUT OF horrible nightmares to find myself lying on
a bed in a small unfamiliar room. I felt miserably weak and sick.
I went off, almost at once, into a second stupor, not so deep as
the first, but even more nightmarish. Again I came to, struggled
for a while to retain consciousness, and lapsed a third time into
darkness; after which I lay between sleeping and waking for I
don't know how many hours. At last the sound of a door shutting roused me sharply, and I saw the Chief of Bulnid standing
by my bedside.

"Well, sir," said the Chief after a long silence. "Have you
anything to say for yourself?"

"Nothing," I answered proudly. "I reserve my defence for the
law courts."

"You will be taken for trial tomorrow," said the Chief. "Till
then you will be confined here. If you are in need of anything,
ring this bell and you will be attended to."

He went out. I lay in a drowsy condition for some time
afterwards, but strength gradually returned, and I began to be
curious about what had happened. I rang the bell and asked for
wine and newspapers. The latter made all clear in a moment.
The forces of the Middle Zone had taken the field armed only
with a soporific gas. With this they had crumpled up our whole
army a few hundred yards in front of their lines. The sleeping
invaders had then been systematically disarmed, and on recov-
ery dismissed to their own territory, all but the leaders who were
now lodged in custody. About a hundred of the Middle Zoners

had been killed or wounded by the shots of the Twilighters before their batteries had come into action. On our side no blood at all had been spilt, except for a few men wounded by the discharge of rifles dropped by themselves or their comrades in their paroxysms. Altogether it was a pretty inglorious tale.

Early on the following day I was conveyed in a closed car to the law courts; but instead of being brought up for trial immediately I was led into a small private room where a most unpleasant ordeal awaited me. It appeared that the question had been raised whether I was really a human being, and so entitled to a trial, or whether I should be destroyed offhand as a dangerous animal. This difficulty, I feel sure, had been suggested by Mr. Yasint, who had taken a violent prejudice against me on account of my criticism of Rathean economic ideas. Anyway, a scientist, a diabologian, and one of the Gogaleths had been told off to find out whether I was human or not, and between them they gave me the very devil of a time. When they had finished they took me into court, where the Gogaleth gave the bench a summary of the result of the inquiry. It was doubtful, he said, whether the race to which the prisoner belonged should be classed as a very low type of man or a rather high type of ape. They had not allowed themselves to be influenced by what they had learnt of the physical aspect of the creatures, though the general conformation of the head, particularly in the oph-thalmic region, was undoubtedly simian. Their researches had been mainly conducted into our mental and physiological characteristics; and on this basis the evidence was uncertain, confused, and contradictory. Our quarrelsomeness, ferocity, vindictiveness, and general love of mischief were markedly simian indications, as were our acquisitiveness, our mania for collecting useless things, our vanity, our addiction to meaning-less chatter, our gluttony, and our insatiable sexuality, which was tempered only by irrational taboos. On the other hand, it was evident that we had some rudimentary reasoning powers,

of which, however, we made very little use, and that we could
both speak and write, and had even some primitive artistic
instincts. Again, traces of elementary religious ideas were obviously discernible in our composition, though it was doubtful if
we had any deeper ethical conception than the animal notion
of reward and punishment. The examiners, therefore, begged
to report that they were unable, in the time at their disposal,
to come to any definite conclusion as to whether the race in
question were human or not; but they considered that it was
sufficiently probable to justify the court in giving the prisoner
the benefit of the doubt.

With this recommendation the Gogaleths concurred, and
the trial began. My guilt, of course, was self-evident, but, the
hearing was a long one. There is no need to describe the whole
of the proceedings, which were excessively boring, but 1 will try
and set down what 1 remember of the Chief Gogaleth's

After a full examination of the facts of the case, he said, I
had been found guilty of taking part in a conspiracy against
the peace and order of the world a consequence of which large
numbers of people had been killed and injured, the population
of a whole continent had been roused to anger and violence
against their neighbours, and the remainder of the world had
been compelled to take defensive measures which involved
grave disturbance of soul, the rousing of some of their lowest
instincts, and their training themselves for the performance of
tasks which were as repugnant as they were degrading. These
facts were beyond doubt or dispute, and I had admitted them.
But I had pleaded in mitigation of my offence that I had been
inspired by good motives, and though the court was not concerned with motives, since its function was not to pronounce
judgment upon offenders, but only to protect society against
mischievous conduct, nevertheless the plea had been examined
in view of its possible bearing upon the steps which that protection might require. The first of these good motives to which I

had laid claim was a genuine sympathy with the hard condition of the Twilight population, and a consequent resolve to remedy it. "After a most exhaustive psychological examination," he continued "we find that this motive, if existent at all, was so small as to be of no account. However, small as it is, we shall hold it to your credit, and have decided to grant you what alleviation of your remorse may follow from the information that henceforward their needs shall be the first charge on the surplus energy and resources of their fellow-tribes.

"The second good-motive which you allege is an honest desire to assist the progress of this world by imposing upon it the social-economic system which has conferred such benefits on that from which you have come. We have satisfied ourselves that this motive did actually occupy a very prominent place in your mind. But that only confirms us in our opinion that you are an extremely dangerous person. In the course of a prolonged and tedious cross-examination you utterly failed to produce any facts which disprove the *a priori* arguments which have prevented us from adopting a system of economics based on money and the principle of exchange. On the contrary, the conditions which you have described as obtaining in your world have perfectly confirmed all the conclusions to which abstract reasoning had already led us. For you must not imagine that this idea is a novelty in Rathé. Indeed it has always been a favourite theme with those cranks, Utopians, and other feeble-minded dreamers, who imagine that the admitted disadvantages of our existing system of fellowship and co-operation would vanish under a system of competition and exchange. But, as our economists have pointed out, a system of exchange, though excellent in theory, cannot work out in practice. They have demonstrated that the inevitable tendency of money would be, sooner or later, to lose its character as a symbol and acquire a real value— or at any rate a value which would be esteemed as real. If it be decided that so many coins shall represent a suit of clothes for exchange purposes, inevitably the corollary will arise that the coins and the clothes are of the same value, or, worse still, that the coins and the thought and labour that made the clothes are of the same value. Money would thus cease to be a symbol of exchange and become a commodity. It would rise or fall in value like a commodity, and like a commodity could be hired or purchased. But unlike a commodity it could be accumulated, and would not wear out. So, like any imperfect symbol, it would obscure instead of clarifying. Even you, with your limited brain, would laugh at the idea of paying anybody a year's supply of commodities in return for a day's work: yet you think it perfectly natural to pay him their equivalent in coin. Even your undeveloped moral sense would recognise the iniquity of allowing one man to monopolise the labour of ten thousand, and bequeath its fruit to his heirs and descendants; yet it is a part of your law that he can do so with the symbolic representation of it. Your whole civilisation is, in fact, founded upon a fallacy which two seconds of clear thinking would expose, though God knows its fruits of horror and suffering should make you execrate it without any brainwork at all.

"To our minds the sequence is as clear as daylight. Inevitably the money must accumulate in the hands of a few: and those few not the wise and the good, but the merely acquisitive, who are held in least esteem in our world, though so highly honoured in yours. As it thus accumulated, the system of exchange would, equally inevitably, give place to a system of pay and service. One part of the community would become the hired servants of the other part, and would be paid not according to their needs, but whatever minimum sum they could be induced to accept. Mankind would thus be cleft into two classes: one working (where it worked at all) for profit; the other toiling for mere existence under a compulsion no less real because the whips and chains would not be visible.

"To bolster up this preposterous arrangement there would

arise, or be invented, a vast sham Science of Finance, which nobody could understand except a few people too stupid to understand anything else. According to this perverted science it would be perfectly possible and logical for a man to starve in the midst of plenty, or to be workless amid a shortage of production. It could prove scarcity to be better than abundance, or a stone or a dog of more value than a man. It could prove birth a calamity and fertility a disease. All government and all education would be conducted in accordance with this science, so that all social and personal evolution would be perverted by it. The acquisitive type of man—the lowest type—would be exalted at the expense of all others. The highest types—those for whom some external idea is more important than their own personal wants, such as the religious thinker, the artist, the scientist—would be compelled, unless exempted by some accident of fortune—to develop their acquisitive instincts at the expense of their finer qualities, if they were to exist at all. As for the great mass of common folk, on whom the evolution of the race, as a race, depends, they too would be forced into petty acquisitiveness which would nevertheless be insufficient to raise them out of their narrow insignificance. And at the bottom there would be the dregs, the hopeless failures, worse than useless, a contamination to all others.

"According to this sham science the most soul-tormenting absurdities would be practical, and the most horrible injustices would be legitimate. We should have some people, born into the possession of wealth, passing all their lives in idle pleasure, and others working from childhood to the grave for a bare subsistence. We should have wealth wasting in the hands of fools, and the capacities of men of worth wasting for lack of it. Whole countrysides would be swept bare of workers to make playgrounds for the rich; and men would be taken from useful work to stand about as their lackeys. Vast masses of people would lead dreary, narrow, purposeless lives, working at dull monotonous meaningless tasks in other people's service, dwelling in small, ugly houses in cheerless neighbourhoods, with moderate animal comforts, but starved of beauty, art, and joy, and drugged to all thinking. Yet other multitudes would be poor enough to think these rich. Childhood born into these surroundings would have all its rich potentialities blighted like a flower in a dark place. Youth would grow hard and set, like a stunted tree in impoverished soil, or bent and twisted like a plant vainly seeking the light. Young love would be thwarted and made barren, and beauty become the prey of ageing lust. Finally, when the avarice of the rich had made the world desolate for the rest of mankind, these would take counsel of despair and, lest their own increase should starve them, cry "we will breed no more." In short, the consequences of our adopting a monetary system would, say our philosophers, be exactly what you have described as the accepted conditions in the world which you have come from.

"Thus," said the Gogaleth, "the second extenuating plea which you have advanced aggravates instead of mitigating your offence. Nothing remains, then, but to pronounce sentence upon you. Aloysius O'Kennedy, you are a dangerous person, whose continued existence is a menace to the peace of the world. I order therefore that at eight o'clock tomorrow morning you be taken away from here and shot dead in the manner prescribed by law."

"Get along out of that, you goggle-eyed son of a fossilised gorilla," said I. "I'm not afraid of you—you or the bunch of fruit-eating state pensionaries beside you. I don't care a spit in hell for the lot of you. D'ye hear? I'm not afraid of your pop-guns. Shoot till you're black in the face, but you can't kill me. I'm immortal. This isn't the first body I've taken up and laid down. A wanderer among the stars I am, and at home anywhere in the universe, so what's one life more or less to me? That in your eye," says I, spitting on the floor, "and the next world I settle in, I hope it'll be a better one than this."

They were all impressed by my steadfastness in the face of death.

"Well bethought," says the Chief Gogaleth presently. "If that restless spirit of yours should ever return to the world from which it started, here is a hint that may lead its people out of their foolishness. You have seen with what horror we have heard your accounts of those grim and awful wars which from time to time gather all the blasts of your miseries into one vast hurricane of woe. Yet there, in the very abandonment of your folly, you have found the beginning of wisdom, and do not know it. For when your soldiers take the field, how do you pay them? Is it according to merit? Do you pay them according to the number of the enemy they kill, or the value of the information they procure in reconnaissance? Do you stir their competitive instincts with opportunities for high profits? Or keep them up to the mark by fear of short rations? No. You treat all alike, and expect each to do his best, even to the sacrifice of his life. Yet you have repeatedly told us that the same men who for no reward at all will face toil and privation, wounds, danger and death, readily and cheerfully, will not perform the ordinary duties of social life unless bribed with immense rewards, or driven by the fear of poverty. This condemnation of your race, we would have you observe, has not been spoken by us, whose censures you so unreasonably resent, but by you yourself; and it is so contrary to reason that we urge you to reconsider it, and to suggest to your people that if they were to conduct their affairs in peace on the same principle as they conduct them in war, their peace would prove as fruitful in happiness as their wars in misery."

I had said my say, so I made no answer to this tirade. The Gogaleths then rose, and the court rapidly emptied.

Returned to custody at the Palace, I was informed by the Chief that it was customary for a condemned person to be accompanied by one relative or friend to the place of execution, and that if I would name one he would have my message conveyed to him. As all the friends I had in this world were probably in a like case to my own I could make no suggestion, but presently I remembered Mr. Dobyna, the young man I had met on my first entry into Bulnid, and asked that he should be requested to do this last office for me.

Early on the following day he came to the room where I was confined, along with one of the Gogaleths, who had been chosen by lot (according to the law of these people) to be my executioner. Between them I walked to a side-door where an airplane was waiting. We stepped on board, and at once flew to the great Cemetery. There there was enacted a scene which reproduced exactly that which I had observed as a spirit not so long before. We stepped out among the litter of bones. The executioner fixed up his apparatus. Dobyna walked with me to the place where I was to stand, gave me a few kindly parting words, and left me to face the instrument of death.

I stood with closed eyes, waiting.

CHAPTER XLVI

The Procession of the Gods

IT ISN'T EVERYBODY THAT suffers two deaths in a lifetime: and here am I due for a third sooner or later. This second death was a far more unpleasant experience than the previous one, which had been only a sort of spiriting away, for Ydenneko's body had been genuinely killed at last, and I felt a frightful pang in parting from it. May my next be a quiet one!

I was so stunned by the shock of dissolution that Rathé had slipped far away from me before I realised that I was still a living spirit, drifting again into that outer blackness which had so terrified me at the beginning of my adventures. But then I had been a lusty soul fresh from a live body, with powers only waiting to be discovered; whereas now I was a mere wraith, a dead man's ghost, abjectly will-less. I wanted to grasp at any of the rare worlds that at wider and wider intervals went rolling by, but I could not do it. My very wanting was feeble, and growing feebler: my power of willing was gone. So out, out, out I went, beyond the last of the stars, out into the night. With incredible speed the material universe abandoned me, shrank till it was only a glimmer like the tail-light of a receding car, and vanished. I was alone, utterly and completely alone.

So at least it seemed for a moment. Then I realised that the universe had not quite vanished. It still remained as a barely discernible speck of brightness no larger than a pinprick. And the whole black immensity around me was dotted over with millions of such specks. I was poised, in fact, in the very heart of a universe of universes, right in the immoveable centre of

things, and there passing into nothingness. All that remained
of Aloysius O'Kennedy, the Me that was in him and made him,
was going out like the last red point on the wick of a blown-
out candle. And it was just then that I realised somehow that
Aloysius O'Kennedy was not such an important person as I had
always imagined him. I looked at him in a queer detached sort
of way as if he was somebody else, and asked myself what on
earth he had ever been up to. A living soul in a body that he had
to feed and clothe and wash and take care of, what had he done
with his life? He worked to feed himself, fed himself that he
might work again; worked at no task worth doing, a mere convenience to others, without responsibility, without pride or joy
in performance, with his mind always on the end of the week,
wishing his life away for a brief spell of fruitless amusement.
He had never thought anything worth thinking, or known anything worth knowing. What was he up to? What was he for?

It was a funny thing, but my faith must have been dead in
me at that moment, for it never occurred to me to think that
of course after all his trials he would go to his eternal reward.
That idea was as far from my mind as if I had never heard it,
and those two questions kept repeating themselves without
ever recalling it to my memory. Instead there came over me
an extraordinarily urgent desire to find something that should
make Aloysius O'Kennedy worth while.

With that the life seemed to revive in me. I became stronger. I
called out to the universe: "A purpose for Aloysius O'Kennedy!"
and waited for an answer.

Then it seemed to me that a sort of smudge appeared in
the limpid depths of space, and, growing steadily, came gliding
towards me as an enormous cloud. Seated upon it was a monstrous being of terrible aspect. It had the head of a bull and
the teeth of a tiger, and hands like eagles' talons all slobbered
with blood. And towering over me it spoke, saying: "I am the
lord thy God, and my name is Moloch. Tremble and adore me.

Thou shalt hack thy flesh in my honour and bow the necks of thy children before me. Thou shalt fear my temper and do honour to my whims. The black cat shalt thou cherish, and turn away the thirteenth guest. Thou shalt worship me with blood and thy wailing shall be as music in my ear. Bow down and adore me." And he gnashed his teeth, belching out blood and gobbets of flesh.

But I said: "Vile and abominable creature, you are no god for me. I do not believe in you, and I do not worship you." And at that the monster vanished.

Then there came rolling towards me a second cloud, and there was seated upon it a tremendous old man with proud fierce eyes and a long curling beard. With one hand he fondled a naked girl who sat on his knee offering him wine in a cup; with the other he crushed and mangled an unfortunate poor wretch who was bound to a wheel beside him. And he said to me: "I am the lord thy God, and my name is Zeus. Eat, drink, and be merry, for tomorrow you die. But keep thy fingers from my cup, and thine eyes from the woman of my desiring. And lest thou not prosper, bow down and adore me." Then he swilled off the wine, and crushed yet again the bruised body on the wheel, and kissed the girl between the breasts.

So I said: "Away, you improper person. Away, you old hypocrite. I do not believe in you, and I will not worship you." And cloud and god passed on their way.

Then there came a third cloud, and seated upon it was an ancient man as huge as a mountain, and he with three eyes. One of them was mild and credulous and one of them fierce and spiteful, and the third blind. His face was changeable and capricious, and he held in one hand a bunch of lollipops, and in the other fire and brimstone. And he said to me: "I am the lord thy God, the Omnipotent-Benevolent; who made the tiger and the fawn, the sparrow and the sparrowhawk, the lamb and the liver-fluke; who invented cancer and leprosy and tubercle, and earthquake and famine and pestilence. I am the All Just; who chose one people, and left the rest to wallow in idolatry and abomination. I would have all men know the truth: therefore I spoke only to the West, and left the East in darkness; and to the West I spoke in so uncertain a voice that my words were interpreted in seventy senses, and men thought to please me by burning one another over the difference. I am he who damned mankind for one crime, and demanded a worse crime in reparation for it; and all this without imperilling my immutability. I am the Omnipotent-Benevolent; and if my deeds seem to belie my character, remember also that I am inscrutable. Believe in me, and you shall dwell in eternal bliss: reject me, and you shall be delivered to eternal torment. Now take your choice, remembering that your will is free."

So I said: "I believe."

"Do you?" said the god.

"Certainly," I replied.

"You think me a perfectly credible figure?"

"I do."

"Think again, Aloysius," said the god.

"Lord," I said, "don't ask me to do that. I was always told not to question your ways, and that thinking would destroy my faith. Maybe you remember the time you called in the Assyrians to chastise the Israelites for idolatry, and how, when the Israelites repented, you sent your angel to slaughter the Assyrians in their sleep. Well, when I was a little chap and knew no better, I asked my teachers how a just god could do a thing like that; and they told me that whatever you did must be just, and not to ask wicked questions. So now don't ask me any, but take my word for it that I believe in you, and want nothing but to go up to heaven as soon as may please you."

Here a change came over the appearance of the god. His blind eye vanished, and the other two fixed me with an awful look. The lollipops and the brimstone also disappeared.

"Heaven, Aloysius?" said the god. "Do you think you are fit for heaven?"

"I hope so, lord," I said humbly. "I never set up to be anything of a saint, but I never meant any harm, and what I did I'm sorry for, and won't ever do again."

"I was not thinking of your sins," said the god.

"I thought they offended you, lord."

"Offended Me!"

"Well, don't they?" I said.

"O come, Aloysius. Do you really believe that any sin of which You are capable could move Me to anger?"

"Lord, lord," I said, "don't harass me with questions I can't answer. I've told you I believe in you. Isn't that enough?"

"Do you believe this of me?" demanded the god relentlessly.

"Don't you want me to believe it?" I asked.

"Never mind what I want, Aloysius. Do you believe it? Do you think so highly of yourself and so lowly of me?"

"Whatever you say, lord," I said. "Was there no harm in my sins then?"

"You should be the best judge of that, Aloysius. No doubt they have harmed you: but they could not possibly affect me."

"Well, can I go up to heaven, lord?" I asked.

"There is nothing to prevent you, Aloysius. But you must not expect to enjoy it."

"Why not, lord?"

"You have not the capacity."

"I don't understand you, lord."

"Well, tell me this, Aloysius. Have you ever read any poetry?"

"No, lord."

"Or listened to a symphony?"

"No, lord."

"Or contemplated a picture?"

"No."

"Why?"

"I couldn't be bothered."

"Why, then, you have answered your own question, Aloysius. These things are foretastes of heaven, shown to you darkly through the instrumentality of fellow mortals. And if such poor samples are too much for you, how shall you endure the glory of the whole kingdom?"

"Well, I don't think it's fair," I said. "When I think of all the things I haven't done, to be deprived of my reward like this!"

"Reward, Aloysius?" said the god.

"Yes, lord. The eternal happiness you promised me if I was good."

The god smiled and said: "Do you really believe that any deed you could do could merit eternal happiness?"

"Well, it seems reasonable enough," I said. "As I said before, I haven't been exactly a saint, but I wouldn't have been half as good as I was if I hadn't expected something in return for it."

"Indeed?" said the god.

"Well, what's the use of being good if it's to make no difference in the hereafter?"

"It would have made a difference in yourself, Aloysius."

"That's not much of an incentive," I said.

"Do you think," said the god, "that Omnipotence has nothing better to do than to bribe you into making the best of yourself and terrify you out of doing yourself injury? O, Aloysius, at your pride the stars laugh."

"I suppose I was wrong if you say so," I said. "But if there's no heaven and no hell, what's to become of me? I can't spend eternity floating around here in the darkness."

"Indeed?" said the god. "And do you expect to live eternally, Aloysius?"

"Surely," I said. "Why not?"

"Man," said the god, "speak not so lightly. Eternal life is not the pleasure you fancy, but a burden to be borne only by the strong. You cannot bear it, Aloysius. You have not done anything to train yourself. You have never once tasted freedom or responsibility, or cultivated any of the powers of your soul. You are as fitted for eternal life as a baby to climb mountains."

"That's not my fault, lord," I said.

"What does it matter whether it is your fault or not? We are not now apportioning blame, but reckoning up facts."

I was struck dumb by those remorseless words. The god, reading the tumult in my soul, said:

"Is it not strange that, craving life as you do, you have done nothing to enable you to attain it? Had you but married one of those women you poisoned your soul by lusting after, you might have handed on that craving to another, and who knows but in a hundred generations it might have become a will directed by intelligence."

"What do future generations matter to me?" I said. "I haven't been treated fairly, that's all I can say. If I'd only known this before, what a different life I'd have led!"

"Not so different as you think, Aloysius," said the god. "After all, even with the incentive you imagined, were your strivings after righteousness very exhausting?"

"Maybe not," I said, "but wasn't it just as well, seeing that nothing was going to come of them."

The god gave me a queer look at that. "Aloysius," said he, "if I were omnipotent, would I have made a mistake like you?" Then he uttered a deep sigh. "How long, O Man, how long?" he said, and then cloud and god passed out of my sight.

For a long time I looked into emptiness; but presently there came another cloud, and there was sitting on it a hard-faced woman in a red cap. She had a steel triangle in one hand, a hypodermic syringe in the other, and a flayed dog writhing beneath her feet. She said to me: "I am the lord thy god, who brought thee out of the land of freedom and out of the house of temptation. Grovel and adore me."

"What is freedom?" I asked.

"Now is my labour justified," said the goddess triumphantly. "Deprived of his freedom, man no longer misses it. Therefore he is better without it. Quod erat demonstrandum."

And she said: "I am the greatest of all the gods. For the other gods made man, and man overthrew them: but I am the god that man found it necessary to invent.

"Jehovah said he had made the world in seven days: and I proved that that s impossible, and man knew Jehovah for a liar. But I said chance had made the universe in a million centuries and men believed me.

"Jehovah said, increase and multiply: but I said, the increase of population is by geometrical progression, but the increase of sustenance is only by arithmetical progression.

"Jehovah said, thou shalt not kill: but I gave you reasons for killing anybody you dislike sufficiently, or whatsoever you may find expedient.

"Jehovah said, thou shalt not steal: but I said, enclosure and consolidation make for economy and efficiency, and trustification is an inevitable economic development; and again I said, property is theft.

"Jehovah said, thou shalt not commit adultery: but I said, sex is the causative factor of all psychological phenomena.

"Jehovah said, man is not flesh alone, but spirit: but I said, that is not an argument with which a secular civilisation need feel itself called upon to deal.

"And there was one who commanded that you love one another: but I proved by statistics that seventy-three per cent of the democracy are criminals, loafers, wastrels, morons, and feeble-minded degenerates.

"Thus I confounded and overthrew all the gods, and there is no other god but me."

Then the goddess looked at me with a contemptuous stare, and she said: "You are poor, poor fool?" I said, "Yes." "And overworked?" "Sometimes." "And your work is uninteresting to you?" "So-so." "You are ignorant?" "More or less." "And you have little joy in your life?" I agreed. "And you are sick some-times, in trouble often, and ruled always by fear?" "Well, within limits." "And you are a person of no account, with no hope of ever being other than you are?" I admitted it. "Therefore," says the goddess decisively, "the sum of your pleasures is less than the sum of your pains. Therefore your life is not worth living. Therefore you were better dead. Why do you not die at once?" "God knows," I said, "but I prefer to live." "Avaunt, fool," said the goddess, and vanished.

After that there came another cloud out of the void, and lolling on it was the queerest figure that ever you saw. It had the head and bust of a woman, but the rest of it was more or less masculine. He was fat and glossy and greasy. Two jets of perfume, springing out of his own breasts, played on his nostrils. "I am Beauty and Love," he said, smiling lusciously. "I am the great god Moderntwaddlums. Am I not adorable?"

"You are not," I said disgustedly.

The god smiled more treaclishly than ever, and said: "How delightfully frank and downright you are, my brilliant young friend. There is nothing that pleases me better. O, why cannot we all be frank and free and fearless?"

"I don't know," I said.

"Then I will tell you," said the god, suddenly taking on a solemn expression which suited him very badly, and speaking with the portentousness of one who is about to deliver a weighty revelation. "It is because we are prudish, and fettered, and cowardly."

"You've hit the nail on the head first time," I said.

The god gave a perfectly ghastly smirk at this, and said: "There is no problem in the universe that I cannot solve with equal celerity."

"You're the most remarkable god I've met yet," I said.

"Ah!" said the god, expanding, "that is because I combine in myself the best qualities of all the gods. Moloch, of course, is

démodé, though his cat still has its votaries among quite smart
people. But the glorious freedoms of Zeus, the subtle intellec-
tuality of Reason, and the emotional and artistic grandeur of
Jehovah are all to be found in me, purged of any contamination with the disagreeable and the inconvenient. Indeed I am
a most obliging god. I will take any shape you like; put any
interpretation you will upon your desires; and justify in your
own judgment anything you have done or wish to do."

"That sounds very nice," I said, "and so accommodating a
god ought to be encouraged. But before committing myself too
finally, I should like to have your views on things in general, so
that I may know exactly where I stand."

"That is very reasonable," said the god. "Very reasonable
indeed, and, I may add, broadminded. Well, my brilliant and
free-spirited young man, the first and fundamental article of my
creed is simply this: that love justifies all things."

This was rather disappointing. I don't know what exactly
I had been expecting, but not that bunk certainly. Besides, I
didn't know what the dickens it meant.

"Excuse me," I said. "I don't quite understand that remark."

The god looked annoyed. "What is your difficulty," he asked.

"Well," I said, after thinking hard for a moment, "what
would you think I meant if I said to you: 'Cabbage justifies all
things'?"

"Nothing at all," said the god, looking more displeased still.

"Well, that's my case," I said.

"My dear young man," said the god, "you wrong your own
intelligence by such a comparison. Love—you know what Love
is?"

"Yes. Don't you know what cabbage is?"

The god looked as if he'd like to blot me out of existence,
but he controlled himself and said with pitying gentleness: "I
am afraid I have found a prudish and primitive streak running
through your frank modernity."

"Maybe," I said. "But I haven't a lot of use for love anyway. Do you mean that if I was gone on a girl it would be no harm if I pinched a watch for her?"

"My friend," said the god, "you are disappointing me sorely with your crudity and insensibility. If a phrase of such deep and subtle significance as that which I used can be translated into everyday language without alteration or impoverishment of its meaning, it means this: that there is no such thing as right or wrong; only the agreeable and the disagreeable; and no reasonable god could expect people to do anything that is disagreeable, or refrain from doing what is agreeable."

"Perhaps you wouldn't mind being a little more explicit," I suggested.

"Certainly," said the god, brightening up and fitting on his smile again. "Though apparently you are not troubled with that deeper and grander sort of Love that tramples honour, discipline, decency, and other people's happiness under foot, still you must be possessed in some small degree of the joy of living. Let that get its grip on you. Dance, lad. Dance while you're young to keep yourself young. Dance when you're middle-aged to prevent yourself getting old. Dance when you're old to make yourself young. Don't take on responsibility too early, or you'll be old before your time. Young people must be free to have a good-time, and how can they keep a car if they're tied down by children? Live your own life: Life isn't your concern anyway. Live your own life, even if you spend it hopping from one bedroom scene to another. Live your own life, even if that means playing and kissing away the earnings of other men. You aren't responsible for the way things are managed, so you may take the world as you find it. Other people would have a good-time if you were down and out: why shouldn't you have a good-time if—"

"Excuse me," I interrupted. "There's one unpleasant fact that you don't seem to be aware of."

"There is no fact so unpleasant," said the god, "that we cannot shut our eyes to it."

"Yes," I said. "When the misfortune is someone else's. But as it happens the misfortune is my own. All this advice of yours is wasted on me. I haven't enough money to do anything really wicked—anything really agreeable, I mean."

The god started like a lady shocked by a vulgar expression. Then he spat at me and said: "Out, you base plebeian! My doctrines are not for you. The full free life can only be sustained by a system of privilege, which must be based upon the labour of the unintelligent and undistinguished. Pff! you conventional creature. I will waste no more time on you." And the god drifted off very high and mightily after the others.

I watched to see if there were any more gods coming out of the void; but there were none. I was alone, and feeling more miserable than ever.

"This is a most unsatisfactory universe," I said.

"Do you think it should have been cut to your measure?" came a Voice in reply.

Then I perceived that a deeper darkness loomed in one quarter of the night. Slowly it grew larger and blacker till it filled half the firmament, and began to assume a definite shape— the shape of a long lean person sitting upon a gigantic throne. There was no need for him to speak. I knew at once who it was. It was the Devil himself.

"You needn't think I'm going to worship *you*," I said.

"I do not desire your worship," said the Devil. "I leave that to the gods, who care for such toys."

"You speak very high and mightily," I said. "Is your pride not broken yet? Do you still think yourself greater than God?"

"I am greater than any god you can create," said the Devil.

"I create a god?" I said. "What do you mean?"

"You have just created five," said the Devil.

"O," I said. "Were those not real gods?"

"There are no gods," said the Devil, "but those that you create in your own image and likeness."

"You mean that I imagined them? Then I must be imagining
you too."

"No," said the Devil. "You cannot imagine me. I am the
unimaginable and the undeniable. I am Darkness. I am the
enemy of the gods. I am he that has marred all the gods of your
making. I stand between you and the god that is to be."

At these words the black shadow swelled up again as if to
overwhelm creation, and at that I closed up all my faculties in
dread of what might happen. An age of suspense passed before I
ventured to look forth again. When I did so, there was nothing
to see but the myriad light-specks of the universe.

CHAPTER XLVII

Return

AND NOW A BLACK despondency settled upon my soul, and once more my vital spark began to sink. But just as I thought I was really gone, a faint luminosity, coming into being, arrested my attention. Very slowly it increased in brightness, at the same time taking on form and substance. As I watched it, fascinated, I thought I could detect two eyes staring at me out of its swirling depths. Presently, as it became more substantial, these appeared to be framed in one of those grotesque faces that you see in the coals of a dying fire, which gradually became more and more human, until, lo and behold, it was the very likeness of old Mr. Murphy, the fellow who had despatched me on this adventurous trip. There was his face, ghostly but perfectly recognisable, gazing at me in the centre of creation, and out of it was a thin streak of light tapering down to one of the innumerable pinpoints in the enveloping night.

What happened just then I can't describe. The expression of the eyes seemed to draw me towards them. Then they vanished, and I was flying at a frightful speed after a light that retreated even more swiftly before me. On, on, on we rushed, faster and faster, the light gobbling up the silver thread that held it, like a spider returning to its web, while I followed headlong, willy-nilly, in its wake.

What distance we traversed, and what time we took to do it, heaven only knows. They seemed infinite. Ages passed before I saw any sign that I was getting nearer to anything; but at length I perceived that the spark at the end of the silver thread was growing larger. In time it became a star, shining in the midst of the firmament. Then as I came nearer still, it split into a cluster; and the cluster rapidly became a constellation, which spread itself out before me like the spilling of jewels. Into it I plunged, speeding towards one single star that shone in its depths. Past blazing suns and rolling worlds I flew once more, the star of my aim waxing ever brighter, till it was a boiling white ball of flame with numerous lesser lights circling round it. Somehow my course was diverted towards one of these, which in turn increased until it had become a great silver moon revolving slowly beneath me. Then, by an indescribable transition, the whole spectacle changed. I was again in yellow sunshine, and there was old Mother Earth slowing up like a train arriving at the platform. Asia sauntered past from Kamschatka to the Ural Mountains. Europe rolled leisurely into view: first Russia, then Germany, then France, then England, and at last Ireland, half smothered in clouds, with a black blob on its edge that must have been Dublin.

At the first touch of the sunshine my guiding light had vanished, and the incredible speed with which I had been fetched from the remotest parts of space had suddenly ceased. I was now floating downwards like a feather from the sky, and, passing through the layer of clouds, found myself fluttering over a part of the country that was quite unfamiliar to me. Then the force which had already brought me so far gripped me again, and, as helpless as a straw in a whirlpool, I rushed earthwards.

All went black. I felt as if I was being smothered in blankets, and began to fight blindly for breath. It came at length in great gasps that shook and tore me as in those last dreadful moments on the battlefield of Yllab. But soon they became easier, and a warm comfortable tingle spread itself through me. Somewhere or other a dog barked.

CHAPTER XLVIII

Waking

I OPENED MY EYES, and there was Mr. Murphy anxiously staring down at me. But I wasn't in my digs at Stoneybatter. I was in the open air, lying on my back in an ashpit, in the shadow of a great castle, with a view of mountains behind it. I tried to sit up, but, whatever they had been up to with my body during my absence, it had been so ill used that I sank back with a cry of pain. Mr. Murphy, who was kneeling among the ashes and the cabbage stalks by my side, thereupon gave me a dose of sal volatile; and presently, after assisting me from the ashpit to a grassy bank nearby, and placing his rolled up coat as a pillow under my head, he gave me some hot tea out of a thermos flask, and some cheese sandwiches, which I tucked into very heartily. Being then somewhat refreshed, contrary to Mr. Murphy's advice, I again attempted to rise, in which I succeeded at last with some difficulty, being rather light in the head, and my feet deucedly painful. My word, but I did feel queer and all-overish. My body had been so stretched and wrenched and pulled out of shape that I hardly knew it for my own. The feel of it was loose and unfamiliar—like as if it was a suit of clothes that had been worn by somebody three sizes too big for it: which indeed was exactly what had happened, as Mr. Murphy presently confessed to me, and as he has promised to tell you any time you please, so as to prove the truth of what I'm telling you by a perfect alibi.

The ashpit in which I had come to earth was in a corner of the kitchen garden of Castle Boodleguts in Glengariff in the County Kerry, a most interesting and picturesque locality. So, when Mr. Murphy saw that I was fit to stand, he gave me another sup of the tea and suggested that we should be moving on, as the owner of the place was particularly hard on trespassers, and we were liable to be discovered there any time by his gardeners or scullions. We therefore took the nearest way to the boundary of the demesne, Mr. Murphy assisting me as well as he could, as my feet were almost unwalkable-on. When we reached the high road, a carter who happened to be passing offered us a lift into Bantry, where we slept that night, afterwards taking the train to Cork, and from there back to Dublin.

So that's the whole of my story, Mr. Gallagher, and every word of it as true as if I was kneeling before the priest in the confessional. And I think that in such exceptional circumstances you might stretch a point and take me back into my job, in which I assure you I will do my best to give you complete satisfaction in the future. And hoping this finds you as it leaves me at present.

Thus far the narrative of Mr. Aloysius O'Kennedy; and here endeth the Second part of the comical epic Tale of the Adventures of Cuanduine.

PARIS, September 1925.
LONDON, April 1928.

EIMAR O'DUFFY (1893-1935) was born in Dublin. Both a participant in and, beginning with the publication of his first novel in 1919, a critic of the Irish nationalist movement in the first decades of the twentieth century, O'Duffy devoted much of his prolific fiction writing to the satirizing of modern Irish culture.

MICHAL AJVAZ, *The Golden Age.*
The Other City.
PIERRE ALBERT-BIROT, *Grabinoulor.*
YUZ ALESHKOVSKY, *Kangaroo.*
SVETLANA ALEXIEVICH, *Voices from Chernobyl.*
FELIPE ALFAU, *Chromos.*
Locos.
JOAO ALMINO, *Enigmas of Spring.*
IVAN ÂNGELO, *The Celebration.*
The Tower of Glass.
ANTÓNIO LOBO ANTUNES, *Knowledge of Hell.*
The Splendor of Portugal.
ALAIN ARIAS-MISSON, *Theatre of Incest.*
JOHN ASHBERY & JAMES SCHUYLER, *A Nest of Ninnies.*
GABRIELA AVIGUR-ROTEM, *Heatwave and Crazy Birds.*
DJUNA BARNES, *Ladies Almanack.*
Ryder.
JOHN BARTH, *Letters.*
Sabbatical.
Collected Stories.
DONALD BARTHELME, *The King.*
Paradise.
SVETISLAV BASARA, *Chinese Letter.*
Fata Morgana.
In Search of the Grail.
MIQUEL BAUÇÀ, *The Siege in the Room.*
RENÉ BELLETTO, *Dying.*
MAREK BIENCZYK, *Transparency.*
ANDREI BITOV, *Pushkin House.*
ANDREJ BLATNIK, *You Do Understand.*
Law of Desire.
LOUIS PAUL BOON, *Chapel Road.*
My Little War.
Summer in Termuren.
ROGER BOYLAN, *Killoyle.*
IGNÁCIO DE LOYOLA BRANDÃO, *Anonymous Celebrity.*
Zero.
BRIGID BROPHY, *In Transit.*
The Prancing Novelist.

GABRIELLE BURTON, *Heartbreak Hotel.*
MICHEL BUTOR, *Degrees.*
Mobile.
G. CABRERA INFANTE, *Infante's Inferno.*
Three Trapped Tigers.
JULIETA CAMPOS, *The Fear of Losing Eurydice.*
ANNE CARSON, *Eros the Bittersweet.*
ORLY CASTEL-BLOOM, *Dolly City.*
LOUIS-FERDINAND CÉLINE, *North.*
Conversations with Professor Y.
London Bridge.
HUGO CHARTERIS, *The Tide Is Right.*
ERIC CHEVILLARD, *Demolishing Nisard.*
The Author and Me.
MARC CHOLODENKO, *Mordechai Schamz.*
EMILY HOLMES COLEMAN, *The Shutter of Snow.*
ERIC CHEVILLARD, *The Author and Me.*
LUIS CHITARRONI, *The No Variations.*
CH'OE YUN, *Mannequin.*
ROBERT COOVER, *A Night at the Movies.*
STANLEY CRAWFORD, *Log of the S.S.*
The Mrs Unguentine.
Some Instructions to My Wife.
RALPH CUSACK, *Cadenza.*
NICHOLAS DELBANCO, *Sherbrookes.*
The Count of Concord.
NIGEL DENNIS, *Cards of Identity.*
PETER DIMOCK, *A Short Rhetoric for Leaving the Family.*
ARIEL DORFMAN, *Konfidenz.*
COLEMAN DOWELL, *Island People.*
Too Much Flesh and Jabez.
RIKKI DUCORNET, *Phosphor in Dreamland.*
The Complete Butcher's Tales.
RIKKI DUCORNET (cont.), *The Jade Cabinet.*
The Fountains of Neptune.
WILLIAM EASTLAKE, *Castle Keep.*
Lyric of the Circle Heart.
JEAN ECHENOZ, *Chopin's Move.*

STANLEY ELKIN, *A Bad Man.*
The Dick Gibson Show.
The Franchiser.
FRANÇOIS EMMANUEL, *Invitation to a Voyage.*
SALVADOR ESPRIU, *Ariadne in the Grotesque Labyrinth.*
LESLIE A. FIEDLER, *Love and Death in the American Novel.*
JUAN FILLOY, *Op Oloop.*
GUSTAVE FLAUBERT, *Bouvard and Pécuchet.*
JON FOSSE, *Aliss at the Fire.*
Melancholy.
Trilogy.
FORD MADOX FORD, *The March of Literature.*
MAX FRISCH, *I'm Not Stiller.*
Man in the Holocene.
CARLOS FUENTES, *Christopher Unborn.*
Distant Relations.
Terra Nostra.
Where the Air Is Clear.
Nietzsche on His Balcony.
WILLIAM GADDIS, JR., *The Recognitions.*
JR.
JANICE GALLOWAY, *Foreign Parts.*
The Trick Is to Keep Breathing.
WILLIAM H. GASS, *Life Sentences.*
The Tunnel.
The World Within the Word.
Willie Masters' Lonesome Wife.
GÉRARD GAVARRY, *Hoppla! 1 2 3.*
ETIENNE GILSON, *The Arts of the Beautiful.*
Forms and Substances in the Arts.
C. S. GISCOMBE, *Giscome Road.*
Here.
DOUGLAS GLOVER, *Bad News of the Heart.*
WITOLD GOMBROWICZ, *A Kind of Testament.*
PAULO EMÍLIO SALES GOMES, *P's Three Women.*
GEORGI GOSPODINOV, *Natural Novel.*

JUAN GOYTISOLO, *Juan the Landless.*
Makbara.
Marks of Identity.
JACK GREEN, *Fire the Bastards!*
JIŘÍ GRUŠA, *The Questionnaire.*
MELA HARTWIG, *Am I a Redundant Human Being?*
JOHN HAWKES, *The Passion Artist.*
Whistlejacket.
ELIZABETH HEIGHWAY, ED., *Contemporary Georgian Fiction.*
AIDAN HIGGINS, *Balcony of Europe.*
Blind Man's Bluff.
Bornholm Night-Ferry.
Langrishe, Go Down.
Scenes from a Receding Past.
ALDOUS HUXLEY, *Antic Hay.*
Point Counter Point.
Those Barren Leaves.
Time Must Have a Stop.
JANG JUNG-IL, *When Adam Opens His Eyes*
DRAGO JANČAR, *The Tree with No Name.*
I Saw Her That Night.
Galley Slave.
MIKHEIL JAVAKHISHVILI, *Kvachi.*
GERT JONKE, *The Distant Sound.*
Homage to Czerny.
The System of Vienna.
JACQUES JOUET, *Mountain R.*
Savage.
Upstaged.
JUNG YOUNG-MOON, *A Contrived World.*
MIEKO KANAI, *The Word Book.*
YORAM KANIUK, *Life on Sandpaper.*
ZURAB KARUMIDZE, *Dagny.*
PABLO KATCHADJIAN, *What to Do.*
JOHN KELLY, *From Out of the City.*
HUGH KENNER, *Flaubert, Joyce and Beckett: The Stoic Comedians.*
Joyce's Voices.
DANILO KIŠ, *The Attic.*
The Lute and the Scars.
Psalm 44.
A Tomb for Boris Davidovich.
ANITA KONKKA, *A Fool's Paradise.*

GEORGE KONRÁD, *The City Builder.*

TADEUSZ KONWICKI, *A Minor Apocalypse.*

The Polish Complex.

ELAINE KRAF, *The Princess of 72nd Street.*

JIM KRUSOE, *Iceland.*

AYSE KULIN, *Farewell: A Mansion in Occupied Istanbul.*

EMILIO LASCANO TEGUI, *On Elegance While Sleeping.*

ERIC LAURRENT, *Do Not Touch.*

VIOLETTE LEDUC, *La Bâtarde.*

LEE KI-HO, *At Least We Can Apologize.*

EDOUARD LEVÉ, *Autoportrait.*

Suicide.

MARIO LEVI, *Istanbul Was a Fairy Tale.*

DEBORAH LEVY, *Billy and Girl.*

JOSÉ LEZAMA LIMA, *Paradiso.*

OSMAN LINS, *Avalovara.*

The Queen of the Prisons of Greece.

ALF MACLOCHLAINN, *Out of Focus.*

Past Habitual.

RON LOEWINSOHN, *Magnetic Field(s).*

YURI LOTMAN, *Non-Memoirs.*

D. KEITH MANO, *Take Five.*

MINA LOY, *Stories and Essays of Mina Loy.*

MICHELINE AHARONIAN MARCOM, *The Mirror in the Well.*

BEN MARCUS, *The Age of Wire and String.*

WALLACE MARKFIELD, *Teitlebaum's Window.*

To an Early Grave.

DAVID MARKSON, *Reader's Block.*

Wittgenstein's Mistress.

CAROLE MASO, *AVA.*

HISAKI MATSUURA, *Triangle.*

LADISLAV MATEJKA & KRYSTYNA POMORSKA, EDS., *Readings in Russian Poetics: Formalist & Structuralist Views.*

HARRY MATHEWS, *Cigarettes.*

The Conversions.

The Human Country.

The Journalist.

My Life in CIA.

Singular Pleasures.

The Sinking of the Odradek.

Stadium.

Tlooth.

JOSEPH MCELROY, *Night Soul and Other Stories.*

ABDELWAHAB MEDDEB, *Talismano.*

GERHARD MEIER, *Isle of the Dead.*

HERMAN MELVILLE, *The Confidence-Man.*

AMANDA MICHALOPOULOU, *I'd Like.*

STEVEN MILLHAUSER, *The Barnum Museum.*

In the Penny Arcade.

RALPH J. MILLS, JR., *Essays on Poetry.*

CHRISTINE MONTALBETTI, *The Origin of Man.*

Western.

NICHOLAS MOSLEY, *Accident.*

Assassins.

Catastrophe Practice.

Hopeful Monsters.

Imago Bird.

Natalie Natalia.

Serpent.

WARREN MOTTE, *Fiction Now: The French Novel in the 21st Century.*

Oulipo: A Primer of Potential Literature.

GERALD MURNANE, *Barley Patch.*

Inland.

YVES NAVARRE, *Our Share of Time.*

Sweet Tooth.

DOROTHY NELSON, *In Night's City.*

Tar and Feathers.

WILFRIDO D. NOLLEDO, *But for the Lovers.*

BORIS A. NOVAK, *The Master of Insomnia.*

FLANN O'BRIEN, *At Swim-Two-Birds.*

The Best of Myles.

The Dalkey Archive.

The Hard Life.

The Poor Mouth.

The Third Policeman.

CLAUDE OLLIER, *The Mise-en-Scène.*

Wert and the Life Without End.

PATRIK OUŘEDNÍK, *Europeana.*
The Opportune Moment, 1855.
BORIS PAHOR, *Necropolis.*
FERNANDO DEL PASO, *News from the Empire.*
Palinuro of Mexico.
ROBERT PINGET, *The Inquisitory.*
Mahu or The Material.
Trio.
MANUEL PUIG, *Betrayed by Rita Hayworth.*
The Buenos Aires Affair.
Heartbreak Tango.
RAYMOND QUENEAU, *The Last Days.*
Odile.
Pierrot Mon Ami.
Saint Glinglin.
ANN QUIN, *Berg.*
Passages.
Three.
Tripticks.
ISHMAEL REED, *The Free-Lance Pallbearers.*
The Last Days of Louisiana Red.
Ishmael Reed: The Plays.
Juice!
The Terrible Threes.
The Terrible Twos.
Yellow Back Radio Broke-Down.
RAINER MARIA RILKE,
The Notebooks of Malte Laurids Brigge.
JULIÁN RÍOS, *The House of Ulysses.*
Larva: A Midsummer Night's Babel.
Poundemonium.
ALAIN ROBBE-GRILLET, *Project for a Revolution in New York.*
A Sentimental Novel.
AUGUSTO ROA BASTOS, *I the Supreme.*
DANIËL ROBBERECHTS, *Arriving in Avignon.*
JEAN ROLIN, *The Explosion of the Radiator Hose.*
OLIVIER ROLIN, *Hotel Crystal.*
ALIX CLEO ROUBAUD, *Alix's Journal.*
JACQUES ROUBAUD, *The Form of a City Changes Faster, Alas, Than the Human Heart.*

The Great Fire of London.
Hortense in Exile.
Hortense Is Abducted.
Mathematics: The Plurality of Worlds of Lewis.
Some Thing Black.
RAYMOND ROUSSEL, *Impressions of Africa.*
VEDRANA RUDAN, *Night.*
GERMAN SADULAEV, *The Maya Pill.*
TOMAŽ ŠALAMUN, *Soy Realidad.*
LYDIE SALVAYRE, *The Company of Ghosts.*
LUIS RAFAEL SÁNCHEZ, *Macho Camacho's Beat.*
SEVERO SARDUY, *Cobra & Maitreya.*
NATHALIE SARRAUTE, *Do You Hear Them?*
Martereau.
The Planetarium.
STIG SÆTERBAKKEN, *Siamese.*
Self-Control.
Through the Night.
ARNO SCHMIDT, *Collected Novellas.*
Collected Stories.
Nobodaddy's Children.
Two Novels.
ASAF SCHURR, *Motti.*
GAIL SCOTT, *My Paris.*
JUNE AKERS SEESE,
Is This What Other Women Feel Too?
BERNARD SHARE, *Inish.*
Transit.
VIKTOR SHKLOVSKY, *Bowstring.*
Literature and Cinematography.
Theory of Prose.
Third Factory.
Zoo, or Letters Not about Love.
PIERRE SINIAC, *The Collaborators.*
KJERSTI A. SKOMSVOLD,
The Faster I Walk, the Smaller I Am.
JOSEF ŠKVORECKÝ, *The Engineer of Human Souls.*
GILBERT SORRENTINO, *Aberration of Starlight.*
Blue Pastoral.
Crystal Vision.

Imaginative Qualities of Actual Things.
Mulligan Stew.
Red the Fiend.
Steelwork.
Under the Shadow.
ANDRZEJ STASIUK, *Dukla.*
Fado.
GERTRUDE STEIN, *The Making of Americans.*
A Novel of Thank You.
PIOTR SZEWC, *Annihilation.*
GONÇALO M. TAVARES, *A Man: Klaus Klump.*
Jerusalem.
Learning to Pray in the Age of Technique.
LUCIAN DAN TEODOROVICI, *Our Circus Presents...*
NIKANOR TERATOLOGEN, *Assisted Living.*
STEFAN THEMERSON, *Hobson's Island.*
The Mystery of the Sardine.
Tom Harris.
JOHN TOOMEY, *Sleepwalker.*
Huddleston Road.
Slipping.
DUMITRU TSEPENEAG, *Hotel Europa.*
The Necessary Marriage.
Pigeon Post.
Vain Art of the Fugue.
La Belle Roumaine.
Waiting: Stories.
ESTHER TUSQUETS, *Stranded.*
DUBRAVKA UGRESIC, *Lend Me Your Character.*
Thank You for Not Reading.
TOR ULVEN, *Replacement.*
MATI UNT, *Brecht at Night.*
Diary of a Blood Donor.
Things in the Night.
ÁLVARO URIBE & OLIVIA SEARS, EDS., *Best of Contemporary Mexican Fiction.*
ELOY URROZ, *Friction.*
The Obstacles.
LUISA VALENZUELA, *Dark Desires and the Others.*
He Who Searches.

PAUL VERHAEGHEN, *Omega Minor.*
BORIS VIAN, *Heartsnatcher.*
TOOMAS VINT, *An Unending Landscape.*
ORNELA VORPSI, *The Country Where No One Ever Dies.*
AUSTRYN WAINHOUSE, *Hedyphagetica.*
MARKUS WERNER, *Cold Shoulder.*
Zundel's Exit.
CURTIS WHITE, *The Idea of Home.*
Memories of My Father Watching TV.
Requiem.
DIANE WILLIAMS, *Excitability: Selected Stories.*
DOUGLAS WOOLF, *Wall to Wall.*
Ya! & John-Juan.
JAY WRIGHT, *Polynomials and Pollen.*
The Presentable Art of Reading Absence.
PHILIP WYLIE, *Generation of Vipers.*
MARGUERITE YOUNG, *Angel in the Forest.*
Miss MacIntosh, My Darling.
REYOUNG, *Unbabbling.*
ZORAN ŽIVKOVIĆ , *Hidden Camera.*
LOUIS ZUKOFSKY, *Collected Fiction.*
VITOMIL ZUPAN, *Minuet for Guitar.*
SCOTT ZWIREN, *God Head.*

AND MORE . . .

www.ingramcontent.com/pod-product-compliance
Lightning Source LLC
La Vergne TN
LVHW040818031025
822519LV00002B/111